GHOST HOPE

GHOST HOPE
The PSS Chronicles: Book Four

RIPLEY PATTON

Cover design by Scarlett Rugers of The Scarlett
Rugers Book Design Agency
Cover © 2016 by Ripley Patton
Edited by Lauren McKellar and Rachel Barnard
Typesetting and Formatting by Simon Petrie

Library of Congress Control Number: 2016908479
ISBN 978-0-9884910-8-3

Publisher's website: www.ripleypatton.com

DEDICATION

This book is for me because I did it. I invested seven years of my life writing this story, some of them incredibly difficult years, and the story did not fail me the way good story never does.

OTHER BOOKS
BY RIPLEY PATTON

The PSS Chronicles
Ghost Hand (Book One)
Ghost Hold (Book Two)
Ghost Heart (Book Three)

Novellas
Over The Rim (Young Adult Fantasy)

CONTENTS

CHAPTER 1	1
CHAPTER 2	15
CHAPTER 3	29
CHAPTER 4	35
CHAPTER 5	47
CHAPTER 6	61
CHAPTER 7	75
CHAPTER 8	81
CHAPTER 9	91
CHAPTER 10	101
CHAPTER 11	109
CHAPTER 12	117
CHAPTER 13	125
CHAPTER 14	137
CHAPTER 15	143
CHAPTER 16	151
CHAPTER 17	161
CHAPTER 18	175
CHAPTER 19	181
CHAPTER 20	191
CHAPTER 21	197

CHAPTER 22   207
CHAPTER 23   211
CHAPTER 24   219
CHAPTER 25   229
CHAPTER 26   235
CHAPTER 27   245
CHAPTER 28   255
CHAPTER 29   271
CHAPTER 30   277
CHAPTER 31   291
CHAPTER 32   303
CHAPTER 33   311
CHAPTER 34   317
CHAPTER 35   325
CHAPTER 36   333
CHAPTER 37   339
CHAPTER 38   347
CHAPTER 39   351
CHAPTER 40   361
CHAPTER 41   373
CHAPTER 42   379
CHAPTER 43   385
CHAPTER 44   391
CHAPTER 45   395
CHAPTER 46   401
ACKNOWLEDGEMENTS   408
ABOUT THE AUTHOR   409

1

OLIVIA

Someone was standing next to my bed, looming over me.

I threw off my blankets, rolled to my feet, and wrapped my ghost hand around his throat before he knew what hit him.

Even in the dark, I could still see the bulge of Mike Palmer's eyes by the gentle glow of my PSS.

"What the fuck?" I growled, feeling strangely disappointed that my life hadn't truly been in danger. For the last week, Mike, Samantha, Grant, Passion, my mother, and I had been holed up in an old dilapidated house on Burnside Street in Portland, Oregon, and it hadn't stopped raining since we'd arrived. Mike claimed that was normal for Portland in early November. He said we'd get used to it, just like we'd get used to living with the two college dropouts Mike claimed were members of the infamous hacker group B-Ominous. Supposedly, their computers were hard at work scanning the internet for any signs of a CAMFer or Hold resurgence, and we just had to wait. But the rain and the waiting were killing me. I had too much time to think, too many quiet moments to dwell on my captivity at the hands of the CAMFers or replay the look on Marcus's face when he hadn't remembered me. I felt like I was going crazy and I needed something to happen. There had been a time when I could have counted on Mike Palmer to spice up my life with a little arson or double-agent intrigue, but that time had come and gone.

"What do you want, Mike?" I sighed, letting go of his neck.

"I wanted to check on your PSS," he said, eyeing my hand. "See if there was any flickering while you slept."

"Nope," I said, sitting down on the edge of my bed. "No more turning on and off. I told you, it's completely back to normal." I was actually quite relieved. It had felt almost like a betrayal of myself, being able to switch off my PSS.

"Good," he nodded. "I think that means it's stabilized."

"You think?" I raised an eyebrow at him. I was getting tired of guessing how PSS worked and what it could do. What I wouldn't give for some cold, hard facts.

"Yes I do, and I also wanted to give you this." He held something out wrapped in a paper towel and tied with a bread bag twist tie. "Happy birthday," he added.

"Aw gee Mike, you shouldn't have. As in 'you *really* shouldn't have,' because it's the middle of the night. In my room. And it's creepy. Plus, my birthday isn't until next week." How did he even know when my birthday was? Then again, he had been spying on me for the CAMFers most of my life. Mike probably knew way more about me than I wanted to contemplate.

"Just open it," he said, presenting the gift to me again.

"Fine." I took the thing from him. It was surprisingly heavy for its size. I tugged at the twist tie and the paper towel fell open. I stared down at the rock in my hand. The rock inscribed with my father's name and the dates of his lifespan. The rock I'd pulled out of my own psyche to save myself and everyone I cared about.

"Where did you get this?" It wasn't possible. I had given it up. Used it to cause a cataclysmic displacement.

"In the cave in the desert," he explained. "When I went back in looking for signs of Kaylee, it was right where you'd been lying, pressed into the dirt. I found these too." He stuck a hand in his pocket and pulled out the dog tags Marcus had made from Passion's blades, holding them out to me.

"They came with us," I said, taking the tags, holding them alongside the stone and brushing my fingers over both. "It must be because we're connected to them. And that's why your matches came with you. But shouldn't this rock be inside Grant's cube? I used them together."

"I did a thorough search," Mike said, shrugging. "If the cube had been there, I would have found it. But don't worry. It just means your power is unpredictable, like Kaylee's. That's why the two of you scare the CAMFers and The Hold so much. They can't control what they don't understand."

"Yeah, well, neither can I," I said, setting the tags and the stone on my bedside table. "Hey, wait a minute." I turned back to Mike. "You've had these since the cave and you didn't tell me?"

"The timing wasn't right," he said. "But now I have to go and I'm not taking them with me."

"You have to go? What the hell does that mean?"

"Come on, Olivia, we both knew this was coming. I shouldn't have stayed as long as I have. Kaylee is out there, and my cover was never blown thanks to you and what you did at the dome. If the CAMFers or The Hold have her, I need to find her and get her away from them. And if they don't, I have to get to her first."

"Okay," I glanced down, looking for my boots. "I'm coming with you." This was the answer to all my problems. I could go with Mike to find my sister and fight Holders and CAMFers again. I could get out of my own head, not to mention escaping the constant rain and my overly-protective mother.

"Nope. Not gonna happen," Mike said firmly. "You're gonna stay here and hold down the fort. If I find Kaylee, I'll let you know and I'll do my best to bring her back. But I can't make any promises. You know that."

Of course he didn't want me tagging along. The reason he had to go find Kaylee was because I'd messed up his first rescue attempt by randomly displacing everything and everyone at the compound. Our group, those of us who'd woken up in a cave in the middle of the Oregon high desert, had managed to walk back to the highway and hitchhike to Portland. But we still had no idea what had happened to everyone else. Hell, we had no idea what had happened to the entire compound structure. The B-Ominous guys had shown me satellite images of where it had once been in a valley on the Warm Springs Reservation. All that remained was a crater the size of a stadium. Yeah, I'd done that.

"So, you're leaving *now*?" I turned to look at the glowing red numbers on my alarm clock. "At 3:32 am on a Saturday morning? You're trying to avoid my mother, aren't you?"

"Exactly." He nodded.

There was only one thing my mother was more passionate about than repairing our relationship, and that was finding my sister. If she knew Mike Palmer was leaving on that very mission, she'd want to go. "She's going to be pissed," I warned him.

"She'll get over it. She has you to worry about, and she'll be extra distracted with your *special day* coming up."

"Oh, God, please tell me she's not throwing a party," I groaned. "I asked her specifically *not* to."

"You won't get that information out of me," Mike said, grinning wickedly. "I'm a highly-trained double agent, remember?"

Shit. She was throwing me a party. "Please," I begged. "Take me with you."

"Not this time, kiddo," he said, his face going all serious. "You have work to do here. You wiped the CAMFers and the Hold off the map, but something has to fill that void and people are going to look to you for what to fill it with."

"No one's going to look to me," I scoffed. "Maybe to Samantha, or Marcus, wherever he is, but not to me."

"Well, we'll see," Mike said, clapping me awkwardly on the shoulder. "I'll keep in touch through B-Ominous as much as I can. And all of you can stay here at the house as long as you need to. I've got it covered financially."

That was generous of him. Then again, he sort of owed me a house since he'd burned mine to the ground. My mom had also given up her practice and my dad's entire art collection trying to find me after I'd run away, which left us with very few resources and nowhere else to go. Passion was pretty much in the same boat. And Samantha refused to make contact with her parents, even if we could locate them, which, so far, we hadn't been able to. The Hold and CAMFers seemed to have gone underground since the displacement, though I wasn't fool enough to believe either was gone for good.

Of all of us, Grant was the only one who still had a home and a family to go to. He'd called his parents to let them know he was okay, and I'd even gotten to talk to Emma. Still, I hadn't heard Grant mention going home or back to college in Indy. I had a sick feeling he was lingering to see if I had feelings for him when I finally got out of my funk. If I ever got out of my funk.

I looked up to see Mike already at the door, his hand on the knob.

"Hey," I said and he stopped, glancing over his shoulder. "Be safe."

He nodded and slipped out into the hallway, closing the door silently behind him.

I sank down onto my bed in the dark, feeling the panic rise up in my chest. That was all I ever felt anymore, a terrible, indefinable fear. My mom was convinced I was suffering from post-traumatic stress disorder because of what the CAMFers had done to me. She'd never understand none of that had been worse than losing Marcus. The thought of him is what had kept me alive. He was the first person I'd really loved since losing my father. And now, not only had he forgotten me and what we'd had, but I didn't even know where he was.

Sometimes, I found myself wishing the displacement had been something else—like an explosion or a raging fire. At least if I'd died, I wouldn't have to feel this constant agony over what had happened. And, despite being a licensed psychologist, my mom couldn't help me. She couldn't diagnose or prescribe meds for her own daughter. It would be unethical.

But I guess it was perfectly all right to traumatize me by throwing an eighteenth birthday party I didn't want. Crap. I was never going to get back to sleep now, and Mike's sudden departure had made me curious about his hackers. Had they made some discovery he hadn't told me about? Had they found a clue to my sister's whereabouts?

I got up and slipped out into the upstairs hallway, skirting past my mom's bedroom, then the room Mike and Grant had been sharing, and finally Passion and Samantha's room. The bedrooms had just sort of fallen out that way, which was good. I didn't want any of them to know how often I woke up from my nightmares, sweating and biting back screams of terror.

As I descended the stairs to the main floor of the house, the skunky aroma of pot wafted around me. We hadn't seen much of the hackers. They slept in the basement apartment during the day and worked at night, and for that I was grateful. My mom was having enough trouble with the whole sharing-a-house-with-strangers-thing as it was. Personally, it didn't bother me. My standard of living had changed considerably since spending two weeks in a cement cell being tortured.

When my bare feet hit the cold tile of the kitchen, I scurried across it and slipped through the dining area to the hackers' lair, a room that had once been the front parlor of the house. It didn't have a door, just an open archway, and I thought I'd just stand there a moment, spying on the hackers and their nefarious activities unseen.

The glow of six computer monitors and the glint of a joint were the only things lighting the room as the two young men tapped away on their keyboards, headphones on and oblivious to the world around them. The closest monitor was scanning satellite pictures, flipping through them so fast it was just a blur of color, though every once in a while it would pause and process an image for a second longer.

The monitor next to that was doing some kind of map scan in infrared.

Another screen revealed a rousing game of *League of Legends*, and I experienced a flash of extreme gratefulness that I hadn't caught anyone watching porn.

Suddenly, the guy closest to me turned, caught sight of me, and practically jumped out of his skin.

"Whoa. Fuck!" he said, dropping his joint as the other guy swiveled toward me too, both of them pulling off their headphones as they turned.

"Hey, Olivia," the second guy said, smiling warmly. "What can we do for you?" If I remembered right, this was the one named Chase and the other one went by the nickname T-dog.

"Sorry I startled you," I told them both. "I couldn't sleep, so I thought I'd see what you were up to."

"No problem," Chase said. "Why don't you pull up a chair?"

"Really?" I grabbed one and rolled up between them.

"You wanna smoke?" T-dog asked, looking on the floor for his joint. He had dreadlocks and a black Apple logo, morphed into a skull and crossbones, tattooed directly over his Adam's apple.

"No thanks," I said. "My mom would kill me."

"How about some Cheetos then?" he asked, pulling an open bag from behind his computer monitor.

"Sure," I said, reaching my ghost hand into it and snagging a handful.

"You ever smoked a Cheeto?" T-dog asked me.

"Nope. Can't say I have."

"Don't," he said, "It ain't good." His eyes followed my ghost hand, transfixed, as I raised the Cheetos to my mouth. PSS had that effect on people. Especially high people.

"Your hand is awesome," he said. "I've never seen PSS up close. Can I touch it?"

"T-Dog, man," Chase scolded, "Don't be a—"

One of the computers started beeping frantically, the one that had been scanning satellite pics. It had stopped on an image and was flashing GPS coordinates in the corner of the screen.

"We got it," T-Dog said excitedly, turning to the monitor. "We found the dome."

"45.8431 degrees north, 119.4381 degrees west," Chase read. "We're in luck. That's Oregon—about 170 miles northeast of the point of origin, and the compound appears fully intact, dome, sub-stories, and everything."

I stared at the blurry grey-green screen, wondering how they could tell any of that.

"Holy shit," T-dog exhaled, glancing at me. "You moved an entire complex almost 200 miles and nothing fell apart? What about soil displacement? If that thing landed fully intact in a new location, what happened to the dirt that used to be there?"

"I don't know," I said, feeling like an idiot. I was as amazed and mystified as he was by what I'd done.

"Maybe she displaced the soil to somewhere else," Chase said. "Tee, zoom in and enhance the resolution."

My eyes were glued to the screen as the image magnified and came into focus.

I'd never actually seen the CAMFer compound from the outside. I'd been drugged when they'd taken me in, and I'd spent most of my time there on the lower levels. I had been in the dome portion once, and I knew the basic layout of the compound enough to tell that the thing on the screen was definitely it. The terrain around it, on the other hand, was like nothing I'd ever seen. There was a grid of lighter gray lines on a field of lumpy brown rectangular berms all spaced evenly apart and encompassing the entire aerial satellite image. Whatever it was, it was huge.

"What is that?" I asked, my heart dropping into my stomach. "A cemetery?"

"Hmm, no." Chase frowned, typing something into his search engine and scrolling down a list of articles. "That" —he said, scanning some text—"is the Umatilla Chemical Depot, once the largest cache of chemical weapons in the world. Thankfully, it was decommissioned a few years ago and all the chemicals were destroyed."

"Is there still a military presence?" T-dog asked.

"Shouldn't be," Chase answered. "It says here all military personnel and staff were relieved or relocated early last year, and since then the land, all twenty thousand acres of it, has been stuck in some kind of legal limbo. The government had promised to release it to local interests at no cost, but they apparently had a change of heart, resulting in multiple lawsuits against them."

"Ah, poor govey-wovey," T-Dog crooned mockingly.

"So," Chase said, "with that much land and no personnel presence, it's likely no one has noticed the compound is there."

"What kind of security are we looking at?" T-dog asked.

Chase typed in a new search and scanned more text. "It's pretty old-school. The entire area is surrounded by a high-voltage military-grade fence, but the remote electronic security is way out-of-date. It hasn't been updated since they started the decommissioning process a decade ago. We should be able to get in and find exactly what we need with no trouble."

"Get in?" I choked out. "Why in the world would you want to do that?" I'd spent two weeks clawing my way out of that hell hole, and these guys wanted to go back?

Chase turned to me. "The CAMFers and The Hold had closed computer networks. Neither was connected to the internet or anything we can hack, unless we can physically access those networks ourselves. We get into that compound, and we have every piece of information on PSS the CAMFers and The Hold have ever collected. Better yet, we keep them from recovering it."

"But what if the computers aren't in there? What if they displaced separately?"

"If the entire building is intact, there's a good chance the computer systems are too," he reasoned.

"But you don't know for sure," I argued.

"There's only one way to find out," Chase said. "The information from those networks would be invaluable."

"But what if the CAMFers are still in there?" I asked, staring at the image on the screen.

"Let me run some scans," Chase said, typing quickly. "We should be able to tell with some degree of certainty."

Suddenly, satellite images of the compound began flicking across the screen from different times of the day and night, some of them in infrared, but all obviously from Umatilla. He paused on a final image, the date blinking in the corner. It was Umatilla the day before I'd displaced the compound.

"There's no indication of activity inside or outside since you moved it," Chase said. "And it appears to be powered down. There haven't been lights or power surges of any kind. So, I'd say it's highly unlikely anyone's there."

"In that case," I said, feeling fear creep up my spine. But at least this fear was real and of my own choosing. "When do we leave?"

"Our van is already geared up and ready to go," Chase said, grinning. "But Mike thought you'd be way harder to convince."

"Did he?" Mike had planned this all along. He'd set the hackers looking for the compound and he'd expected me to go with them. "How far away is this place?"

"About a three-hour drive on I-84 east," T-dog answered.

The clock on the closest computer monitor said it was 4:00 a.m., and my mom didn't get up until 6:00. But if I disappeared on her again, she would never forgive me. I was going to have to tell her something. Besides, it would probably be better to make our run for the dome at night under cover of darkness.

"We could leave tonight around 7:00," I suggested. That would give me time to come up with an angle to convince my mom to let me go, but not enough time for her to overthink it. "Does that work for you guys?"

"Let's make it 9:00," Chase said. "Tee and I have been up all night, and I want to get a decent day's sleep before I have to drive."

"Okay." I nodded. "I'll be ready."

2

DAVID MARCUS

"Come on, David, stop dragging your feet," Reiny called over her shoulder. She and Kaylee, walking hand in hand, had gotten a few yards ahead of me on the one-lane, dirt road which cut through the middle of Warm Springs. The name of the road, Hollywood Boulevard, had to be ironic because there was nothing Hollywood about the ramshackle little reservation village. And I *was* dragging my feet. Partly because I was still recovering from almost dying in the desert a few days ago, but mostly because this was not the way I wanted to spend my Saturday morning.

"Oh for Christ's sake, it's not a death march," Reiny said. "We're just going to the Christmas bazaar."

She stopped in the middle of the road to wait for me. Kaylee stopped too, peeking out from under her hood and giving me a shy smile.

"Why is the Christmas bazaar the second weekend of November?" I complained. "And we're Native Americans. We don't believe in Jesus Christ or Santa Claus, do we?"

"No, we don't." She frowned. "Well, some of us do, but that's not important. The bazaar is about building community and fostering creativity. Oh, and also about sticking it to Thanksgiving because we sure as hell don't celebrate the European invasion of our lands that culminated in the deaths of more than twenty million of our people."

"Now there's a cause I can get behind," I said. "Sticking it to the white man by buying one another's hideous craft projects. That will teach him."

"Listen, you smart-ass," Reiny said, pulling Kaylee back toward us and looping her free arm through mine. "The reason we're going is to get you two out of the house and build your strength back up. And because I saved your life, you're going to come quietly and like it."

"We would have found water eventually," I argued. But honestly, she'd totally saved Kaylee and me. After we'd woken up in the middle of the high desert, disoriented from whatever Kaylee's sister had done to us, we'd wandered for two days without food or drink. We'd been dehydrated, sunburned, and on our last legs when Reiny and her brother, Lonan, had ridden out of the hills on horseback and rescued us. They'd brought us back to the reservation and the village. They'd fed us, housed us, and nursed us back to health. Yeah, Reiny had saved my ass and I owed her big time, but I was worried about Kaylee. She wasn't used to people or crowds. She wouldn't understand the stares or laughter. She was completely innocent of this world, and I wasn't. I knew what kind of abuse people could dole out just because someone was different, and Kaylee was about as different as they came.

"She'll be fine," Reiny said, reading the worry on my face. "You'll both be fine. Now, come on." She tugged at me and the three of us moved forward, arm in arm in arm.

I will be fine, Kaylee said into my mind, and I glanced at her in surprise. *We're all touching,* she explained. *So, I can use Reiny's mind to connect with yours, like skipping rocks from one pond to another. Except, I've never actually skipped rocks. I've only read about it.*

"We'll find you a pond and we'll skip some rocks," I told her.

"Stop it, you two," Reiny scolded. "We're almost there, so none of that."

"And that's exactly why this is a bad idea," I said. "She doesn't understand. What if she accidentally mind-speaks to someone and—"

I won't. I promise. Cross my heart, Kaylee said. *I won't even talk to you two, just to be sure.*

"See? She understands," Reiny said, guiding us into the Warm Springs Elementary School, which also doubled as the Community Center. "Now, go have some fun." She let go of my arm, moving away to greet someone she knew at one of the food stands near the door.

The place was packed wall-to-wall with people—more people than could possibly live in Warm Springs. All around the perimeter, there were tables and stands set up, selling everything from beads and bone jewelry, to blankets and baskets, to band t-shirts and used electronic devices. A few of the booths had food, and there were a couple of tables piled with old toys someone's kids were hoping to make a little cash on.

Kaylee and I were immediately swept up in the line of jostling people circulating the gym and she clung to me at first, pressing herself into my side like a scared child. It was hard to believe she was older than me. Over the past few days, I'd come to think of her as a little sister, and even now I could see people responding to her petite stature, assuming she was, at most, in her early teens. The hooded sweater-coat Reiny had given her, pieced together from numerous brightly-colored sweaters and falling to her knees, only added to the illusion of someone young, shy, and in need of protection. All it had taken was one look at her pixie-like, glowing face for me to fall completely under her spell.

But I wasn't sure the population of Warm Springs would respond the same way. Plus, I knew something they didn't. I knew that beneath Kaylee's innocent and childlike exterior, there was power beyond measure. During our time together in the desert, I'd discovered that she could soothe someone and mind-speak to them with just a touch. And I had a feeling I hadn't seen the full depths of her abilities yet. No wonder the CAMFers and The Hold had kept her balanced between them for so long. But they couldn't have her back. I had to keep her out of their clutches. I'd promised her that. I'd promised her she'd never be a prisoner again.

"You wanna buy something, or you just gonna stand there holding up the line?" the guy behind me growled. I looked up to find myself standing in front of one of the toy tables where Kaylee had been checking out an old etch-a-sketch. Only she wasn't there anymore. Shit. I couldn't see her anywhere. She'd been right beside me a moment ago.

"Kaylee," I called, pushing through the line.

"Hey, wait your turn, buddy," someone said, shoving me back.

"Kaylee," I called again, looking over people's heads, searching for the multi-colored hood of her sweater-coat.

There she was, three booths ahead, the wrinkled, long-faced guy behind it frowning at her. By the time I reached them, it was obvious she'd worked her silent magic on him. He was chatting away about art and sculpture, which was apparently what he called the odd arrangement of recycled crap he was selling. It was amazing how people never noticed that Kaylee didn't speak. They talked to her like they would their cat or their dog or their horse, not needing anything in return but the privilege of interacting with someone so wonderfully other.

"Kaylee," I said, trying to calm my racing heart. "Don't get ahead of me like that. I didn't know where you were."

She turned to me and held up a smooth silver cube, about the size of a Rubik's cube, the question in her eyes obvious.

"You want to buy *that*?" I asked. Of all the things at the Christmas bazaar I thought might fascinate Kaylee, a metal cube was not one of them. Then again, she loved that magic eight ball of hers. I guess someone raised in a dome all their life could be entertained by almost anything.

"She has a good eye," the guy at the booth said, scrutinizing me. "That there is a bonafide alien artifact. I found it in the desert, and it ain't made from any metal known to man. Now, in my day, people came out here just for a hope of a glimpse of a UFO, but not anymore. People don't believe in mystery these days. They think we're it. Us and the stuff right in front of our faces. But you and I know different," he said, his glance falling on Kaylee, then flicking to my chest and finally back to my face. "There's way more to this world than meets the eye."

What was the old coot getting at? That Kaylee was a mystery, or that I was? Did I know this guy? Fuck. Would I even remember if I did?

"You don't need this," I told Kaylee, taking the cube from her and putting it back on the table next to another one exactly like it. Reiny had generously given me a couple of twenties to spend, but I couldn't justify blowing it on junk when Kaylee and I were literally borrowing the clothes on our backs.

"Of course, she don't *need* it, boy." The old guy scowled. "Ain't nothing in this gym anybody needs."

Well, he had a good point, but I really didn't like the way he'd called me boy.

Kaylee picked up the cube again, this time holding it out to me more emphatically. Then she picked up the other one and held it out too, her eyes determined.

"No way. We're not getting two of them," I told her. "They're exactly the same."

"No two artifacts are the same," the junk man said. "Besides, they're more valuable as a set."

"You really want these?" I asked Kaylee, and she nodded adamantly.

"How much?" I asked the old guy.

"Thirty bucks for one. Fifty for both."

"I'll give you twenty for one," I said, slapping the bill down on the table.

"Deal," he said, snatching up the money. "One mysterious cube sold to the young buck and his alien princess side-kick."

I grabbed one of the cubes and handed it to Kaylee, gently pushing her into the flow of people toward the next table.

She looked back, glancing at the other cube longingly, but it was soon out of sight and, I hoped, out of mind.

We made the rounds, Kaylee stopping at every booth and admiring each person's selection with unfeigned interest. Yet, underneath it, I could sense some subtle impatience in her. Was she getting overwhelmed? I noticed she'd tucked the cube in one of her over-sized sweater pockets, the one opposite the pocket she kept the eight ball in. A cube and a ball. Simple shapes for a girl who'd lived a simple life, just one more reminder of how ill-equipped she was for the complex world she now found herself in.

Finally, we finished the craft booth circuit and ended up at the food tables where Reiny handed us each a cob of corn on a stick, dripping with butter. Then we had to have some fry bread and some fudge, which Kaylee loved. By that time, the crowds were dying down and the vendors began putting away their wares.

"So, did you have a good time?" Reiny asked as the three of us stepped outside to walk back to her place.

"I made it out alive," I said. "And Kaylee bought an alien artifact."

"Excellent," Reiny said, turning to Kaylee. "Can I see?"

Kaylee reached into her pocket and pulled out the cube, handing it to Reiny.

"Hmm, very mysterious," Reiny said, turning it in her hands. "Definitely from another planet." She handed it back to Kaylee, who put it in her pocket and went skipping ahead of us. When she was out of earshot, Reiny turned to me. "See? I told you everything would be fine. Kaylee is different, I know, but she has an innate charm that disarms people."

"Maybe, but the more people she interacts with, the more likely her whereabouts will get back to the CAMFers or The Hold."

"We don't even know if The Hold or the CAMFers still exist," Reiny argued. "The compound is gone. I've seen the crater where it used to be with my own eyes. And your uncle hasn't contacted me, which makes me think The Hold is out of commission."

God, I hoped she was right, and that she was telling the truth. I knew it was a risk to stay with Reiny considering her past employment with Uncle Alex. She'd sworn she wouldn't give Kaylee and me up, even if he did contact her, and what choice did we have? Kaylee and I had nowhere to go. But I knew my uncle would rebuild. He wasn't the kind of man to let anything stop him. The loss of the compound and Kaylee were just temporary glitches in his plans. When he did resurface, I wanted to be indebted to Reiny as little as possible.

"Hey, here's your money back," I said, pulling the leftover twenty from my pocket.

"Um, okay." Reiny took it, a funny look on her face. "You do know you have money, right? You don't have to keep borrowing from me."

"What are you talking about?"

"Oh, crap. You don't remember. I'm so sorry; I should have told you sooner. You have a bank account with a million dollars in it. It's a trust fund settlement from the train collision awarded to you on your eighteenth birthday."

"I have a million dollars?"

"Yep," Reiny said, smiling.

"With what bank?"

"I have no idea," she said, her face falling.

"And neither do I," I pointed out. "I also don't know my account number, my password, my PIN, nor do I have any legal documentation that proves I'm David Marcus Jordan."

"Well, we can work on the documentation part, at least," she said. "You were born here on the rez, right? So, we should be able to scrape up a birth certificate. But yeah, I see your point. Why don't you keep this then?" She handed the twenty back to me with a fifty tucked under it. "I know you're good for it."

Ahead of us, Kaylee had reached Lonan and Reiny's tiny shack of a house, but instead of going inside, she waited for us on the stoop. Sitting down in the sun, her face masked by her hood, she took out the cube I'd bought her and inspected it.

"I'm going inside to make some sandwiches for lunch," Reiny said, patting Kaylee on the head as she stepped past her. "You two still need more meat on your bones." She and Lonan didn't make much working at Kah-Nee-Tah, and feeding and caring for me and Kaylee had to be costing them. If I did have a million dollars, I would definitely pay them back for all they'd done for us.

I felt Kaylee's small hand slip into mine. *Look,* she said, holding the cube toward me in her other hand, the metal now glowing a soft, pulsing blue.

"What are you doing?" I asked, trying not to sound alarmed.

I'm just feeling it, she said matter-of-factly. *I can sense the boy it came out of. He's that way.* She pointed to the west. *But way too far to walk.*

"The boy it came out of?" I repeated. "Wait, that thing came out of someone with PSS?" She'd told me about her sister's abilities. She'd told me all about Olivia, the girl I'd supposedly been in love with. Kaylee wasn't the only one in her family wielding immense power.

No, silly. Kaylee mind-spoke to me. *It's a cube, not an artifact. It came out of the boy without PSS. You know, Olivia's friend—the one who visited the dome with her.*

"This is from the dome?" I grabbed it out of her hand. "Why didn't you tell me?"

I thought you knew, she said defensively. *You were there when she pulled it out of him and used it to amplify her stone.*

"You mean when she blew us all to hell?" Back at the dome, with Dr. Fineman screaming in my face that he'd killed my sister, I hadn't exactly been paying attention to what anyone else was doing. I knew there had been an embrace between Olivia and the guy she was with, and then she'd had something in her hands. A moment after that, everything had been sucked into a tunnel of darkness, including me, and I'd woken up in the middle of the desert with Kaylee bending over me. "This is what obliterated the compound?" I held the cube out, barely stopping myself from flinging it away. "What about the other one? The one we didn't buy. That was from the dome too?"

Of course. Kaylee said. *I thought you didn't want it because Olivia pulled it from the doctor and you hate him.*

The other cube had come from inside the man who'd killed Danielle.

"If we had the other one, could you feel where the doctor was, just like you can feel the boy with this one? Could it lead us to him?"

Yes, Kaylee said, sounding puzzled. *But why would we want to find him? We just got away.*

To kill him, of course. To end the man who'd killed my sister. Thankfully, Kaylee could speak into minds, but she couldn't read them. She couldn't sense the gut-wrenching, soul-ripping hate I felt for Dr. Julian Fineman. But I couldn't just run off after him. I had Kaylee to think of now, and the last thing I wanted was to lead her right back into his clutches. Maybe there was a way to protect her *and* get my revenge. But for that, I'd need the other cube to trace the doctor. "You're right," I said, composing my words carefully. "We did get away. But I think these cubes are important. Don't you?"

Yes, she said, eyeing me. *They're important to Olivia. That's why I wanted both of them, but you said no.*

"And I was wrong," I admitted. "I should have listened to you. Reiny might know the guy who was selling them. Maybe we can still get the other one."

Good idea, Kaylee said, taking the cube back and sticking it in her sweater pocket just as the door opened behind us and Reiny called out, "Time for lunch."

The BLTs Reiny had made smelled delicious. So did the apple pie she was baking in the oven. And Lonan returned from caring for the horses just as we sat down at the table. But after what Kaylee had told me about the cubes, I could barely eat. We had to get the other one before that old coot sold it to someone else.

"Hey," I said to Reiny, leaning back in my seat and trying to sound casual. "Did you see that guy we bought that cube from?"

"Nope," she said. "We were swamped at the corn booth, so I didn't notice. Why?"

"There was another cube," I explained. "Kaylee really wanted the set, but I was worried about money. But now that I know I'm a millionaire, I thought maybe I could get her the other one."

"Oh, that's so sweet of you," Reiny cooed.

"What did he look like?" Lonan asked. "I'm pretty familiar with all the vendors. I used to help them set up when I was a kid."

"He was older and native, with long hair," I said.

"You've just described every person in the village," Reiny said, laughing.

"What did he have at his booth?" Lonan tried again.

"Lots of random metal made into weird sculptures. They were car parts mostly, I think."

"That would be Gordon Lightfoot," Lonan said, glancing at Reiny. It was subtle and quick, but I didn't miss the look that passed between them. "He's named after the Canadian folksinger."

"Never heard of him," I said. "So, does this guy live on the reservation? Because I was thinking I could walk over and see if he'd sell me the other cube."

"Well," Reiny said, "it just so happens that Gordon's partner, Mia, is the tribe registrar. She should be able to provide you with an official birth certificate, so if you're going over there you could kill two birds with one stone. They live on the other side of the rez, and I have to work tonight, but Lonan could ride over with you."

"I promised I'd haul some firewood up to the lodge this afternoon," Lonan said. "But we could go right after dinner."

"That would be great," I said, just as Kaylee began tugging at my sleeve.

"Yeah, yeah, of course you can come," I told her. She loved the horses, and they loved her, and she'd been begging Lonan for a night ride for days.

3

OLIVIA

"If you think, for a minute, I'm going to let you out of my sight again," my mother said, clamping her lips into a firm, thin line, "then you are sorely mistaken."

"Mom, come on, it's just a little road trip. I'll get to see some scenery. It will be therapeutic." That was my cover story: that the hackers had invited me on a scenic drive up the Columbia River Gorge. But I'd known it was weak, and everyone had been so upset about Mike leaving in the middle of the night, I'd put off broaching the subject until now, at dinner. And it wasn't going well, even though it wasn't completely a lie. We did have to drive up the Gorge to get to the Umatilla Chemical Depot, and I would no doubt see some scenery along the way. I hated lying to my mom, but her reaction was exactly why I had to. She would never let me go if she knew what the hackers were really up to.

"No," she said, crossing her arms over her chest. "Absolutely not."

"I can't hide in this house forever." I tried to reason with her while simultaneously looking around the table for support from Grant, Passion, and Samantha. I'd hoped their presence might make my mom more receptive. "Sooner or later you're going to have to let me start doing normal things like going outside and driving around. Otherwise, the CAMFers have won, and I've just exchanged one cell for another."

I was working her hard, pulling out the "they've won" argument, and I knew it.

"It's too soon," she said, her eyes pleading with me. "You have no idea what it was like not knowing where you were or if you'd ever come back, wondering if you were even alive. Don't ask me to do this. Not yet." Her begging nearly broke my resolve. Her hair was growing back into a pale, gray spike that made her look like a surprised hedgehog. She'd shaved her head after I'd left last time, like someone dying of cancer. I didn't want to hurt her again. I didn't want to lie to her. We'd promised not to fight anymore. We'd promised to hear one another out and be reasonable. But if she wouldn't even let me out of her sight, what was I supposed to do? How could I be honest with her and still live my life?

"Mike obviously thought it was safe enough to leave the house," Grant said, trying to help.

"Yes," Samantha jumped in. "Olivia, what did Palmer say before he left? He must have had some plan for what we should do while he's gone."

"He didn't tell me anything specific," I said. I certainly wasn't going to recount Mike's ramblings about people looking to me for guidance. That was Samantha's thing, though I'd heard her say more than once that she'd led people to the slaughter at the Eidolon and didn't deserve to lead anyone ever again. I suppose I wasn't the only one in the house suffering from PTSD.

"Listen." I turned back to my mom. "All I want to do is get out of this house for a little while. That's it. Chase and T-dog have promised we'll be back by tomorrow evening." They hadn't, but surely we would be.

Compassion and fear battled in my mother eyes.

"Mom," I pleaded, "It's just one night and one day. I'll be fine."

"Okay," she exhaled, her face softening and a calmness settling over her. "You can go."

"Really?" I couldn't believe she was caving so easily.

"It's such a good idea, in fact—" she nodded— "that I think we should all go. You kids have had it rough, and I've never seen the Gorge myself. I can rent a van, and we can even stay more than one night. Who's up for a road trip?" she asked enthusiastically.

"No, that's not—I'm not sure that would be cool," I scrambled. "I mean it's the hacker's trip and I was just tagging along for the ride."

"Well, that's the only way you're going," my mom said, crossing her arms over her chest. "Take it or leave it. And I'm sure they won't mind.

They seem like nice boys." She didn't mean it. What she really meant was, "They seem like derelict potheads I would never let my daughter ride in a vehicle with."

"Yeah, but can we afford this?" I asked. "A rental car and a motel for all five of us is going to be expensive."

"I think we can manage," she said. "I still have some funds from my private practice."

"No, really, you guys don't have to come." I looked around the table at my friends, hoping one of them would rescue me from this disaster.

"Are you kidding? I love road trips," Grant said, smiling at me with a glint in his eyes.

"Me too," Passion chimed in. "What time are we leaving?"

"Well, the plan was to leave at 9:00 tonight," I stammered, glancing at the clock in the kitchen. It was already 6:25. Surely my mom couldn't arrange a rental van in less than three hours. She never went anywhere without planning weeks ahead and confirming multiple times. The Sophie Black I knew didn't have a spontaneous bone in her body. There was no way she was going to pull this off. She had to be bluffing. Maybe she thought if she threatened to come, I'd back down. Well, I would call that bluff.

"So, I guess we'd better get packing," I said, getting up and putting my dishes in the sink.

To this day, I don't know how she did it, but two and a half hours later, at 8:55 sharp, my mother was parked outside the Burnside house in a rental van.

While Grant, Passion, and Samantha loaded our luggage into the back, I stepped away to intercept

Chase and T-dog at the curb next to their beat-up VW Westfalia.

"Hey," I said, cringing a little and gesturing at the rental van behind us. "Sorry about this, but my mom wouldn't let me come without an entire entourage. She's a little overprotective at the moment."

"Um, okay," Chase said, pulling the door to the Westfalia open. From the outside, it appeared to be your typical hippie camper, but the inside was like something out of a techno-thriller. There were computers and various pieces of electronic equipment covering every nook and cranny. The interior of the pop-up housed some kind of satellite array. "So, you told the rest of them about finding the compound?" he asked.

"Not exactly," I said softly, smiling and waving at my mother. "They think we're driving up the Gorge for some sightseeing, but don't worry. I'll figure out how to tell them before we get to Umatilla."

"Okay," Chase said, shrugging. "You're the boss."

"No, I'm not," I snapped. Why was everyone trying to make me the leader of everything? "I'm just—I'm your equal," I said more gently. "We're all just people."

"Right," he said, glancing at T-Dog as they climbed into the Westfalia. "She's just people like us, Tee."

"Nah," T-Dog said, his eyes mocking me. "She's special. We all know it. We have finally found The One."

"Very funny," I growled. "This is not the Matrix. Just drive and try not to lose us." I told them, marching back to the van and my mother.

4

DAVID MARCUS

The firewood job went faster than Lonan expected, so we ate an early dinner, geared up the horses, and were on our way to Gordon and Mia's before sunset. Even so, I was surprised we were visiting the old couple so late in the day, but I certainly wasn't going to object because I really wanted that cube.

A twenty-minute horseback ride later, across the dusky hills of the rez, and we came upon a giant junkyard. Burnt out and smashed cars were everywhere. There were rusted appliances stacked like totem poles and a giant sculpture made of hubcaps welded together. In one massive pile of metal, probably twenty feet high, a huge red backhoe jutted out, its shoveled arm seemingly frozen in the act of trying to unbury itself. It reminded me of a book I'd loved as a kid about Mike Mulligan and his steam shovel, Mary Ann. But this Mary Ann hadn't made it out alive.

"Hold it right there," a gruff voice called, and a short knight in bizarre piecemeal armor stepped out from behind the mountain of metal, wielding a flaming blowtorch. The knight raised a gloved hand, pushing up a faceguard and revealing a middle-aged, but still beautiful, native woman.

"Hey, Mia," Lonan greeted her. "I brought some visitors."

"You know we hate visitors," she replied, teasingly, dialing down her blowtorch.

"They bought something from Gordon at the bazaar today and were hoping to buy another one. Plus, David here,"—he gestured at me—"was born on the rez and needs a birth certificate."

"You bought one of my sculptures from Gordon?" she asked, her face suddenly beaming at us. "Which one?"

"No, not a sculpture," I clarified. "A metal cube. He said he found it in the desert."

"Oh." Her face fell. "Of course. I spend hours and days creating unique hand-crafted art, and all that old man has to do is go out in the desert and pick up junk and it sells. Such is the life of an artist, I guess. Anyway, he's around back in his studio." She gestured toward the far side of Trash Mountain. "I'm in the middle of something, but when I'm done I'll come inside and put on my registrar hat."

She knocked her faceguard back down and her blowtorch flared to life as she turned away from us.

"Come on," Lonan said, getting off his horse. "We'll walk them from here. They get skittish in close quarters like this."

Kaylee and I got down and followed him, leading the horses through a labyrinth of debris to a tiny house with a shack hanging off the back of it like a tumor.

We tied the horses to the porch rail and Lonan pointed at the door of the shack. "That's his studio."

"If he just collects junk, what's the studio for?" I asked, staring at the door.

"He's also a painter," Lonan said.

The way he said it was strangely weighted, as if the word "painter" carried some deeper significance. And then I remembered the look he and Reiny had exchanged at lunch when they'd first mentioned Gordon.

"A painter," I echoed, thinking of the mural at Kah-Nee-Tah Resort. The painting that resembled me titled *Ghost Heart*. "You mean *the painter*?" I stared at Lonan, the pieces finally falling together. "Gordon painted the mural?"

"Yes." Lonan nodded.

"Okay, now I really want to talk to him," I said, charging up to the shack door and rapping on it with my fist.

As it opened, I could feel Kaylee come up behind me.

"What do you want?" Gordon demanded, standing in the doorway of a softly lit painting studio. There was paint on his face and in his hair, and he was holding a wet red brush in his hands.

"I—we came to buy the other cube," I said, gesturing at Kaylee. "She wants the set."

"Do you now?" He scrutinized us. Behind him, I could see portraits covering the walls, amazingly done, brightly colored portraits in a similar style to the mural, but more refined. And on the easel in the corner, where'd he'd just been working, was the beginning of a new one of a small girl in a rainbow-hued sweater-coat, her glowing face peeking out from the hood. He was painting Kaylee.

"Let's cut to the chase," I said, more desperate than I realized. "That mural you painted at the lodge—it looks like me." This was not the way to get what I wanted. The direct approach never worked. If you wanted something you had to be sneaky about it, but I just couldn't seem to help myself. "But I've never met you. At least, I don't think I have."

"We've never met, not until today," Gordon said, turning to put his brush in a jar full of clear liquid before turning back to me. "At least not in the flesh."

"What the hell does that mean?"

"It means you should learn some respect for your elders and the spirits of your ancestors," Gordon Lightfoot snapped. "Your grandparents would be grieved their grandson has turned into such a chooch."

A chooch? I had no idea what that meant, but it obviously wasn't good. "So, you knew my grandparents," I said, an anger growing in me. "Big deal. They're dead, and my parents with them. My ancestors didn't stick around long enough to teach me anything, and as for their spirits—"

David, Kaylee's voice whispered in my head, *calm down. He isn't our enemy, and we need his help.* She held my hand, pulling me back from lunging at him.

"No, listen. I'm sorry," I said to Gordon, composing myself and squeezing Kaylee's hand. "That was rude. I—it's just—"

"You want answers," Gordon finished for me, his eyes suddenly gentler. "And you're wrong about your ancestors. You have your grandmother's fire and tenacity. Come into the house," he said, stepping past me and Kaylee out into the junkyard.

He led all three of us to the front door and into a cozy living room surrounding a small wood stove radiating warmth. There were pictures all over the walls, not paintings but photographs and articles and newspaper clippings, many of them in black and white. A few were framed, but most were just tacked or glued to the wall, their edges curling, their captions fading.

Gordon invited us to sit, but Lonan said something about coyotes and needing to check the horses, and he quickly went back out. I sat in an old stuffed chair by the fire and Kaylee sat on the floor at my feet, watching the flames through the little woodstove's window. Gordon went to wash the paint from his hands in the kitchen. When he came back, he crossed to one of the few framed color photos on the wall, a picture of a bunch of young people from the 70s or 80s trying to look cool, like they were posing for an album cover or something. He took the picture down and brought it over, handing it to me, then sat heavily in one of the two remaining chairs by the fire. "Recognize anyone?" he asked.

Of course, I found her face immediately. My mother. A much younger version of her than I remembered as a child, but I'd seen similar pictures of her from her college days. Always, she'd looked gentle and motherly to me, but not in this photo. In this one, her expression was so angry and defiant; it was almost like seeing myself peering out of someone else's eyes. Standing next to her was another face I recognized, though not nearly as fondly. It was Uncle Alex, much younger too, but not as fierce. In fact, he appeared strangely unsure of himself, as if my mother had dragged him along to a party he hadn't wanted to attend. I scanned the group for my father, but he wasn't there. I did, however, find Gordon, a much younger version of him but still obviously older than the other ten people. He stood slightly apart from them in the back row, almost as if he was their leader or teacher.

"So, you knew my mother, my uncle, *and* my grandparents," I said. "Is this where you tell me you're my long-lost relative or something?"

"We are both people of the Tenino," Gordon said. "But no, we're not closely related. I knew your family through the tribe and your mother and uncle took a painting class from me in college. Except it wasn't actually a class. That was just a cover for what we really were."

"And you were what, exactly?" I asked, trying not to laugh because he'd made it sound so mysterious.

"These days, I suppose they'd call us terrorists," he said matter-of-factly. "Back then we called ourselves activists. Are you familiar with NAM?"

"The Native American Movement? Yeah, I've read a little about them. But I thought they were based on the East Coast."

"There are smaller branches out here in the west," Gordon said. "And this"—he gestured at the photo—"was one of the core groups at the height of the movement."

I scanned the picture again, impressed by its diversity. There were two women other than my mom, one native but one obviously white. And among the seven younger males, there was an Asian guy, a black dude, and two white guys, one with sunglasses, a ball cap, and a beard like the Unabomber, though the others looked rez enough. "Nice picture," I said, holding it out to give it back to Gordon. "But what does NAM have to do with the mural or the cube?" I wasn't surprised my mom had been an activist. Her entire life had been dedicated to setting wrongs right, and ultimately it had gotten her killed. As for my uncle, he'd probably joined just to make himself look good.

"That picture was taken the night before we did something particularly bold and stupid," Gordon said, finally taking it from me, his hands shaking a little. "Something that was my idea and ended in the death of four of these young people."

Kaylee was still at my feet, her eyes fixed on Gordon now, listening.

"There was a government facility built on tribal land," Gordon continued, running his brown, paint-stained fingers over the picture. "We wanted to show them they couldn't take what was ours and get away with it. Their security was weak and we thought, if we could prove that, there would be media attention and an investigation. Maybe they'd even shut the place down." He looked up at me, his eyes haunted.

"Seven of us broke into one of the buildings while four stayed outside to keep watch. We were just going to move stuff around and tag the building with some grafitti. We weren't even going to take anything. Your mother had the spray paint and she was writing on one of the walls. I shoved a crate aside to give her more room and it bumped into another one. To this day, I don't know exactly what happened. One second, everything was fine, the next second we were on our knees, coughing and gasping for breath."

My mother had struggled with asthma for as long as I could remember. I'd always assumed she'd been born with it, but what if this had been the cause? Gordon didn't look so healthy himself. There was just something about him that seemed off. But he was an old guy who thought aliens really existed, so obviously he wasn't all there. I mean, he seemed to believe what he was telling me, but that didn't make it true. My parents had never told me any of this.

"Whatever was leaking," Gordon went on with his tale, "I took the worst of it, but your mother was a close second. It filled the room and our lungs. We tried to crawl out on our hands and knees, but then we started going into convulsions. I saw your uncle try to drag your mother out, but they were both too weak, and then I lost consciousness. We all did, drowning in the poison inside that building."

I didn't know what to say. I could see the scene in my head as if Gordon had painted it for me.

Kaylee was clutching my leg and whispering, *it will be okay, it will be okay*, over and over again in my mind. I wasn't sure if she was talking to me, or herself.

"Then when the concentration of that gas, or whatever it was, reached a certain point," Gordon continued, "it erupted—or something. I wouldn't call it an explosion because there wasn't any heat or fire. But the entire building and everything in its immediate vicinity was vaporized, leaving only a crater."

"Wait, what?" I leaned forward. "But how did you escape the building?" He'd said earlier that four people had died, and it obviously hadn't been him or my mom or my uncle, so that left the other people in the building. "Did the ones outside come in and get you?"

"No." Gordon shook his head. "They didn't know what was happening until it was too late. When those of us who'd been inside regained consciousness, we were lying in the crater and they were gone. The vehicles we'd driven and everyone and everything in them. Obliterated."

"But that's impossible," I said, staring at him. "How could you survive inside if the people outside didn't?"

"I don't know," he said, sounding like a bewildered child. "To this day, I don't know. Maybe we were in the eye of it, or the building protected us."

"The building that was completely gone?" I asked, incredulous.

"I know it doesn't make sense, boy," he snapped. "If I haven't figured it out in thirty-three years, you're certainly not going to solve it in ten minutes. You're not going to solve it at all. It's a mystery.

If I've understood anything after all this time, I've come to understand that. Not everything is explainable."

"So what happened then, after you woke up with my mom and uncle in a crater?" Not that I believed him. This story was getting crazier and crazier, but I'd humor him a little longer if it got me what I'd come for.

"The seven of us woke up surrounded by armed guards and government workers in hazmat suits," Gordon went on. "The guards grabbed us and hauled us away. They made us sit in the desert, coughing and hacking our lungs out for two hours. We demanded medical attention and they ignored us. We began to fear they were just waiting for us to die. I tried to get up and a guard pinned me to the ground, a gun at my head. Gradually, our symptoms started to lessen and a woman, who seemed to be in charge, came over and waved some kind of device up and down our bodies. Then she nodded to the guards, and they took us outside of the facility and let us go.

"We were still dizzy and disoriented, but we managed to walk to the nearest hospital. It was late at night. There wasn't a car on the road. At the hospital, we told them what had happened, but they couldn't find anything wrong with us. They ran all kinds of tests. Everything came back negative. So, they sent us home. We might have convinced ourselves it had all been a bad acid trip, except you could see this strange cloud hanging in the sky above the facility for days afterwards, like a fading Polaroid."

"Yeah, and four people were dead," I said, pointing out one of the biggest holes in Gordon's story.

There were lots of them, but this one was gaping wide enough to drive a semi through. "What about that?"

"There was no evidence," He answered. "No proof of anything. I told their families what I could. Most of them didn't believe me. There were investigations, but they led nowhere."

"Then why tell me?" I stood up and stepped over Kaylee, pacing across the room, trying to rein in a sudden surge of anger and grief. I hadn't been there. This wasn't my fault or my responsibility. So, why did I feel as if I'd just lost those friends myself? "Even if any of this is true"—I turned back to Gordon—"maybe my mother never told me because it's a fucking horrible story which accomplished jack shit. You guys thought you were standing for something, but look what it got you. Your friends were killed. No one believed you. You didn't change anything. That's just fucked up."

"Yes, it is," Gordon agreed, "if that were the end of the story."

"What? There's some kind of great moral, some Indian wisdom you're now going to impart to me about how not fucked-up a world is where shit like that happens?"

"No," he said, grimacing. "I thought you wanted answers about the mural."

Kaylee was touching Gordon's leg now. He hadn't seemed to notice, but I knew what she was doing. She was making him feel better. Maybe he didn't deserve to feel better. Maybe none of us did.

"What does any of this have to do with the mural?" I asked.

"Well," he said, taking a deep breath, "we all came back here that night after we left the hospital. Everyone was scared to go home. We were in shock. What if the government changed its mind and came for us? What if we were going to die slowly, over the course of days or weeks? We needed to process what had happened, to make sense of it, even if only a little. So, we each took turns describing what we'd experienced, piecing together each tiny detail to understand the whole. I was the first to admit that while I'd lain unconscious in that building full of gas, I'd had a vision. And as I described it to the others, their eyes grew rounder and their heads began to nod and they began to add their own accounts because we'd all seen something similar."

"And what was that?" I asked reluctantly, not sure I wanted to hear any more of Gordon's old man delusions.

"You," he said. "I saw you. And your mother saw your sister."

5

DAVID MARCUS

I stared at Gordon Lightfoot. "You're telling me you saw me in a chemically induced vision fifteen years before I was born, and my mother saw Danielle?" I barely stifled a laugh.

"Yes." He nodded. "Every one of us saw a different young person with PSS ten years before it existed. This man"—he pointed at one of the white guys in the photo—"is Stephen Black. He saw Kaylee."

"Stephen Black? That's her father," I blurted.

"I know," Gordon said without batting an eye. "He went on to become a very accomplished painter." He suddenly looked down at Kaylee, who was leaning against his knee. "Of course you can see it," he said, handing her the photo and pointing. "He's the one in the middle there."

Shit. She was mind-speaking to him and he didn't realize it. She could trick people that way for a while. She'd tricked me at first but, later, I'd noticed her lips weren't moving when I heard her voice. Gordon would notice too. And that would be dangerous.

"Whatever we were exposed to," Gordon said, "the visions were ours. They couldn't take that from us. Stephen painted his, and I painted mine, first just on canvas, but eventually the tribe commissioned the one of you to go on the wall at the lodge."

This was crazy. It couldn't be true. My parents would have told me. They wouldn't have lied to me about something this important.

"I think I've heard enough," I said, moving toward Kaylee. Someone was outside, sneaking up on the house. I had seen a bulky form out the window I'd been standing near. Why had I come here and brought Kaylee to the home of a lunatic, surrounded by a labyrinth of junk an entire army of CAMFers could hide in? I'd been lulled into a false sense of security by Reiny and Lonan and the tight-knit community of the rez, but the reservation was no protection from CAMFers.

"Come on, Kaylee." I took the photo from her, handing it back to Gordon and pulling her up. "Time to go."

"You think I'm lying?" Gordon asked, a new edge to his voice. "Why would I make this up? What could I possibly gain?"

"I don't know," I said, turning toward the door just as Mia came in. She'd taken off her armor and helmet, but her face was still rosy from the heat of her welding.

"Are you leaving already?" she asked, surprised.

"He thinks I'm lying or crazy," Gordon told her. "Just like the rest of them."

"Oh, give him some time, you gruff bear," she scolded, sounding half-amused, half-annoyed. "You can't spring this kind of news on someone and expect them to gobble it up like candy. That story is hard to believe and you know it. As for you two"—she turned her eyes on me and Kaylee—"you can't go yet." She shooed us back toward the chairs and the woodstove. "Lonan tells me you were born on the rez, David, and need proof you exist for the white man. How a piece of paper can do that better than a body standing smack in front of them, I'll never understand. But hell, they pay me to shuffle their papers, so who am I to complain about it? Now, when were you born?"

I told her my birthday, and she turned to a large filing cabinet in the corner of the room. "While I'm doing this," she said, flipping through faded manila folders, her back to us, "Gordon can go fetch you that thing you wanted. What was it again?"

The cube. In all the mayhem and ridiculous revelations, I'd completely forgotten why we'd come in the first place. We had to get that cube, and I'd possibly just blown our only chance by shitting doubt all over Gordon's story. Did he or Mia have any idea what they had in their possession? Probably not, or they wouldn't have been selling it at the bazaar. How could they know? To anyone without Kaylee's powers, it was just a weird metal cube.

"I'll go get what you really came for then," Gordon said, setting the photo down, his voice dripping with sarcasm. "No more of this nonsense about your mother or NAM. The boy needs his alien artifact." He got up and went into another room.

Kaylee stood and stared after him, a look of concern on her face.

"You kids don't mind him," Mia said, still flipping through folders. "He hasn't been feeling himself lately. I think it's his heart, but the man's so stubborn he won't go see the doctor in town. And here it is." She turned, waving a paper in her hand. "Your birth notation, exactly where it should be. Now I just have to transfer it over to an official certificate, put a seal on it, and stamp it with my registrar stamp, if I can find it. Gordon," she called, "have you seen my registrar kit?" But she wandered into another room before he could answer.

Gordon came back, the cube in his hand, and held it out to me. "I'm not lying," he said, "or crazy. It happened just like I said. Your grandparents had similar visions of people with PSS years before we did, and they weren't being gassed when they had them. I know you've heard that story, and it must mean something. Maybe what we did was foolish and dangerous, but it was part of something bigger."

I reached out and took the cube. I didn't want to argue with the guy, but now he was dragging my grandparents and their grand delusions into this, and that pissed me off.

"Maybe you all saw what you wanted to," I said. "Something to help justify what you'd done and the loss of your friends." My mother and uncle passing out and having visions similar to their parents was understandable. Those images had been described to them their entire childhood. They'd been held up as something huge and spiritual and important. My mother or my uncle could have described them to Gordon and the group before the gas accident. Maybe they'd all shared a group hallucination, or pretended they'd had one afterwards to comfort themselves. There had to be some explanation other than the one Gordon was offering. Because he wasn't offering an explanation, really, just some revised version of The Hold's mythological fairy tale about PSS.

"Here it is. All done," Mia said, coming back into the tension-filled room like a breath of fresh air and handing me a crisp, very official-looking birth certificate. "The white man will be able to see you now," she teased, winking.

"Thank you." I took it, folded it up carefully, and stuck it in one of my pockets, then dug in my other one for the money Reiny had given me. "How much do I owe you, for both the cube and the certificate?"

"Oh, none of that," Mia said. "They're gifts. You're practically family now, and we don't take money from family."

Family. That was a laugh. Everyone in my family was dead, but at least I had the cube and we could get out of here. I turned, looking for Kaylee, but she wasn't behind me. She wasn't anywhere in the room.

"She was here a minute ago," Mia said, glancing at the door. "Maybe she slipped out to go find Lonan."

I hadn't heard the door open or close. Neither had they, and I could see that realization dawning in their eyes.

"Kaylee," I called, battling to keep the fear out of my voice.

"I'll check the bathroom," Mia said. "Gordon, you check the den." She went one direction and he went the other, back to the room he'd come from when retrieving the cube.

I went into the kitchen. She wasn't there. I glanced out the window, but it had gotten very dark since we'd come into the house and I couldn't see a thing. I looked down at my empty hands. Gordon had given me the cube, but I didn't have it now. By the time Mia had handed me my birth certificate, I'd used both hands to fold it up and put it away. I didn't have a pocket big enough to hold the cube, but Kaylee did. Had I handed it to her without even remembering? Or had she slipped it out of my hand when I'd been arguing with Gordon? Shit. Kaylee was gone and the cube with her. My heart was hammering in my chest. Where were they? How could they both have been taken right out from under my nose? Even if Kaylee had just wandered outside and gotten lost in the maze of junk, she'd be terrified. Or maybe this was exactly what Gordon and Mia had planned all along. Lure us with the cube. Set their trap. Take the cube *and* Kaylee as the prize.

"Kaylee!" I yelled, moving back into the living room, not sure if I should yank the door open and search outside, or demand that Mia and Gordon give her back to me. Before I could do either, the door opened, her small hooded face peering in. "How did you get out there?" I demanded, grabbing her by the arms. "We didn't know where you were. Don't scare me like that."

I'm sorry, she whimpered in my mind. *You and Gordon were angry and it scared me. I didn't want you to fight.*

"Did you take the cube?" I asked, shaking her a little.

You gave it to me, she said, her eyes wide. *Don't you remember?*

I didn't and that scared me shitless. I had lost my memory, but I couldn't lose my mind. I had to get a grip, had to pull myself together.

"Let go of her," Gordon growled, striding toward me, his fists clenched.

I let go of Kaylee's arms, preparing to defend myself, but she stepped between us, holding her arms out and halting Gordon's advance.

"I wasn't hurting her," I told him. "I was just worried."

"You're nothing like my vision." He scowled at me. "What I saw—what I painted was a man of strength and insight, a spiritual leader. But you're just a snot-nosed, terrified kid with no idea which end is his head and which is his ass."

"Gee, so sorry I don't measure up to your make-believe wet dream of me," I shot back. "I'm sure there's a guy out there somewhere with a PSS chest who will meet all your expectations."

"No, it's you," he said, shaking his head in disappointment. "But you have no idea what you're doing."

"Oh, leave the boy alone," Mia chided, coming up behind him. "You were a young fool once too, and that didn't stop you from acting way too big for your britches. You should go," she said, skirting around Gordon and holding the door open for Kaylee and me. "We'll see you again soon, I'm sure, when the time is right."

God, I hoped not.

"Yeah, goodnight," I said, pulling Kaylee with me into the night, hoping we were headed toward Lonan and the horses.

When we got back to Reiny and Lonan's house, Kaylee immediately excused herself to the bedroom she shared with Reiny, saying she was tired. I thought she might be mad at me for grabbing her and scolding her back at Gordon's. Or maybe she just wanted to check out the cube in private. Either way, I could give her a little space. I wanted to talk to Reiny and Lonan about Gordon.

As I began telling Reiny what had gone down, she didn't seem as surprised as I thought she'd be. In fact, about five minutes into recounting Gordon Lightfoot's unbelievable story, I realized something.

"You already knew this," I said, staring from her to Lonan and back.

"Yes," Reiny sighed. "Mia is our aunt. We grew up hearing Uncle Gordo's story, along with dire warnings never to share it outside the family or the Mah-zame would come and snatch us from our beds."

Now that I knew, I could see the resemblance between Reiny and her aunt. They were both beautiful, strong women. But why keep the relationship from me? Why not tell me before we'd headed over there? The secrecy didn't make sense. Unless they were still hiding something, and immediately I knew they were. There was still some secret I hadn't earned and maybe never would. "What's a Mah-zame?" I asked, hoping to dig deeper without seeming to.

"The sherriff, or cops in general," Lonan answered. "Basically the rez boogie man."

"And what's a chooch?" I asked. "Your Uncle Gordon called me one."

"It means idiot or moron," Reiny said, her face flushing red.

"Don't worry." Lonan smiled. "I'm sure it was a term of endearment."

"Yeah, I don't think so. Anyway, if this was the great family secret, why tell me? I'm not family." Mia had tried to say I was, but we all knew that was just something people said to make you trust them.

"Isn't that obvious?" Reiny asked. "Your mother and uncle were there. That makes it your family secret too. We thought you deserved to know."

"Is that how you ended up working for Uncle Alex and treating me? Because he and your uncle share this secret?"

"Sort of," Reiny said, looking uncomfortable. "I mean, that's how I knew who he was. I'd heard Uncle Gordon talk about him. But your uncle didn't seek me out to treat you. That was later. When he originally hired me, it was to be a research assistant for a medical study he was conducting on PSS. Then the tribal council roped me into giving him an ultimatum about the compound, and I thought for sure he'd fire me. He probably would have too, except then he found you and needed help bringing you back from the dead."

"A study on PSS? What kind of study?" The rest of it, I had already figured out. But this was new.

"A highly illegal one," she said. "Pete and I were scanning medical records from the entire US database, searching for certain, subtle, indicators of internal PSS."

"Indicators? What indicators?"

"Ghosting on X-rays. Unusual blood labs. Certain types of feedback on electrocardiograms and ultrasounds. We identified sixteen specific anomalies and your uncle had a program designed to assess and calculate the probability, given a combination of those variables, that each patient had some manifestation of PSS, no matter how slight."

"And what was the outcome? What percentage did you come up with?"

"Ninety-eight percent," she said, her eye locking with mine.

"Ninety-eight?" I repeated. I couldn't have heard right. She must have said "point eight." Given how rare experts claimed PSS was, even eight percent would have been a huge stretch from the currently held norms. But ninety-eight was ridiculous. "That isn't possible," I told her. "That would mean only two percent of the people in your study didn't have PSS."

"That's correct." She nodded. "But it wasn't just

the people in the study. We ran a similar search on the medical records of a few other countries as well. The results came out virtually the same. There was a discrepancy of only three-tenths of a percent."

"Then your indicators were wrong," I said. "You started with a false hypothesis, so you ended up with incorrect data." Maybe I didn't have a high school diploma, but medical science had always been a fascination of mine, for obvious reasons. If you could learn it on the internet, I had. What she was saying just didn't add up.

"We thought so too, at first," Reiny admitted, "until your uncle went one step further. He brought in a cross-section of the actual patients and we did full diagnostics on all of them. The indicators weren't false and neither was the percentage. 98.4% of the patients we tested had PSS, some only in trace amounts on a cellular level, but it was there and identifiable if you knew how and where to look."

"But that—how can that be? It doesn't make sense." I seemed to be saying that a lot lately.

"It actually does make sense on a genetic level," Reiny said. "If PSS is some kind of mutation or evolution of human DNA, it would manifest slowly and incrementally in a majority of the population. Only in rare cases, like yours, would it be externally obvious. And internal PSS is hard to detect. Our medical machines and tests aren't designed to identify it as anything but a mistake or a glitch in the system. But once we identified the pattern in those glitches, it became clear. They weren't mistakes at all. They were undeniable evidence of a global phenomenon."

"And you have proof? You have the stats and the case studies of the patients? I want to see them." I would have to see it to believe it, and even then.

"*I* don't have them," she said. "Your uncle kept everything on a closed network, and Pete and I were searched every time we logged in or out, plus we signed a non-disclosure agreement which I'm technically breaking by telling you any of this. I'm not sure what plans he had for the information but he was keeping it under very tight wraps."

Of course, the last thing Uncle Alex wanted was for the world to know that almost everyone had PSS. If his special Marked Holders were suddenly just like everyone else, his position of power went straight out the window.

"So, you did this research in Indy, or at that farm?" I asked. Maybe there was some way we could get our hands on it.

"Neither," Reiny said, avoiding my gaze and glancing at the door to her bedroom as if she was afraid Kaylee would hear. "We did it at the compound," she finally whispered, her eyes coming back at me.

For a moment, my brain just couldn't make the connection. Reiny couldn't be saying she'd worked at the compound where I'd been held and tortured, and my sister killed. The compound where Kaylee had been a prisoner all her life. And once I understood that was exactly what she meant, I still couldn't say anything. I didn't have words, just feelings rushing over me like a hot wind. It didn't matter that she would have been on The Hold side, or for what purpose.

There were no sides to that place in my mind. It was all one, horrible, hellhole and anyone associated with it was my enemy. Pete had worked there as well, both of them doing my uncle's bidding, possibly at the very same time the CAMFers were killing Danielle.

"Did you work there too?" I asked Lonan, slamming my fist down on the table.

"No," Lonan said, "I didn't."

"Fuck you!" I screamed in both their faces. I reached into my pocket and pulled out the money Reiny had given me, throwing it at her. "I don't want this. I don't want help from people like you." She flinched away from me, tears in her eyes, and I was glad.

As I charged out the front door of the house into the dark desert night, I heard Reiny weeping behind me and Lonan's gentle voice consoling her, saying "It will be all right. Just let him go."

6

OLIVIA

"**O**livia!" My mother's voice jolted me awake.

I sat up in the rental van's passenger seat, wiping drool from my cheek. The hackers' Westfalia had stopped in front of us at a massive gate rising out of the darkness, topped with barbed wire and sported several *Danger: High Voltage* and *No Trespassing on Federal Land* signs.

Shit. We were at Umatilla, and I'd fallen asleep, like I always did in a moving vehicle, before I'd explained anything to my mom.

"Olivia Anne Black," she said, pointing at the gate. "What is that?"

"Um—I don't know," I stammered. "We must have taken a wrong turn."

"Are we there?" Grant asked groggily from the back. It sounded like I wasn't the only one who'd taken a nap.

"Well, we're somewhere," my mother answered testily. "What the hell is he doing?"

She was referring to T-Dog, who had gotten out of their van carrying something bulky under his arm. When he set it down and started fiddling with a controller in his hands, I realized it was one of those personal drones. Suddenly, the little thing lit up and went whirling into the air, kicking up dust and flying over the gate. On the other side, it dipped down and stopped, a green light flashing on its undercarriage as it hovered over some kind of control panel. As I watched, a green light began flashing on the panel too, like they were communicating with one another. Because they were. The hackers had started hacking into Umatilla.

I could feel my mother turning toward me, a question in her eyes, her lips parting to ask it.

Headlights, high and wide, flashed in the rearview mirror, blinding me. They were barreling down on us, but I only heard the rev of the engine just before the crunch of impact.

The whole van jerked forward, shoving us toward the back of the Westfalia and stopping only inches from its rear bumper.

"What the fuck?" Grant yelled, and I heard cries of alarm from Passion and Samantha.

My seatbelt dug into my waist and my shoulder, but the airbags hadn't deployed, so that was good.

In front of us, T-Dog scrambled back into the Westfalia and slammed his door. The gate started to open, the drone hovering on the other side, still blinking green.

There was another crunching sound and a slight tug backwards. Then, more revving.

"Shit! Hold on. They're coming again," my mother said, jamming the van into drive and laying on the horn like a mad woman. We couldn't go anywhere. The Westfalia was right in front of us and some lunatic was behind us, gearing up to rear-end us a second time.

"We have to go through," I told my mom, gesturing at the gate.

"I know," she said, glaring out at the Westfalia and revving our engine now. "Get out of my way, you little fuckers," she mumbled under her breath, laying on the horn again and not letting up.

The vehicle behind was almost upon us. I could hear it coming.

Up ahead, T-dog glanced at me in his side view mirror, but it was too dark to read his expression. Had the hackers set us up? Was this their doing?

The gate was open wider now, maybe wide enough for the Westfalia, but would it be enough for our bigger van?

"Hold on," my mom said, glancing in the rearview mirror and slamming her foot on the gas.

I braced myself, this time for impact from the back and front, but it didn't come.

We surged forward, gently kissing the back bumper of the Westfalia, both of us racing through the still opening gate. I heard a horrible sound, metal screeching against metal, and sparks flew in a shower away from us as the huge closures of the gate scraped down both sides of our van.

As soon as we were free and clear, the Westfalia veered off to the right and pulled to a stop. As we drove past, I could see T-Dog holding the drone remote out his window, working it frantically, trying to close the gate before our attackers made it in. But he wasn't fast enough. The pick-up truck that had rear-ended us roared forward, squeezing through just like we had. For a moment, I thought it had a really weird hood ornament, but then I realized it was the drone, flying low and toward us in front of the truck.

"Get higher," I murmured to the little thing. As if hearing me, it did, rising above the front of the truck only to plummet a second later just as the vehicle overtook it.

And then it was gone, sucked under the huge wheel of the big truck with a soft crunch and a shower of shrapnel spraying from its undercarriage.

"Stop the van," I told my mother, but she'd already turned and was pulling up alongside the Westfalia.

"Who the fuck is that?" I shouted out my window at Chase, pointing at the truck as it pulled up, headlights blinding us all, the gate clanging shut behind it.

"I have no idea," he shouted back. "But I think we're about to find out."

A truck door slammed.

A dark form moved, crossing the dusty swathe of its high beams, and a man emerged, tall, wrinkled, and tan, wearing cowboy boots and a cowboy hat.

I had never seen him before, but he reminded me a little of Clint Eastwood and everything about him screamed CAMFer, especially the long rifle dangling from his right hand.

"Everybody stay here and let me handle this," I said. I was out the door before my mom could protest. If the CAMFers were here for me, I wasn't going to let them have anyone else I cared about. Not this time.

But Chase and T-dog were already out too, T-Dog holding the drone controller dejectedly in his hands.

"Hey!" Cowboy CAMFer yelled, looking us over and gesturing to the signs on the fence. "You kids are trespassing."

"You from the government?" I asked, fuming, but trying to keep myself in check.

"Nope," he said, spitting something black from between his teeth, his eyes flicking to my ghost hand and back up to my face. "Can't say that I am."

"Then we're not the only ones trespassing," I pointed out.

"Are you crazy?" my mother demanded, charging up from behind me. "You almost killed us," she said, getting right up in the guy's face and wagging her finger at him. She was so mad, I don't think she even noticed the gun. "It's the middle of the night, we take an innocent wrong turn, and suddenly we're being rear-ended, bullied, and told we're trespassing on land you forced us to drive onto. Do you have insurance? Because that—" she pointed at our van— "is a rental, and I'm not paying for the damage *you* just did to it."

"A wrong turn?" he said. "I don't think so. These two—" he gestured at T-dog and Chase—"just cracked a high-level government security gate."

"We weren't trying to crack anything." T-Dog jumped in. "We just got lost, man, and Chase was like, 'Whoa, that's a massive fence, dude. Let's fly your Phantom over it.' And technically it wasn't trespassing because airspace is in the public domain. But that drone cost me five hundred dollars. Why'd you have to smash it?" T-Dog bent down and picked up a piece of what had once been his drone, cradling it in his palm. It was a pretty good shtick. I almost believed it, but I doubted this guy would.

"You're saying you *accidentally* opened it?" Cowboy scoffed. "Boy, I wasn't born yesterday. I know exactly who you are, with your hippie vans and special drones. You tree huggers always send women and children to do your dirty work."

Tree huggers? What the hell was this guy talking about?

"Who is this wacko and why did he ram us?" Grant asked, joining the group with Passion and Samantha hand-in-hand right behind him. Grant was acting casual, but I saw him glance at the rifle and then back at me.

I shook my head, ever so slightly. The last thing we needed was someone playing the hero. It was looking more and more like this guy wasn't a CAMFer, but just some local lunatic. And apparently, he thought we were environmentalists or something. He was sizing us up now, his eyes scanning our little group, pausing a moment on Samantha's PSS ear, curious and calculating, but not hostile. He hadn't reacted to my ghost hand either.

Then, it finally dawned on my mother that this crazy old coot had a gun, and she went straight into therapist mode. "I'm not sure who you think we are," she said calmly. "But this seems to be a case of mistaken identity. Why don't you explain to us why you're here, and what this place is, and maybe we can all sort it out together."

"I'm here because this land is rightfully mine," Cowboy said. "It belonged to my family for generations and was forcibly taken from my grandfather by the government before World War II so they could turn it into a chemical depot."

"Chemical depot?" my mother repeated, glancing around worriedly.

"So, wait, do we need hazmat suits or something?" Chase asked.

I had to admit, he and T-dog were doing an amazing job playing dumb. If hacking didn't work out for them, they could definitely seek an alternative career in the performing arts.

"If you've put these kids in any danger—" my mother began.

"You'll be fine," Cowboy cut her off. "They destroyed the chemicals years ago, and they promised to give this land back to the people of Hermiston, but now, suddenly, they're gonna charge us for it," his voice grew passionate. "Never mind that our families have lived within reach of some of the most dangerous chemical weapons on earth for generations. Never mind that my kids grew up constantly in fear for their lives, carrying shelter-in-place kits to school every day and enduring the monthly evacuation drills. And then there's our livelihood, our family farms gone to shit, because who wants to buy anything grown next to a chemical depot? I'll tell you who. No one. They owe us this land, see."

"That is obviously horribly unjust," my mother said in her best therapist voice. "No wonder you're up-in-arms about it. But I'm still not sure I understand why you rear-ended our van."

"Well," he said, "We're not the only ones with a claim in all this. Now that the rights to the land are up in the air, everyone wants a piece of it. The natives. The military. The preppers. The tree huggers. That's who I thought you were because of your hippie van and your drone. The tree huggers use them sometimes to get footage of the wildlife. And they've been rumors going around that certain groups are trying to get onto the land and use some kind of loophole in the Homestead Act to solidify their claim, so when I came upon your vans and saw the gate start to open—"

"You assumed that's what we were doing," my mother finished for him.

"Yes, ma'am," he said, looking sheepish.

"Well," she said, smiling at him, "I assure you we were doing no such thing. I'm Sophie Black," she introduced herself. "I'm a psychologist from Illinois and this is my daughter, Olivia, and her friends. We've all been through an ordeal recently and we're driving from Portland up the Gorge for some much-needed rest and relaxation. But it was late, and we made a wrong turn, and the boys foolishly got out to test their drone, at which point you damaged our vehicle and pulled a gun on innocent kids." Man, she was really milking the "innocent kid" thing, and it was so NOT true, but it seemed to be working, so I certainly wasn't going to stop her.

"And I'm mighty sorry about that, ma'am." Cowboy tipped his hat, suddenly going all southern gentleman on her. "I'll put this away," he added, stepping back to the open window of his truck and setting his rifle inside on the seat. Then, he reached into his glove box and pulled out a card, crossing and handing it to her. "The name's Wade Hermiston, and here's my insurance information. But I'd sure appreciate you reporting this as an accident, you know, just like I'll report that your kids here *accidentally* breached military security and trespassed on federal land."

He wasn't going to report this. What he'd just done to us would get him in a ton of legal trouble and hurt his court case.

"Of course, I'll report it as an accident," my mother said, "Just a minute," she added, turning toward the van. "I think the rental insurance information is in the glove box."

"No, that's all right," he said. "My truck is fine." He was right. The old thing had a huge bumper with hardly a scratch on it. "Do you need directions to somewhere?" He offered politely. "I know this area like the back of my hand."

"Yeah, about that," T-dog said grimly, bending down and picking up a few more pieces of his pulverized drone. "I don't think any of us is getting out of here anytime soon." He stood, glancing at the gate. "That thing locked up again as soon as it closed."

"So, can you open it?" I asked Chase and T-Dog, all three of us huddled around the control panel of Umatilla's main gate.

"You're never gonna crack that code manually," Wade Hermiston called from behind us where he was leaning against his truck making small talk with my mom.

"Ignore him," I told my new hacker friends. "You guys were made for this."

"Sorry," Chase said somberly. "No can do."

"What?" I whispered. "Why the hell not? You're telling me you brought an entire van of electronic hacking equipment and you can't reopen a simple gate?"

"Oh, we can open it," T-Dog said, keeping his voice low. "We can open it *and* close it. In fact, we can open all four security gates on this property and shut off their voltage, as well as intercept any new code changes that might be issued remotely. We could do all that the moment the drone linked to the control panel and uploaded the security information to our computers in the van. Not to mention, we have several more drones with us."

"Then why'd you just say you couldn't hack it?" I asked, totally confused.

"Because," Chase explained, "if we open this gate, Wade Hermiston is going to be suspicious all over again. He'd probably insist on escorting us off this land at gunpoint, and then we lose access to the compound and he and his vigilante townspeople keep us from ever coming back."

"Right." I let out a sigh. "Good point. So, we pretend we're trying and we fail, and then what?"

"We find the dome," T-Dog said, shrugging.

"With him tagging along?" I groaned.

"You have a better idea?" Chase asked.

"You ain't getting it, are you?" Wade Hermiston called to us loudly. "I told you, but you kids these days think you know everything about technology."

"He seems harmless enough," I said, glancing back at the old coot. "How far is the dome from here?"

"About fifteen miles due north," T-Dog answered. "It's pretty much smack in the middle of the depot."

"Okay," I said, racking my brain for a plan. "Do you have any video equipment in the van?"

"Sure," Chase said. "We have a couple of hand cams."

"Good. Here's what we do. We want to get to the dome, right? And Wade Hermiston wants the world to know how the government is shafting him and his entire town. So, you guys act all interested and tell him you're up-and-coming documentary filmmakers. That's why you had the drone, for cheap aerial shots or something. Anyway, stroke his ego. Tell him this is the best underdog story you've ever heard and you want to film him and get footage of the entire depot. And, if he lets you do that, you'll make sure when we all get out of here that everyone who's ever used the internet sees his story."

"That gives us an excuse to head north to the compound," T-Dog said, sounding impressed. "But what about when we actually get to the dome?"

"I guess we act like we have no idea what it is, but it's cool-looking, so you guys want to film it. That gives us an excuse to go inside. And Wade's probably going to assume it's all part of someone's diabolical plot to take the depot from him, so that might play right into our hands."

"You kids ready to give up yet and let a seasoned adult get us out of here?" Wade yelled.

"And exactly how are you going to do that?" I yelled back.

"I have a friend who lives just north of the depot," he hollered. "If we can get his attention by flashing our headlights, he'll come to our rescue."

North of the depot. It was like the fates were playing directly into our hands. And that totally freaked me out because I wasn't used to things going my way pretty much ever.

"Excellent," I whispered to T-Dog and Chase, "He wants to head north, so let's make him a movie star along the way. And when we get to the compound, we can send him further north to signal his friend while we stay back and get some extra footage."

"Whoa," T-Dog purred. "You're good."

The first part of our plan worked flawlessly. T-Dog and Chase gave an incredible performance. Even those of us who knew they were hackers began to believe they were also passionate part-time filmmakers. When they pulled the small, hand-held cams out of their van to back up our charade and filmed a short clip of Wade Hermiston telling his story, I could practically see tears in the old guy's eyes. And best of all, I could tell my mother was completely convinced.

"Well, isn't this a little surprise side-adventure?" she said, putting her arm around me while T-Dog and Chase showed Wade his footage. "Are you feeling okay? I know getting rear-ended like that was a little traumatic."

"Mom, I'm fine," I assured her. And yes, I still hadn't told her about why we were really at the depot. But as T-Dog had pointed out, I was pretty good at winging it, so I figured when we drove up to the dome, the right words would come to me.

After T-dog and Chase had shot a few more dramatic scenes on location at the gate, we all piled into our respective vehicles and headed north, Wade Hermiston leading us. Mom even let me drive the van, despite the fact that it was against the rental agreement. But she was exhausted and frazzled and, let's face it, I wasn't likely to damage it any more than it already had been.

Driving through Umatilla at night was like driving through a strange apocalyptic world. The road we followed was just hard-packed dirt, so there was always a shroud of dust billowing around us. As our headlights cut through this self-made haze, bizarre forms rose out of the darkness on either side of us. Strange hummocks, covering the underground chemical storage barracks, flashed passed at perfectly spaced intervals.

According to Wade's earlier narrative, they were called igloos and there were exactly 1,000 of them. Originally, there'd been 1,001, but somewhere along the way Umatilla had experienced an unfortunate accident, an explosion that had left only a crater where one of the bunkers had been. That was why they'd been built spaced so far apart. So that one going off wouldn't trigger a domino effect of Armageddon across the entire depot.

"This place is eerie," Grant said from the back. "It's giving me the creeps."

"I don't know. I think it's kind of serene," Passion countered.

Finally, about ten miles in, the scenery changed. The constant array of bunkers ceased, making way for an arrangement of abandoned buildings, looking like some kind of industrial ghost town.

In front of me, Wade's truck sped up, passing between two huge, hanger-like buildings. I followed, foot on the gas, glancing at the building to my right with its large doors hanging open, revealing a hauntingly empty interior.

"Olivia!" my mom screamed, and I jerked my eyes back to the road just as something charged out of the dark and darted directly in front of the van.

Oh shit.

I swerved just in time and missed it, but it didn't matter. There wasn't just one. There were hundreds of them, leaping and scampering across the road in a giant herd. The one I'd missed bolted away, flashing a big, glowing, heart-shaped butt as it went.

And then we were slamming into the next one.

7

DAVID MARCUS

I don't know how long I'd been running in the desert, or how far I'd gotten from Reiny and Lonan's. I wasn't aware of the night, or the cold air, the sand under my feet, or the stars hanging above me. I might as well have not been in my body, as little as I cared for anything but escaping the anguish inside of me.

I'd held the crushing guilt and grief at bay for days, comforted by the presence and touch of Kaylee. But now that I was on my own, I had no choice but to face it. My one job in life had been to protect my sister, and I had failed. Not only that, I'd led her into danger. I'd practically handed her over to the CAMFers, and then I'd had the audacity to survive instead of her.

She should have lived. She had been the good one. The one who could still love and trust people, despite everything that had been done to her. She could heal people. Of course, she'd never been able to heal me on the inside where it really mattered. I had been broken for way too long. We'd both known that. But she'd loved me anyway, even when I was angry and bitter. Even when I was terrified and paranoid. Even when my only power was the useless act of saving myself over and over again. Danielle had always understood me. She had been the one person who truly had. How could I go on without her?

Maybe I couldn't.

Or maybe I could and I didn't want to.

Miles of running later, I found myself on top of a sandy hill: sweaty, panting, and standing on the ridge of a tableland overlooking a large valley. The valley floor was black and barren, only a few twisted, burnt-out tree stumps peppered around the large, football-field-sized crater at its center.

My body had known exactly where it was going, even if my mind hadn't.

This was where Danielle had died, where I had lost her. If she had a burial site, this was it, this giant gouge in the earth where the compound had once been.

I stepped over the steep edge of the hill and started to run down it. Toward the bottom, my feet couldn't keep up. I was going so fast I pitched forward, head over heels, a rock pounding into my shoulder, dust filling my mouth, the earth and sky spinning out of control around me.

I bounced the last few yards, the wind knocked out of me as I landed at the bottom on the valley floor. My vision was blurred and my face was wet. There was blood on my hands and leaking from a tear in my jeans. It stung and felt good, all at the same time, the bruises and cuts protesting as I pushed up onto my hands and knees.

I got up and walked past dead trees to the outer rim of the crater, looking down into it.

Everything was gone. Danielle. The buildings and the dome. Everything and everyone who had ever worked there. The power to do that—to remove an entire building, all its sublevels, its foundation and systems as if they'd never existed—was both impressive and terrifying. Olivia Black, reportedly my girlfriend, had scoured the world clean of the CAMFers and The Hold. Whatever our relationship had been in the past, I certainly wouldn't get on her bad side if we met again.

I don't know how long I stood there. The stars cycled across the sky. The moon rose. Coyotes howled in the distance and the sound so perfectly encapsulated how I felt that I threw back my head and joined them.

The howling came closer, answering my own, at first hesitant and questioning, then more sure. I knew I was calling them to me, but I didn't care that it was dangerous. I wanted to see them. I wanted to be seen.

I heard a noise behind me, the slightest sound, and turned to see the silhouette of a lone coyote on the ridge.

Her eyes glowed, reflecting moonlight, as she inspected me. I don't know how I knew it was a she, but I did. If Danielle's spirit lived on, I would want it to look like that. Fierce. Free. Dangerous. Wild. All the things life had never allowed her to be.

"Hello," I said, and the creature startled a little, obviously insulted that what she'd come to find was only an odd upright human. But she didn't run.

"I don't know what to do." I told her, stepping forward, my foot sinking into the sand and hitting something solid that didn't feel like a rock.

She darted away, her tail swishing at me as she ducked behind the hill and disappeared.

I reached down and felt the edge of something wooden and man-made jutting from the ground.

I crouched and dug around the edges of whatever it was, following the rectangular line the wood made. One corner was buried deeper than the others, but I eventually got it all pulled up, dirt cascading off of it to reveal a painting. The frame was black and burnt in places, and I couldn't really see the picture because the canvas was caked in sand.

I shook it, knocking the sand away and slowly uncovering the dark painting beneath. It was a portrait of Kaylee. Not just any portrait, but the exact one I'd remembered seeing in my uncle's collection when I was a kid. Gordon would claim it as proof of his vision story. My uncle had used it in other ways. Everyone I knew had their own version of the truth about PSS, and I was getting a little tired of it.

How had the painting gotten here? Surely my uncle hadn't kept one of his most prized art pieces at the compound. Yet, here it was. And for some reason, it had only displaced a few feet instead of miles like Kaylee and I had.

I glanced up to where the coyote had been.

I don't know what to do, I'd said to her, and one step forward had landed me on a picture of Kaylee.

I didn't believe in visions or signs. It had just been coincidence, a freak of chance.

Still, hadn't I promised to help Kaylee? Hadn't I vowed to protect her the way I hadn't protected Danielle?

Gordon's story about what he'd done with my mom and uncle didn't change that. Reiny's confession that she'd worked at the compound didn't either. As for the whole thing about almost everyone in the world having PSS? I was still processing that.

"Okay then," I said, taking a deep breath and hefting the painting of Kaylee onto my shoulders. I hadn't been worried about her during my run in the desert, probably because I knew, deep down, I could trust Reiny and Lonan. But I wasn't used to trusting people. Hopefully, they'd accept my apology for going off on them, and we could start again. Because the truth was I needed their help. And I wanted it.

When I stepped onto the porch, Lonan opened the door before I'd even reached for it.

He glanced at the painting on my back, then gestured for me to come in.

"I'm dirty and bloody," I said, reluctant to mess up the house Reiny kept so neat.

"Don't worry," Lonan said. "We'll get you cleaned up. But don't be loud. Reiny and Kaylee are asleep."

I slipped inside, leaning the painting against the wall and taking off my sand-filled shoes.

"What's with that?" Lonan asked. "You rob a museum or something?"

"No." I turned it around so he could see the front. "I found it near the compound's crater, buried in the dirt."

Lonan stared at it, his eyes a little wider, and nodded. He didn't ask me why I'd been at the crater, or why I looked like the desert had beaten the crap out of me. That was one thing I admired about Lonan. He was a man of few words, but when he spoke you knew it was going to be worth something.

"Go get cleaned up," he said, pointing toward the bathroom.

No reprimand. No guilt trip about what I'd said to them. Reiny had saved my life at least twice. Together they'd housed me and fed me and treated me like family. And instead of thanking them, I'd made them feel like shit. Lonan had obviously let it slide right off his back, but Reiny was another story. I'd hurt her badly. I knew that, and I had to try and fix it.

"I'm sorry about before," I told Lonan. "I—it won't happen again, and I'll apologize to Reiny first thing in the morning."

"Good." He nodded, giving me one of his rare smiles.

8

OLIVIA

The rental van was fucked. I could see that even before we all climbed out. The entire front end was crumpled and the engine hissed steam, plus it had a new hood ornament. A bloody, flailing hood ornament in the last throes of death, its doe-eyes still locked on me as the light slowly faded from them.

No, not the light. The PSS.

"Not your fault," Wade said, coming up beside me and looking down at the poor animal. "I shoulda warned you. Since the army left, and with no natural predators inside the fence, the pronghorn population has exploded."

"I didn't see them," I stammered. "They darted from behind the building."

"Olivia, it's okay," my mother said, putting her arm around me. "No one was hurt. See, Grant is fine. So are Passion and Samantha." There they were, my passengers, safe and sound. But someone was hurt. Didn't she see the animal dying right in front of us?

"They're fast," Wade said. "Fastest land mammal in the western hemisphere, and that was a big herd."

"Oh my God, did you see that?" T-Dog asked as he and Chase came running up to the scene of the crime, their van parked behind ours. "They had PSS." He held his camera's playback screen up to show me. "Every last one of them."

I watched the recording of the pronghorns as they went streaming across the road in front of our smashed van, flashing PSS horns and butts, legs and flanks, eyes and ears. In a couple cases, it looked like the entire animal was PSS. They were glow-in-the-dark animals, and I'd still managed to hit one.

"I didn't hear them," Samantha murmured, watching over my shoulder. "Why didn't I—" She stopped mid-sentence, glancing at Wade and clamping her mouth shut.

"Oh, they're so beautiful," Passion said, joining Samantha.

"They're mutants," Wade said, frowning. "Supposedly, the government cleaned this place up, but I guess some damage can't be undone. Still, no reason to let it suffer. I'll get my gun to put it down." He turned, walking toward his truck.

The pronghorn had stopped flailing, but it was still looking at me with those PSS eyes. In all my life, I'd never heard of animals manifesting PSS, yet Wade seemed to be taking it in stride. He'd called the pronghorn mutants, but he hadn't said a thing about my ghost hand, or Samantha's PSS ear. All this time I'd thought we were luring Wade deeper into the depot, but what if he'd been luring us?

"I should have never let you drive," my mom said. "This is all my fault."

"No, it's not," I assured her softly, keeping my voice low so Wade couldn't hear. He was reaching into his truck now, pulling out his rifle. "None of this is your fault, Mom. It's mine. We didn't come to see the Gorge. That was a lie. We came to find the dome. It's here on the depot and the hackers need to get into it and access the computers. I'm sorry I lied to you, but I don't trust this guy at all, so I need you to hold it together for me, okay?"

Her fingers dug into my arm as I spoke, but she didn't say anything. She didn't reproach or scold me. Then Wade Hermiston was back in our midst, hefting his gun.

"You'd better move clear and turn away," he said, grabbing the rear legs of the pronghorn and pulling it off the hood of the rental van. It thumped to the ground in front of the grill, bleating weakly in protest or pain, probably both.

The others were moving to the side of the van where they wouldn't be able to see, and my mother was pulling me with her.

"No." I turned back to Wade Hermiston. "I hit it." I walked up to him and held out my hands. "It's my responsibility."

I was afraid my mother would protest, but again, she didn't say anything. They all just stood, staring at me in shock. Except Wade. His eyes locked with mine, calculating, weighing, his sense of country honor and stark justice warring with the unnatural act of handing his weapon over to a stranger.

"All right," he said, a certain respect glinting in his eyes as he handed me his gun. "You know how to use it?"

In lieu of an answer, I checked to make sure my mom and the others were at a safe distance.

Then I turned back to the pronghorn, flicked off the safety, pointed the barrel at its head, and pulled the trigger.

For a split second afterward, I was tempted to raise the gun and point it at Wade. I truly didn't trust him and, with the gun, we'd have the upper hand. But then the image of Yale and Nose, lying on the ground in pools of their own blood, came to me. My friends had died. The pronghorn's eyes were now hollow soulless sockets. If Wade Hermiston was my enemy, I would beat him some other way.

"Your van's front axle is broke," he said. "It ain't going nowhere. I can ride two of you in my cab if the rest of you can fit in the hippie van."

"Thank you," I nodded, handing his rifle back to him. "We'd appreciate it."

We were ten miles down the road when a dark spherical shape appeared in the distance, slowly filling the windshield.

"What the hell is that?" Wade barked, his foot slamming on the brakes.

"Looks like a dome," I said, glancing at my mom and hoping she wouldn't give anything away. I'd insisted on being one of Wade's passengers. She'd insisted on being the other one, of course, leaving Grant, Passion and Samantha to ride in the hacker van. She'd even made me take the passenger seat while she sat in the middle of the bench between Wade and me, as if that would keep me safe. And maybe it had helped because he'd at least tucked his rifle away again.

"But that—I've never seen that before," Wade said, sounding seriously afraid. "It can't be here."

He swerved his truck off to the side of the road and jammed the stick into neutral. The dome loomed on the horizon, but it was difficult to judge distance in the dark, expansive desert. I had to admit, if I hadn't known what it was I would have been spooked too. From where we were, it looked like a crashed spaceship or some kind of alien bubble colony.

"What's up?" Chase asked, pulling up next to us in the Westfalia. "Why'd we stop?"

"Because of that," Wade pointed at the dome.

"Probably some evil government secret," Chase said, a wicked twinkle in his eyes. "Let's go check it out." He pulled in front of us, taking off down the road.

"Hey, come back here!" Wade called out his window, but it was too late. "Damn kids," he mumbled under his breath, giving my mom and me a dirty look as he popped the truck back into gear and we tore off after them.

Five minutes later, we pulled up to the compound. The Westfalia was parked near one of its oversized doors, and Chase and T-Dog were already at work, their cameras in hand, directing Grant, Passion, and Samantha to stand next to the door for perspective.

As Wade, my mom, and I climbed out of his truck, Chase directed his camera light up, flashing it across a symbol of The Hold stamped on the door.

"Stop right there," Wade Hermiston said, and I turned to see him aiming his gun directly at my mom. "I'm not an idiot," he said, nodding at the dome. "You knew this was here. Who the hell are you people?"

Then, from behind us came a horrible groaning noise, like an armored beast waking up from deep inside a cave. Wade's eyes startled away from us, following that sound.

My mother sprang forward, even before I could, but her target wasn't Wade Hermiston. It was me. She tackled me like a linebacker, both of us falling to the ground just as gunfire rained down around us.

Wade's rifle rang out once in response, and then he was on the ground too, dust and bullets exploding around him. Desperately, he began to army crawl back to the open door of his truck as fast as he could.

"Don't shoot. Don't shoot!" I heard T-Dog yell. "We're unarmed."

I turned my head to see him, Chase, Grant, Passion and Samantha plastered to the ground near the Westfalia, their arms splayed out in surrender.

The door of the compound was open, a lone silhouette standing smack in the middle of it, hefting an assault rifle.

Wade Hermiston's truck revved to life and he peeled out in reverse, his headlights flashing across my mom and me. He was leaving us. The fucker had a gun and he was leaving a woman and a bunch of teenagers at the mercy of an unknown armed maniac.

Gunfire sang again, pinging against the body of the truck, as Wade tore off northbound, disappearing into the dark desert night.

I pressed against my mom, curling myself around her. Would the gunman turn his sites on easier prey now that Wade and his rifle were gone? Were we all going to die because I'd been stupid enough to bring us here?

"Uh-oh," my mother whispered, her eyes round with surprise as she raised a bloody hand between us. "I think I'm hit."

"What? Where?" I asked stunned, staring at her hand, unable to see a wound.

"My leg," she said, looking down, both our eyes falling to the hole in her jeans and the slick, dark blood seeping from her thigh.

No. No, no, no. This could not be happening.

"Put your hand on it and press down hard," I said, managing to keep my voice calm as I guided her bloody hand back to her leg. "It's gonna be okay. We'll get help." Where was I going to get help? We were in the middle of the desert, miles from the nearest hospital. Blood was welling up from between her fingers now. Her eyes were losing focus. She needed a tourniquet.

"My mom is hit!" I cried out in utter panic, not caring what the gunman did, just thankful he'd stopped firing. "I need something to stop the bleeding."

I heard voices calling to one another, feet shuffling, people moving toward me, but none of it really registered. I just kept holding my mom and talking to her. "Mom, I'm here. Everything's going to be okay. I've got you."

"I know you do." She smiled weakly. "You've got me. And I've got you."

"Where is the entry wound?" someone asked in a clinical, doctory voice, and a large, sandy-haired man crouched next to me, an AK-47 slung over his shoulder. He tugged at his waist, pulling off his belt. I might have been intimidated by his weapon and his size if it weren't for the fact that he looked like death warmed over. He was gaunt, pale, and had a large bandage taped to his neck.

"Pete?" my mother said to him, her voice a mixture of pleasure and pain. "How did you get here?"

Was she hallucinating, or did she actually know this guy? Because I'd never seen him before in my life.

"I wish I knew, Sophie," he said, gently wrapping his belt around my mother's thigh and synching it like a pro.

The guy who'd shot my mom was an old friend? WTF?

"The last thing I remember," he went on, "was charging toward the compound dodging gunfire with you. The next thing I know, I wake up inside with a hole in my neck, no power, and not a soul left but me. That was two days ago, and frankly, at first, I thought I'd died on that ER table and woken up in hell."

"Oh, you poor thing." My mother sighed, closing her eyes.

"Is she okay?" I begged him, whoever he was. "Help her, please."

"She just passed out," he said. "Let's get her inside."

"No." I grabbed his arm. "She needs a hospital. We can take her in the van." I gestured toward the Westfalia, my eyes taking in the two front tires, now utterly flat, two more victims of this guy's marksmanship.

"We don't have time for that. She needs treatment now. Take her in," he said. And then arms were reaching out for her, Grant and T-Dog, lifting her together and carrying my mom toward the dark maw of the compound. Meanwhile, Chase hopped in the van, started it up, and drove it limpingly toward the doors. Of course, we needed the van and its equipment inside with us, safe and sound, in case Wade Hermiston came back.

"I'm so sorry." Pete turned to me. "I thought you were CAMFers. The guy in the truck—he had a gun. I should never have fired like that, but two days alone and injured made me a little jumpy."

"You shot my mom." I glared at him and his pitiful apology.

"I know," he said. "The good news is I'm a certified nurse and EMT, and there's a fully equipped infirmary inside. Now, let's get in there so I can get that bullet out of her," he said, standing up and offering me his hand.

And I took it, pulling myself up, dusting myself off, and walking back into the compound with some guy named Pete.

9

OLIVIA

"Who is he exactly?" I asked, pacing outside the glass doors of the infirmary. Inside, my mom was laid out unconscious on a gurney being operated on by a complete stranger—who had shot her in the first place—while Grant held two phone screens over her leg for lighting.

Everything had happened so fast. The rush into the darkened compound. Someone pointing at a crank and barking orders for me to shut and lock the big bay door manually after Chase drove the van in. When I'd finished that, I'd turned to find myself in a huge room filled with computer workstations and overturned chairs, and its newest feature—a Westfalia parked to one side. Chase had hopped out, his arms full of cords and equipment.

When T-dog had joined him a moment later, the stain of my mother's blood fresh on the front of his t-shirt, he'd pointed me toward the back, to a smaller room off the larger one where Grant was already inside helping this guy, Pete, remove a bullet from my mom's leg in nearly pitch-black conditions.

"Pete worked for my father," Samantha said. "He was one of the people hired to nurse David back to health, but on our way into the compound, the CAMFers shot him. He's a good guy. Your mom is in good hands."

"I should be in there," I said, moving toward the doors.

"Olivia," Passion stopped me, holding me back. "Pete knows what he's doing. Going in there is only going to distract him."

"You don't understand," I said, pulling out of her grasp but moving away from the doors. I couldn't watch my mother die. "I lied to her. I brought her here. That bullet was going to hit me, but she pushed me out of the way."

Passion followed me, taking my hands in hers, stubborn in her calmness. "She's going to be okay," she said. "And if you really think your mom believed this was a sight-seeing trip, you're even more gullible than you think she is. She knew all along this was about the CAMFers and The Hold. I mean, come on. Palmer leaves and the very next morning you're chomping at the bit to get out of a house you'd refused to leave for a week? Your mother isn't stupid. We all knew this wasn't a vacation, and that's exactly why we came. You don't have to do it alone anymore, Olivia. In fact, you don't get to. We're all a part of it now."

"She knew?" I asked, stunned. "You all knew?"

"We knew something was up," Samantha said, shrugging. "We weren't sure exactly what. I guess we're still not sure, but whatever it is, we'll follow your lead."

There it was again—someone insisting I lead them. Samantha James, born leader and heir to The Hold, was following *me*. I didn't even know what to say to that. Except, obviously, it was time to tell them what was going on.

"Okay, so, the hackers located the compound by satellite last night," I explained. "They told me if we could get in, they could access all the data about PSS the CAMFers and The Hold have ever collected. And they were pretty sure we'd be the first ones here since Umatilla is deserted. But we thought it would be a quick in and out. We didn't expect to run into Wade or this Pete guy. I don't even understand why or how he's still here."

"He'd just come out of surgery when the displacement happened," Samantha said. "Maybe it doesn't work on people who are unconscious."

"I guess that could be it," I admitted.

"So, we get the information from the computers and then what?" Passion asked.

"We keep it away from them, and we look at it, I guess." God, that sounded lame and not a decent reason to get my mom shot. I hadn't really thought beyond that, though, because I'd been too desperate to get away and distract myself like a selfish idiot. After everything the CAMFers had done to me, surely I wanted more than just stealing their computer files.

When I'd stood in the dome and banged my dad's rock against Grant's cube, I'd had a vision for something better, a world where people with PSS weren't feared or lauded. Where we were just people like everyone else. That had been Marcus's dream and I'd caught it from him, tagging along for the ride. But now he was gone and I was here, poised on the verge of accessing information about PSS the world had never seen. Information was knowledge, and knowledge was power. If this worked, we were going to have power, and everyone was looking to me for what to do with it. That scared the shit out of me, but at the same time, it felt amazing. I wasn't sure why they'd all picked me as their designated leader, but I really didn't want to disappoint them.

Samantha and Passion were still looking at me, expectantly.

"Then," I said, my voice gaining confidence, "we separate the truth from all the lies they've been spreading for years. We uncover everything we can about PSS and our powers, and we blast that information all over the internet."

"It's a good plan," Samantha said, smiling, just as a few small lights and the red exit sign over the bay door flickered on, bathing the room in a soft glow.

"Woo-hoo!" T-dog called from across the room. "That's the emergency lighting, which should give us a few hours of visibility to figure out how to restore the entire system."

"How are there any lights in this place?" Passion asked, looking at me. "Did you displace the entire power grid along with the building?"

"The whole compound is solar-powered," Pete said, pulling his surgical mask off as he walked up to us. He still looked pale, but maybe it was just the weird lighting. "This place was designed to be off the grid. I was actually trying to figure out how to get the power back on when I heard your vehicles pull up outside."

Grant came up beside Pete, and I peered between them, trying to catch sight of my mom.

"I got the bullet out and, thankfully, it didn't hit her femoral artery," Pete assured me. "I'm giving her pain meds and fluids by IV. She's stable but she'll be out for a while. Do you want to see her?"

"Sure, and thank—"

Pete's eyes started to roll back in his head, and he stumbled sideways into Grant, who was already shoving an office chair under the big guy's ass.

"Get some water," I said.

"I've got some in my bag in the van," Passion said, running for it.

"I'm okay. Really." Pete insisted. "I just haven't stood for that long in a while. When I woke up yesterday, I pretty much stayed in the infirmary and hydrated myself. I was afraid if I got up I'd pass out."

"Here's some water," Passion said, running up and handing him a water bottle. "When's the last time you ate?"

"I don't know," he said between sips. "The night we left Kah-Nee-Tah to come here."

"That was over a week ago," Samantha exclaimed. "No wonder you almost passed out."

"A week ago?" Pete said, choking on a gulp of water. "I—that can't be right. I mean, I remember regaining consciousness a few times, but a week? How is that even—what the hell happened and where did everyone go?"

"Hate to interrupt," Chase said, joining the group. "But we have an issue." He looked at me pointedly. "I need you."

"Okay," I said, glancing longingly in the direction of my mom, but Pete had said she was unconscious. I would check on her as soon as I put out this new fire. "Can you guys bring Pete up to speed?" I asked Passion, Samantha, and Grant. "And find him something to eat, while you're at it."

"Yeah, sure," Grant said and the girls nodded.

"What's up?" I asked Chase, as he led me to the van.

"We have a problem at gate four," he said, ushering me inside and pointing to a monitor which showed a gate, just like the one we'd entered Umatilla through, hanging wide open in a mangled mess. "It's the one at the north end of the depot, and he drove right through it." Chase rewound the feed a few minutes to show me footage of Wade Hermiston ramming his truck through the gate in a shower of sparks and tangled metal. It took him a couple runs to breach it, but he was obviously very determined. "I didn't notice it until a few minutes ago," Chase admitted. "I was helping T-dog get the auxiliary power up and running. Not that we could have done anything anyway."

"Great," I said, "After what Pete did, Wade will be convinced we're one of the lawsuit groups enacting some kind of hostile takeover. He's going to come back with his people." How long would it take Wade to get back to Hermiston and raise a mob of angry farmers? The corner of the monitor said it was 3:07 in the morning. God, no wonder I was so tired. "Are you guys into the computers yet?" I asked.

"No." Chase shook his head. "We can't even access them until we restore full power, and then it depends on how difficult the security is. Best case scenario, it will take two or three hours to break into the network, and that's just on this side. The CAMFer system is completely separate, so it will probably take that long as well. Plus, there's the issue of getting into that side of the building. We lucked out having Pete open this side for us, but it won't be that easy getting into the dome or the CAMFer side."

"And that's in-and-out? You guys said you could do this fast."

"That is fast." He glared at me. "For anyone else this would take days."

"But it's not fast enough. Wade is coming back. And what about the broken gate? Is that going to flag anyone's attention?"

"It shouldn't. All the camera and security information feeds directly into this van now, and we've created a false loop for anyone monitoring it from the outside. At least, until the van battery runs out. But we should have the full power of the compound to hook into by then."

"Good." I took a deep breath. Wade was going to come back before we could get the job done. I was sure of it. But, we couldn't just cut our losses and run. After all the trouble we'd gone to, including my mom getting shot, we had to get that data. Besides, she wasn't in any condition to be moved, and Pete wasn't in great shape either. And then there was the issue of vehicles. I'd killed the rental van and the Westfalia had two flat tires. Besides, I was pretty sure Chase and T-dog wouldn't leave their equipment behind. So, we had to stay. "Okay." I exhaled. "How secure is the building without power? Can we keep people out?"

"I think I can shed some light on that," Pete said, coming up to the open van door, accompanied by Grant. Pete's color was better, probably due to the half-eaten cereal bar in his hand. "The big bay doors, as you know, can be opened, closed, and locked manually, and I think they'd withstand a significant onslaught. But there are other smaller entrances throughout the compound that rely heavily on cameras, alarms, and electronic security deterrents. Without electricity or the manpower to guard them, it wouldn't take much more than a crowbar and some brute force to get in. That's another reason I came out, guns blazing, when I heard someone outside. Anyway, the point is, if you're worried about an exterior assault, it's an issue, at least until we have full power. Once we have it, though, there are ways to make this place an impenetrable fortress."

"Right, but if Wade comes back in force like I think he will," I said. "How do we get out and past him once we have the data?"

"What data are you looking for?" Pete asked. Apparently, Passion and Samantha hadn't explained that part to him. If he worked for Alexander James, what we were trying to do might be a problem for him.

"All of it," I said. "Everything we can find about PSS from both sides. We're going to take it and use it to make The Hold and the CAMFers obsolete."

"I see," he said, nodding. "You really are as tenacious as they say you are."

I wasn't sure who "they" were, but I'd take it.

"Once we have the files," Chase said, "we can utilize them from anywhere. The van has its own satellite link, so we can connect to the internet. And I can route us through multiple VPNs so it won't be traceable. Location isn't an issue."

"Yeah, but we can't stay here indefinitely," I pointed out. "This is federal land and, eventually, the government is going to notice what's going on and remove everyone."

"Probably," Chase said, "but we'll have the data by then. We might be charged with trespassing, but I doubt anything more severe than that. There's going to be a lot of confusion with all these people and the mystery of where the dome came from."

"Waiting it out shouldn't be a problem," Pete said. "This place was made to be self-sustainable for a large population. There are storage rooms full of food and basic supplies, and staff quarters for a hundred people, plus a full commercial kitchen, a cafeteria, and a hydroponic garden, and that's just on The Hold side. I don't know what they have on the CAMFer side."

"The accommodations aren't quite as nice," I said, dryly. "But yeah, they have a similar set-up."

"So, hypothetically, we could stay here indefinitely if we had to," Chase pointed out. "But not without power. When the compound landed here, the backup power failed to reboot, so all the interior doors, except the infirmary, engaged in an automatic, manual lock down. That means we're stuck in this area for now. We can get the main power up. That's not a question. And once it's up we can get the data and gain access to the entire compound."

"Then get it up," I said. "And do it as fast as you can."

10

OLIVIA

Sleep. Sometimes, if I was exhausted enough to forgo the nightmares, it was a wonderful thing, even draped between two computer chairs in a giant abandoned compound under threat of attack. It had probably helped that my mom had finally come to, insisted she wasn't going to die, and ordered me to get some decent rest somewhere other than the chair by her bedside. And that had been fine with me. I'd just been glad she was alive and in mom mode again.

But restful sleep, like all good things, must come to an end.

"Olivia," Chase said, and I opened my eyes to find him standing over me. "Wade is back."

I sat up, noticing I wasn't the only one who'd crashed. Passion and Samantha were curled up on top of a desk together. Grant was sleeping on two chairs like I was. And Pete had found another hospital gurney and parked in it just outside the infirmary, probably to be close to his patient. He wasn't asleep, though. I saw him turn his head our way as Chase woke me.

"Do we have power?" I asked groggily, realizing the stupidity of my question even as I asked it. The compound was still dark, the computers off and quiet.

"Almost," Chase said. "I finally found the problem, and T-Dog is working on it right now."

"And how close is Wade?"

"I think you should come see," he said, quietly, cautiously. There was something he didn't want the others to hear.

"Okay." I got up and followed him to the van.

As we stepped inside he said, "After you told me you thought Wade would come back, I set up an online alert for anything related to Umatilla and the lawsuit. A few hours ago hits started to ramp up on a couple of obscure forums and social media groups. T-dog and I didn't see it, at first; we were both so focused on the power issue."

"What does that mean? What are you talking about?"

"It means we have more to worry about than Wade and his people from Hermiston," Chase said. "Somehow, the other groups got word that he was mustering his people. They must have thought he was making a move for the depot, and it acted like a domino effect. As soon as we realized what was happening, we sent some of the drones out on a surveillance circuit."

"Other groups? How many?" *Fuck. Fuckity fuck fuck.*

"Take a look." He pointed at the monitors.

On one screen, by the dim light of dawn, Wade's pick-up was barreling across the depot, followed by a stream of farm trucks, dusty station wagons, and rusty RVs. There were maybe twenty vehicles, most of them packed to the nines, so maybe a hundred people or more.

However, there were three more screens feeding from three more drones, all showing armies of vehicles headed in our direction.

"They broke through the other gates," Chase explained. "And the electricity on the fence is completely down now. I'm assuming these are the preppers." He pointed to the screen with a neat convoy of about fifty Humvees and retired military vehicles streaming across it. "And these are the environmentalist." He indicated a smaller group of hybrid and electric cars and minivans, very much out of place on the dusty desert roads. "So, this must be the tribes." He gestured to the smallest group of vehicles making their way confidently across the depot toward us.

"How long until they get here?"

"Ten minutes max. Maybe a little sooner. Wade's group is ahead of the rest."

"Then what are you doing standing here?" I practically shoved Chase out of the van. "Get me that power up now."

"Yes, ma'am," he said, turning and running off in the direction of the power grid panel they'd been working on for hours.

"What's going on?" Pete asked, sticking his head into the van. "We got trouble?"

"Yes, we have trouble," I groaned, as Grant and the girls joined Pete at the van's sliding door. "I seem to have displaced this compound to the one piece of dessert everyone and their mother has a claim to." I pointed at the screens.

"Holy shit," Grant said. "What are they going to do when they get here?"

"I don't know." I shook my head. "The preppers probably have weapons. And I'm sure Wade's group does, considering what happened the last time he was here."

"Again, I'm sorry about that," Pete said. "I had no idea one bad decision would come back to bite me in the ass with such a vengeance."

"What about the gun you had?" Grant asked Pete. "We have at least one weapon."

"Except it's out of ammunition," Pete said, cringing. "I'm a medic, okay? I had no idea how to use that thing."

"But where'd you get it?" Grant asked.

"I found it just inside the bay door on the floor," Pete answered.

"Someone probably dropped it when they got displaced," Samantha said.

"But there must be more where that came from," Grant pointed out. "A place like this has to have an armory, doesn't it?"

"Yes," Peter nodded. "There's one on the lower levels, which we can't get to until the power is back on."

"Maybe when they get here, they'll all just fight each other," Passion said hopefully.

"I doubt it," Samantha said. "We've provided them with a common enemy."

"Then what are we going to do?" Passion asked, her voice filled with fear.

"We keep them out until the guys get the power up," I said, looking to Pete. "You know the building. Where are we most vulnerable?"

"There are three smaller access points to this room," he said, pointing to the dim glow of several exits signs. "We could barricade them with desks and chairs."

"Okay, do it," I told them. "But be careful with the computers. We need them intact. And don't let him overdo it," I said to Grant, indicating Pete. "The rest of you do the heavy lifting." I turned back to the screens. They were getting closer. All those cars filled with hostile people.

Behind me, I could hear the frantic scrape of desks and the noise of heavy furniture being moved.

On the monitors, the four convoys converged on the compound. Of course, Wade led them right to our big bay door.

Wade jumped out of his truck, rifle in hand. Other people were getting out too, a few from the lead vehicles of each group. Some had guns. Most didn't. They were yelling at each other and gesturing at the dome, a mob of confused humanity. The drones didn't have audio so it was a bit like watching a silent movie, except from the air. Thankfully, the group was focused on the big door. They hadn't noticed the smaller entrances, but they would. Once they tried battering the bay door without success, they'd look elsewhere.

"We got it. We got it!" Chase called, and I turned to see him running toward me. At the same moment, there was a surge of sound and light and energy as every electronic device and system in the building turned back on. The central heating whooshed to life. The computers hummed, their screens flickering, and finally the overhead lights flared, blinding us with their radiance. There were sounds I didn't recognize, things beeping and flashing and alarms wailing down distant and empty corridors.

I stepped out of the van, moving to meet Chase, planning to congratulate him on his perfect but terrifyingly close timing. Maybe even give him a hug.

But he wasn't looking at me anymore. He was glancing to the right, the elation on his face turned to horror.

I followed his gaze and saw the bay door opening slowly and mechanically, all on its own. A puff of dust gusted under the expanding opening, and I thought I caught a glimpse of Wade Hermiston's boots, the cries of the mob ringing in my ears.

"Get out of the way," Chase yelled, shoving me aside as he climbed into the van and threw himself at one of the keyboards.

"The door is opening," I cried, as I crawled in after him. "Why is it opening?"

"I don't know," he snapped, typing frantically. "The power reboot engaged the entire security system, and I can't stop it because we haven't actually accessed it yet."

"What do you mean you can't stop it? You have to. We cannot have that door open. We cannot let those people in. Do you understand?"

"Yeah." He nodded numbly. "Let me do it."

"Okay." I jumped out of the van, scanning the room. Pete, Grant, and Samantha were at the manual door lock, trying to engage it, but it obviously wasn't working. The gap had increased, widening by inches. Any moment it was going to be high enough for those people outside to crawl under. There was no sign of Passion. Maybe she was back in the infirmary with my mom. The cacophony of sound and light washed over me. I tried to focus, to think of some way to help, but this room, this moment washed over me, a crashing wave of everything I'd experienced since I'd left Greenfield. There was no hiding. No escape. No safe place I could barricade myself into—not even my own head. There would always be people coming after me, no matter where I went. They would always find a way. The fear would come. The pain. The lies. The hate. Who was I to think I could stand against it? Change any of it? I was only a girl with a ghost hand.

"Olivia," a voice said, muffled. Grant was bending over me, touching my arm gently. "Are you all right?"

I was on the ground outside the van, curled into a ball, my hands pressed over my ears. My face was wet and my body was shaking. "The door?" I asked, trying to look past him, but there were too many people in the way. Chase and T-Dog. Passion, Pete, and Samantha too—all of them standing over me.

"We got it just in time," Grant said, helping me sit up. "Samantha remembered the override code from when she saw her dad type it in. You should have seen Wade Hermiston. He was trying to crawl under the door. I've never seen an old guy backtrack so fast."

"They didn't get in?" I asked, dragging in a ragged breath.

"We're locked in tight, safe and sound," Pete said, taking my other arm as I stood up. "How about you? Seems like you were having a bit of a panic attack there."

"Yeah." I exhaled. "I guess so."

"He looks pissed," Grant said, pointing toward a security monitor positioned over the bay door, now come to life and featuring Wade Hermiston's face scowling up into the camera from outside. He raised his gun and shook it, his mouth forming obscenities I couldn't hear as an angry mob swirled silently around him.

11

ANTHONY

I wasn't dead.

As long as I could feel the pain, I wasn't dead.

That was what I told myself every time I woke up in the dark.

The dark was good. It kept me from seeing the gory stump at the end of my right arm.

Fineman had done that to me. Fineman and his obsession with those fucking PSS freaks. He'd always been a sympathizer, agreeing to keep that defective pet in the dome for all those years. He'd mutilated me for doing exactly what he should have done to that minus bitch Olivia in the first place, but apparently cutting off my hand hadn't been enough. He was a sicko.

A lunatic who liked to fuck people in the head. So, he'd left me in this cell to rot, and he'd left something else with me, something to taunt me while I died.

It hadn't been in my cell at first. Not that I remembered. Then again, I'd been in and out of consciousness. No, I was sure it hadn't been there when the guy came to cauterize my wound. The lights had still been on then, and I hadn't seen it. So, maybe Fineman had brought it after I'd passed out.

And when I'd come to later, I'd moved my leg and brushed against it on the cold cement slab, sending it clattering to the floor. The cell was pitch black, so I couldn't see what it was, but it sounded hard and metallic, like something I could use to escape. So, I'd gotten down on the floor, searching for it.

I'd led that search with my right hand, until it had brushed up against the thing on the floor and pain had surged up my arm, almost knocking me out again. But I'd fought it off, cursing myself for forgetting I didn't have a fucking right hand anymore. Then I'd reached out carefully with my left hand, running my fingers along the outline of the object.

When I'd realized what it was, I'd almost laughed.

The thing on the floor in front of me was the PSS-severing knife Fineman had invented to save his precious test subjects from certain death. It was the knife I'd used to cut off Olivia Black's defective hand. He must have put it in my cell, tossed it in like trash, because to him it was.

Fineman had claimed the knife hadn't worked. He'd said I'd fucked up and it hadn't gotten Olivia's sample. But I knew that wasn't true. I'd felt it take her PSS, and I'd seen her empty, useless stump afterwards. There was no doubt it had worked. If Fineman had ruined the sample later, how was that my fault? Fuck him. It wasn't on me if he'd screwed up.

But finding the knife had given me hope. If he'd put it in my cell, he'd come back to rub it in my face. Or question me. I could still tell him about Palmer, how he'd wanted to get rid of that bitch as much as I had—how he'd egged me on. And I could rat out the guys who'd helped me drag her to the interrogation room. I still had options. Or so I thought.

Except Fineman never came back. No one did. I hadn't seen or heard a soul since the guy who'd cauterized my stump had left. Shortly after that, the lights had gone out and everything had grown eerily silent.

That's when I started to really freak out.

The compound had always been too quiet, so different from the woods where I grew up. The longer I'd been here, working and living underground like a rodent, the more it felt like nothing could touch me, but there had always been sound, and light, and the shift of air as the building recycled it. I'd always had a sense of people going about their business above me.

But the moment I'd discovered the knife in my cell, the silence and stillness became so deep, it was as if nothing existed beyond those four stone walls—like I was the only one left in the world.

It had been days since then, and no one had come for me.

It had been so long since I'd eaten, I didn't feel the hunger pangs anymore.

The water in the toilet tank I'd been drinking had run out a while ago. My lips were chapped and bleeding, and I eagerly licked away the blood that seeped from them.

I was weak, barely able to clutch the knife, but I hadn't let go of it since I'd found it. It was something to hold on to. Something other than the darkness and myself.

Of course, I'd tried to use it to hack at the door lock and the hinges, but the damn thing wasn't made for real cutting. It had been designed to harvest PSS, not for a prison break.

Maybe that was the joke. Maybe Fineman, sick fuck that he was, hoped I'd get desperate enough to try and use it to cut my own throat. It would take a long, agonizing time to end myself that way. Was that what he wanted?

It didn't really matter anymore. I was going to die, one way or another. That had become clear. The gunshots I thought I'd heard a few hours ago—was it hours or days?—they'd just been a hallucination. No one was coming for me. It was almost over.

Something had obviously gone wrong. I knew that now. Not just with me and the knife, but with everything.

If Fineman had won the great conflict he'd been planning against The Holders to take the dome, he would have come to gloat. If he'd lost, the enemy would have come for me by now.

But this solitary, silent death made no sense.

I curled up in a ball on my slab, trying to preserve warmth, my back toward the wall and the knife pinned between my knees so I wouldn't drop it. I couldn't trust my remaining hand or my fingers to hold anything. That's how weak I was.

I focused on resisting the darkness crowding into my head, not sleep or dreams, but the bottomless pit of unconsciousness. If I went there again, I wasn't coming back.

I closed my eyes and took a deep breath. And then another, feeling myself begin to slip away.

Light flashed against my eyelids, white and hot, and I opened them, blinded by the lightbulb in the ceiling, blazing like the sun. Then the door to my cell made a clicking noise, a sound I'd heard a thousand times before, the gentle snick of the lock mechanism disengaging. A draft wafted over me, slight and warming as if the entire compound had exhaled, and the door swung open.

I sat up, my head spinning, and yanked the knife from between my legs, holding it out unsteadily, brandishing it against whatever was coming. Were they here to hurt me again? Or had they come to kill me?

But there was no one behind the door.

It opened slowly, revealing the well-lit hallway beyond it, completely empty.

I could hear the hum of the compound's systems coming back on-line, all the familiar sounds I'd grown used to while living and working there.

I stood up, shakily, clutching the knife with all my strength, still unsure. Was this a trick?

I was dizzy and weak, yes, but now adrenaline was pumping through my veins at the thought of freedom and escape. The door to my cell was open.

I stumbled across the threshold and out into the hallway. All the other cell doors were hanging open and unlocked. There was only one thing that could do that: a full loss-of-power reboot. They'd mentioned that in my training and laughed, saying it would never happen. There were too many back-ups, they said. Too many checks and balances between the two sides to protect against that sort of vulnerability.

I took a few more hesitant steps down the hallway.

From behind me came a buzz and a grating sound.

I whirled around, brandishing the knife, as every single cell door on the block slammed shut simultaneously, their mechanical locks clicking into place.

The power reboot had triggered a full security reset. If I'd hesitated any longer, I'd still be in that fucking cell.

What the hell was going on?

I should have stopped and answered that question. I should have assessed the situation like my old man had taught me, but I didn't.

Instead, I raced down the hallway into the elevator and hit the button for the staff cafeteria. No one was there, of course—it was obvious the entire compound had been abandoned—but there was a faucet, and cups, and food. I ate and drank until I threw up. Then I ate and drank again, selecting more carefully. There was plenty of stuff that hadn't gone bad, that wouldn't go bad for a very long time. I was glad I'd thrown up the first round. In my weakened state, food poisoning could kill me.

Or whoever had turned the power back on would.

I started rummaging through kitchen drawers until I found the knives. I took the sharpest three, putting one in my boot, one in my belt, and one in my jacket pocket. Everything was so much more difficult with my dominant hand gone, and I wasn't even sure I could still wield a weapon effectively, but at least now I was armed with more than Fineman's useless PSS knife. And yet, I couldn't bring myself to ditch it, so I cut a black garbage bag into a long strip, tied it to the damn thing, and slung it over my shoulder. It felt kinda like a gun. Maybe if I ran into anyone, they'd mistake it for one.

I considered running, but I was in no shape to go anywhere. The food and water had helped a little, but just finding the knives had exhausted me and my wrist was throbbing. There was no way I'd survive ten minutes out in the desert. Especially not with a bloody stump and filthy bandages. Infection would kill me as sure as anything. I needed fresh dressings and antibiotics. I'd find both in the infirmary. Plus, there'd be pain meds.

As I left the kitchen, I noticed a security camera pan my direction, triggered by my movement. I quickly slipped behind it, pulled the knife from my belt, and severed the connection at its back. The less evidence I left of my presence the better. On the way to the infirmary, I skirted other cameras, making sure I was always outside their range. Fineman might have stripped me of my keys, weapons, and high-level clearance pass, but I still knew a few tricks.

Once I'd taken out the infirmary camera, I scored antibiotics, pain killers, and bandages. I popped a handful of pills, sterilized and rewrapped my stump, pulled a gurney out, and lay down for a minute, just to rest my eyes. It was a stupid move, but between the exhaustion, the food in my belly, and the medication, I could barely stand, let alone think straight.

As soon as I lay down, my head began to spin. My body felt like it was falling, and I started to hear voices, like an angry mob, screaming and banging to get in.

Shit. What the fuck had I taken? I reached for the bottles on the counter to check the labels, but my stump knocked them to the floor, pills scattering everywhere like gentle rain.

I liked rain.

It had always put me right to sleep back home.

The pitter-patter of gentle rain on a tin roof.

It was—so—fucking—nice.

12

DAVID MARCUS

I woke to the sound of muffled voices and a beam of sunlight streaming through a crack in Lonan's bedroom curtains, nailing me right in the face.

From the intensity of the light, I was guessing it was late afternoon. I'd slept long and hard after my run and tumble in the desert.

I untangled myself from my sleeping bag on the floor and slowly stood up, ignoring the throbbing pain in my knees and shoulder. The muted voices coming from the living room grew louder, and I realized it wasn't just Reiny and Lonan. Someone was here. More than one person. And the discussion was heated.

I limped carefully to the door and opened it quietly, just a crack, listening.

"—should tell him everything," a familiar husky female voice said. It was Mia, Reiny's aunt.

"No," Gordon countered. "He didn't believe me last night. What's the point in telling him the rest? Besides, he stole from us."

Stole from him? I'd offered to pay for the cube and the birth certificate. What the hell was he going on about?

"We don't know that," Mia said. "You misplace things in that junk heap of yours all the time."

"I didn't misplace it," Gordon growled. "It was in the den when I went to get the cube. I saw it with my own eyes, and now it's gone."

So, he wasn't talking about the cubes. He thought I'd taken something else, and he had his old-man-panties in a twist about it. Like I'd want his desert crap.

"I don't trust him," he went on, "If he was missing until sunrise, as Lonan says, he could have met up with someone and told them everything."

"He didn't meet anyone," Lonan said calmly. "He just needed some time alone. That's all."

"Then how do you explain the painting?" Gordon huffed. "Last night, he's never heard of Stephen Black or the visions, and this morning he shows up with that. You really think he just found it in the desert?"

"You find weird shit in the desert every day," Mia pointed out. "And you've heard Reiny and Lonan explain about the displacement. Don't hold it against the boy because he found that painting and you didn't.

"Fine," Gordon snapped, "What about the news from the tribal council this morning? You think that's just a coincidence?"

"That has been brewing for weeks," Reiny said. "David had nothing to do with it."

"I still don't trust him," Gordon said. "He's not interested in the truth. We haven't kept this under wraps for all these years to put it in the hands of a fool."

"He's not any more of a fool than you were at his age," Reiny said, sounding pissed. "And he's a part of this whether you like it or not."

"I don't like it." Gordon huffed. "He isn't what I expected. He's too damaged."

Ouch. I guess that's what I got for eavesdropping. Then again, I'd already known I didn't measure up to Gordon's standards. I'd also known they were holding out on me last night, and this conversation proved it.

"Well, we have to tell him about the council meeting," Reiny said, her voice getting louder as if she'd turned her head toward Lonan's bedroom door.

And that was my cue to exit before she realized I'd been listening.

I pushed the door open and came out, running my hand through my hair and yawning.

"Hey." I stopped and stared, as if I were only just discovering there were guests in the house.

They were all sitting at the table in the dining room, which was really just a corner of the living room, crowded with a table and some chairs. Kaylee was off to the side, sitting in her favorite overstuffed chair and playing with her magic eight ball.

"David," Reiny said, standing up nervously. "Did we wake you?"

Her genuine concern made me feel like a complete dick. I'd treated her horribly last night, and I'd promised Lonan I'd apologize as soon as I saw her. I just hadn't realized I'd have to swallow my pride and do it in front of Gordon.

"No, it's fine," I said. "But I owe you an apology. Last night, I acted like an ass. And I'm sorry to you two as well." I turned to Gordon and Mia. "What you told me was a lot to take in, but that's no excuse." I was lying. I wasn't sorry for how I'd reacted to Gordon. But buddying up to him was probably the best way to uncover the secrets he was keeping.

"See?" Reiny said, turning to her uncle. "We can all sit down and have a rational conversation together."

"A rational conversation about what?" I asked, pulling up a chair.

Gordon Lightfoot frowned and crossed his arms over his chest. It was going to take more than a little placating to change his opinion of me.

"There was an emergency tribal council meeting this morning," Reiny said, sitting down again as well, though she looked far from relaxed. "Our tribal association was contacted by the Confederated Tribes of Umatilla, who have been in a legal battle with the government over land near the Columbia Gorge. Apparently, last night, it escalated, and the tribes made a move onto the land. Now, they're calling for all available local tribes to join them in solidarity. They think the more people we have, the more likely their claim will be honored."

"You mean it's like a sit-in?" I asked, genuinely surprised. "I thought those got played out in the 70s."

"At least my generation stood up for what they believed in," Gordon said.

"I assume that means you two are going," I said, ignoring his jibe. It made sense. Gordon and Mia were retired hippies or whatever. They could leave their artsy junkyard and go protest without losing their livelihoods.

"We are elders of the Warm Springs tribes," Gordon said. "Of course we'll go."

"Reiny and I are going too," Lonan said, looking at me. "Which leaves you and Kaylee with a choice. You could stay here, but Reiny and I will be packing up most of the food and supplies from the house to take with us."

"We'd really like you to come," Reiny added. "Gordon and Mia have an RV and plenty of camping supplies for all of us."

"What about your jobs?" I asked. "The resort is just going to let you go?"

"People are stepping in to cover for those of us who can go," Lonan explained. "This is more important than checking in guests and cleaning rooms."

"Yeah, but the tribes are never going to win this," I said. "You realize that, right? The government can't concede on land ownership to native people, not even a little, because as soon as they do it opens a whole can of worms calling the origins of this entire country into question. I mean, it's noble and everything, but it's a complete waste of time."

"See?" Gordon said, waving his hand at me in frustration and glaring at Reiny. "I told you."

"Told her what? That I'm a realist?" I couldn't kiss Gordon's ass, no matter how hard I tried. He was just so infuriatingly out of touch.

"Listen, you two," Mia said, pinning first Gordon and then me with her eyes. "Stop acting like children. You're going to have to set aside your differences and make this work."

"She's right," Reiny agreed. "David, if you think it is a waste of time, then don't come. Lonan and I can vouch for you and get you a fill-in job at the resort."

"What about Kaylee?" I asked. "I'm not leaving her here alone every day."

"Kaylee will have to make her own decision," Lonan said.

We all turned to look at her, and she set her eight ball aside, smiling at us. Then, she slid from her chair and sidled up next to me, slipping her hand into mine. *It sounds like an adventure straight out of a book,* she said. *I want to go.*

I didn't have to tell anyone what she'd said. It was obvious by the expression on her face. I was afraid she was going to be disappointed if she was expecting an adventure, though. This sit-in thing could be a risk, but I doubted it. Anytime the tribes protested anything, the world ignored them, so it might actually be a great place to hide. Still, I wasn't looking forward to camping in the desert when it had almost killed us not so long ago.

I turned to Reiny. "I guess we're coming with you."

Reiny glanced at Mia, and Mia glanced at Gordon. There was something else they weren't telling me.

"The facility we told you about last night," Mia finally said, "the one your mother, and uncle, and Gordon broke into. It was a government chemical arms depot that was decommissioned a few years ago. It's on the Umatilla land."

That was why Gordon thought I'd met with someone. If he believed I'd set this whole land-grab thing in motion, he had vastly overestimated my abilities.

"So, what's there now?" I asked.

"Abandoned buildings and pronghorn, mostly," Reiny said. "But it's tribal land and the government promised to return it to the Umatilla people."

I could tell by the look on Gordon's face that a government promise had nothing to do with it. He wanted to go back to Umatilla for reasons of his own. He just wasn't willing to admit it.

"So, when do we leave?" I asked.

"As soon as we can," Mia said. "We'll pack up the truck, and Reiny and Lonan can drive it. Gordon and I will take the RV and you and Kaylee can ride with us."

"I'll have to make arrangements for the horses," Lonan said. "And Reiny can work on covering our shifts at the lodge. We should be able to get it all taken care of by tonight."

"We'll see you at our place tonight then," Mia said, as she and Gordon got up and hurried out.

13

JASON

The sound of the dogs baying grew louder, closer, more urgent. They had my scent, but it didn't matter. I was too winded to run anymore, so I huddled in a patch of brambles next to a stream, muddy, shivering, and waiting for the inevitable.

My old man was going to kill me this time. I'd pushed him too far. And I should have known better because he'd been on one giant alcoholic binge ever since I'd appeared out of thin air and fallen smack into the middle of his late-night poker game, scattering chips everywhere.

That's what that bitch, Olivia, had done to me. One minute I'd been at the compound in the dome trying to help save her, the next she'd thrown me right back to him. And not just me, but the bullet too, the one she'd taken from me and crammed into Fineman's cube: it was in my fucking pocket when I landed.

My father and his drunk poker friends were so freaked out, they fucked me up pretty bad. They searched me and found the bullet, but my old man just laughed and shoved it back in my pocket. "You keep that," he said. "Maybe someday you'll have the balls to use it on yourself."

That had been nine days ago. Nine days of living in the kennel with the dogs, just like old times. The same dogs howling after me now. They weren't pets or companions. They would bleed and tree me as fast as any prey they'd been set on. My old man treated me like a dog, but the dogs had always known the difference.

The third day in the kennel, he'd pulled me out to interrogate me, and I'd told him most of it. Not the part about wanting to kill him. He already knew that. And I left some other things out, but I told him enough that he got the picture. Fineman had gone to war against The Hold without him, cutting my old man out of the action, even after he'd done all the doctor's dirty work and killing at the Eidolon.

It only confirmed what the others were telling him—all the scattered compound CAMFers who'd been streaming into the lodge daily, each with their own story of how and where they'd ended up. He questioned every one, and not a single soul had seen Fineman. It seemed the doctor had disappeared without a trace, leaving the field wide open for my old man to lead the new order of CAMF.

That should have made him happy. It was what he'd always wanted.

But it wasn't until he'd come to me this morning, his meaty fists gripping the bars of the kennel, that I'd discovered what was really bothering him.

"Did you see Tony at the dome?" he blurted.

"What? No," I answered, surprised. A few months before I'd gone off with Marcus, my step-brother, Tony, had been recruited for a special CAMFer assignment. My old man had been so proud, his perfect son going off to the perfect job, following in his footsteps. My brother hadn't said goodbye to me, and no one had bothered to tell me where he'd been assigned.

But now I knew.

My step-brother had been working at the compound.

He'd been displaced just like me.

Except, he hadn't come back.

My poor old man was stuck with the son he loathed while the one he really wanted was missing. And the irony of that was so funny, I couldn't help but laugh. I didn't just snicker either. No, I threw back my head and laughed hard, and I didn't stop, even when I heard the kennel keys jingling against the bars. I didn't stop when he reached in, dragged me out by my hair, and punched me in the temple.

"Shut up!" he yelled, punching me again, making my ears ring. "Shut up, you fucking piece of shit."

"No," I said, grappling with him, trying to get out of his grasp. "I'm never gonna shut up. You'll have to kill me to shut me up, just like you did ma."

He backed off then, suddenly letting go of me, fear creeping into his eyes. "Your ma fell down the stairs in a drunken stupor and broke her neck," he said, but his voice was weak and unconvincing.

"I saw you shove her," I said. "Tony and I both saw you do it."

"No." He shook his head. "Tony told the truth to the police. She tripped and fell."

"Tony lied to protect you."

"Tony did what any good son would do," he said, glaring at me.

"I'm your son," I spat, yanking up my pant leg to show him the undeniable evidence of my PSS, "and I have this. Do you really think they'll let you lead CAMF when your son is a freak? Even if you kill me, they'll remember. They'll talk about it even more. Because killing me doesn't change the fact that I was born this way and I'm your son."

"Your ma was a whore and everyone knew it," he said. "You're not my son, and you never have been. If that shit was in my genes, Tony would have it too. But he doesn't."

"Maybe," I said, shrugging, smiling, "unless his mother was the whore and he's the one who's not your son."

I knew I'd crossed the line, even before he grabbed me and threw me from the kennel. He was screaming incoherently, spit flying from his mouth. The dogs leapt against the bars of their cages, barking and fueled by his fury. I was running before he'd pulled out his gun, dodging between trees, headed for the stream. I ran as fast as I could, escaping into the woods and using every trick I knew to hide my trail, but it hadn't worked.

They were coming now, the dogs who had been my kennel-mates for much of my life. Their baying echoed louder and louder in my ears. From where I cowered, I thought I could hear the splash of their paws in the stream, and in the distance, the calling of men, deep voices booming back and forth. "This way. He's over here."

When they found me, my old man would finally kill me and put us both out of our misery.

"Get up," someone hissed, grabbing me from behind and yanking me to my feet.

I turned, expecting to see one of my old man's hunters, but instead I found myself staring at Mike Palmer.

"Cover your face," he ordered, pulling a small bottle from his pocket and spraying something all over my clothes, my boots, and where I'd just been sitting. I covered my mouth and nose just in time to avoid the worst of it, but there was no mistaking the smell of skunk oil. Hunters often used it to mask their human scent from prey, and it also worked on dogs. Our hounds were trained not to hunt skunk. As soon as they hit that patch of scent, they'd go off my trail. My eyes watered and my throat clenched, but it was worth it. Mike Palmer had just saved me, and he was spraying himself now.

He put the can of skunk scent away and turned, stepping into the water and heading up-stream, gesturing for me to follow.

And I did. What else was I going to do? With Palmer, I might get away. With the dogs and my old man, I'd run out of chances.

When the baying of the hounds had mostly faded behind us, I took a few quick steps, forcing my boots from the sucking stream muck, and caught up with him. "What are you doing here?" I asked.

"I was just passing through when I heard the dogs," he said. "But I guess now I'm saving your ass."

Just passing through? Yeah, we both knew that was bullshit. Palmer had been a major player in Fineman's regime. Maybe he knew where the doctor was. Maybe he'd come here spying for him, gathering information on my old man's doings. Mike Palmer was not my friend. I would have killed him back in Illinois, if Olivia hadn't stopped me, and we both knew it.

The stream grew deeper and we clambered onto the bank. Then it got wider, opening up to a small waterfall, and we stopped there as Palmer surveyed our surroundings. I'd been to the waterfall many times. The hunters liked to stop there for lunch, a swim, and some cold beers. The baying of the dogs had died out long ago, but that didn't mean we weren't still being hunted. Men could track without the dogs, if they were good enough. My old man wouldn't give up so easily, but I was parched, so I crouched down on the bank and filled my hands for a quick drink.

"Your father appears to be rallying an army," Palmer said.

It wasn't a question, so I didn't answer it. There had always been whispers at the lodge that Palmer was a double-agent for The Hold. I didn't believe it.

Especially after I'd seen him kill their most treasured PSS pet at the dome. The Holders would never forgive him for that. Which meant right now he was a man without a hole to shit in, and that kind of man was very dangerous. When I finally stood up, wiping my mouth with my sleeve, he was staring at me, his eyes scanning my face.

"You don't look like your brother," he said.

I did my best not to react, turning toward a thick bush to piss before responding. "He's my step-brother," I said, flicking myself dry and zipping up my fly.

"When I spoke to your father, he seemed very concerned for his welfare."

Palmer had balls if he'd strode right in and talked to my old man. I'd give him that. Did he really know something about Tony, or was he just baiting me? That tactic had worked on my old man, but it wouldn't work on me.

"I don't give a fuck about my step-brother," I said. "I just want to get out of here. So, where are we going?"

"Well, I'm going to Indianapolis," he said. "If The Hold is still intact, that's where they'll be, and I need to gauge their next move. As for where you're going, that's up to you. I just got you away from the dogs. I'm not adopting you or anything."

"You'll just let me go?" I asked, surprised.

"Sure," he said. "You have money or a place to crash?"

"No," I said. "Not really." I had the money Mr. James had paid me to shoot Samantha, but I'd locked it up in the barn back in Indiana. But if I could get back there, I might be able to work that angle again.

Marcus's uncle paid well, he didn't treat me like a dog, and it was really my only option. I'd just have to be careful around Palmer. He'd probably sell me to the highest bidder. Then again, maybe that wouldn't be so bad. "I've been back with my old man for days," I said, a plan forming even as I said it. "I've heard and seen things. If you need an in with The Hold, you could offer me up as a rat."

"And you'd be willing to play that out?" he asked, raising an eyebrow.

"If I have to."

"Fine," Mike Palmer nodded. "You can come. But you screw me over and you won't live to regret it. Is that clear?"

"Got it." I nodded.

Then he led me to a pick-up truck parked in some brush near the boundary line of my old man's land. We drove to a rundown motel to grab his gear and try to shower the skunk smell away. While I was in the bathroom toweling off, he opened the door and handed me a wad of clean clothes. I put them on. They must have been his because they were way too big, but there was a belt so I just cinched everything up.

After Palmer took his shower, we packed, left the hotel, and ended up outside some skanky gay bar in Fort Worth. Palmer got out, went in for about ten minutes, and came back with a fake ID. The name on the license was Bubba Lynch and it said I was eighteen. It even sort of looked like me if you squinted real hard.

"It's close enough. Hold these," he said, shoving two plane tickets to Indy into my hands.

At the airport, Palmer pulled out some kind of badge that got us through security without a search or any questions.

I slept most of the flight. An airplane seat was a hell of a lot more comfortable than the floor of a dog kennel. Palmer slept, too. He didn't seem nervous about entering The Hold's main territory, especially for a guy who'd killed their most valuable asset. Then again, I'd never seen Palmer nervous. Maybe The Hold was in shambles like CAMF. Or maybe Palmer had something to offer them even more valuable than me. Then it hit me: he must have been looking for someone back on my old man's land. My guess would be Olivia. With Kaylee gone, whoever had Olivia had the power. The two of them had certainly wielded more than their fair share of it. That was for damn sure. And all I'd ended up with was the inability to jump off a cliff.

When we landed in Indy, three Hollywood-looking thugs met us at the gate and immediately escorted us to a limo at the curb.

"Who are these guys?" I asked Palmer as we climbed into the back. "Where are they taking us?"

"You said you'd give information to The Hold," he said, "so why beat around the bush? I called Mr. James from the motel back in Texas while you were in the shower. He's expecting us."

Fuck. Palmer didn't kid around.

The limo drove straight to the James mansion where the man himself was standing on the steps, waiting for us. He looked desperate. Hell, he smelled desperate. Last time I'd seen him, he'd been King of the World about to dominate the CAMFers and take the dome. He'd fallen a long way since then.

"Michael," Mr. James said, opening the door, practically pulling Palmer out, and giving him a hug. "How is Samantha?" he asked softly, still embracing him. "Is she safe? Does she hate me?"

"Yes, and yes," Palmer answered, pulling away. "But she'll get over it."

"I got a call while you were on the plane," Mr. James said, still keeping his voice low. "Kaylee and David were seen a few days ago on the Warm Springs reservation in Oregon and my—"

"Good," Palmer interrupted him, casting his glance my way, clearly unhappy I'd overheard that.

So, Kaylee was alive, and she *was* the one Palmer had been searching for on my old man's land. He must have faked killing her back at the dome. I'd always thought a knife was an odd choice of weapon for that whole scenario. Guns were much more efficient. Anyway, it sounded like Marcus was with Kaylee. I guess there was no doubt now that Palmer had been playing both sides. Damn, the guy was good. He'd certainly fooled me. And I hadn't missed the comment about Samantha either. She was off somewhere, still pissed at her dad. I'd seen an old, torn luggage tag from Portland, Oregon, on Palmer's bag back in the motel in Texas. That must be where Samantha was and her lesbo lover, Passion, was probably with her. This was all information Palmer and Mr. James obviously didn't want me to know. Now that I did, what were they going to do about it? Hopefully, not kill me.

"Hello, Jason," Mr. James said, holding out his hand. "It's good to see you again."

"You too, sir," I said, shaking his hand. And I almost meant it.

"It's good timing, actually," he said, a glint of something more devious flaring in his eyes as he gestured his men to take the luggage inside. "I present my case to the new Hold council tomorrow night." He was still speaking softly, even though we were standing outside, just the three of us. "It was going to be a challenge with certain key witnesses missing, but at least now I have some backup."

"You're going to put him on the stand?" Palmer glanced at me, sounding surprised. "Are you sure that's a good idea? He has no stake in Hold politics."

"All the better," Mr. James replied. "No one would suspect him of lying for me as they might have with Samantha or Passion. And he was at the Eidolon as well as the dome. It's perfect."

"I don't know, Alex," Palmer said. "It could get messy. What if they—"

"I'll do it," I interrupted Palmer, looking directly at Mr. James. "But I want double what you paid me last time." Last time two of my friends had been killed, and I'd had to jump off a cliff while being shot at by a helicopter. But Mr. James had taken care of me afterwards. He'd paid me and housed me and treated me like a man.

"It's a deal," Mr. James said, laughing at my boldness.

"You don't even know what it is yet," Palmer said to me.

"You want me to tell a bunch of Holders that Mr. James is the good guy," I said. "And leave out anything else. Sounds simple enough."

"And there will be a small demonstration," Mr. James added.

"A demonstration of what?" I asked.

"It's better if we don't explain until the time comes," Mr. James said, giving a sidelong glance toward the double front doors. "Not all of my employees are as loyal as they once were. But come in." He gestured toward the house. "You both must be exhausted."

14

DAVID MARCUS

"**P**ut it there," Gordon grunted, directing me to an open space in the RV's lower storage compartment.

Gordon and I had come to an unspoken truce, at least for the time being. He told me where to put things, and I obeyed like a good little soldier. With as much as we were stuffing into the mammoth camper, you'd have thought we were prepping for Armageddon.

I slid the case of canned applesauce into the slot, and headed back to Mia in the pantry for more supplies. As I approached the back door, I could hear the television broadcasting the local evening news. Mia had turned it on, hoping to catch something about the occupation at Umatilla. I very much doubted she would.

But when I opened the door and walked in, Mia, Lonan, Reiny and Kaylee were all standing in front of the TV. I caught a brief glimpse of a reporter, back-dropped by a huge broken gate. She was saying something about "live, exclusive, breaking news."

Mia turned to me and said, "Go get Gordon. Now."

I didn't have to. I could already hear him clomping in behind me, and Lonan moved aside, giving us both a better view.

The scene on the screen now featured a helicopter flying over a strange bumpy desert at sunset, the reporter's voice narrating. "We have some footage here of the depot taken earlier this evening," she said. "The ground formations you're seeing are actually underground igloos once used to store chemical weapons. Thankfully, all those weapons were destroyed several years ago, with only the igloos and a few other abandoned buildings left on the premises. That is until yesterday when, during a peaceful occupation of the contested land by local special interest groups, this strange new structure was discovered."

I stared at the screen as the helicopter flew over the dome and compound. There it was, just like I remembered it, whole and smack in the middle of a new piece of desert.

"No group currently on the ground is claiming responsibility for the structure," the reporter continued. "Initial reports seem to suggest that it materialized overnight. As you can see, there are lights on in the building, but witnesses on-site say it is locked up tight and impenetrable. Producers here at KTWO news have contacted the US Military's Base Realignment and Closure Commission, the branch now responsible for the decommissioned base, but they have not yet responded to our queries. As for conjectures that this is some kind of secret military facility, that remains to be seen. Whatever it is, rest assured KTWO news will keep you up-to-date and informed on the latest developments."

I turned to Reiny and Lonan, fighting to keep my cool. "Did you know about this?"

"There were vague rumors at the council meeting," Reiny said. "But we couldn't be sure."

"But you knew it was a possibility, and that's the part you weren't telling me." I glanced at Kaylee, trying to gauge her reaction, but she was staring at the television, transfixed by a commercial for cat litter. "You were going to take her back to the dome and not even tell her? What the hell?"

"No," Reiny said, shaking her head. "That's not—"

"Bullshit," I spat. "The CAMFers could still be in there, or The Hold. They could both be there, for all you know."

"Have some respect, boy," Gordon said, looming in my direction.

"Gordon," Mia said, taking his arm and pulling him back.

"David," Lonan said, taking my arm in a similar way, "calm down. We did not know the compound was there. Now we do, and so do you and Kaylee. It must have displaced to Umatilla and has only now been discovered. If anyone managed to remain inside, they could still be there, that's true. Or they might have left. Or someone completely new could have stumbled upon it and powered up the lights. We have no idea, which is one of the reasons we need to go."

One of the reasons. So, there were still others they weren't telling me.

"We're wasting valuable time," Gordon said. "We need to leave now. As soon as that story goes live on the larger networks, all hell is going to break loose."

"Go start up the RV," Lonan told him, nodding toward the door. "We'll be out in a minute."

Gordon frowned, but he and Mia headed out.

"We're going," Lonan said, looking from me to Kaylee. "You need to decide if you are."

Kaylee was still staring at the television, which was back to the news and rattling on about some giant weird mound of dirt that had recently been discovered just outside the town of Oymyaken, Siberia, the locals claiming it had mysteriously appeared overnight.

"Kaylee," I said, crouching down and putting my face level with hers. "If you're afraid, we don't have to go."

Her eyes finally flicked from the TV back to me, locking with mine. *It's like magic,* she said, her voice in my head full of wonder. *It tells stories like the pictures in my mind when I read. How does it do that?*

"It's just a TV," I explained. "Didn't you have one in the compound?" Reiny and Lonan didn't have a TV, which I'd thought was odd, but it had never occurred to me that Kaylee had never seen one.

No. Just books, she said. *They didn't let me have electronic devices. Of course, I've read about them, but I never imagined it was so—realistic. It's just like seeing the world, except flatter and in a square frame. Oh, and I want a kitten. I've always wanted a kitten. Can we get one?*

"Maybe. Listen, I need you to understand—If we go with Reiny and Lonan, we're going back to the dome. I know it frightens you, but—"

The dome doesn't frighten me. She laughed. *But I liked flying over it like a bird. That was amazing.*

"So, you're okay with this?"

Sure, she said, smiling.

Did she have any concept of what I was asking her?

"David," Reiny said, bending down, her eyes pleading with me. "We need to go."

"Okay." I nodded.

15

KAYLEE

L iving in the tiny house with Lonan, Reiny, and David had been nice. We'd eaten around a table, the way families did in books. Real life was sometimes like books, but not always. Books were cleaner. There wasn't so much dirt and mess, and things weren't as random. In a book, I could eventually figure out why something happened, because everything in a good story happens for a reason. But out in the world things were always happening—things no one would ever bother to write about—just a whirlwind of meaningless moments I was constantly sifting through, trying to find the thread of the story and where it was going.

But now the calm, homey, dinners were done.

Everyone was frantic because the dome had been on the television. And I knew what that meant: the climax of the story was building. Things were going to start happening, important things way better than quiet conversations around the dinner table.

David took my arm and escorted me to Mia and Gordon's giant house-bus. On the way, I saw Reiny and Lonan climbing into the truck, their PSS sparkling at me in the dark. Reiny's was minuscule, a pin-prick of light close to her heart, and Lonan's was a soft glow near his left temple. Often, the location of the PSS inside someone told me something about them. People who manifested it in their torso area were usually caring. People with PSS in their skull, like Lonan, were usually thinkers. And people with PSS in their extremities, like my sister, were people of action.

David had been very surprised when Reiny had told him that almost everyone in the world had PSS, but I'd been able to see that all my life. Most of my abilities hadn't manifested until recently, but that one had been with me for as long as I could remember. David tried so hard to pretend he didn't care about others, but his entire chest was PSS, so I knew better. I also knew it helped him to think I needed his protection. It made him feel better. So, I let him think it.

I sat down on a cushioned bench in the bus, across from my father's painting of me, which I'd insisted we bring. I was glad David had found it. Even if my father was dead, I had finally seen him in Gordon's picture, and I could tell by his painting that he'd loved me. I wasn't sure if my sister did. Back in the compound, she hadn't really known who I was.

She'd just needed my help. Then she'd sent me away in the displacement, landing me with David and his memory ball. I'd assumed that was all part of her plan—that she knew what she'd been doing. But then I'd begun to wonder. What if it had been a mistake? Or even worse, what if she'd sent me away on purpose because she didn't like or want me. That happened sometimes in books. Sad, tragic books.

Then there was my mother. I'd never met her or seen her. Mothers were always important in books. The desire I felt to see my mother, to touch her and know her and be held by her: it was more than any words that could be written.

Mike had promised to reunite me with her. He'd promised to give my family back to me.

But something had gone wrong with his plan. I knew that now, and my best chance of correcting it was back at the dome. To find Mike and my family again, I must start there.

I glanced around the inside of the bus, taking it all in. It had a tiny kitchen and bathroom. They were so cute, and I wanted to touch everything. I wanted to open the cupboards and peek into every nook and cranny, but David sat down next to me, all serious and tightened up like a coiled spring. I could feel the tension in his body calling out for me to touch it and relieve it, to siphon it off like I'd been doing for days.

Instead, I reached into my right pocket, touching the memory ball. David called it the magic eight ball, and he thought it was a toy. It hadn't taken me long to realize he didn't know what it really was, or what it held. At first, I'd thought people in the world must know everything, but now I understood how much there was to know. As soon as I'd figured out what was inside the black ball, perhaps I should have told him. They were his memories, safe and sound, not lost forever like he thought they were. If I'd been a character in a book I was reading, I would have been screaming at me to tell him.

But I didn't. That was my first untruth—unless you counted the note I'd slipped to Olivia in her cell telling her not to trust Grant. That was a test, a first tiny tasting of deception that hadn't worked. I had no reason not to trust Grant, other than the fact that I'd had my sister to myself before he'd come along. Jealousy. That was always in books, and I had been thrilled to feel it burning in my bones. And then I'd written the lie: *Don't trust the boy.* Because I could. Because I didn't want her to.

She'd ignored me and trusted him anyway, and ultimately it had gotten us all out of the dome. So much for my first lie. I thought then deception must be a thing that only worked in books, or I was just terrible at it. Now, I knew you simply had to practice a little. It was like learning an instrument. It never sounds good the first time you play.

So, I didn't tell David about his memories. After all, what was the point? I couldn't give them back to him. There was only one person who could do that, and it would only hurt him to know something so dear was so close, yet so far out of reach. That was where telling the truth versus lying got tricky. It wasn't black and white like I'd thought it would be. It was very, very gray.

The house-bus rumbled to life, the vibrations of the engine coming straight up through my seat. I jumped, startled, then nestled back into the bench cushion because I wanted to feel it more. It felt good. Of course, I'd read about all kinds of transportation in the dome library—trains, planes, buses, ships, cars, trucks, and everything in between. But I'd never actually ridden in a vehicle, and it was one more thing books hadn't quite rendered completely. And even though I knew it was coming, I was still surprised when we started to move, the bus lumbering around in a bumpy circle before finding the main road.

It's a moving house, I mind-spoke to David. *It feels almost alive like it's growling or purring at us. Or it's just eaten us and is running away to digest us in its lair.*

"You've never ridden in an RV?" he asked.

I've never ridden in anything, I told him. *Just on top of horses, but that's nothing like this.*

He smiled and shook his head, then looked out the back window as if he thought someone might be following us.

With all the excitement about the dome, he seemed to have forgotten about the cubes. He hadn't said a thing about them since we'd come back from Gordon and Mia's last night. I certainly hadn't forgotten them. They were in the other pocket of my sweater, even now, and I stuck my hand in, touching their hard corners, just to be sure because I'd told David yet another lie. I couldn't read who the cubes belonged to or where that person was. That was the thing about cubes. They were blanks. The glowing I'd shown David on Reiny's steps had all been a trick using my own PSS. Of course, I'd known what the cubes were as soon as I'd seen them at the bazaar. And maybe they couldn't lead me anywhere, but they were powerful all the same, extremely powerful when combined with a PSS artifact. My sister would want them back. Or Mike would. So, when David had only let me have one and shoved me away like a child, I'd been very angry.

It had also been my first realization that people out in the world had a different plotline than my own, perhaps even in opposition to mine. David was living his own story, and I was only a minor character in it. I began to understand that if I wanted to help my sister and be reunited with Mike and my mother, I would have to take charge.

That's when I'd told David we had Grant's cube and I could tell where he was. I lied well that time, and it worked exactly as I'd hoped. David had taken us straight to Gordon and Mia's, desperate to get the other one. Now I had them both in my pocket, side by side. Oh, and then there was the other thing I'd found and taken, the thing in Gordon's den pulsing with PSS and calling to me. It had been easy to slip away while he and David were fighting. Even easier to slip through the wall of the house and hide it carefully inside my boot, then scurry around to the front door as if that was where I'd been all along. I wasn't sure why Gordon had been hiding that slim, sharp knife, pulsing with the PSS of a dead man. But it was mine now. Once we'd arrived back at Reiny's, I'd kept it out of sight until I could sneak it into the bag they'd given me to pack for the dome.

Mike Palmer had always said I knew nothing of deception.

He'd also said I was one of the quickest learners he'd ever met.

"Don't be afraid," David said, scooting closer to me on the bench and putting his arm around me. "It's going to be okay. I promise."

I'm not afraid. I smiled up at him as the RV rumbled on. *Not even a little.*

16

JASON

The testimony about the Eidolon was easy. The Hold council, a group of seven people sitting behind a huge table, including that asshole, Holbrook, and Mr. James's wife, called me as a witness and asked a shit-ton of questions about what I'd seen and what I'd done. There were a lot of pissed-off-looking adults in the audience, and a handful of kids my age, glassy-eyed and battle-worn. I didn't recognize any of them specifically, but I knew that look. They were survivors of the Eidolon and had probably already given their accounts. So, I stuck to the truth, mostly. I did skip the part about shooting Samantha at Mr. James's request, and I neglected to mention my newly-acquired ability. Oh, and I certainly didn't tell them the massacre had been my old man's handiwork. I thought I'd recognized some of his men that night, and he'd confirmed it with his boasting back at the lodge. Fineman had hired them to run The Holders off the cliffs so they could be captured down below by the doctor's men. But my old man hadn't exactly followed the plan.

The entire time I talked, Mrs. James glared at me. She was sitting next to Holbrook, leaving no question about her loyalties now. She must have been faking her cooperation at the farm, or what she'd learned about Mr. James at the compound had been the last straw. Whatever. She was a two-faced bitch with secrets of her own. She knew I'd shot her daughter at her husband's request, but she didn't bring that up. She was still protecting her own interests.

When the council was done with their questions, Mr. James got up and started asking me about what had happened after the Eidolon.

I told them Passion and I had run, and how we'd gotten caught. I described how Holbrook's people had treated us like criminals. How he'd drugged me and locked me in a crate, and that got him some nasty looks. Then I tried to make Mr. James sound really good, explaining how he'd gotten me out of Holbrook's clutches, taken care of all of us at the farmhouse, nursed his nephew back to health, and tried to rescue Olivia from the CAMFers.

"Yes, Yes," Mr. James said, sounding impatient. "But back at the farmhouse, do you remember my medical assistant, Reiny, giving you a shot, something she referred to as a vaccine?"

"Yeah," I nodded, wondering what the hell that had to do with anything. "She said it was for some virus going around Oregon."

"Well, that wasn't precisely the truth," Mr. James said, pacing toward the council. "You see, when we gave my nephew, David, an emergency blood transfusion after the Eidolon, we discovered something very unique about the donor's blood. Her plasma was PSS, and not just any PSS. It had a unique property, a stabilizing element we'd never seen before."

"We don't care about your little experiments," Holbrook growled. "They can't bring our children back or protect them from the CAMFers."

"Actually, they can," Mr. James said, pulling a minus meter out of his jacket pocket.

"What the hell?" Holbrook leapt up. "How dare you bring that in here?"

"Alex!" Mrs. James said, standing up and glaring at her husband. "They used one of those to torture Luke." She glanced toward a stocky, dark-haired boy in the audience, who was now staring at the minus meter in Mr. James's hand, his face gone completely pale and still. The woman next to him, obviously his ma, was clutching his arm and glaring down Mr. James with utter hatred in her eyes. This kid Luke hadn't just been at the Eidolon. He'd been one of those taken and tortured by Fineman. What the fuck was Mr. James thinking pulling out a minus meter in this crowd?

"I know what they did to your son with this," James said to Holbrook, holding up the meter.

Fuck. That kid was Holbrook's son? Shit, this was outa control.

"But what if I told you," Mr. James continued, glancing at Luke, "that I could guarantee this device could never be used against him again. Or against anyone with PSS. What if my little experiments, as you call them, resulted in the discovery of a vaccine that makes PSS completely impervious to extraction?"

Holy motherfucking shit. Passion's blood could do that? Was that her power? There was no way. James had to be bluffing. I could see everyone in the room thinking the same thing. Holbrook didn't believe him. That was obvious, and the council and the gallery had broken into a loud uproar, voices yelling over voices.

"Silence! Order!" Mrs. James called, banging a gavel on the table in front of her. The room quieted down, mostly, and she turned to her husband. "Can you prove this?" she asked, hope swimming in her eyes. "Do you have evidence to back up this claim?"

"Yes," he said, turning to me. "Jason, pull up your pant leg."

"Wait? What?" I stammered as he approached me with the minus meter. Oh, fuck no! Is this what he'd meant by "a little demonstration"? You couldn't pay me enough money for this shit.

"Get the fuck away from me." I stood up and pushed my chair back, ready to bolt.

"Jason," Palmer said from behind me, putting his hand gently on my shoulder. "It's okay."

"No way," I said, shaking my head.

"You didn't even tell this boy you were going to do this?" Holbrook laughed bitterly. "You're as bad as the CAMFers, Alex. You're exactly like them, scaring and torturing innocent children."

"No," Mr. James said. "The vaccine works. We tested it. You have to believe me. Think of how many lives we could save and protect—"

"I'll do it," a quivering voice came from the audience. It was Luke. "I'll take the vaccine right now, and he can do the test on me."

"Son, no," his father begged, the blood draining from his face.

"You don't have to do this, Honey," his mother said from his side, clutching his arm. "You've been through enough."

"No," Luke protested, his voice growing stronger, the room gone suddenly and absolutely silent. "When the CAMFers had me, I was terrified. I thought I was going to die. The things they did to me in my cell were bad enough. Then, one day, they chained us all together, and gagged us, and took us into a room where another captive was. They threatened her and hurt her, because they wanted her to do something to us, something horrible. She refused, so they pulled me out of the line. They were going to hurt me, but one of the other guys— he stepped forward. He volunteered to be tortured in my place. Do you understand that?" he asked, those dark bottomless eyes falling on me, then on Mr. James, then back to his dad. "They did horrible things to him instead of me, and I just stood there watching."

"It's not your fault, Son," Mr. Holbrook said, his voice ragged. "It's this bastard's fault." He gestured at Mr. James. "Not yours."

"Arguing about whose fault it is accomlishes nothing," Luke said. "If there's a way to stop them from ever doing it to anyone else, I want to help."

I had to admit, the kid had balls. He was an idiot to volunteer, but still, he had balls.

"That's very mature and noble of you, Luke," Mr. James said, "but I'm afraid it takes the vaccine twelve to fifteen hours to become fully effective. Jason here had it well over a week ago. If I gave it to you we'd have to wait—"

"You do this and he's back on top," Palmer murmured in my ear. He was still standing behind me, making sure I didn't run. "He'll go after your father. You know he will."

My old man had used a minus meter to punish me a few times. One short zap to my PSS leg had been much worse than the burning cigars he'd sometimes pressed against my arms. This kid Luke's story was nothing. He hadn't really suffered. He was a pussy.

But he was a pussy who'd just volunteered for this, and he wasn't even getting paid.

"Fuck it. I'll do it," I said, shaking Palmer off and stepping toward Mr. James.

"Good," Mr. James said, relief in his voice. "Thank you, Jason. Go ahead and sit down. It won't hurt. I promise."

I sat back down in my chair, trying to stay cool, calm, and collected, but mainly I was hoping I wouldn't piss my pants. When I reached down to pull up my pant leg, my hands were shaking. I rolled up the cuff, revealing the leg I'd been shamed for all my life, but no one in the room made a sound. No one mocked or abused me.

As Mr. James approached, flicking that minus meter on, the memory of that soft buzz in the air, the calm before the pain, made me squirm in my seat and I felt Palmer's hand settle on my shoulder again, to pin me or comfort me, I wasn't sure which. Mr. James bent down, holding the minus meter near my leg, and some part of me hoped someone, anyone, would jump in and object the way Luke's parents had for him.

But no one did.

The room was absolutely silent, every eye on me.

I caught Luke's gaze, and he held mine like he was staring straight into my soul.

The minus meter crackled with energy.

Luke glanced away, and I squeezed my eyes shut, waiting for the pain, for a sensation, for anything. I counted to ten, every muscle in my body tensed.

"There, you see?" Mr. James said, standing up, the minus meter powering down in his hands. "It had absolutely no effect on him or his PSS."

I opened my eyes and bent over, stunned, staring at my leg. He'd done it? He'd actually done it and I'd felt nothing?

"We're still not sure what all the applications for the vaccine might be," Mr. James was saying to a now very receptive and captive audience. "We know it stabilizes PSS to the point that it cannot be extracted, disrupted, or compromised. This"—he crossed to the council's table and set the minus meter in front of them—"is no longer a weapon or a torture device. It is now nothing more than an overdesigned flashlight. And this,"—he turned to the audience and pulled a small syringe of glowing blue liquid from his pocket—"is the promise that your children need never fear the CAMFers again."

In a moment, the room was in utter chaos. People stormed Mr. James, begging to have their kids be first in line for the vaccine. Holbrook and his wife were among them, looking sheepish and completely appeased. Mrs. James was hanging back in the crowd, but it was obvious she had been won over too.

Mr. James was back on top.

An hour or so later, after a lot of handshakes and small talk, Palmer and I rode back to the mansion in the limo, but Mr. James stayed behind to bullshit more people and carve out his reclaimed kingdom.

Palmer leaned back against the black leather seat, flipping through stuff on his phone.

"You know it doesn't matter, right?" I said to him.

"What doesn't?" He mumbled, not even looking up.

"The vaccine. The immunity to minus meters. All that shit back there. My old man isn't going to use minus meters. He's going to use guns. He's a hunter, not a scientist, and he hunts to kill." Just like Mr. James, my old man would never give up. He wouldn't let anything stop him—including having a son with PSS. And despite my taunts back in Texas, I knew the CAMFers would follow him, because they already were.

Palmer looked up. I had his attention now. "The vaccine hasn't been fully tested yet," he said. "It may have other applications."

"It's not going to save their lives, and you and I both know it."

"Maybe not. But it will give them hope and courage. It already has. And with Alex back in control—"

Palmer's phone pinged in his hands—not a ring tone but a message alert, soft and insistent.

He touched the screen and a satisfied grin spread across his face. He tapped the screen a few more times, scanning and swiping.

"Just a minute," he said, dialing quickly. "I need to make a call."

After a couple of rings I heard a deep, male voice on the other end, a voice I recognized immediately. "What is it?" Mr. James asked.

"The dome just broke onto the national news circuits," Palmer said, grinning. "It's all over the internet too. I thought you'd want to know."

"But it's too soon," Mr. James said. "You told me we'd have more time."

"No." Palmer countered. "I told you we wouldn't have control over the timing. Things like this have a life of their own. Besides, the faster it builds, the better for us. But we need to leave tonight. Tomorrow morning at the latest."

"I can't leave this soon," Mr. James said, sounding frustrated. "I need more time to solidify my position here. I have to call in my people and that's going to take a few days. I bail now and Holbrook is right back in the driver's seat. But I want you to go, and take the Williams boy with you. I should be able to send some men by tomorrow evening."

"There's no sign of military intervention yet," Palmer said, "but when there is, we'll need them."

"You know I have your back," Mr. James said. "Take the jet tonight."

"Will do," Palmer said, hanging up. Then he turned to me and asked. "Did you follow that?"

"Someone found the dome and Mr. James wants us to secure it?" It would burn my old man so hard if the Holders got the compound. There were CAMFer secrets in there dating back to the early years of PSS. And of course, The Hold had secrets of its own within those walls.

"Close enough," Palmer said. "We're flying to Oregon. Tonight."

I didn't like Oregon. Last time I'd been there, the place had spat me right back to Texas. But if there was money to be had and I could screw my old man at the same time, I was in. "What's the pay?" I asked.

"I might as well put you on the payroll," Palmer said, typing something into his phone. "How does this look?" he asked, holding the screen out to me with a very adequate number on it.

"Looks good," I said, trying not to sound surprised.

"Just to be clear," he added. "*I'm* paying you that, not Mr. James. You understand?"

"Yeah, I get it." He wanted my loyalty if it came to betraying Mr. James and, for that price, he had it.

"Here. Watch this." He handed me his phone.

It was playing a news video with half a million hits and counting. There was someone talking, a woman rattling off hype and then helicopter footage of the dome lighting up the desert like a fucking UFO. And there were crowds, tons of people, too many to count, milling around it like ants around an ant hill.

17

JASON

Four hours later, at about midnight, Mr. James's private jet hit the ground in Oregon and we exited the plane right into the middle of the high desert, a dirt landing strip trailing off into the distant shrub.

There was a vehicle waiting for us, a beat-up truck with an even more beat-up camper top on the back of it. It reminded me of some of the rigs back home guys took into the woods during hunting season, cooking their food over a fire every night and shitting in the bushes.

"Get the bags," Palmer ordered, as he moved toward the truck. I had one small duffle, filled with a few items Mr. James's staff had scraped up for me before we'd left. Palmer had two huge bags. So, I threw my duffle over my shoulder and reached down to pick up his two, but they felt like they were full of bricks. Fuck that. I wasn't his valet. I dropped them at my feet, and looked up to see Palmer talking to some old guy who'd climbed out of the truck. I walked over, and I could tell Palmer was pissed.

"That's not the arrangement we made," he said, holding out an envelope. "I pay you and we take this heap of junk off your hands, no title or paperwork involved, but we're not renting it. That's not the deal."

"Buying was the deal a few days ago," the old guy said, frowning. "Things has changed around here since then. You know how much a camper is worth in these parts now? Ten times what you got in that envelope. Probably more. So, I'm not selling, but I'll give you a ride to the dome and rent you all the camping gear you'll need. Hell, I'll even bring you back to your posh jet when you get tired of the noise and the people and the dirt. But I'm not selling Ole Betsy here. That's the deal. Take it or leave it."

"You'll rent us equipment?" Palmer asked. "Everything we need to camp, including food and water, for as long as we need it. And how much is that going to cost me?"

"Four hundred a day," the guy said, glancing between Palmer and me. "Two for you, and two for the boy, and I'm the best price around. I guarantee it. And all the stores is sold out of everything, so don't go thinking you'll be able to get it yourself."

"The stores are sold out because you unloaded them," Palmer said, his nostrils flaring. "You bought them out so you could run this game on every idiot coming into town. That's called extortion where I come from."

"Here we call it good business," the old guy said, spitting into the dirt. "I'm giving you a fair price."

"And that price won't go up," Palmer said. "You gonna guarantee that too?"

"Well now," the old coot said, one of his eyes twitching, "that ain't really up to me, is it? It all depends on the free market. Things is getting dearer and dearer around here. You better take this deal while you still can. That's all I'm saying."

"You promised to sell me this camper for this price." Palmer held out the envelope of money again, his voice gone hard. "*You* better take that deal *while you still can.*"

"Then I guess we got nothing more to talk about," the old guy said, turning back toward his battered truck.

It was fast.

One minute the guy was reaching for his driver's side door. The next he was on the ground, blood pouring into the sand under him, his pained eyes staring up at the starry night sky, his breath coming in desperate gasps.

I hadn't even seen Palmer pull the gun that was now in his hand.

"I told you to get my bags," Palmer said calmly, his eyes still on the old geezer dying in the dirt.

"Yes, sir." I turned on my heels and hurried to obey. I wasn't afraid. Palmer wasn't going to shoot me. But he'd certainly just earned my respect.

As I bent to get his bags, hefting the heaviest one over my shoulder, another shot rang out—Palmer putting the old guy out of his misery.

By the time I got back to the truck, he was pulling the body into some shrubs and kicking sand over it.

I was still standing next to the pick-up like an idiot, when he came back, keys in hand.

"Give me that." He took his heavy bag from me and unzipped it. It was full of guns and ammunition. He pulled out a handgun and held the grip out to me. "In case we meet any more extortionists," he said. "Unless you'd rather have the shotgun in the cab he was reaching for." He nodded toward the truck's interior.

"I'll take this." I palmed the gun he was holding out, then slipped it into my waistband. Some weird shit was going down in Oregon already, and I was glad to be armed. Plus, it meant Palmer trusted me.

"Let's load up," he said, leading me to the back of the truck and putting one of the old guy's keys into the door of the camper so we could throw our bags in.

The lock clicked and he pulled the door open.

"Holy shit!" I said, confronted with a solid wall of sleeping mats, tents, and pillows. I could see a camp stove wedged in between the softer stuff as well, and a new lantern still in its box. There wasn't an inch of room in that camper left unstuffed.

"Fuck," Palmer said. "We'll have to put our bags in the front with us, and unload this stuff when we get to the dome. If that old bugger was right, there should be high demand for it."

"So, we're the new extortionists?" I smiled at Palmer.

"Looks that way." He grinned back.

We climbed into the cab, jamming our bags between us, and Palmer put the old truck into gear.

Almost as soon as we cleared the little airport, it became obvious that the world had gone bat-shit crazy. There were hitchhikers everywhere, holding up flashlight-lit signs that said things like *UFO or bust* and *Take us Home to the Dome*. We passed groups camping along the roadside, many of them families, sitting in lawn chairs outside their RVs like they were vacationing at the beach. And then there were cops patrolling the area, lots of them.

"I don't see any state troopers," Palmer observed. "But they'll be calling them in soon, if they haven't already."

"What the hell is this?" I asked, nodding out the window. "Why are they here?"

"Because the world is changing, and they can feel it," he said. "They don't know how, or why, or even what it means, but they've come looking for answers."

"From a fucking dome in the desert? How is that going to answer anything?"

"The dome is just a rallying point, like a porch light drawing moths at night. It's only a symbol."

"But when moths fly to the light, they fucking die."

"Yeah, well, no analogy is perfect," Palmer said, frowning.

"With all these people here, the compound must be trashed by now. You really think there's going to be anything left to secure?"

"It's already secure," he said. "Olivia's inside with her mom, Samantha, Grant, and Passion, plus a group of hackers and Pete Hardy. They found it a few days ago and locked down the compound before anyone else could. But the area is contested government land.

It's an old chemical depot, and there are a bunch of special interest groups vying for it. When they discovered the compound and an occupying presence, they got a little riled up. Now with it all over the news, we've got this." He gestured out the window.

"So, this is a rescue mission?" I asked, still confused. "Mr. James wants us to get his daughter and his information out safely?"

"This isn't about what Alex wants," Palmer said, navigating a sharp turn in the road a little too fast. "We're way beyond that. He thinks in terms of his own little empire, but this is way bigger than The Hold. It's bigger than Fineman, your father, or the CAMFers. We're here to facilitate the beginning of— What the fuck?" He slammed on the brakes, sending me hurtling toward the truck's dashboard.

I caught myself before my head hit the windshield. We'd almost rear-ended the car in front of us and there were red taillights streaming into the distance beyond it. Further down the road there were flashing lights too, the red and blue strobe of numerous cop cars.

"Dammit," Palmer said. "That's why there were so many people camping off the road. They've got road blocks at the entrances."

Even as he said it, a batch of vehicles passed us in the other lane, obviously motorists who'd been turned away at the gate.

"Fasten your seatbelt," Palmer said, checking his rearview mirror and putting the truck in reverse. "We need to find another way in."

There was already a van behind us, and more cars piling up, but Palmer still managed to pull a U-turn with the awkward camper. When he merged into the other lane, right in front of an oncoming RV, they had to slam on their brakes to avoid hitting us. The old Indian guy behind the wheel scowled and his wife flipped us off, but Palmer didn't even acknowledge them.

"Is there another way?" I asked, as he gunned the gas and we took off back the way we'd come.

"There's always another way."

We were maybe five minutes down the road when I noticed a guy my age on a dirt bike, off to the side. He was waving at us vigorously, gesturing for us to pull onto the shoulder.

Palmer saw him too and slowed, but just before we reached him, the biker took off, veering straight into the desert down a dusty trail.

"It's a service road," Palmer said, swerving onto the shoulder, following the bike.

"And who's the biker?"

"I have no idea. But I guess we'll find out."

Headlights flashed in the rearview mirror, almost blinding me. It was the RV. They were following us and they weren't happy, that was for sure.

Palmer didn't seem to care. We couldn't see the biker anymore, but he'd led us down this road and Palmer seemed determined to follow it to the bitter end.

And then we came to the end—a huge, fortified, chain link fence twenty feet high and stretching in either direction as far as the eye could see. Palmer almost ran into it, barely stopping in time. The dirt track we were on ran straight up to the fence and continued on the other side.

We weren't alone, either. The biker rode out of the shadows, another dozen dark forms on dirt bikes joining him on either side of our truck. Several of them dismounted, wielding baseball bats. And the RV had pulled up right behind us, blocking us in.

"Shit," I said.

"They have bats. We have guns," Palmer pointed out. "Just let me do the talking."

The leader, the one who'd led us into this trap, pulled up next to Palmer's window, his bike buzzing like a hornet and kicking up dust.

"Hey," he yelled over the noise of the engine. "You're not Bernie."

"He's sick," Palmer said, without missing a beat. "He asked me and my nephew here to take over."

"Then what the hell were you doing at the road block?" the biker asked, shutting his bike off. He was young, probably younger than me. "Didn't he tell you about the new route?"

"He said something," Palmer explained, "but you know Bernie. He never gets it right."

"Good thing I saw you then," the biker smiled, glancing behind us. "Who're your friends in the RV?"

"Don't know," Palmer said. "They just followed us."

The biker gave the big vehicle a second look. "Not a problem." He shrugged. "If they can pay, we'll let them through. You got your entry fee?"

"Sure." Palmer reached into his pocket, pulling out the envelope full of money he'd offered to Bernie earlier. "Here." He handed it to the biker who immediately flipped it open and started counting.

He was only a few bills in when I heard one of the RV doors slam and the crunch of sand underfoot.

"What the hell is going on?" a gruff voice asked.

"Wait your turn, old man," Biker Guy said. "You're next in line."

But Palmer had gone rigid at the sound of that voice, his hand sliding toward the gun in his underarm holster.

"This guy was driving like a maniac," the old Indian said, coming up to Palmer's window and glancing in. "He almost—" He stopped, his mouth falling open, his eyes bulging. "Nathan," he hissed on an exhale, his entire face gone pale like he was seeing a ghost. "What—how on earth—but you're dead."

The biker stopped counting money, looking curiously between Palmer and the Indian.

"You got me confused with someone else," Palmer said, his cheek twitching. "My name's not Nathan, and I've never been dead."

"I know you," the old coot insisted, his right hand drifting to his chest and clutching it, his eyes drilling into Palmer. "I would know you anywhere." He sounded weird, breathy, his voice barely audible. "How did you survive? What about the others? Where have you been all this time?"

And then the guy went down, like a felled tree. One minute he was standing, the next he wasn't.

"Move," Palmer yelled, shoving his door open, slamming it into Biker Guy and sending him and his bike flying. Palmer crouched over the Indian guy, who'd collapsed in a heap just outside the truck door, and I heard Palmer whisper, "Gordon, can you hear me?"

Then he was yelling at Biker Guy again, who was just getting up, the envelope of cash still clutched in his hand. "I think he's having a heart attack. Call 911," Palmer ordered.

"I'm not calling the cops, man," Biker Guy said. "This gate isn't exactly legal. Is he dead?"

"Not yet," Palmer said, putting two fingers on the old man's neck.

Just as I scooted across the seat to get out and help, a female voice cried, "Gordon," and the woman from the passenger seat of the RV threw herself down at the old guy's side. "Gordon, oh my god, please wake up," she pleaded, tears streaming down her face.

"How far to the nearest hospital?" Palmer asked Biker Guy.

"There's one in Hermiston," he answered.

"I'm—not—going—to—that—hospital," Gordon said, opening his eyes. "I'd die first."

"Do you have any aspirin?" Palmer asked the woman. "It might help."

"I think so." She nodded, turning toward the RV and yelling, "David, bring the aspirin. It's in the pouch on the back of my seat."

At the sound of that name, Palmer and I locked eyes.

It couldn't be. What were the odds? There were a lot of Davids in the world and this was probably just some random David, not the one I'd known as Marcus. Not *the David*.

But in my gut, I knew it was him, even before he ran up carrying a bottle of aspirin.

I had to hand it to him. Marcus—I still thought of him by that name—always played it cool. He paused, only for a moment, looking from Palmer to me, before he tossed him the pills and said, "What the hell are you doing here?"

"Wait. You two know each other?" Gordon wheezed, trying to sit up.

"We three," Marcus clarified. "This is Mike Palmer. And that's Jason Williams. They were at the dome when it displaced."

"You were at the compound?" Gordon asked, glaring at Palmer.

Palmer ignored the question, just like he had Marcus's. Instead, he told the woman to help Gordon sit up while he opened the bottle of pills. "Chew these, don't just swallow," he instructed, slipping two aspirin between Gordon's lips. "They taste bad, but they work better that way."

"Is he going to be all right?" the woman asked, clutching Gordon's hand as he chewed.

"You should get him to a hospital," Palmer said.

"I'm not going to a goddamn hospital," Gordon growled. "I'm fine, Mia." He took her hand "Just help me up. Reiny and Lonan are waiting for us in there." He gestured at the fence. "We have to get in tonight. No more delays."

"There's an emergency medical tent inside," Biker Guy spoke up, a couple of his cronies standing behind him. "And it seems like Bernie gave you enough to get the RV in too." The money was nowhere to be seen. He'd already pocketed it, and he probably thought we'd been trying to rip him off since it was obvious we knew Marcus, at the very least. Maybe he even thought we'd faked Gordon's heart attack.

"Anyway," he said, "you all better get moving and out of the way. We've got more customers coming down the road." He gestured at a group of headlights off in the distance, moving quickly toward us, led by the single light of a kid on a motorcycle.

"But how do we get in?" Mia asked, looking up at the fence in our way.

"Like this," biker guy said, whistling loudly and waving his hand as more forms appeared on the other side of the fence. They reached their arms up, pulling down dark lines of rope or chain, and suddenly a huge flap of the fence rolled upward, leaving a gaping hole a little bigger than the RV. "You've got about five minutes to get through before we close it for the next batch," Biker Guy warned.

"You said you have people inside already." Palmer looked from Gordon to David. "How did you manage that?"

"We left together in two vehicles," Marcus explained. "Unfortunately, on our way here the RV's fuel pump went out, so we sent them on ahead while we stopped to get it fixed. That was yesterday, before the roadblocks went up. When we got turned away, we didn't know how we were going to get in. Then you pulled out in front of us, and here we are."

"Time is ticking, people," Biker Guy said. "You going in or out?"

"In," Palmer and Gordon said in unison.

"Gordon," Mia said, fear in her voice. "You're sure?"

"Yes, I'm sure," Gordon insisted.

"I can drive the RV," Marcus offered.

"Then let's load up," Palmer said, helping Gordon stand and handing him off to Mia and Marcus.

Palmer watched them head back to their vehicle, his eyes scanning its dark interior and narrowing slightly.

I followed his gaze, but all I saw was the soft glow of an interior light winking out.

"What is the chance we'd run into them?" I asked, as we climbed into Bernie's pick-up.

"There's no such thing as chance," Palmer said, starting up the truck, as Biker Guy waved us through the fence, the RV following behind us.

18

MIKE PALMER

Driving across the dark dust bowl of Umatilla in a beat-up truck, it all came rushing back to me—another night just like this one, long ago, a group of us sneaking through the fence, though we'd cut it open ourselves back then. Another vehicle's headlights flashing behind me, just like they were now. I had to shake off the feeling of deja-vu. Had to remind myself that had been another lifetime. I wasn't a young, idealistic, FBI agent working his first assignment and trying to change the world. I was older and wiser. Now, I understood you don't change the world—it changes you.

It had certainly changed Gordon. Seeing me alive after all these years had nearly killed the old bastard.

And him refusing to go to the hospital — if he died out in this desert, it would be his own damn fault. He was as stubborn as ever. That much hadn't changed. If he lived, he was going to grill me about where I'd been all these years. I wouldn't be able to avoid it forever.

I should have known he'd come to the Umatilla when he saw it on the news. How could he resist? And of course, he'd managed to get his hands on David Marcus and Kaylee at the reservation. I'd seen her glowing face peering out from inside the RV. And that hadn't really surprised me either.

Everything was falling into place. And now that the world was seeing events unfold via the news and social media, there was no stopping it. The road blocks didn't matter. People would come. They would get through just like we had, and those who didn't would still see. The more the officials tried to stop it, the more people would want in. The more they tried to cover things up, the more would be revealed.

The end game was coming.

I glanced over at the Williams kid sitting next to me. He looked like his mother, and he had her sensitive nature too, though it had nearly been beaten out of him by his piece-of-shit father. The boy was a bit rough around the edges, but he had potential. In fact, he reminded me of myself at his age. I'd recognized that when I'd let him beat the crap out of me outside of Greenville. He knew how to cause pain efficiently, and he wasn't squeamish about it. He had balls and good intuition, plus he was more than proficient with a gun, and he knew how to shut the hell up even when something was eating at him like it was now.

He wanted to ask me about Gordon, had been itching to ever since we'd come through the fence. But he'd waited, biding his time, staring out the window and watching the evenly-spaced hummocks roll by. He was a good kid, but I could see his patience was wearing thin.

"You knew that guy Gordon," he finally said, turning toward me. "I heard you say his name before his wife did."

"Yeah, I knew him, but it was a long time ago. Another life ago."

"Is that why he thought you were dead?"

Ahead, a small sign at the side of the road flashed in my headlights and I slowed the truck, pulling up next to it and stopping. The RV pulled up behind me, but no one got out.

"Stay in the truck," I ordered Jason as I opened my door.

I stepped around the pick-up and walked to the tiny sign situated in front of a giant, shallow crater in the desert. Six hundred feet to my right was an igloo and six hundred feet to my left was another one.

Incident 47, the sign read. *Complete and catastrophic disintegration. Four casualties.*

How nice of them to erect a marker. To finally admit that something had happened that night, thirty-three years ago.

Such a touching memorial.

Except for the fact that it was wrong.

I hadn't died the night Gordon had led us here to work his little act of protest. And the others waiting outside the igloo with me hadn't died either.

We had been displaced. I'd ended up in a mountain snowdrift in Norway, stunned, alone, half-frozen, and 4,600 odd miles from where I'd been a moment before. If not for the kindness of an elderly Norwegian couple who'd found me and taken me in, I might have died of exposure that night.

And I'd thanked them by lying about my identity, falling in love with their only daughter, getting her pregnant, and leaving her, never to be heard from again.

It had been a dick move. I'd known it then, and I knew it now. But I'd also known myself and I was a lot of things, but father-material wasn't one of them.

I'd come back to the States, of course, and discovered I had a little brother. My grieving parents had replaced me, but I didn't blame them. I couldn't really explain where I'd been all those years or why. Chase was young enough to accept the mystery of it, but the rest of my family, not so much. So, I started a new life again with a new name and set out to discover what had happened to me, and what it meant.

That night, when Gordon led his band of rebels into Umatilla, I was supposed to call in backup to catch them in the act and arrest them, but I hesitated a moment too long. And everything changed.

Now, I stood in front of that sign, the wind blowing dust in my face, and I fought the urge to turn and glance at the RV. It was foolish to hope Gordon would come out and stand with me, that he would clap me on the back and we would look at what we'd done, together, and assure one another it could still be fixed. Because Gordon was in worse shape than either of us had let on. No, I would have to honor this memorial alone.

Complete and catastrophic disintegration, the sign said. That part, at least, was accurate. Being suddenly unmade, your very essence dissolved and put back together somewhere else—it does something to you and you have to find out what, and why, and how. Those questions, plus the strange circumstances of my daughter's birth back in Norway, drove me to seek an explanation at all costs.

That was how I fell in with The Hold. I wanted answers, and when I finally located Alex, I thought he might have them. He invited me into his fold with open arms, trusting me instantly because of our shared experience at Umatilla. Or maybe he just wanted to keep me close and make sure I never revealed our mutual secret. Whichever it was, he assigned me to the compound to be the main protector of his precious infant Kaylee. It was a terrible idea. She cried whenever I came near and screamed when I held her. But slowly, the trust between us built. I never let anyone see it, the way she softened me. It was a weakness, and I knew it. I didn't deserve to have a little girl love me. Not after I'd abandoned my own child like a coward.

So, years later, when Alex asked me to disavow The Hold, leave the dome, and go infiltrate CAMF on a long-term mission, I did it. I left her. I ripped her clinging, crying, snotty five-year-old form from my leg like an old Band-Aid, and I went away. I did my goddamn job and got in good with the CAMFers, aligning myself with a new and rising scientist in their ranks, Dr. Julian Fineman. He was a genius and a fucking mad man. It took me seven years and a lot of unspeakable acts to fully earn his trust. Those were dark years for me. Very dark. When Julian assigned me to the quiet little town of Greenfield to pose as their fire chief and keep tabs on one defective, it had been a relief. It had also been my chance to sneak back to the dome occasionally and report to Alex face-to-face.

And visit Kaylee.

She hadn't forgotten me. Far from it.

She'd idealized me.

I was the one who'd escaped the dome and lived in the real world. And I'd come back for her finally. To save her and set her free.

It was only when she told me that, looking up at me with those deep, dark, trusting eyes, that I realized it was true. From that day forward, I no longer worked for Alex or Fineman. I worked for her.

No, I hadn't died as a result of incident 47.

But I had been changed.

The whole world had.

It just didn't know it yet.

"You gonna stand there all night staring at that sign or what?" Jason called from the truck.

"No," I answered, turning away from it. "Let's get to the dome."

19

OLIVIA

It took over forty-eight hours for Chase and T-Dog to hack into the dome portion of the compound, and I think it was a serious blow to their egos. They kept apologizing and trying to explain to me, in very technical terms, why it was taking so long. And I just kept saying, "It's okay. We'll get there."

My first step back into that huge, open space was somewhat surreal. A clear desert sky spread over me, giving the illusion that I was outside, which was nice after being trapped in The Hold's windowless computer lab for so long with only cold fluorescent lighting. Even better, the noise of the mob outside was barely a murmur inside the dome. I could almost forget they were out there. I could almost forget we were trapped as precisely as the tiny mouse in the game of *Mouse Trap*.

Then, I had to remind myself that my sister had been trapped here all her life. This had been her home, and if she could live and thrive in it, so could I. We had so many resources at our disposal, and I had good, competent people with me. Chase and T-Dog seemed to think working from inside the compound might actually be an asset, rather than a detriment, and Pete agreed.

"You gonna let us in, or just stand there gawking in the doorway?" Chase teased from behind me.

"Oh, sorry." I stepped fully into the dome and moved aside so the rest of them could enter.

Chase and T-Dog came through first and crossed to the far door, immediately plugging their laptops into various control panels. "This should go much faster, now that we know what we're dealing with," Chase assured me.

Passion and Samantha came in next. They both looked around, taking in the homey furnishings, the ornate tile floor and plush rugs, the rows and rows of library-sized bookshelves filled with books. It was all exactly as it had been before I'd displaced it. Off to one side, behind one of the many oriental screens that divided the room, the corner of my sister's four poster bed was just visible.

"Wow. It's really not that bad," Samantha said, and then she looked at me guiltily. "I mean, it was still wrong, keeping your sister trapped here all her life. I'm not trying to excuse—"

"Samantha, it's okay," I said. I knew what she meant.

The dome had a certain serenity. It didn't give off a prison vibe at all. It felt more like a museum or an old library, somewhere you'd talk in hushed tones and accidentally learn something.

Grant and my mom came in next, her limping and him assisting her across the threshold. Grant had been here before. With me. But we hadn't exactly gotten the scenic tour. My mom, on the other hand, had never seen the place they'd hidden her first born child away from her for years, and I didn't miss the haunted look in her eyes as she entered. This had been Kaylee's home, instead of our house. And maybe the furnishings were nice and the ambiance wasn't bad, but Kaylee had still been a prisoner here, unwillingly separated from her family.

My mom limped forward and slipped her hand into mine. "So, this is where she lived," she sighed. "I know it's foolish, but some part of me was hoping—when we opened that door—that she'd be standing here waiting for us."

"Mike will find her," I said, squeezing her hand. "He'll get her back for us."

Finally, last but not least, Pete stepped into the dome.

"Grant," he said. "Why don't you come with me and we'll take some inventory. I'd like to know what we've got here, and what we need to bring in from the rest of the compound." They both moved away, disappearing beyond the screens.

Pete was a good guy. I'd figured that out after only a couple days of living with him. During that time he'd nursed my mom back to health, sourced us numerous necessities from The Hold side of the compound, and helped Chase and T-Dog identify the most important files on The Hold's computers, including the ones about the research he'd done with Reiny on internal PSS, and the files on the vaccine Mr. James had made from Passion's blood, both of which had been huge revelations to the rest of us. Passion was still in shock. But she was also thrilled. She finally had a power and it was a pretty awesome one.

And it had been Pete's idea to make the dome our base of operations once we'd hacked into it. The dome was way more secure than the outer areas of the compound, plus we could see the sky. But that also meant we'd have to move some beds and other resources into it to make us all comfortable.

Yeah, Pete had been such a huge help, I'd almost forgiven him for shooting my mom.

Almost.

"Let's go check out the library." I said, helping my mom along and waving for Passion and Samantha to join us. I'd only met my sister briefly, and most of that time I'd thought she was an apparition or a dream, but you could tell a lot about a person by looking at the books they read.

I had other motives as well. Getting lost in one of Kaylee's books might help me forget that every hour there were more people outside, gathering and building some kind of weird, refugee-like city in the desert. I'd seen it on the drone footage. I'd also seen them amassing on the feeds from the outside cameras. And this morning, Chase had shown me several news clips from the internet urging people to stay away from Umatilla for purposes of "national security and public safety."

But it didn't matter. They just kept coming by the thousands. Something was happening out there way beyond the scope of the original special interest groups— something wild and beyond our control, drawing people from all walks of life. And we were the center of it, like the cast standing backstage on opening night of a sold-out play. The only problem was we didn't even know what play we were performing. What did those people out there want from us?

"That looks comfy," my mother said, pointing to a leather chair near a table sporting a stack of magazines. I deposited her in it, then made my way to one of Kaylee's bookcases, running my fingers along the spines while Samantha and Passion wandered off to an area with a bunch of potted plants and trees.

My hand stopped on a book with a familiar title. It was The Bone Road by Mary Holland, its paperback pages tattered and worn as if it had been read a thousand times. I slipped the book from the bookcase, and it fell open instantly to a place where a page had been torn out. Page forty-seven was missing. So was page one hundred and thirteen. Those were the pages Kaylee had written me notes on when I'd been alone and desperate in my CAMFer cell. This was the book she'd torn them from, and she'd obviously loved it so much I could almost feel her presence leaking from it. There were random notes scrawled in the margins too. Our handwriting was sort of similar.

"Hey, Olivia," Chase called from across the room. "Check this out." He pointed up at the dome, then tapped a button on his laptop.

Immediately, the entire glass ceiling overhead went opaque, dispersing the sun's morning glare into a gentle, ambient glow.

"Oh, that's nice," my mom said from her chair, her face buried in her magazine. "It was getting too bright in here."

"Chase did it," I told her, pointing upward as I put The Bone Road away. "But I have no idea how."

"It's a built-in feature," Pete said, walking up to us with Grant in tow. "Not only are the glass windows of the dome solar panels, they've also treated with something called electrochromic film. It's sort of like very expensive contact paper that can be stuck to any smooth, clear surface. Then, by running a very low electrical current through the film, you can change the transparency of that surface. The technology's been around for a while, but the application on the dome is a little more advanced than most."

As if on cue to the phrase "more advanced", we were suddenly plunged into darkness and the entire night sky hung over us, a full moon rising. Stars twinkled and a satellite passed overhead. If you'd asked me if it was real, I would have sworn it was, except I knew it was morning.

"What is going on?" Samantha's voice called anxiously from a few feet away.

"It's okay," Pete called back. "Chase is just running a demo of the dome's projection capabilities."

And the dome changed again, the world around us painted by an incredible red and orange sunset.

Then another flicker, and there were foreboding storm clouds gathering over the desert and racing toward us, lightning rippling across a dark purple sky.

Another flicker and it was the crack of dawn, the sun just peeking its pale morning face over the horizon.

Then it was back to opaque, Grant, Samantha, and Passion all standing around me with their mouths hanging open.

"That was spectacular," my mom said, grinning from her comfy chair.

"It's done with digital projectors," Pete explained, pointing around the dome to several devices mounted on the floor near the outer walls.

"But why would The Hold or the CAMFers install something like that?" I asked, puzzled. "It seems like a lot of trouble just to pretty up a prison."

"Well, originally, there was just the opaque option to keep down the glare and heat," Pete said. "It was a climate control feature. The projectors and the skyscape displays came later. They're the product of a few bored techies working long shifts. They used to mock them up and test them on their lunch hour, much to everyone's delight."

"Can it be seen from outside the dome as well?" Grant asked.

"Yep." Pete nodded. "It projects through the glass onto the other side. And it can do video too."

"So, this building is basically a giant drive-in theater," my mom said.

"I never really thought about it that way, but I guess so," Pete said, smiling. "Except it doesn't have audio. Although, there are external speakers mounted on the outside of the compound for announcements and alarms that could probably be hooked up to it."

"Can we see it again?" Passion asked.

"Sure," Pete said, giving Chase an encouraging wave.

Chase waved back, tapped at his laptop, and the dome started to play its skylight demo again.

But this time, as it flashed its fancy skies, I wasn't filled with child-like delight or wonder. Instead, I was trying to figure out how I could use it to my advantage. Thanks to Mr. James's research, we now had scientific proof that people with PSS weren't freaks. In fact, just the opposite. People without any PSS like Grant and Dr. Fineman were the true anomalies. But you couldn't just tell people the world was different than they'd always thought and believed. It wasn't that simple. Most people didn't want to know the truth. Most people wouldn't take the news that there was a ninety-eight percent chance they had internal PSS as calmly as Chase, T-dog, and my mother had.

No, before we could show people what we'd learned about PSS, we had to make them want it. We had to change their minds, but before we could do that, we had to change their feelings.

And I suddenly had an idea for exactly how to do that.

To make it as effective as possible, though, I needed something I could only get from the CAMFer side of the compound.

The second demo run was done, and Chase set the dome back to opaque to protect us from the glaring sun. I looked around at my friends, my mom, these people I knew I could trust.

This dome wasn't a prison anymore. It was our fort, and I wasn't just going to hold it down and wait for Mike Palmer or someone to come rescue us. The way I saw it, we had a captive audience. We might as well give them a show.

"Yes!" T-Dog yelled from across the room.

"We got it," Chase called, grinning and pointing to the door that led to the CAMFer side. It was hanging open.

I smiled, feigning excitement. This is what we'd come for, to get all the dirt and research the CAMFers had on PSS—to understand what they'd been doing all these years and why, so we could use it against them. I knew that, and I'd known all along it would mean entering the CAMFer side and facing all my personal demons. But now that the door was hanging open—

I squared my shoulders and walked over to Chase. "Can I talk to you for a minute, alone," I said, hoping T-dog wouldn't take it personally.

"Sure," Chase said, sounding concerned. "Everything okay?" he asked as we walked away from that looming door.

"Yeah, I'm good. I just need you to get me something from the CAMFer computers. It's top priority, but please don't mention it to anyone else." And then I told him what I wanted.

"Sure. I can get that for you," he nodded, his brow creasing, "but are you sure—"

"Yes, I'm sure."

After that, Pete rounded us up and paired us off kindergarten-buddy style so we could cover more ground exploring the CAMFer side. I was paired with him.

Passion was with T-dog. Samantha was with Chase. And Grant volunteered to stay back in the dome with my mom.

My heart skipped a beat as Pete and I stepped over the threshold into that familiar hallway—the same hallway Grant and I had once been marched down accompanied by armed CAMFer guards. But it was okay. I was in charge this time. I wasn't a prisoner, and there was no one on the CAMFer side to hurt me.

20

ANTHONY

Waking up was like coming out of a deep fog. Murmuring voices echoed in my head, and I didn't know where I was or what had happened to me.

No, wait. They'd cut off my hand. I remembered that much, and I looked down, hoping it had simply been a bad dream.

But my hand was gone, a hideous, crusty stump where it once had been, now throbbing with pain.

I slowly sat up on the gurney. There were pills scattered all over the infirmary floor, some long and white, some short and blue, and I remembered spilling them right before I'd conked out. I had no idea how long I'd been out, though. It might have been two hours or two days. But I felt rested, so that was good. My foggy vision had cleared, and I was so hungry my stomach was growling like a wild animal.

It had been stupid to fall asleep like that. I had to be more careful. I swung the PSS knife around to my back and crouched down on the floor, trying to figure out the best way to scoop up hundreds of pills with only one hand. I would sort them later. I had just propped one of the bottles between my legs to hold it steady when I heard the voices.

Real voices, muffled and distant, but coming closer. They must have been what had woken me in the first place. Someone was on the CAMFer side of the compound moving toward me, not one person but a whole group.

Fuck.

It was too late to duck out without knowing exactly where they were or which direction they were coming from. I'd have to hide, but my only real option was under the gurney. So, I ducked into its undercarriage, pulled the sheet down around the sides, slipped the knife from my jacket into my left hand, and tried not to breathe or move.

"Here it is," a man's voice called from right outside the infirmary door. "Just where I thought it would be."

"Good for you," a female voice answered teasingly, and I clutched the knife handle so hard it bit into my palm. I knew that voice. It was her. Olivia. The freak I'd guarded until she'd killed Major Tom and I'd severed her PSS hand. She was here.

They both came in, two sets of feet were all I could see, and right away the man's shoe crunched down on one of the pills.

"Whoa," Olivia said. "What a mess. Looks like someone was in the middle of filling a prescription when I displaced them."

"I hope not," the guy said, lifting his shoe and stepping more carefully as he moved into the room, the second pair of smaller feet following him in. "Those two drugs are a bad combination. They'd knock out an elephant."

"Here's one of the bottles," Olivia said, leaning over and picking it up with her PSS hand.

I made a sound then. I know I did. Deep down in my throat and barely contained. I had cut off that hand. I had seen it gone. And I had lost my own hand for taking it. There was my stump, resting in my lap. If my hand was gone, her hand should be gone. Except, I'd just seen her use it.

"Are they something important?" Olivia asked. "Should we pick them up?"

If she did, if she crouched down to gather those pills, she'd see me.

I held out my knife, ready for her. Ghost hand or not, I'd cut that bitch. I'd cut her over and over until she couldn't come back.

"You're kidding, right?" the guy asked, sounding appalled. "There's no five-second rule with medication."

"Right. Sorry," she said, and I heard the slight plastic snick of her setting the bottle on the counter.

"Besides, there's plenty more where these came from," the guy said, moving to the cabinet. "Especially now that we have two infirmaries to pull from." I could hear him opening the cabinet doors. "Excellent," he muttered. "I need more of this for your mother. Oh, and this will come in handy. They're well stocked over here."

It took about ten minutes for them to fill the duffle bag they'd brought. The entire time, I sat, sweating and trembling, curled under the gurney. Even after they'd left the infirmary, I stayed, folded in on myself, clutching my knife and shaking because they were still out there. Not just Olivia and the man, but the whole group, calling back and forth to one another as they ransacked the compound and took whatever they wanted. It sounded like there were six or seven, and they were so confident, and casual, and cocky, that my fear slowly turned to white hot rage. What would my old man say if he saw me cowering under a table? I was a Williams and we did not hide: we hunted.

I quietly extracted myself from under the gurney and grabbed as many of the antibiotics off the floor as I could, jamming them into my pocket. I'd have to endure the pain, or come back when I could for different pain killers. Then, I palmed my knife and checked the door. I couldn't see the intruders and their voices were distant.

I didn't understand how, but Olivia was alive and well, and she had her hand back.

The Holders must have won the conflict for the dome. They must have ousted Fineman and rescued her and somehow restored her PSS. And now that they'd broken through to the CAMFer side, they would take everything.

That minus bitch thought she was safe here in her ivory tower. She thought she'd won.

I should have cut off more than her hand when I'd had the chance. I should have ended her. I had been too soft.

But not this time.

21

DAVID MARCUS

"I'm not going to the medical tent," Gordon insisted, sipping at his coffee as Kaylee buttered him some toast. "I feel better. I'll be fine."

I should have waited until Mia had come back to broach the subject. She'd gone off to find Reiny and Lonan. Still, even with her here, the conversation would have been the same. Arguing with Gordon was like banging your head against a brick wall. It hadn't done any good last night when we'd arrived at the dome either. Plus, we'd had no idea where the medical tent was. Now, in the bright morning light, the large white tent off to the east with the Red Cross flag flying over it was pretty obvious. But Gordon had insisted we find Reiny and Lonan before we did anything else, and I couldn't exactly drag him away against his will. I couldn't drive him either. As soon as we'd pulled onto a dusty patch of earth last night, vehicles and campers had parked around us blocking us in. By the time we'd woken up this morning, you couldn't see the end of them, which made me think there had to be more than one illegal entrance into the depot. Those locals must be raking in some serious cash.

Maybe Gordon was okay. His color was better, and Kaylee's touch seemed to help. She was sitting next to him now at the little fold-down RV table, close enough that their legs were touching. She looked well-rested. She must have slept better than I had last night, but then she'd gotten the bed over the cab and I'd slept hanging off the edge of a skinny-ass bench seat.

Kaylee glanced up and caught my eye. *He's okay for now*, she mind-spoke to me. *I'll keep close to him and let you know if anything changes.*

It took me a moment to realize I'd heard her without any physical contact.

"How did I just hear you?" I blurted. Then I turned to Gordon, blinking and trying to come up with a good reason to have blurted it.

"I can hear her too," he said. "I know she's telepathic."

The more I talk to someone the easier it is to make myself heard without touching them, Kaylee explained. *And it helps if I'm upset.*

"Are you upset with me?" I asked.

A little, she answered. *You made me hide in the RV last night when I could have helped Gordon. You can't keep me hidden away forever, you know? I might be a freak, but I still deserve to have a life.*

"A freak? Kaylee, that's not what this is about. It's just too dangerous. We don't know who we can trust, and if there are CAMFers—"

That's the same thing you said at the reservation, and people saw me and it was fine, she insisted. *Besides, you can't stop me from doing what I want. I'm not a child. I'm older than you are. And I didn't escape being a prisoner in a dome to be kept prisoner by you.* She tossed her head and raised a hand, pulling aside one of the RV window curtains behind her and looking out. *I'm not hiding anymore. There's a whole world out there and I intend to see it.*

"Sounds like she knows what she wants," Gordon mumbled between bites of toast.

"No, it sounds to me like your pig-headedness is contagious," I said, throwing my hands in the air. "Forgive me for trying to keep both of you alive." I knew Kaylee wasn't a little girl, but she still needed protection. "Listen." I reached past her, pulling the curtain shut. "Mike Palmer is out there, and we barely lost him last night. If it wasn't for the traffic and the dust, he might be camping right next to us, and I don't want him anywhere near you."

Mike Palmer isn't dangerous, Kaylee said, as if explaining something to a toddler. *He helped me escape when no one else would. He isn't who you think he is.*

"Ain't that the truth," Gordon murmured.

God, I wanted to pick that man's brains about how he knew Palmer, but he was holding those cards very close to his chest. That was yet another reason to worry for Kaylee's safety. Everyone was hiding things, especially crotchety old Gordon. I could feel people and events stacking up, colliding with one another, racing toward an outcome I couldn't possibly predict, and it scared the hell out of me.

Suddenly, there was a loud knock, the RV door rattling on its hinges.

"Who is it?" I called, crossing to the door and grasping the handle.

"Mike Palmer," a deep voice said. "And you might want to remember you've got thin walls and close neighbors. I heard you arguing from three camps away."

There was no point in panicking, or running, so I opened the door and faced him head on. He was standing at the bottom of the RV's two metal steps.

Kaylee pushed past me and flung herself into his arms. He barely caught her, looking almost as startled as I was.

"All right, kiddo. It's good to see you too," he said, peeling her from his chest and setting her down on her feet next to him. "By the way"—he turned back to me—"you didn't lose me last night. We're camped a few rows over. I just thought I'd give you some space. Plus, we had gear to unload before we could use the camper and it took a while. Jason's over there selling the last of it as we speak. But"—he peered past me at Gordon—"I thought you might want help getting this stubborn old coot the medical attention he needs."

"I'm not going," Gordon growled.

"Gordon," Palmer said, climbing the steps and pushing past me. "At the very least, you need some oxygen and a good once over."

"I'm fine," Gordon insisted, showing no signs of budging from behind his little table. "Sit down, Nathan. You and I have a lot to talk about."

Palmer sat across from Gordon at the table. Kaylee took her spot back at Gordon's side, and I swiveled the front passenger seat around and sat in it.

Maybe Kaylee was in danger from Palmer. Maybe we all were, but better to have him here right where I could watch him, than out there somewhere doing who knew what. Besides, I was pretty sure Gordon and Palmer were about to spill major info on what the hell was going on.

"Okay, let's talk," Palmer said. "What is it you wanted to say?"

"I don't know where the hell you've been or what you've been doing all these years," Gordon said, "but we started this mess and it's time to finish it."

We started this mess? What did that mean? I knew why Gordon felt responsible, but why would he include Palmer? Unless—I turned, scanning Palmer's face. Had he been the guy in that picture of the NAM group, the one with the beard and glasses? Oh shit. It was him.

"It isn't you and me who are going to finish this," Palmer said. "We had our chance. Now, it's their turn." He nodded at me and Kaylee.

"They're not ready," Gordon said, glancing at me. "What if they botch it?"

"They can't do worse than we did," Palmer said.

"Maybe not," Gordon conceded. "Did you have a vision of PSS during the blast? The rest of us did."

Gordon had thought Palmer was dead, which meant Palmer had been one of the people outside the building who'd supposedly been disintegrated.

"Yes," Palmer said, blinking. "I had visions."

"And what about your body?" Gordon asked excitedly. "Did anything unusual happen to your body afterwards?"

"What do you mean?" Palmer asked.

Gordon set his coffee cup down and scooted on the bench a little. Then he bent over and began unlacing his right boot. It was such a weird thing to do in the middle of a conversation, and Palmer seemed as puzzled as I was. Gordon yanked off his boot and pulled down his sock, a familiar glow filling the RV.

Fuck me. Gordon Lightfoot had a PSS foot.

"When did this happen?" Palmer asked, his face void of expression.

"It changed a few days after Umatilla," Gordon said. "One day I put my boot on a normal foot, and the next time I took it off, it was like this. Hell, discovering it scared the tar right out of me. There wasn't a hint of this when they inspected us at the hospital. I know that much. They never would have let me go if there had been."

My mind was reeling. Gordon, a guy decades older than the first recorded occurrence of PSS, was sitting in front of me with it. He was the first case, not Thea Frandsen of Norway or Kaylee. And he hadn't been born with it. It had been a side-effect of the gas explosion he and my mother had caused.

"And you're the only one this happened to?" Mike asked.

"As far as I know," Gordon said. "Then again, I thought you were dead until last night. What about the others? The ones outside the bunker with you?"

"They survived as well," Mike said. "We all displaced to different locations, but I didn't know that at first. I found out later. And if they manifested PSS, they certainly didn't tell me about it."

"Perhaps it affected me most because I was closest to the gas," Gordon postulated, putting his sock and boot back on.

I stared at the two of them, utterly stunned. Did they not understand what this meant?

Gordon Lightfoot and his band of vandals had *caused* PSS. My own mother, and my uncle, and the two men in front of me. They were the reason I'd been born with a giant hole in my chest filled with blue energy. They had inflicted a birth defect on innocent children and an ethereal epidemic on the entire population of the planet. True, only eleven people had been directly exposed to that unknown chemical agent, but it had altered their DNA in some way. Gordon's had obviously changed almost instantly, but in the others it must have lain dormant until they'd reproduced, passing on PSS to their offspring. Still, that didn't explain everything. There were thousands of cases of PSS worldwide, and that didn't include the more subtle, internal PSS Reiny and Pete had discovered from my uncle's research study. So, how could one localized incident have impacted human DNA on a global scale?

Wait. What had Gordon said when he'd described that night? *You could see the strange cloud in the sky for days afterwards, like a fading Polaroid.* No, not a Polaroid. More like the eruption plume of a volcano. I'd read once that the gas and ash from volcanoes get incorporated into the atmosphere almost immediately, traveling thousands of miles a day and encircling the earth in a matter of weeks. Whatever gasses had combined and combusted in that little building thirty-three years ago had not stayed put. Instead, the agent created by that reaction had been quickly disseminated all over the world. PSS was in the very air we breathed and the water we drank. Gordon Lightfoot and his little NAM group had perpetuated the biggest environmental accident known to mankind, and they'd managed to keep it a secret for decades.

Now it all made sense, my mother's driving guilt. Her obsession with protecting my grandparents from The Hold and protecting The Hold from itself. No wonder she'd almost ruined her marriage trying to micro-manage the impact of PSS on those around her. Every day she'd had to look at Danielle and me, knowing it was her fault—that her rash, youthful actions had burdened us forever.

"I know what you're thinking," Gordon said, his eyes locked on mine. "You think it was our fault." There was true grief in those eyes and a lifetime of agony and remorse. I could see it there, but I didn't care.

"Yeah, because it was," I spat at him.

"No." Gordon shook his head. "The government made those chemicals. They're the ones who stored them dangerously and without adequate security. And after the accident, they did nothing. They didn't help the victims. They didn't warn people or investigate. They just covered it up and pretended it never happened."

"Informing the populace would have been a mistake," Mike interjected. "You can't tell people an unknown chemical agent was released into the atmosphere, but you don't know what it is or what it will do. That would have caused global panic. I'm not saying it was right, but I understand why they didn't tell people."

"So what?" I demanded. "Instead, you keep an entire planet in the dark and when their kids are born with glowing chests and hands years later, you kill their parents, abandon them, and let some maniac scientist torture them for sport? No shit, we can't fuck this up any worse than you guys did."

David, Kaylee said. *Calm down, please. Don't you understand it could have been so much worse?*

"Worse?" I exhaled, thinking of my sister and what had happened to her. "How could this be any worse?"

I'll tell you how, Kaylee said, her voice firm and almost scolding. *That agent the accident created, that combination of random chemicals never meant to be joined—by every right of chance and logic, it should have wiped mankind off the face of the earth. But instead, it revealed the power and light inside of us. Instead, it gave humanity the ability to manifest our true, ethereal, eternal, selves.*

"Are you serious?" I laughed bitterly.

"Yes, she's serious," Palmer said, standing up. "And it's about time you stopped feeling sorry for yourself and got with the program. Teenage angst is not going to fix this."

"Fix this?" I scoffed, standing up too so he couldn't loom over me. "Nothing is going to fix this."

"Really?" Palmer asked. "Look around you. It's already started. Why do you think all these people are here?"

"They came for some kind of land grab," I pointed out. "Those people out there don't know anything about PSS or the accident. They're campers and hitchhikers and homeless people. They're not going to unite and magically fix a problem you guys created years ago."

"Not magically, no," he said. "But Olivia and some of the others have possession of the dome along with all the data from The Hold and the CAMFers. With that information, we may be able to turn the tide of public opinion. At the very least, we can offer people the truth about PSS."

Olivia was in the dome? How long had Palmer been keeping that under wraps?

"The truth about PSS? You mean the truth that you caused it?"

"If it comes to that, yes," Palmer said, staring me down. "Are you and me gonna have a problem?"

Stop it, both of you, Kaylee cried inside my head. *Something is wrong with Gordon. He needs help. Now.*

Palmer and I turned toward her. Gordon was slumped across the table, Kaylee standing over him, her hands pressed to his back and tears streaming down her face.

22

DAVID MARCUS

"**H**elp me get him out of here," Palmer ordered, as Kaylee moved out of our way.

Despite the table and the close quarters, we each managed to get an arm under one of Gordon's and maneuver him toward the narrow RV door, but I didn't see how all three of us were going to fit through it.

Kaylee slipped around me, opened it, and we came face-to-face with Mia. Lonan and Reiny were standing behind her at the bottom of the RV steps.

"What happened?" she cried, grabbing Gordon's limp hand.

"I'm fine," Gordon mumbled, coming to a little and lifting his head at the sound of her voice.

"Bullshit," Palmer said. "Your lips are blue. You need oxygen. And we're taking you to the Red Cross Tent right now. Lonan, give us a hand."

By the time we maneuvered down the steps, Lonan had somehow taken my place under Gordon's left arm.

"Clear the way!" Palmer bellowed, as he and Lonan lifted Gordon off his feet and charged through the camps, making a bee-line to the medical tent.

"Come on," I said, grabbing Kaylee's hand, the rest of us following as fast as we could, winding through a dusty crowd of concerned onlookers.

When we finally got to the tent, we found Palmer just inside, drilling the terrified, white-clad attendants on what kind of training they had for treating acute heart failure. Further in, Gordon was on a gurney in a small alcove wearing an oxygen mask, Lonan standing over him looking helpless.

Mia rushed to Gordon's side, bursting into sobs.

"Now, don't do that," he said, as he took her hand, his voice muffled through the mask. "We always knew I'd go before you."

"They've radioed for an evac helicopter," Palmer told us, striding over. "It'll be here in ten minutes if we can make room for it to land. Let's go." He looked at Lonan and me. "Time to move some campers."

"No," Gordon said, pulling his oxygen mask aside a little. "I need to talk to David."

"You should save your strength," Mia pleaded with him.

"It will only take a minute," Gordon insisted, looking from Mia to Palmer.

He and Palmer stared at one another a moment longer, and then Palmer simply nodded, gesturing to Lonan, and the two of them left. As soon as they exited the tent, we could hear Palmer bellowing, "Move these fucking tents! Move these vehicles now, people! We have an emergency helicopter coming in any minute."

When I turned back to Gordon, he reached inside his shirt, pulled something out, and handed it to me. As I unfolded it, I realized it was the picture he'd shown me back at his place, the one of the NAM group who'd raided Umatilla. He'd taken it out of the frame and there was something scrawled on the back, a list of names in faded pencil.

"I want you to have that," he said. "Make sure your generation understands. Don't let them make the same mistakes we did."

"I'm sure we'll make our own mistakes," I said, knowing it was already true.

"Then make them count." He smiled, or it might have been a grimace of pain. It was hard to tell.

He turned to Reiny. "You and Lonan must watch out for the tribe's interests."

"You're going to be fine," Reiny assured him, clutching his hand and squeezing it.

"The helicopter is almost here," Palmer called, sticking his head in the tent door. "We've cleared room for it to land. Get him ready," he barked at the Red Cross workers, and they scrambled like rats, descending on Gordon and shoving the rest of us out of the way.

I could hear the chopper in the distance now, buzzing like an angry wasp. The tent sides were heaving against the down thrust of the chopper blades and, for a moment, I felt overwhelmed by a sense of déjà vu, as if I'd been in a tent with a helicopter buzzing over it before.

And then the medical workers were wheeling Gordon's gurney out the door, Mia clinging to him, the tent flaps whipping violently as they passed through them.

Kaylee, Reiny, and I went outside, holding our arms up to our faces against the dust and wind.

Several guys jumped out of the chopper and loaded Gordon into it, pulling Mia in as well.

The medics began working on him immediately, attaching their monitors even before they shut the door and lifted off into the sky.

23

KAYLEE

The world around us seemed unaware that we'd lost Gordon. Our grief and fear meant nothing to them. Even as we walked back to the RV, they had already returned to their normal banter and excitement, as if Gordon no longer existed—had never existed. And that was almost as scary as feeling the energy ebb from his heart as I'd held his hand. To these people, Gordon was only a background character in a story they had never read.

Living in the dome, I'd been the center of everything. Every person who'd come there, came to see me. Every conversation had been with me or about me. Every event had concerned me.

But out here in the real world, it wasn't like that. I was only one person in an endless ocean of people, each one convinced they were the apex of the events swirling around them. It was both terrifying and exhilarating, this constant effort to mean something. And now perhaps Gordon would be done with it. The sadness of that only made me want to try harder. I had found Mike, or he had found me. It didn't matter which. We were back together. And there was the dome, looming on the horizon, just within reach. My sister was in there. My mother too. Mike had whispered it to me when I'd hugged him. They were here.

When we arrived back at the bus, Reiny made lunch, but I could tell she was holding back tears. Lonan was quieter than ever. David kept folding and unfolding the photo Gordon had given him. And Mike looked stricken. As for me, I felt strangely reluctant to touch anyone, as if I only had enough comfort to sooth myself, and barely that.

After we ate, we all went to Lonan and Reiny's camp to pack up their stuff. They'd decided to stay in the RV with David and me because the local weather was predicting a rare desert storm for the evening. Plus, we had room now. I was thrilled that Reiny let me sweep out the tents and roll them up, and even under the hot sun in a dry desert with Gordon gone, the sound of children giggling and playing nearby made me feel better. At least on the inside. On the outside, every part of me was coated with a layer of dust. It was in my hair, up my nose, on my neck, and even in my teeth. Without thinking, I took off my light cloak and swung it around, doing my best to shake it out.

The giggling I'd been hearing suddenly stopped, and I looked up to find three children standing at the edge of the nearest camp, gawking at me.

"Whoa," the littlest boy said, waving a stick at me. "You're freaky cool-looking. What happened to your skin?"

"Abram, hush! That's not polite," an older girl scolded, though I could read in her eyes she was just as curious.

"She has PSS," the other boy said, proud to be the expert. "It's just the way she was born."

I nodded and smiled at all of them, folding the cloak over my arm instead of putting it back on. I had told David I wasn't going to hide anymore. Why not start now?

"Is PSS contagious?" little Abram asked, sounding almost hopeful. "Can we catch it from her?"

"No," Expert Boy said. "It's just like being born with red hair, or brown eyes, or a birthmark on your arm. Except way cooler."

"Do you glow in the dark?" Abram asked me, excitedly.

I nodded, showing them the glow of my hand under the cloak.

"That's awesome," Scolding Girl jumped in. "You don't even need a flashlight, or a lantern, or a campfire when you go camping. I want PSS!"

"Does it hurt, though?" Abram asked, stepping closer. "Does it feel like real skin?"

I shook my head at the first question and held out my arm in response to the second, offering him a touch.

"Can't you talk?" he asked, his eyes gone huge and concerned. "Or did a cat get your tongue?"

"Kaylee can't talk," David stepped up, coming to my rescue, alarm radiating off of him. This was his worst nightmare, people seeing me and asking me questions. "And it has nothing to do with a cat," he added, managing a smile.

"Children, who are you talking to?" A woman came around the tent and stopped, her eyes falling on me.

For a moment, I was tempted to run. Was this the part where she gasped in horror and raised a mob to kill me, like in *Frankenstein*? No, that was silly. I wasn't a monster.

"I'm sorry," the woman said, nodding at the children. "Were they bothering you?"

I shook my head adamantly, smiling, and David said, "They were just curious. It's fine."

"Are you leaving?" she asked, nodding at our rolled up tents.

"Yes," David said, lying through his teeth, always trying to protect me. "We heard there's a big storm coming tonight, so we're packing up and heading home before it hits."

"We heard that too," the woman said. "But after the Dome Show, we're determined to stick it out and see what happens."

"The Dome Show?" David asked.

"Didn't you see it?" There was excitement in her voice.

"It was so cool!" little Abram chimed in.

"I saw it first," his sister declared.

"No, I saw it before you did," her older brother argued.

"Early this morning," their mother went on, right over the top of their bickering, "the entire dome turned as white as frost, and then it started flashing the most amazing images—beautiful skyscapes and landscapes, one right after the other. People were staring and cheering, everyone climbing out of their tents to see it. And then it paused for a moment and did it all over again. Didn't you notice it had changed?" She pointed toward the dome.

David and I both turned, staring at its newly opaque surface. Of course, I wasn't surprised. I'd seen the projection program run numerous times. But I was glad my sister had discovered it and the crowd had enjoyed it.

"I guess we missed it," David said. "We had a pretty hectic morning."

"Everyone's saying it's a sign," the woman told us. "Someone is obviously in there, and they're trying to tell us something. I think what we saw this morning is only the beginning. So, storm or no storm, we're sticking it out."

"Well, good luck with that," David said, sarcasm tinging his voice.

And the woman didn't miss it. She frowned, took little Abram's hand, and said, "Come on children, I need your help getting the rain flies up. And best of luck to you," she called over her shoulder as they turned back to their camp and disappeared behind a huge green tent.

You didn't have to be so rude, I told David. *They were nice people.*

"You should put your cloak back on," he said, ignoring my comment.

No, I said, handing it to him. *But you're welcome to wear it if you like.*

"Kaylee," he called after me as I marched past the truck and walked proudly through the neighboring camps on my way back to the RV.

And yes, people stopped and stared. They murmured and some gasped. A few small children even followed in my wake, chanting "Glowy girl. Glowy girl. Where are you going Misses Glowy Girl?" I think I liked that best of all.

When I was almost to the RV, the truck drove by, maneuvering slowly and squeezing between the tents and pop-ups.

David was hanging his head out the window, frowning worriedly, but I caught a glimpse of Mike, Lonan, and Reiny holding back grins.

Back at camp, Jason was waiting for us.

"Gordon had to be medically evacuated," Mike told him. "Mia went with him."

"Is he gonna be okay?" Jason asked.

"We don't know," Reiny answered. "But I'm going over to the Red Cross tent right now to see if they have any news. Lonan and David, can you start dinner?"

"Sure," David said, looking at me and expecting me to follow him, but I just crossed my arms over my chest until he went inside with Lonan. He was going to have to learn I wasn't his pet project.

As soon as Reiny left, and Lonan and Marcus had gone into the RV, Jason pulled a handful of money out of his pocket and held it out to Mike. "I sold all Bernie's stuff," he said.

"Did you take your cut?" Mike asked.

"Of course," Jason nodded.

"Good," Mike said. "Keep the rest too, because I have a job for you. I want you to go back to the spot we came in last night, and give that money to the guy in charge as payment to hold the fence open for the rest of the evening. Based on the rate they charged us that should be enough, but I want you to stay and make sure they do it. You got that?"

"Yeah, I got it," Jason said, stuffing the cash in his pocket and marching off into the crowd mumbling something about wasting good money on moths.

24

OLIVIA

We should get back to the dome," Pete said at my shoulder. "It's getting late, and I promised your mother we wouldn't stay over here too long." Had she made him promise so she wouldn't worry? Or had she guessed how hard this would be for me?

I'd been fine while Pete and I raided the infirmary and searched the upstairs CAMFer rooms. Well, mostly fine. I kept having the strange feeling someone was watching us, but I didn't tell Pete that. My fears were my own to deal with.

Then, we'd gone downstairs and the feeling had dissipated, only to be replaced with something worse.

Memories.

We were standing in Fineman's lab now.

"This is where we're going to find what we really need," I told Pete, crossing to one of the large cooling units and pulling it open. Inside were shelves packed row upon row with small glass vials glowing blue with PSS. I shuddered to think how many of them represented people the doctor had killed. I bent down, scanning toward the back, and found the vials labeled David Marcus Jordan and Danielle Elizabeth Jordan.

The fridge next to that one was full of PSS samples too, their labels yellowed, faded, and beginning to peel. A name caught my eye and I reached in, pulling out the vial and staring down at it.

Gilbert Lee Long, it read, with a long serial number after the name.

"How did Fineman get Yale's PSS?" I asked, holding it out to Pete. "He escaped the CAMFers with Marcus in California and was killed at the Eidolon. Fineman never extracted him."

"That's a health industry number," Pete said, pointing at the label. "All hospitals use them. This part is the date, this is the patient ID, and this portion indicates the hospital of origin and the department. Based on its number, that sample came from the obstetrics unit of a hospital in California shortly after Yale was born."

Pete and I searched through the rest of that fridge, and found old hospital samples for everyone who'd been on David's list except for Marcus. There was even a sample of my PSS and Kaylee's.

"Marcus wasn't born in a hospital," I pointed out.

"True," Pete said. "I doubt they took a sample on the reservation. It appears to me Fineman was conducting a study, comparing the hospital samples to the new ones he was taking."

"To find out what?"

"He must have been trying to track some kind of change between the two. I'll ask the hackers to scan for the numbers in the CAMFer data base. That should lead us to the files on whatever he was doing."

"Good idea," I said, hoping we could finally crack the code on what Fineman's twisted mind had been up to.

While Pete jotted down the numbers, I moved to the wall and opened a tall cabinet. It was filled with PSS tools and torture devices, including various types of minus meters, though the knife made out of Passion's blades was mysteriously missing.

I closed the cabinet and turned to the far end of the lab, facing the door to the interrogation room where I'd been tortured and beaten.

"Olivia," Pete said, coming alongside me. "We don't need to go in there."

Was that true? Maybe I did need to? Maybe I had to go down to the depths of my cell too, and into the dark morgue with Major Tom to get over this horrible fear they'd instilled in me.

Fuck.

Was Major Tom still down in that death drawer, waiting for me, or had I displaced him?

The thought of any part of my power touching his dead, lacerated body was too much. I leaned over and puked under the nearest table.

"I told you," Pete said, putting his hand gently on my shoulder and handing me a handkerchief to wipe my mouth. "It's time to take a break."

"Okay," I nodded.

Upstairs, we found the others ready to head to the dome as well. Chase and T-dog had downloaded all the CAMFer files and could process them from the van. Samantha and Passion had sourced a duffle bag of useful supplies, including some sweets and chocolate. And Pete gave the hackers the vial numbers from the lab, and they said they'd search for them.

So, we made our way to the dome door and Chase unlocked it, letting us back into our new domicile.

"Hey honey, I'm home," Pete called good-naturedly.

"Well, it's about time," my mother called back. "I made sandwiches."

After a late lunch, Samantha, Passion and I had dish duty. I was pretty distracted, absently rinsing a plate when Passion nudged Samantha and said, "Tell her."

Samantha frowned, shaking her head.

"Tell me what?' I asked.

"It's nothing, really," Sam said. "You have enough to worry about."

"If you don't tell her, I'm going to," Passion said, crossing her arms over her chest.

"Fine," Samantha said, turning to me. "It's just—I haven't been able to hear anyone's PSS since we got here. Back in the van, I didn't hear the pronghorns, but I had my earbuds in, so I thought maybe that was why. But since then, all I can hear is this rushing sound, like when you hold a shell up to your ear, only much louder. It's gotten worse since we've been in the dome, and it was even louder over on the CAMFer side today. And it's actually really starting to worry me."

"Yeah, that's not good," I said. "Do you think it could be all the PSS samples over there, or maybe one of Fineman's experiments interfering with your ability?"

"I don't think so," Samantha shook her head. If something over there had been the source, I should have been able to pinpoint it."

"Maybe it's all the people outside. I mean, now we know most of them have PSS."

"No," Samantha said, sounding frustrated. "This isn't—human. It has no personality or melody. It's just big and relentless, like the ocean beating against the shore."

"And it scares her," Passion said.

"Yes," Samantha whispered.

"I'm so sorry." I reached for Samantha's hand and squeezed it. "I think you should check in with Pete, just in case it's something medical, and I'll ask Chase if he has any ideas. Maybe he can think of a way to trace it. And I want you to tell me if the sound changes, in any way."

"Yeah, okay," Samantha nodded. "Thank you."

"No problem. And while I'm thinking of it," I turned to Passion. "I have something I need to tell you." I pulled the dog tags from my pocket and held them out. "Mike found these in the cave. He gave them to me before he left Portland."

She stared down at them. "I can't feel them anymore. Isn't that weird? I had no idea you had them."

That was strange, and in the context of what Samantha had just shared, the two things might be connected. If something in or near the compound was interfering with PSS resonance that could explain both Samantha's deafness and Passion's inability to feel the tags.

"Anyway," Passion said. "I don't want them." She reached out, closing my fingers over the tags. "They're yours now."

When we went back upstairs, we found Pete and Grant moving beds and furniture from the Hold staffer suites into the dome, while my mother directed them. Samantha and Passion quickly joined in, arranging the screens to give us each, at least, the illusion of privacy.

As for me, I went off looking for Chase and found him in the van alone, which was perfect. First, I told him about Samantha's hearing issue and my theories about something interfering with PSS resonance. He said he'd run some tests, but he didn't have much confidence in his equipment to discern something like that.

"Well, do your best," I said. "I know I've put a lot on your plate. Were you able to get what I asked for from the CAMFer files?"

"Oh, right." He reached into his pocket and held out a USB stick. "It wasn't hard to find," he paused for a moment, "but I just want to say, the stuff you went through, I don't even know —"

"Thank you," I interrupted, palming the stick and standing up to leave. The last thing I wanted was his pity.

"I did the edits you asked for," he added, looking a little sheepish. "But I tweaked them a little. I hope you don't mind."

What the hell? Why had he messed with my stuff? Maybe pretending to be an amateur documentarian had gone to his head. Still, he'd done me a huge favor by even getting it. And here he was, still slaving away over the CAMFer files for me.

"That's fine." I tucked the USB into my pocket. "And thank you again."

"No problem." He smiled. "Consider it an early birthday present."

"Oh God," I groaned, slumping back into my seat. "Did my mom tell everyone?"

"That you turn eighteen tomorrow? Yes, she blabbed to all eight of us," he teased. "Why do you think Passion and Samantha raided the CAMFer kitchen for chocolate and cake mix? Oh, and be sure to pretend you don't smell the baking wafting up from downstairs after dinner. We're supposed to keep you busy and out of their hair."

"They're throwing me a party in here?" I was stunned. I thought for sure I'd avoided the whole birthday thing when we'd left Portland, but apparently not.

"Ah, it's just a little one," Chase said. "You'll survive."

"Yeah, I guess so." I sighed. "Hey, did you find anything on that information Pete gave you from the labs?"

"Yeah, we found some matching files. From what we can tell, Fineman was trying to reverse-engineer PSS. Using various samples, he was tracing its evolutionary journey back through each individual's DNA. Pete thinks he was attempting to find the origin and exact makeup of the PSS gene."

"To what end?" I wondered out loud. "What good would that do him?"

"Well," Chase said, "we use the same principle in hacking. If you can figure out the origin and makeup of a code, you can usually break it."

"Break a gene? Can that even be done?"

"Hypothetically, yes," Chase admitted. But Pete says reverse-engineering like that is nearly impossible without access to some portion of the original sample—sort of like cloning a dinosaur without dinosaur DNA. You might be able to figure out where a dinosaur came from, what it looked like, and how it behaved, but you can't reconstruct one without some element of the stuff it was originally made from. Anyway, there are still some encrypted files we haven't cracked that might shed more light on it. We should have them by tomorrow sometime, *just in time for your birthday*."

"Stop it," I said, punching him in the arm.

He rubbed it and grimaced like I'd really hurt him. Then his face went all serious. "Hey, I have something I need to confess. We weren't totally honest with you back at the house. Mike wasn't, and I wasn't, about who we were."

I felt alarm suddenly creep up my spine. What did he mean? Were they fucking CAMFers? Had this all been an elaborate trap to get me back into the compound?

"It's nothing to be afraid of," he said, reading the look on my face. "It's just that Mike and I are brothers, and I thought you should know."

"Mike Palmer is your brother?" I echoed dumbly.

"Yes," Chase nodded. "My less-handsome, much-less-talented older brother."

"But he's old enough to be your dad."

"Yeah, I know. It's a long story, but basically, I didn't find out I had a brother until he showed up on our doorstep when I was thirteen. My parents thought he'd died before I was born, so they never bothered to tell me about him."

"Wow, you and I have more in common than I realized," I marveled.

"Exactly." Chase grinned. "We both belong to the Society of Secret Siblings. It's a small but elite group."

"Yes, it is," I nodded, noticing for the first time what a nice guy Chase was. And cute. And smart. He had a curl in his dark brown hair that hung over his forehead and reminded me of Superman.

"There's something else," Chase pinned me with his fine green eyes, his voice excited. "Mike is here, at the dome right now, out there in the crowd. He messaged me late last night that he'd arrived. And he's not alone. He has Kaylee, David, and Jason with him."

"You've been in contact with him?" I stammered. "And they're all safe?" Until that moment, I hadn't realized how much I'd been afraid I'd hurt Kaylee or Marcus during the displacement. Sometimes my nightmares were about that very thing. Kaylee displaced underground, buried alive. Marcus with only his arm sticking out of a wall of granite. The relief washed over me in waves. They were safe. They were here. But they might as well have been a million miles away if they were outside the dome.

Unless.

"Can we get them inside?" I asked Chase.

"I think so," he said. "We could sneak them in one of the side entrances after dark. There's a big storm coming tonight. It's been all over the weather feeds. It might be our best opportunity. But I should probably check with Mike first. He may have other plans."

"What do you mean *other plans*?" I glared at him. "I need him in here. I need all of them in here. You tell him we found the fucking fort, now he damn well better get in here and help me hold it down."

"Yes, ma'am," Chase said, a smile quirking at the corner of his lips. "I can send the message, but I can't guarantee how soon he'll respond. My brother doesn't always consider communication a priority. He's more of an action guy."

"I know. Just do it. Oh, and let's keep this between you and me for now. It would kill my mom to know she was this close to Kaylee. If we can't get them in, she'll be devastated." This had to work for so many reasons. For their safety. For my sanity. For my mom and my sister's long-awaited reunion, and ultimately for my plan to work.

And, if I was brave enough to admit it, for my reunion with David Marcus Jordan, the boy I loved who had no memory of me.

25

JASON

I wasn't an idiot. When Palmer sent me to hold the fence open, I knew exactly what he was up to. He could preach all he wanted about herding moths and helping people, but he didn't fool me. So, I wasn't surprised when at dusk, after hours of RVs and camper vans streaming through, a large convoy of fancy SUVs with dark-tinted windows showed up.

At first, the biker guys seemed confused. These weren't their usual customers and their leader stopped the first vehicle and began questioning the man behind the wheel. My guess was he could smell the money. Or he thought they were undercover cops.

I was out of earshot, but I saw Biker Guy wave his bat at the line of SUVs. "Too many," he seemed to be saying. "It'll cost you."

Palmer might have done something, but he'd sent me, and I didn't feel like risking myself for a bunch of Holders. They had way more firepower than I did anyway. Better to watch and see how it all panned out. But I did step deeper into the shadows of some scrubby bushes growing along the inside of the fence, just in case things got sticky.

And fuck, was I glad I did.

The guy in the front car pulled out a gun instead of money. He flashed the piece at Biker Guy and said something, obviously trying to intimidate him.

Biker Guy backed off a little, pretending to be afraid, but I didn't miss the quick flick of his hand as he signaled his crew.

The open fence immediately came crashing down and the bikers scattered into the night, but not before their leader brought his bat down on the windshield of the lead Hold car, shattering it into a hanging web of frosty glass.

The driver and the guy riding shotgun jumped out, but there was no one to shoot. The bikers stationed on the inside of the fence had fled too. I could still hear them buzzing off into the distance behind me, but I seriously doubted they were abandoning their posts forever. This was a huge money-grab for the locals. They wouldn't give up so easily. My guess was they'd gone for reinforcements.

More well-armed Holders climbed out of their cars, cautiously looking around, so I hid myself even deeper in the shadows. Several men came over and inspected the fence, banging their fists against it like Neanderthals. I'd seen how the locals had rigged it. The two pulleys that raised the cut portion were inside the fence, and it took a person on each to work it. I couldn't let The Holders in by myself, even if Palmer wanted me to. Which, of course, he did.

I was standing there trying to figure out what to do about that when all hell broke loose.

Several trucks pulled up around the SUVs, screeching to a halt, shrouding the night in dust and flashing headlights.

Gunfire rang out—numerous shots volleying back and forth between the trucks and The Holders. Men barked orders. Someone cried out for help.

I realized I was down on the ground, my gun out in front of me, peering between the leaves of the plant I'd been hiding behind, but I couldn't see much.

If the guys in the trucks were the backup for the bikers, I was impressed. They'd come fast, furious, and ready to fight.

Palmer was not going to be happy about this. Obviously, he'd meant for me to get The Holders inside, but how the fuck was I supposed to do that now?

The SUVs were peeling out and pulling away as more trucks descended upon them. It looked like the locals had routed them out.

I heard a truck door slam, and the crunch of boots in the dirt as several men approached the fence line, just on the other side from where I lay hidden.

"Well, that wasn't so bad," a voice said, the man unzipping his fly and beginning to piss through the chain link right onto the bush I was hiding under. "Now we just have to figure out how to get this open."

"It's a simple pulley system on the other side," a second voice said. A voice I knew all too well. "And it's a good thing for you this fence is no longer electrified," my old man added, unzipping his fly and adding his stream to the pitter-patter soaking into the sand near my head. "Have Barry and Clint use some rope to climb over. We'll be through in no time."

"Yes sir," the first guy said, zipping back up.

How had my old man gotten here this fast? He must have flown from Texas as soon as the dome hit the news, which meant he probably had no idea I was here too, and I really wanted to keep it that way. Besides, I had to get back to Palmer and tell him the Holders hadn't gotten through. And that the CAMFers were about to.

Slowly, carefully, I slipped my gun back into the underarm holster Palmer had given me, turned myself around, and started army-crawling in the direction of the dome.

When I was sure I was far enough away not to be seen, I got up and walked, then ran.

To get to the fence, I'd hitched a ride with a hot blonde girl and her brother in a dune buggy. And to get back, I'd been counting on hitching a ride in one of the cars entering through the fence on their way to the dome, but that was not an option now. But it would take me hours to get back to the dome on foot. I had to find another way.

That's when I saw someone coming—a row of single headlights, with a set of larger ones barreling behind them. As they came closer, I could hear the familiar buzz of the dirt bikes. The bikers and their reinforcements had finally arrived.

I ducked off to the side, out of their path, and the bulk of the group went speeding past, kicking up sand and dust, whooping and hollering. Some of the bikers still had their bats, but others now had guns, and the men in the backs of the trucks were heavily armed.

Poor fools. They had no idea what they were heading into. They'd picked a fight with Mr. James's rich city security, and were now racing into battle with a completely different enemy. My old man would annihilate them.

Still, even a short delay played to my advantage.

Now, if I could just find a faster way back.

More headlights were coming, three more trucks, and behind them two straggler dirt bikes bobbing over the sand, one considerably behind the other.

I searched the ground and found exactly what I needed—a stick about three feet long.

As soon as the trucks passed me, I charged into the wake of the dust they'd left, making a trajectory for that final bike, the stick in my hand. I had never been good at math, but a word problem suddenly flashed in my head.

If a dirt bike traveling at X miles an hour, crosses the path of a desperate human traveling Y miles an hour, and a stick whacks that biking motherfucker across the chest, the biker's velocity is reduced to fucking zero and the bike is mine.

Of course, it didn't exactly work that way.

Instead, halfway to the bike, I could tell I was going to miss it. It was moving too fast, and I was moving too slow. I tried to speed up, tried to veer more sharply to meet it, and that's when I tripped on something. To this day, I have no idea what.

I pitched forward, face first, my arms splayed out, the stick flung from my hand. I closed my eyes, bracing myself to tuck and roll when I hit the ground.

Except I didn't.

I opened my eyes, the wind rushing past my face, to find myself flying through the air straight at the biker.

He looked to the side, eyes widening in the narrow window of his helmet visor, but it was too late.

I grappled for whatever I could, snagging one of his elbows and yanking him off, both of us hitting the ground together. The bike kept going a few yards before it tipped over into the sand, the motor revving. At that point, it pretty much became a wrestling match. He was scrawny but feisty. When I tried to break away and run for the bike, he grabbed my boot and pulled me back. When I felt his hand grip my ankle, I freaked out and kicked him in the helmet with my other foot. That bought me a few seconds, and I made it to the bike and got it upright, but the engine had died. I just barely got my foot on the kickstarter before the guy was all over me again, pinning me from behind and trying to wrench me off the seat. I twisted, slamming my heel down to start the bike, while at the same time pulling my attacker inward so his calf pressed against the exhaust pipe. It only took a moment before his pants were smoking and he was screaming like a girl. He let go of me then, writhing away.

As I drove off, I could hear police sirens wailing in the distance back toward the fence. Good. They would delay my old man that much longer. And so would the weather.

There was a storm coming.

I could feel it in the air.

26

MIKE PALMER

As soon as I heard the dirt bike pull up, I stepped out of the RV to investigate.

It was Jason, covered in sand with blood dripping down his face, which did not bode well for the mission I'd sent him on.

"What happened?" I asked. "Your forehead is bleeding."

"The CAMFers," he said, turning off the bike and wiping at the cut, his fingers coming away bloody. "They showed up right before the Holders got through. There was a fight and the locals closed the gate. I had to steal the bike to get back, and the owner put up a fight."

"Did the CAMFers get through?" I asked. "Did you stay to see that much?"

"I don't think so," he said. "I heard the police arrive on my way back, so I doubt it. But they will. It was my old man."

"That's not good. I was counting on Alex's men to get here before him." It seemed nothing was going my way today. First, we'd lost Gordon, though Reiny had found out he was in stable condition in a hospital in Portland, awaiting heart surgery. That tricky old bastard, living all this time with a PSS foot. I'm not sure why it surprised me so much that I wasn't the only one who'd kept secrets all these years. I'd almost told him, back in the RV, how I'd seen my daughter in a dream ten years before she was born, her own tiny glowing foot peeking out from a blanket. He would have understood it was more than just a dream: it was a foretelling. But I didn't tell him because I didn't want to see the look of disappointment on his face when he realized I'd abandoned Thea before she was even born. I'd told myself I was protecting her and her mother. I'd told myself that lie for a very long time.

"So, what do we do now?" Jason asked.

"Take that to the camper," I gestured at the bike. "I don't want to have to explain it to the others. Grab the bag with the guns and your stuff. Then meet me back here."

"What are we going to do?"

"I think our best option is the dome," I said. "It's the only place we'll be safe at the moment, and from there we can work on more options. Now, all I have to do is convince them," I added, nodding toward the RV.

"Good luck with that," he said, starting the bike up and peeling out in the dirt, just as a thunderclap rent the sky.

"Try to make it back before this storm hits," I called after him, hoping he heard me. The kid was smart and tough, but I hadn't missed the fear in his voice when he'd told me his old man was here. He'd be back as soon as he could.

I headed inside. Reiny and Lonan had been cooking dinner when I'd come out to talk to Jason. David and Kaylee had been cutting vegetables for a salad. None of them were going to be happy with the conversation we were about to have, but it had to be done. Not just because of the arrival of the CAMFers, but also because I'd gotten a message from Chase requesting our presence.

As I stepped through the door, David's glance was sharp with suspicion, but Kaylee gave me a smile.

"I have some bad news," I said, catching Lonan and Reiny's attention immediately. "Don't worry, it's not Gordon. But Jason just got back from the fence and told me the CAMFers are here."

"This is exactly what I was afraid of," David said, standing up in a panic.

"They're not inside yet," I explained. "They got stopped by the cops, but it's only a matter of time before they get through." They didn't need to know Alex's forces were coming as well. Telling them that didn't fit my needs at the moment.

"Then we have to leave tonight," David said. "Before they get here. We're sitting ducks in this RV. Shit. How are we going to get it out? There's no room. We're jammed in."

"We can't," I said. I wasn't going to mention Bernie's camper or the fact that we'd all fit in the back easily now that we'd emptied it. That was not the direction I wanted to steer this. "That's why we have to head to the dome. It's the safest place for us."

"What?" Lonan, Reiny, and David blurted in unison.

"This storm that's coming will be the perfect cover," I explained. I could already hear rain tapping on the roof. "Everyone will be tucked into their tents. No one will see us. And the dome is the most secure place we could possibly go."

"Secure?" David laughed. "You've got to be kidding me. That dome is exactly why the CAMFers are here. They came to take it back. That's the last place we should go."

"I've already told you," I said. "Olivia and some of my people are in there. They've kept this entire mob out for days. That place is a fortress if you know how to lock it up tight, which they do. But we can't stay out here, and running is too risky. Up until tonight, this gathering was more of a coincidental festival than a protest, but that's about to change. When the CAMFers get here, there will be violence. The police are already overwhelmed, which means someone's going to call in the military. We need to be safely inside the dome before that happens. Kaylee is the one most at risk here." I knew that would get David. He was fixated on keeping Kaylee safe. "But it's the safest bet for all of us."

"Lonan and I have a responsibility to the tribes," Reiny insisted. "Gordon left that in our hands. You can't expect us to just run away when innocent people might get hurt or killed."

"We have to warn them," Lonan said, "and the other groups too."

"You've been seen with Kaylee," I pointed out. "That makes you a target."

"Well, I'm not going," Reiny said, crossing her arms over her chest and glaring at me. "Lonan and I will stay out here and risk it. We'll deal with the CAMFers when they come. We can take care of ourselves."

"I'm sure you can," I agreed. I couldn't let them stay behind, though. They were too much of a liability. I'd known this would be a hard sell, but I still had one ace up my sleeve. "Ultimately, it's your choice. But before you make up your mind, I think you should know Pete's in the dome."

"Pete Hardy?" Rainy said, all the blood draining from her face.

"Olivia and her group found him when they arrived, injured and dehydrated, but alive. He never displaced. He was unconscious at the time and that somehow blocked the process."

"How long have you know this?" Reiny asked, her eyes drilling into mine. I had never seen her so angry. For a moment, I thought she might lunge at me. But instead, her rage suddenly turned to sobs. "I thought he was dead," she choked out, burying her face in Lonan's chest as he wrapped his arms around her.

"You are a bastard," Lonan said, glaring over his sister's head at me.

"I know, but I'm the bastard who's going to keep us all alive." The rain was splattering against the windows, and pelting the roof. I'd expected Jason to be back by now. We couldn't wait much longer. I had to get this crew ready to go so we could leave as soon as he arrived. I knew I had Reiny, and Lonan would follow wherever she went. Kaylee would follow my lead. I was confident of that. But I had to let David think he had a choice. "Listen, the decision is yours," I said. "If you're coming, pack light—just clothing and weapons, if you have any. The dome has everything else you'll need. Oh, and wrap that in trash bags and bring it along." I gestured at the portrait of Kaylee propped in the corner. "I don't want anything left behind that links this RV to PSS."

"So, how do we even get in if it's so secure?" David asked. "Are we just gonna waltz up and ring the doorbell?"

"Pretty much," I said. "It's already been arranged. You have ten minutes to get ready, and then we're out of here. I'm going to go check on Jason. He went to get our stuff from the camper, but he should have been back by now."

I stepped out onto the RV steps, scanning the night, the awning protecting me from the worst of the rain. The weather was already pretty nasty, and there was no sign of him. I couldn't afford to go looking for him either. I had to keep this group busy and focused or they might change their minds and scatter on me. Fuck. Where was he? I'd been counting on those guns. Well, there was nothing for it. We had to go and we had to go now. Better to leave one behind than lose the whole group. I tapped out a quick message to Chase on my phone, letting him know we were coming.

Then I stepped back into the RV, relieved to see that everyone was suited up in rain gear and David had the bag-wrapped painting strapped to his back.

Lonan held a rifle and I had my favorite pistol in my underarm holster. Hopefully, that would be enough. "I sent Jason ahead to make sure the way is clear for us," I lied. I couldn't have David or Lonan going all no-man-left-behind on me. Wherever Jason was, he'd scrape by. I was confident of that. "Let's go," I said, gesturing them toward the door. "Lonan, you take up the rear, and let's keep Kaylee in the middle and out of sight as much as possible."

I led the way out into the blustering storm, Reiny and Kaylee behind me, Marcus and Lonan behind them. I knew the general location of the entrance we were looking for, but the closer we got to the dome the tighter the tents and cars were packed, requiring us to navigate between them. Plus, the wind was so strong and the rain was coming down so hard it was difficult to see more than a few feet. But no one was out and about, thanks to the weather.

I stopped for a moment to get my bearings, and Reiny and Kaylee almost ran into the back of me.

"We're close," I told them, raising my voice over the storm and pointing in the direction we needed to head. There was a large encampment full of trucks and RVs between us and the dome, but once past that, we would be in the clear.

Reiny nodded, wrapping her arm more tightly around Kaylee. She was still pissed at me about the Pete thing, but she'd get over it. They'd tried so hard to keep their little romance at the compound a secret, but it had been obvious to me. You couldn't mask attraction like that, and there was no point trying. But love always made you vulnerable and put you at risk.

Even with the rain battering down on her, Kaylee smiled up at me from under the hood of her poncho.

Case in point. Would I be doing any of this if it weren't for Kaylee? Probably not. And when we entered that dome, she'd finally be reunited with her real family, and where would that leave me? But it didn't matter. I would not fail this child no matter what it did to me.

David came up and joined us, with Lonan right behind him. Then I forged ahead, leading them all through the tight maze of tents and vehicles at the edge of the dome.

We easily cleared the final camps and entered the open area surrounding the compound walls.

"Where's Jason?" David asked, glancing around. "I thought you said he was ahead of us?"

"He might already be inside. That's the door." I pointed to a small service entrance on our left. "Let's go." A glance at my watch told me we were right on time.

The moment we stepped up to the door it swung open and I was staring my little brother in the face, T-dog standing behind him.

"Get in here," Chase said, smiling broadly and pulling the door open a little wider.

I ushered Reiny and Kaylee in first, then David and Lonan. As I stepped in, David asked again, "What about Jason?"

"He's either here or he's not," I said, as Chase closed the door, punching in a code to lock it.

"Did someone else get here before us?" Lonan asked Chase. "A young man about your age."

"No, I'm sorry," Chase said, shooting me a look. "But T-dog can stay here in case he shows up."

"You said he was ahead of us," David said to me, accusation in his voice.

"T-dog will wait for him," I said. "He'll make it."

But I was pretty sure he wouldn't.

27

JASON

When I came to, I was sitting in a chair with my hands tied behind my back and a canvas bag over my head. Something warm trickled down my neck, and my skull was throbbing.

Someone had hit me hard enough to knock me out.

Fuck. How had they gotten the jump on me?

I'd taken the dirt bike back to the camper like Palmer had told me to. I'd parked it outside and gone in to change my clothes and grab the bag of guns. I'd stopped for a minute in the bathroom to drain the snake and wash the blood off my forehead, and then I'd stepped outside into the growing storm.

That's the last thing I remembered.

No, there'd been a girl.

She'd come around the corner of the camper just as I'd stepped out. And she'd smiled at me, a sort of wicked little smile, and then pain had exploded in my head and I'd gone down.

She'd been the decoy, the distraction while someone else came up behind me.

I could hear them arguing, a guy and a girl, their voices echoing as if coming down a long tunnel. Obviously, they hadn't realized I was awake yet, so I took the time to try and figure out just how fucked I was.

The air was cool and dry against my damp clothes and skin, so we were indoors, but not someplace heated. An abandoned building maybe, but I couldn't hear rain on the roof or the sounds of the camps around the compound. If the plan was to kill me, they would have done it already. They hadn't even searched me thoroughly. They'd taken my gun, but I could still feel the outline of the bullet in my pocket. Plus, they'd left my feet untied and the ropes around my wrists weren't tight. Whoever they were, they were amateurs. Not my old man's people, that was for sure. So, I could definitely get out of this alive if I played my cards right. But first, I had to find out who they were and what the hell they wanted.

Slowly, I lifted my head and called out, "Hello," trying to sound as pitiful as possible. Let them think I was afraid. Let them think they had the power. "Please, let me go," I pleaded. My voice was muffled by the bag, but they'd get the tone.

"Good. He's awake," the girl said, coming closer, but her voice still echoing strangely. "Let's find out who this fucker is." She yanked the bag off my head, grabbing a handful of my hair with it, pulling me up even straighter in the old metal chair I was tied to.

It was the same girl I remembered from the camper. She was about my age, with shoulder-length red hair and freckles, not bad looking, but she wasn't smiling anymore. She was also wearing black padded dirt bike gear that I vaguely recognized. A tall, skinny guy, also about my age, was standing behind her holding a baseball bat that I would have bet had my blood on it.

Before they could ask me anything, I blurted out, "Please don't hurt me. I don't have any money." As I said it, I scanned the room behind them, but it wasn't really a room. It was more like an old train tunnel or something, which explained the weird echoes. The concrete roof curved over us and there were no windows. Behind the girl and her boy-band-reject friend, there was a metal, vault-like door in the distance, with some kind of weird ventilation system built into it.

"Please, cut the crap," the girl said, frowning down at me. "You had a bag of guns, Mr. Innocent." She pointed into the shadow of the nearest wall where they'd tossed Palmer's weaponry like a bag of dirty laundry. "We're not the thieves here. You are. And we'll ask the questions, starting with why you attacked me, stole my bike, and left me in the desert to die."

Wait, she'd been the one on the bike? I'd jumped a girl? Fuck. That's where I'd seen her biker gear before.

"Come on. Allie. You wouldn't have died," her friend said. "If I hadn't found you, you just would've had to walk back, and you hate walking."

"Shut up, Matty," she snapped, glaring at him. "I told you to let me do the talking. He attacked me. Not you."

"Yeah, listen, I'm sorry about that," I groveled. "I thought you were a guy. I never would have jumped you if I'd known you were a girl."

"Really?" She did not sound happy. "How noble of you. But that doesn't answer my question. See, I already know you're an asshole. That's the one thing about you that's painfully obvious. What I don't know is what you were doing out there at the fence tonight with this." She brushed aside her jacket revealing my chest holster with my gun in it. She pulled out the weapon, brandishing it in front of me. "Did you come with those bastards from the city who opened fire on a bunch of high schoolers? Is that what the bag of guns was for, to kill us all?"

Oh shit. This wasn't good. Matty must have seen me at the fence. Then I'd taken this girl's bike and they'd somehow tracked me back to the camper where they'd found me with Palmer's guns. No wonder they were so fired up.

"Those aren't my guns," I stammered. "And I wasn't with those guys at the fence. I was just trying to get away. But then I told my friend about it, and he thought we should do something to stop them. Those are his guns. I was taking them to him. That's all."

She stared at me, mulling that over, then holstered my gun quickly and efficiently. She knew how to handle a weapon. Too bad she didn't know how to tie a knot worth a damn. I was already halfway out of the ropes around my wrists.

Suddenly, there was a strange roar from outside and something banged against the door. She jumped and Matty whirled around.

"Go check on that," she told him. "I think it was just the wind, but better to be sure."

That's when I realized where we were. We weren't in a tunnel. We were in one of Umatilla's old underground bunkers, lit only by a couple of camping lanterns set on the floor near the door. Other than the lanterns and the chair I was in, the place was completely empty. But the walls were covered in graffiti, things like "Megan is a slut," and "I lick balls," scrawled all over them. The locals obviously spent a lot of time here. But, hey, who could blame them? There probably wasn't a lot to do in a small town like Hermiston but lick someone's balls.

"You really expect me to believe you were bringing these guns to help us?" Allie asked, as Matty went to the door and stuck his head outside, the wind gusting in around us. "I don't buy that for a second. You knew those armed fuckers were coming. That's why you paid to have the fence held open. Then, you wrestled me off my bike and burned my leg on the exhaust." She pulled up her singed pant leg and showed me a nasty red welt on her lower calf. "And I saw your leg," she lowered her voice, moving closer and reaching toward me. "You have PSS."

It was a mistake.

Not just to get close to me, but to reach for my leg. That leg.

Even if I hadn't already been planning it, I would have kicked the fuck out of her just for that. As it was,

I caught her off balance as I swept my right foot up and hit her in the gut, knocking her onto her back.

She landed so hard I heard the air whoosh out of her lungs.

"Hey!" Matty yelled from the door, but I was already up, tossing the loose rope off my hands and reaching for my gun inside her jacket.

Her hands batted feebly at mine, but she was still gasping for breath.

I grabbed the gun and I pointed it at her head, her eyes widening as she looked up the barrel. Out of the corner of my eye, I could see Matty, obviously torn between helping her and bolting out the door.

"Tell him to come here and I won't kill you," I told her. He'd take it better from her than me. He'd do what she said.

She nodded, taking one ragged breath and opening her mouth. "Matty," she exhaled. "Run!"

I turned and took a shot, even as he was scrambling at the door mechanism. It didn't hit him. I didn't want it to. But it did ricochet off the metal and make a terrifying racket.

Allie sat up and tried to knock me aside, so I pushed her down and sat on her.

By the time I turned back to the door, it was slamming shut with a loud bang. The handle on the inside turned and something clanked into place with an unpleasant finality.

"He just locked us in, didn't he?" I asked as she squirmed under me.

"Yes," she panted, baring her teeth and smiling that wicked smile again. "He'll go get my friends,

the ones with the baseball bats, and then you're
screwed."

"More like they are," I said, getting off of her and
checking the chamber of my gun. "How many friends
you got?" I asked, "Because I have seven bullets left
in this gun and a shit ton more in that bag over there."

"You—you wouldn't," she said, sitting up.

"Naw, you're right. I'll just invite them in to beat
the shit out of me."

Outside, a dirt bike started up and peeled out,
buzzing off into the distance.

"Really?" I said. "Your boyfriend would just run away
and leave you here? And you thought I was an asshole."

"He's not my boyfriend," she huffed, standing up
and dusting herself off. "He's my cousin."

"Maybe he's your cousin." I crossed to the door
and yanked on the handle, but it didn't budge. The
metal was thick. There was no way I could shoot it
open. "But I guarantee, he still wants to fuck you," I
said, turning back to her.

"Why, because you do?" she snapped, then she
clamped her lips together and suddenly looked
terrified. It was written all over her face. She'd just
realized we were locked in a bunker, I had a gun,
and I might rape her. But I would never do that, and
I suddenly wanted her to know that.

"Listen, I'm not going to hurt you," I said. "I didn't
let those guys with the guns through. Believe me,
that's the last thing I'd do. You have your bike back,
and I have a lump on my head, so I think we're even.
Just get us out of here before your friends show up,
and we can go our separate ways."

"That's the only way out," she said, gesturing at the locked door, except her eyes said differently, the way they slid off of me like oil off water. She was lying.

"No, it's not," I said, raising the gun and pointing it at her chest. "Show me."

"Seriously?" She frowned at the gun. "You just got done promising you wouldn't hurt me. And either you're a terrible shot or you missed Matty on purpose. Whoever you are, you're not a killer. I know that much."

"Maybe not." I lowered my weapon, pointing it at her right boot. "But I could shoot you in the foot and you'd tell me. You wouldn't bleed out before your friends got here, and anyone can live without a toe or two."

"God, why are you such an asshat?" She sounded genuinely curious. "Is it because you were horribly bullied as a child about your leg?"

"Give me my holster." I gestured at her chest. "If you're not going to show me, I'll find it myself."

"Fine." She took the holster off and handed it to me. "I'll show you, mainly because I don't want you to hurt anyone, and I'd like to get away from you as soon as possible."

"Likewise," I said, picking up Mike's gun bag and slinging it over my shoulder. I'd forgotten how heavy it was.

"Do you have a name?" she asked. "Or should I just call you asshat?"

"Jason," I said, realizing too late it was probably a bad idea to give her my real name.

"Well, Jason." She crossed to one of the lanterns and picked it up. Then she turned to the back of the bunker. "Follow me."

As we approached the back wall, I could see it was covered with a detailed and somewhat pornographic mural. Between the eerie shadows cast by the lanterns and the fleshy artwork, I didn't notice the door until she reached out and pulled it open. She held up the lantern, the light falling onto a long flight of metal stairs leading down into a dark corridor.

"There's a series of tunnels that connect all the bunkers and most of the main buildings of the depot," she explained. "They were added during the decommissioning to help transport the chemicals from the bunkers to the incinerators. Then they cemented a lot of them in and blocked the entrances, so it's like a labyrinth. There are only a few places you can still get out, and they're not easy to find unless you know where to look. So, stay close to me. I've explored most of it, but that was before the dome showed up. I haven't been down here since, and I think it might have collapsed some of the tunnels."

"So, if the wrong tunnel collapsed, we might not be able to get out?"

"I can get us out," she assured me.

"And what about when your friends get here? They know about the tunnels, right? Won't they just follow us?"

"I know the tunnels better than anyone," she said proudly. "Besides, they'll have no idea which route we've taken."

"Okay then. Lead on," I said, following her down into the dark underground labyrinth.

28

OLIVIA

Once I found out that Mike, my sister, and Marcus were outside the dome, I barely knew what to do with myself. I didn't hear the conversation at dinner. I blindly followed the guys upstairs to play cards afterwards. It was easy to pretend I didn't notice that Passion, Samantha and my mother stayed behind in the kitchen, undoubtedly to enact operation "birthday cake." And it took every ounce of effort I had not to ask Chase if he'd heard from Mike yet, but he'd promised to tell me the minute he did. I just had to be patient.

I was picking up cards and tossing them down like a zombie when the storm finally broke over our heads. Being under the dome during a torrential downpour was like being trapped in a reverse snow globe. The world outside was swirling and crazy, but inside it was as calm as ever. Still, the sound of the splashing rain had its usual effect, so I excused myself for a quick trip to the bathroom, and when I came back five minutes later, Grant and Pete were the only ones at the card table.

"Where are Chase and T-dog?" I asked, my heart pounding in my chest.

"Chase got some kind of alert on his laptop," Grant said. "Something about one of the side entrances. He said it was probably a false alarm due to the storm, but they went to check, just in case."

One of the side entrances? Did that mean what I thought it did? If Mike had waited until the last minute to message Chase—which he probably had—this could be it. My sister and Marcus might be inside the compound at that very moment, making their way toward us.

Calm down. You don't even know if they're coming for sure.

And then the door on the CAMFer side of the dome opened, and I turned toward it.

Chase stepped through first, catching my eye and grinning from ear to ear. T-dog followed. Behind him was my sister, enveloped in a rain poncho way too big for her, the hood thrown back, her hair dripping wet, but she was smiling too. Her eyes caught mine, then flicked behind me to Grant and Pete, moving from them to search further, puzzled.

"Go get my mom," I said to Grant. "And the girls too."

He didn't even hesitate. He was gone in an instant.

Right behind Kaylee, a gorgeous, petite, dark-haired woman came in, her eyes scanning much like Kaylee's had, but they found exactly what they wanted. She let out a cry and ran straight into Pete's arms, planting a passionate kiss on him. He did not resist. Not even a little.

After her, came another dark-haired guy I'd never seen, but they looked so much alike they had to be related.

Behind that guy was Mike Palmer, not smiling per se, but giving me a nod of approval.

And last but not least, Marcus slipped into the room, his expression guarded and cautious, a bulky wet rectangular trash bag slung over his shoulder which he immediately set down.

I'd tried very hard not to think about this moment.

I'd already lived through it once. The lack of recognition in his eyes. The way they'd passed over me as if I were a stranger. I did not want to experience that again. Yet here he was. My Marcus. My first love, traipsing into the dome soaking wet, his shirt slicked to his extraordinary chest, his dark hair and intense brown eyes.

Those eyes didn't pass over me this time. They found me and locked with mine, his lips quirking into a familiar cocky smirk. I was staring at him. The longing must have been written all over my face. Hell, it was probably written all over my body.

And he found that humorous, just like he had that first day in Calculus class when he'd caught me checking him out.

Suddenly. Kaylee was grabbing me and wrapping her arms around me.

Little sister, don't be upset, her voice whispered in my mind. *It will be okay.*

Being called "little sister" by tiny Kaylee felt really weird. It was hard to believe she was five years older than me. Mom had explained she'd been a preemie and very tiny when she was born. The fact that she'd been whisked away and raised in a cloistered environment probably hadn't helped. But the family resemblance was undeniable. This was my sister.

I heard a noise behind me, halfway between a laugh and a cry, and my mother crashed into us, enveloping us both in her arms.

After that, the rest of the evening was a whirlwind. Kaylee had rattled stuff off in our minds so quickly, it had been hard to catch it all. *She and Marcus had almost died in the desert. Reiny and Lonan had rescued them. She loved horses and they loved her. They'd seen the dome and kittens on television, and she'd gotten to ride in a moving house bus. But then Reiny's uncle had gotten very sick and they'd taken him and Mia away in a helicopter. But he was going to be okay. The doctors were fixing him.*

Then Mike told us about the locals holding the fence open and about the new iteration of CAMF arriving. Thankfully, the police had stopped them, at least for the time being.

That led to an argument between Marcus and Mike about Jason, who'd apparently gone missing right before they'd gotten the message from Chase to make a break for the dome. Marcus argued they should have waited for him. Mike said Jason could take care of himself and waiting would have been too risky. Personally, I agreed with Mike, but I kept my mouth shut.

Add to that the comedy of several of the new people asking, "Do I smell cake?" and the old crew pretending they didn't hear it even though it sent Passion and Samantha scurrying downstairs to check "the dishwasher". That was pretty entertaining. Of course, the girls brought back food and warm drinks for the new arrivals, and Grant and Pete went and got them towels and dry clothes.

Then there was the fact that Reiny and Pete were obviously in love.

After he and the men had brought up more beds and everyone agreed it was time to call it a night, I was surprised the two of them hadn't slipped away to one of the staff suites for a little privacy. Then again, Pete was the one who'd been pushing for us to stay together in the dome for security reasons.

From where I lay, wide awake in the middle of the night, I could see them, just at the edge of one of the partitions, two forms entwined into one shadow in Pete's bed. Not in a sexual way, but in something just as intimate that made my heart ache.

I glanced at the clock on my bedside table, and there was the USB Chase had given me lying beside it. I'd been so distracted I hadn't looked at the stuff on it yet, but that was okay. I wanted privacy when I watched that footage, and 4:12 am was about as private as it got living in a dome with thirteen other people.

So, I swung my legs over the edge of the bed, pulled on my sweatshirt, grabbed the USB, and slipped between the surrounding screens. There were three places I could access a computer: The Hold computer lab, the hacker van, or the CAMFer computer lab.

The Hold computer lab was the obvious choice, followed by the van. But for some reason, I headed toward the door to the CAMFer side. I'm not sure why. Maybe, I just wanted to prove to myself that I wasn't afraid, that those memories couldn't control me. Or perhaps I wanted to keep the contents of that USB on the side where they belonged—the dark side.

Of course, once I was through the CAMFer door, walking down the long hallway, I realized what a terrible idea it was.

My body began to shake. My teeth were clenched. I was fucking terrified.

Face your fears, Olivia. The CAMFers aren't here anymore. It's just an empty building.

I made it to the CAMFer computer lab without bolting, sat down at the nearest station, and plugged in the USB.

A video file icon popped up immediately, and I stared down at it. I was still afraid, so fucking afraid that it pissed me off. I reached into my sweatshirt pocket, feeling for my dad's marker stone, rubbing my fingers across the inscription. It was a good thing Passion couldn't sense my feelings through the dog tags hanging around my neck. I didn't want her to feel what I was about to feel. Honestly, I didn't want to feel it, but it had to be done.

"You can do this," I whispered, clicking play.

At first, I thought there had been some kind of mistake—that Chase had given me the wrong file. I was not expecting beautiful footage of the dome taken from the perspective of a drone flying over it. There was music in the background, something orchestral that soared and fell, syncing perfectly with the scenery. These weren't horrific clips of what the CAMFers had done to me. It was some kind of short, indie film, one that artfully transitioned from outside the compound to old video footage of the arrival of Kaylee and her captivity. *God, she'd been a cute kid. Who was I kidding? She was still adorable. She had some sort of pixie quality that defied age and made you want to protect her.*

The story Chase had woven continued, depicting the warring factions of The Hold and the CAMFers and how each side had approached PSS in an equally fucked-up way. It showed Marcus and Danielle's capture and torture. Yes, I saw her die in front of her brother, her PSS and her life slowly fading to nothing. I saw myself, a few brief scenes of what had been done to me, and relived it, tears streaming down my face. Then Kaylee entered the story once more. Chase had actually found the footage of her coming into my cell after I'd lost my hand. She touched me and the film cut to a scene of my hand pulsing back to life.

After that, Grant and I were being marched to the dome, climaxing to the final conflict between Mr. James and Fineman, Palmer cutting Kaylee, my hand reaching into myself. Then the screen went black, as if that were the end, except the music from the first scene returned, swelling dramatically. When the darkness had lasted just long enough, the drone soared over the dome once again, the mob outside beginning to amass around it far below.

Finally, there were a few key shots of us inside, working diligently, collecting data, with an emphasis on me and my ghost hand directing everyone.

God, was I really that bossy? And as the music built to its final crescendo, text blazed across the screen in beautiful bold lettering. **Come Home to the Dome.** After which Chase had included GPS coordinates and map links to the dome's location followed by the words, **This is not The End. It is only the beginning.**

When the movie finished, I sat in stunned silence, staring at the screen.

How had Chase made this beautiful, brutal thing? The entire video couldn't have lasted more than ten minutes. God, I would never mock his movie making abilities again. What he had created—it was beyond words. This was a story that could change people's minds about PSS. It explained what the dome was, who we were, and why what we were doing was so important. It was brilliant and powerful, and it was exactly what we needed.

This would be the dome's first drive-in movie. All the people out there who'd been gathering for some kind of show would finally get one.

But it was only the first step. Once we had the public's attention, we could release Pete and Reiny's research and all the incriminating shit from the CAMFers' files. As long as we had the hackers' secure internet connection, no one could stop us. We could release all the PSS content we wanted onto the web, including this movie, and more like it.

A noise snapped me out of my reverie and I turned, looking back through the lab door's little window out into the hallway. There was movement, a dark form and the flash of a pale face. It was there one second, gone the next.

My entire body went cold as if I'd suddenly been submerged in icy water.

You're freaking out. There was no one there.

But I could hear someone, moving quietly, but not quietly enough.

I had no weapon, except for the rock in my pocket and the surge of adrenaline in my veins, but it would have to be enough. I clutched my dad's stone and turned back to the door to find someone staring right back at me.

I jumped up as Marcus opened the door and stepped into the lab.

His eyes flicked to the computer behind me. "What are you doing over here in the middle of the night?" he asked, his voice full of suspicion.

"What are you doing following me in the middle of the night?" I countered. This was the first real conversation we'd had since he'd arrived, and it already sucked.

"I saw you get up and leave the dome," he explained, "and when you didn't come back right away, I was concerned."

"Concerned about what?" I couldn't keep the snark out of my voice. He'd followed me because he didn't trust me. Because he'd never truly trusted anyone in his life.

"You know what? Forget it," he said, running his hand through his hair, his muscles rippling under his t-shirt. "I thought you might be in trouble but, obviously, you have everything under control." He turned toward the door and I realized he was barefoot. He hadn't even taken the time to put on socks.

And he was as gorgeous as ever in just a tee and gray sweatpants, his hair all rumpled.

"No, wait. I'm sorry." My heart leapt when he turned back to me. "I just got creeped out, and you startled me. I should have known better than to come over here in the first place."

"You and me both," he said, smiling a little. "This floor is fucking cold." His glance slid back to the computer. "Why *did* you come over here?"

I guess now was as good a time as any to let Marcus in on my plan. He was probably going to hate it, but I couldn't do much more damage to our relationship than had already been done. I really had nothing to lose.

"I was watching footage Chase pulled for me from the CAMFer side," I said. "Well, it's more than footage, really. He made it into a movie. Want to see?"

"Yeah, sure. Why not?" He pulled up a chair and I sat back in mine, trying not to think about how close he was. And how far away.

"I should warn you. It contains disturbing scenes of you, Danielle, and me."

"Thanks for the warning," he said.

And then I played it for him.

I know I'd just seen it, but I got lost in it anyway. I barely knew I was in that room, sitting next to the boy I loved, watching some of the most horrific moments of our lives. I'd planned to pay attention and gauge his reaction. Instead, I was wrung out like a sponge, my face wet with tears. Again.

"Shit," he sighed, his voice wobbly. "I don't remember most of that. How can I not remember?"

I had the same question, but hearing him voice it with such agony—it tore me up inside.

"So, you're going to show this on the dome, aren't you?" he asked. "That's what the fancy sky show was all about this morning—to prime the crowd out there for this."

"I didn't actually think of it until after the demo," I explained. "Do you think it will work?"

"That depends on what outcome you're expecting. You've got their attention. That's for sure. But I doubt it will work."

I'd known this argument was coming. Marcus was as opinionated as I was. He was also smart, crafty, loyal, and caring. You just had to come at him from the right angle to uncover those attributes, and thankfully I was somewhat at an advantage. I knew him a hell of a lot better than he knew me. So, I wasn't going to argue with him.

"You don't think we should show it?" I asked. "Because I won't without your permission. At least not the way it is now. Chase can edit out the scenes with you and Danielle if that's what you want."

I could see he was surprised by that concession, but if he was the same Marcus I'd known before, the one I'd fallen in love with, there wouldn't be any question about his answer. His mission in life had been to save people from what Danielle had been through. He just hadn't thought quite as globally as this, although, to be fair, he hadn't had the opportunity. And that's exactly what I was offering him. It was strange how our roles had reversed. Now, I was the one trying to change the world and he was the one who needed convincing to join me.

"No. Keep us in," he said, flashing that heart-stopping smirk of his at me.

"Okay, I will." I pulled the USB from the computer. "We should head back to the dome before someone wakes up and comes looking for us." I didn't give a flying fuck about that. The truth was, if he smiled at me like that again, I was going to reach out and touch him, maybe even kiss him. So, I needed to get the hell out of there.

"Wait." He reached down, fumbling at the waistband of his sweat pants, and pulled out a folded piece of paper. "I wanted to show you this." He held it out to me.

"Um, that was in your pants," I said, not reaching for it.

"So, I don't have any pockets. Besides, girls keep stuff in their bras all the time."

He had a point. I reached out and took the thick paper, realizing it was an old photo as I unfolded it. It was a picture of a bunch of young hippies, and I recognized my dad immediately. I also recognized a very young Alexander James, and was that a young Mike Palmer dressed like a serial killer?

"Where did you get this?" I asked.

"Reiny's Uncle Gordon gave it to me," he said. "That's him standing in the back, the older one. That is a group of young Native American Movement radicals he led when he was a college art professor."

"My dad knew your mom and your uncle in college?" I couldn't even process the rest of it. My dad hadn't been a radical anything. He'd been an unassuming painter.

"Yeah," Marcus said. "And that's not all. That group—they made a raid on Umatilla back when it had chemicals, and there was an accident, a leak of some kind, and it changed them. Gordon manifested a PSS foot shortly afterwards. I saw it myself. And the rest of them, at least the ones we know, all had children with external PSS."

I looked down at the photo again, scanning the faces. The beautiful, defiant-looking native woman standing next to Alexander James had to be Marcus's mother. I could see the resemblance as plain as day. My eyes stopped on the man of Asian heritage, then flicked to the African American guy. I knew those eyes. I'd seen them before.

I flipped the picture over. Just as I'd hoped, there was a list of names scrawled in faded pencil on the back. Amidst the names I already knew would be there, and a few I didn't recognize at all, I found Bertrum Faison and Sie Ling.

I turned the photo back over and stared at the only white woman in the group. She could be Jason's mom. It was hard to tell. She would have been using her maiden name back then, and I had no idea what that was.

"Did Jason see this photo?" I asked Marcus.

"No. He was always off running errands for Palmer. Why?"

"I think this is his mom." I pointed to the woman. "Because this is Nose's dad, and that is Yale's. All of our parents were in this group. That's what ties us together. It's why we were on the CAMFer list. It's why they were after us."

"Yeah, okay," Marcus said, sounding impatient. "But you do understand the full implications of that photo, right? The accident our parents caused at Umatilla released a chemical reaction into the atmosphere that could be seen for days. It was distributed like a volcanic cloud across the globe, likely within weeks."

I looked at Marcus, finally comprehending the weight of what he was telling me. "They were ground zero," I whispered, looking down at the photo again. "They started it all right here."

"Exactly." Marcus nodded. "And now they expect us to finish it. Gordon and Palmer, they think we can fix what they fucked up. My uncle is part of it too. They've been manipulating us this whole time toward a specific outcome."

"Maybe," I admitted. "But what choice do we have? Leave the world fucked up just to spite them?"

"I'll admit, it's tempting," he said, grinning wickedly. "But no. Your plan is better. The crowd out there is receptive. They were actually curious about Kaylee, instead of hostile. Maybe the world is finally ready for this."

"Be careful," I said. "Your optimism is showing."

"Ha ha. Very funny. So, what do we do now?"

"We go back to the dome and get some sleep," I said, yawning. "Because my mom is throwing me an annoying-ass birthday party tomorrow—no, actually today—and she's going to expect me to stay awake for it."

"Today's your birthday?" Marcus asked. "How old are you?"

"Eighteen." We'd been chatting so well, bantering back and forth, I'd almost forgotten he didn't remember my birthday, or how old I was, or how I liked to be kissed on the back of the neck. By him.

"Okay then, lead the way, birthday girl." He got up, waving me toward the door.

I tried to hand the picture back, but he told me to keep it, suggesting Chase scan it and do an internet search to see if we could identify Jason's mom for sure.

Then, we made our way back down the hallway toward the dome.

As I reached for the security door keypad, I realized it was flashing green. The door was already open, hanging slightly ajar.

"You left the door to the dome unlocked," I said.

"Sorry," Marcus said, looking properly chagrined. "I was in a hurry, but I really thought I'd closed it."

"It's okay." I slipped through, making sure he locked it behind us this time. "No harm done."

29

ANTHONY

Seeing Olivia cross over to the CAMFer side alone in the middle of the night was more than I ever could have hoped for. At first, I thought I was having a fucking wet dream. What were the chances? From my new favorite hiding spot in the CAMFer security room, which Olivia's people had kindly unlocked for me, I watched her go into the computer lab and sit down at one of the monitors, her back to the door.

I stood up and grabbed my knives, tucking them into place. Too bad her friends hadn't opened the CAMFer armory too, but the knives would do the job.

I took one last look at the camera feed, marveling at my good fortune.

And that's when it occurred to me it must be a trap.

That was the only explanation. Just hours before, I'd seen two of her people cross over into my side, hurry toward one of the smaller entrances, and let five more people in, including Fineman's PSS pet and Mike-fucking-Palmer.

I won't lie, that had shaken me up. I couldn't understand why Palmer was here with her, acting like he was on their side? At first, I'd thought he might be a CAMFer plant. Then it had hit me that maybe he'd been playing both sides all along, but I couldn't believe it. He hated minus freaks as much as I did. He'd been the one who'd encouraged me to cut off Olivia's hand.

The hand she had back.

That's when I'd realized he'd set me up to take the fall for him. Olivia's hand, and mine, had all been part of his plan. Mike Palmer was a traitor to our cause. He'd been one of them all along. I'd gone into a fit of rage then, breaking things, smashing them, almost slamming my stump into a wall like an idiot.

But I'd calmed down, and kept watch, and then Olivia had come on screen into the CAMFer side like a dream. It had to be Palmer baiting me. Somehow, he knew I was here. Still, a trap could be outsmarted and used to my advantage, as long as I was aware of it.

I took a deep breath, sat back down, and scanned the other feeds. I didn't see anything, but her people could be dodging the cameras just like I'd been. Of course, the area right outside the dome door was a bottleneck that couldn't be avoided. I could backtrack that camera's footage to make sure no one else had come through, but I had no idea how far back to look.

Olivia was still in the computer lab, watching some kind of movie. What if this wasn't a trap? What if she was just a fool and this was my one chance to take her out?

I stood up and slipped out of the security room. It was a five-minute walk to the lab, a little longer if I dodged cameras along the way. I moved cautiously, searching the hallway and surrounding area before approaching the door.

When I peered through its little window, I almost expected her not to be there, for it to have been a mirage fueled only by my wishful thinking and need for revenge.

But it was really her.

Alone.

Oblivious.

Vulnerable.

I must have made a noise, because she suddenly turned and I ducked, crouching below the window frame.

Maybe she'd get up and come to the door. Maybe she'd open it and I'd grab that bitch and cut her throat from ear to ear. Let's see her come back from that.

But then I heard a sound from down the hall, and I saw the green flash of the security pad indicating someone was coming through.

I bolted, darting back around the corner, but I made myself stop there. If it was a trap and they were coming in force, I was already screwed. But, if it was just one of the others come to find Olivia, I might be able to take both of them.

I peered around the edge of the wall and saw a guy my age—one of the ones who'd come in with Palmer.

He was barefoot in a t-shirt and sweats, standing and looking in the window just like I'd been a minute ago. As I watched, he reached out, opened the door, and stepped inside, saying "What are you doing over here in the middle of the night?"

Olivia said something in return, but I could barely hear it.

Then the guy stepped inside, pulling the door closed behind him.

They were both in there now, unarmed. It would have been so much easier just to take her. A guy would put up a fight, especially to impress a girl, and he had two hands.

But it had to be done. This was my chance and I had to take it.

I crept around the corner, staying low as I approached the door. About halfway there, I noticed the green light still flashing at the end of the hallway.

Olivia's friend had left the door to the dome wide open.

I stopped for a moment, weighing my options just like my old man taught me.

I could go for the two in the lab, maybe kill them now, but the rest, including Mike Palmer, would know for sure they had an enemy. They would hunt me, and find me, and kill me. And Olivia would still win. I'd seen her army of followers outside on the exterior camera feeds. This was bigger than taking her out. I had to stop whatever she was doing.

If I snuck into the dome now, if I infiltrated their side without them knowing it, I might be able to take them all out, or totally fuck their plans. It would be difficult to remain unseen in the dome area, once daylight hit. But If I could get into the Hold side before daybreak, it should be similar enough to the CAMFer side for me to hide.

I heard music coming through the door of the lab.

She was showing him what she'd been watching, and they'd both be distracted.

I moved, ducking under the window in the door, and made my way down the hall, slipping into the dark, star-studded dome.

30

JASON

"For Christ's sake, admit it," I said. "You have no idea where we are." Allie had been leading us for hours through the maze of tunnels under Umatilla. Every time we came to a junction, she'd peer intently at some piece of graffiti before confidently heading off in a new direction. But I was pretty sure we were lost, and my shoulders were numb from lugging around Palmer's bag of guns. Not to mention, I was pretty sure Allie's lantern was fading.

"No, I know exactly where we are," she insisted. "Trust me, we're almost there. Just three more tunnels and this empties out into the eastern most bunker on the depot. Of course, after that, it's a long walk back to—"

"Shhhh," I hissed, grabbing her arm. "I heard something."

"Don't grab me," she said, "I don't—" and then she clamped her mouth shut because she heard it too.

First voices. Deep and rumbly. Men talking to men.

Then heavy footfalls, lots of them, echoing down the corridor toward us.

"They're coming straight at us," I whispered. "We have to hide."

"Hide where?" she asked. "There's nowhere to hide in a freakin' tunnel."

"Then we have to backtrack," I said softly. "We can take one of the intersections we passed and hope they don't follow."

"Okay," she whispered, turning and hurrying back the way we'd come. I followed, trying to position my body so it would block the lantern light from the group behind us. Whoever they were, I really didn't want to meet them in a dark tunnel underground.

Allie stopped at the next junction, holding the lantern up to the wall.

"Just go," I said. "We're not trying to get anywhere. We just need to get out of their path."

"No, I have an idea. A place we can hide." She took the right-hand passage. "It's really hard to find."

I followed, hating that I was at her mercy. If she panicked and took off on me, I'd never get out of here. Fuck. Maybe we'd gotten completely turned around and the guys following us were her friends with the bats. But they'd sounded older. I was torn between my need to be quiet and my need to know what the hell we might be up against.

We were running now, Allie taking junctions with renewed confidence. The sound of the guys behind us was fading, so I dared to ask another question.

"Who else knows about these tunnels?"

"Just locals, people our age, mostly," she said, taking a quick left. "This guy named Rhino grows pot in some of the bunkers. He's the one who originally made the hole in the fence so he could truck his stuff in and out."

It hadn't sounded like a pothead following us, or a bunch of local teens. It had sounded like an army.

"This way." Allie headed right down another tunnel with a door at the end of it. That was a good sign. We hadn't seen many doors. Most of the tunnels just had open connections to each other. And this door wasn't just any door. It was a hatch with a turning wheel like they have on submarines—a sealed hatch. We might even be able to lock it from the other side.

Allie ran up and gripped the wheel, spinning it loose with only a little effort. She pulled the heavy door open and stepped over the threshold into a much larger space, not a tunnel and not a bunker, but some kind of large circular room.

I stepped in after her.

At the far back of the room was a giant, round, metal tank, so big it reached from floor to ceiling and it was radiating a soft blue light.

"Close the hatch," she said, turning off the lantern to save the battery. "It doesn't lock anymore. Someone broke the mechanism, but I doubt whoever is down here will come this way. There's only one tunnel that leads here."

"Only one tunnel?" I stared at her. "You mean there's no way out? What the fuck? If they come after us, we're trapped."

"They won't come this way," she insisted.

Every instinct in my body was screaming that this was a very bad idea, but I pulled the hatch closed behind me anyway. "What the hell is this place?" I asked, setting down the bag of guns to give my shoulders some relief. I really didn't like how this was all going down. As soon as I'd placed my foot inside that room, something had felt off. If I'd been on my own, I would have gotten the hell out of there. But Allie wasn't afraid, so I held my ground.

"It's just a tank for chemicals," she said. "But don't worry. It's empty. They got rid of all that stuff years ago."

"Then why is it glowing?" I asked. "What if that shit is residual radiation or something?"

"I've been down here lots of times and it's never—" She stopped, cocking her head to listen.

I heard them too. Fuck! They were coming straight down the tunnel toward us.

And we had nowhere to run.

"Get into the shadows," I said, pointing to the darkest part of the room, and shoving Allie toward it. As I turned to pick up the gun bag, I heard her run into something with a muffled oomf. "There are pipes here," she said, "but I think we can crawl between them." She grabbed my hand and pulled me down, guiding me after her through a series of giant metal pipes. I dragged the gun bag over and under, trying to make as little noise as possible. And then we were at the wall, huddled against it and jammed together in what felt like a very tight space.

Strangely, there was rubble on the floor, broken chunks of cement and gritty dust as if someone had been doing construction recently in our little hidey-hole. I put my hand on the wall behind us. It was jagged and broken, crumbling under my touch. Hopefully, it wouldn't collapse on us while we hid. I scooted forward a little to avoid putting pressure on it with my back and pulled the gun bag up against us for further camouflage. Then, I removed my gun from its holster and held it ready.

As my eyes adjusted, I could see we'd crawled up next to the holding tank. We were wedged in a corner between it and the wall. Thankfully, the pipes created a pocket of shadow for us that blocked most of its glow. From my position next to the tank, I could actually see a small section of the hatch door.

It was a good hiding spot. We might get out of this yet, despite Allie's stupidity in leading us to a dead end.

The men's voices grew louder. They were right outside the hatch. The wheel on the door squeaked and began to turn. When it opened, the first thing I thought was *fuck my luck*. They weren't teenagers with bats. Based on their uniforms and gear, they were US military. There were five of them, accompanied by two civilians, a man and a woman.

The man I recognized immediately. It was Dr. Fineman.

The woman was older, in her sixties maybe, but strong and wiry-looking.

Of course, the first thing the soldiers did was secure the room.

Allie and I plastered ourselves even further back in our dark corner, as one of them came our direction, shining a light across the pipes. If he saw me holding a gun, he would shoot us. But if I put it away, he'd hear me and shoot anyway. And honestly, I preferred getting shot to ending up in Fineman's hands, so if it came right down to it—

"Clear," a voice called, and our guy called back, "clear," as he turned away from us.

"All clear," a final voice declared, and I let myself exhale.

Fineman and the woman crossed out of my view, over to the other side of the tank. When we'd first come in, I'd noticed some kind of machine built up against the tank on that side. Based on their location, that's what they'd come for.

"You're sure this will work?" the woman asked.

"Yes, yes," Fineman said dismissively. "I assure you, when you've worked with PSS as long as I have, you begin to understand it on an intuitive level. The fact that it's in its original gaseous form makes no difference to my highly trained senses. Even without the resonator activated, I can tell it's as viable and potent as the day you created it."

"We didn't create it," the woman protested. "I told you, that was an act of terrorism. We simply kept a sample to study in hopes of counteracting the effects of the accident."

"Which you couldn't do, of course," Fineman said. "And then your government pulled the funding on this entire facility and ordered all the chemicals destroyed. But you didn't know how to destroy this one, and so here we are."

"You sought us out and offered your services, Doctor," the woman said, sounding pissed off. "And don't forget I was the one who vouched for you since we'd worked together before. Besides, we're paying you handsomely to dissipate this substance and leave no physical evidence it was ever here. So, you damn well better be able to do that, because if the PSS phenomenon was ever traced back to this location, it would be disastrous for this country on a global scale. Now, let's get on with it."

"Very well," Fineman said. "Your machinery is arcane, but I believe if I adjust the vibrational tone and speed like so, it will begin the process of amplification toward the Ryberg state."

"Toward the Ryberg state?" the woman echoed. "What the hell are you talking about? Amplifying these gasses to the Ryberg state would have repercussions I can't even begin to imagine."

"That's been your problem from the very beginning, Muriel," Fineman said, his voice gone cold and vicious. "Such a tiny imagination paired with such a huge intellect. It's been a terrible waste, I'm afraid."

I wasn't expecting the gunfire—three blasts, discharging almost simultaneously, pounding my eardrums. I know I jumped, and Allie clutched my arm. I barely kept from firing my own weapon out of sheer adrenaline.

Fuck. What had just happened?

"Very good," Fineman said. "With her and her whining chatter ended, I can finally do what must be done."

Suddenly, a strange hum filled the room and the tank began vibrating against my leg.

"There," Fineman declared. "The process has begun."

"What if they send someone to try and stop it?" a voice asked.

"They have no one who could," Fineman answered. "Why do you think they were desperate enough to hire me, a lowly research scientist? Now, let's go."

"What about the bodies, sir?"

"Leave them," Fineman said. "It's fitting Muriel should find her final resting place here, beside her legacy, pitiful as it is."

"Yes, sir."

One of the military guys stepped into my line of sight and opened the hatch. Behind him came Fineman, followed by two more soldiers.

They walked out, closing the door behind them.

"What just happened?" Allie whispered, trembling against me.

"I have no fucking idea," I said, slowly lowering my gun. There was no way I was going to tell her I'd recognized Fineman.

We waited a while, still hiding in our dark hole until we were sure they were long gone. Finally, I told Allie to go ahead and I shoved Mike's gun bag aside, gesturing at the pipes.

She crawled forward, wiggling her fine ass in front of me through the tight spaces.

"There are dead people out here," she said, her voice quivering. "Hurry up."

"I'm coming." I slid the gun bag in front of me.

As soon as I moved away from the tank, I felt a strange sensation near my hip, as if something alive had crawled into my pants and was squirming to get out.

I freaked, banging my head on a pipe, but I did manage to look down just as the bullet slipped from the top of my pants pocket and flew toward the tank.

The harsh tink of metal against metal echoed through the room when it hit.

"What was that?" Allie asked, clambering back over a pipe toward me.

"Nothing," I lied, reaching out and grabbing the bullet, which had stuck to the side of the tank. It was like fighting the pull of a very strong magnet. Once I got it off, though, I wrapped my fingers around it and moved my hand further away. The bullet writhed inside my fist like a living thing trying to get out. I could feel it squeezing between my fingers, the pointy end drilling into my flesh. I wasn't going to be able to hold it much longer. It was cutting into me. I was going to have to open my fist or it would go right through me. "Stay back," I told Allie, warding her off with my other hand. Wherever the bullet went this time, I didn't want her in its path.

I opened my fist and it flew out, zipping through the air straight back to the tank with an even louder tink.

"What the hell are you doing?" Allie asked, crawling up to me. She followed my glance to the bullet pressed up against the tank. "Is that from your gun or one of theirs?"

"One of theirs, I guess," I said. "I tried to pull it off, but it really wants to stay."

"Weird," she said. "Maybe the tank is magnetic or something." She reached out, running her hand over the smooth, curved surface of the tank. "It's vibrating. Was it doing that before?"

"I don't know. But I think we should get out of here. Now."

I hated to do it, but I left the bullet. I didn't really have a choice.

Once we were out of the pipes, I could see the bodies. There were two soldiers, lying far apart, each obviously taken out by one of their military comrades. The old woman, Muriel, was lying near the machine, blood pooling around her. The machine was obviously on now, lights blinking, a low hum coming from it, though it had no on or off button that I could see. If I messed with it, there was a good chance I'd make things worse.

Mike Palmer might know what to do, but he would be in the dome by now. Maybe, if I could get some kind of message to him—

But first, Allie and I had to get out of these damn tunnels.

"Let's go," I said, gesturing toward the hatch. "Get us out of here."

"Okay," she said, "but our safest bet is to go out the way we came in. Otherwise, I'm afraid we might run into more of those soldiers, or worse. Don't worry. If Matty's there, I won't let him hurt you. I promise."

"I won't let him hurt me either." I flashed my gun at her. "You understand?"

"Yeah, I understand," she nodded, leading the way.

It was early morning by the time we emerged into the original bunker where Allie and Matty had tied me up. Sure enough, Matty and his crew were waiting for us with bikes, bats, and a few side arms. After Allie convinced them to put their weapons away, Matty explained he'd sent groups to all the tunnel exits searching for us, and some of them had been reporting unusual activity—such as soldiers going in and out—so he'd thought Allie and I might come back this way. Matty wasn't as dumb as he looked. And he was much braver with all his friends gathered around him.

Allie told them what we'd seen down in the tank room, but they seemed much more concerned about the military presence than anything else. At that point, I donated Palmer's gun bag to them as a show of good faith. It wasn't like I could use most of that stuff anyway. I only had two hands.

Then, much to my surprise, Allie gave me a lift back to Bernie's camper on her bike. The only problem was she didn't leave. Instead, she barged in right after me and sat down on the seat bench as if she owned the place.

"What are you doing?" I asked.

"Keeping an eye on you," she said, smiling.

"I don't think so." I gestured at the door. "Get the hell out."

"Nope." She leaned back, getting comfortable. "I know who you are, and why you're really here, and I want to help."

"I don't know what the fuck you're talking about," I said.

"Yes, you do," she insisted. "You're here because you have PSS." She glanced at my leg. "I'm not an idiot, you know, just because I'm from a small town.

My grandpa was one of the first to see the dome. He caught some people breaking into the depot, most of them our age, and several of them had PSS, just like you. They went inside and they're still in there, doing something. I want to know what that something is, and I think, if I stick with you, I'll find out."

"You're crazy," I'd told her. "And I'm exhausted. So, you can stay here and watch me sleep if you want. But that's all I'm gonna be doing."

I was hoping, when I took off my sweaty shirt in front of her, she'd leave, but she didn't. So, I pulled off my boots and threw myself onto the camper's fold-down bed, pretending to fall asleep. She still didn't leave. After an hour of lying there thinking how badly I needed to get word to Palmer about Fineman and what I'd seen, I opened my eyes and found her still sitting there, watching me.

"Fine," I said, sitting up. "Yes, I have friends in the dome and they're in danger, especially after what we saw down in that room. So, I need to get a message to them. If you wanna help, help me do that."

"I can get them a message," she said. "But not for free. I want something in return."

"What?" I asked. I still had my cut of the camp equipment sales hidden in the camper. I could offer her some of that.

"I'll help you," she said, "for everything you know about the dome."

"So you can tell who? Your grandpa and Matty? The local news stations? I'm not selling out my friends."

"What if I promise not to tell anyone?"

"I wouldn't believe you," I said. "Why else would you want to know, except to use it?"

"I'll show you why." She turned her back to me, pulling her hair off the nape of her neck to reveal a glowing patch of PSS skin. "It's a birthmark," she said, letting her hair drop and facing me again. "I've had it all my life. I'm one of you. And I can help. I swear you can trust me."

I wasn't sure a small patch of blue skin qualified her as "one of us," but if I could use it to my advantage, why not?

"Okay," I said. "You help me get a message into the dome, and I'll tell you what I know."

Allie's secret message system ended up being a bunch of cardboard signs and a dirt bike ride to the nearest compound security camera. We held the signs up, one at a time, and that was it. But I had to admit, it was better than anything I'd come up with. Still, I had no way of knowing if Palmer had seen it. Surely, he'd be monitoring the external cameras, so it should get through.

When we got back to the camper, I told Allie exactly what she wanted to hear. Yes, there were people in the dome with PSS. It had been a secret facility used to capture and torture them, but they'd managed to take it over. Now, they were inside, forming a resistance movement, and I was one of their agents, alerting them to danger outside the dome and vetting new recruits for the cause. And since she'd helped me, she was part of the resistance now. A very important part.

She ate it hook, line, and sinker.

Of course, the downside was I'd never get rid of her now.

But I was too tired to deal with it, so when she lay down on the camper bench seat and fell asleep, I crawled into the bed and did the same.

31

DAVID MARCUS

My first night in the compound hadn't been as bad as I'd feared. Seeing Kaylee reunited with her family had felt good. I'd never seen her so happy, and she was usually happy, so that was saying something. Mike had been a dick about leaving Jason behind, but I'd decided to let it go. Supposedly, Jason was a friend of mine, but he hadn't given me so much as the time of day since I'd woken up at the farm house. I didn't owe him anything. Besides, as far as I could tell, the guy was a douche.

Thing hadn't even been too awkward with Olivia. When I'd noticed her sneak out of the dome in the middle of the night to the CAMFer side, I'd had my concerns. But that had gone nothing like I'd expected.

Well, she'd been defensive at first, but so had I. I guess neither of us had any idea how to navigate this whole we-used-to-love-each-other-but-I-don't-remember-it thing. I mean, I was attracted to her. There was no doubt about that. I'd felt it just sitting next to her in the computer lab. Her eyes were gorgeous. Her body was— anyway, most girls were attractive. That wasn't the point.

What I'd discovered last night was that she was more than attractive. She was smart. Also, a little sassy, which I could appreciate. And she was certainly passionate about changing the world's perspective on PSS, no matter how unlikely that was. I had to hand it to her, she had guts.

As for the movie she'd shown me, I was still processing that. It had been hard to watch. It was even harder to imagine other people seeing me at my most vulnerable. My instinct had been to demand she take Danielle and me out. But I hadn't, because Olivia was just as exposed in that footage as I was, probably more so, and she was willing to risk it.

Those scenes with her helpless against the CAMFers had almost been unbearable to watch. A couple times, I'd glanced at her, marveling, aching for her, wanting to reach out and touch her hand or tell her it was okay. Not because I'd loved her before, but just because we were both human and we'd been through similar fucked-up shit.

But I hadn't done any of that. Olivia hadn't needed me to. In fact, she hadn't even looked at me, though she had cried, big, awful, silent tears running down her face. If she still loved me, I wasn't sure why. A girl that strong didn't need anyone, especially a guy like me.

Maybe she didn't need me, but what if she wanted me?

That was a thought I'd tried very hard not to entertain. I'd come into the compound to keep an eye on Palmer and protect Kaylee, not to get back together with her sister. But the conversation and banter with Olivia last night had been so easy. She liked to tease, and she gave as good as she got. And it was apparent everyone in the dome adored and respected her. Last but not least, she hadn't raked me over the coals for leaving that damn door open. She'd had every right to, but she hadn't.

When we'd gotten back to the dome, I couldn't sleep. I kept thinking about her. It had made for a restless night, and the first thing I'd done this morning was take a long, cold shower.

Yeah, I needed to get a handle on this.

"It's time," Mrs. Black called, managing to swoop into the library area of the dome despite her limp.

It was 11:00 am and we'd all gathered per the instructions she'd given us at breakfast. Well, all of us except Olivia who was still asleep. Of course, I knew she'd been up until 5:00 am, and probably wouldn't appreciate a bedside birthday ambush by everyone in the entire dome, but that's what her mom had planned.

"Come on." Mrs. Black gestured for us to follow her. "Quietly now. Don't ruin the surprise."

As we followed like obedient children, Grant gave me a look that said, "This is not going to go well." Then we both grinned at each other because it was also likely to be highly entertaining.

We all squeezed between the screens, gathering beside Olivia's bed.

She was curled up into a tight ball, her blankets tangled in her legs, her pillow bunched over her eyes to block out the morning light. She didn't look relaxed, but she did look soft and vulnerable and something in my chest clenched at the sight of her.

"Rise and shine, birthday girl!" Mrs. Black cried, leaning over her. "Or should I say, birthday woman?"

"No, mom—" Olivia groaned, jamming her head further under her pillow. "Just let me sleep five more minutes, okay?"

"Olivia," her mother said, sitting down on the edge of the bed and gently shaking her daughter's shoulder.

When she got no response, she turned back to us, smiled, gave us an expectant look and began singing. "Happy Birthday to you."

"Happy Birthday to you," Grant, Reiny, and Palmer joined in.

"Happy Birthday, dear Olivia," by that time I think everyone was singing except Kaylee who was exuberantly mouthing the words.

Olivia moaned loudly and rolled over, pulling the pillow from her face and glancing up through squinting eyes.

"Happy Birthday to you." We all bellowed the final refrain off-key.

"Mom, what the fuck?" Olivia blurted, sitting up and hugging her pillow to her chest. Her eyes flicked to the rest of us, tallying, perhaps already plotting her revenge.

"Watch your language, young lady," her mother said. "I let you sleep in all morning, but now it's time to celebrate."

"All right," Olivia conceded grudgingly. "Just no more singing until I've had a shower. And I'll do that without an audience, thank you very much."

She rolled out of bed and shuffled past us, the group parting as she went. And I didn't miss the glare she gave me, her eyes saying, "Et Tu, Brute?"

She got her shower, and after that her mom's homemade cinnamon rolls for a late breakfast down in the kitchen.

Then we were all ushered upstairs to the dome by Mrs. Black where there was a table with presents, most of them wrapped in plain white printer paper. There were a few cards too, handmade of course, and I'd added my own item to the table with Kaylee's permission.

I could tell Olivia was both embarrassed and touched as we all sat down in a circle of chairs around her and Kaylee handed her the first card.

"It's from Passion and Samantha," Olivia said as she opened it, her eyes scanning the inside. "It says, 'We're glad you were born. We never would have met without you.'"

"It's true," Passion said. "And we owe you a lot more than that."

"And I want you to know," Samantha said. "I will do everything in my power to get your father's work back for you. Even if it means I have to wait to inherit it, you're getting it back."

"Thank you," Olivia said, setting the card aside.

Next came a card from Reiny, Lonan, and Pete, again handmade with messages from each of them.

Grant's card was next, which she read silently, giving him a tender smile.

Was there something between the two of them? Grant had been a captive with her in the CAMFer compound, and that kind of shared experience created an unbreakable bond. I mean, it was obvious he had a thing for her, but was she into him?

Kaylee handed her another envelope from the hackers with the inscription, "Happy Birthday to The One." Apparently, it was some kind of inside joke.

Then, there was a gift from her mother, meticulously wrapped. Inside was a small painted portrait of Olivia and her dad sitting on a green hillside together bathed in the glow of the setting sun.

"Where did you get this?" she asked, barely choking out the words.

"He made me save it for you," her mother said, tears in her eyes. "He was trying to capture what he thought you'd look like as a grown woman. He hated that he was going to miss that."

"But how did it survive the fire?" Olivia asked.

"I kept it at my office," her mother explained. "I knew you'd find it if I'd kept it at the house. And since then, I've carried it in my purse. I wasn't going to lose it."

"Thank you," Olivia said, a tender, intimate look passing between them.

Kaylee was up again, presenting Olivia with a lumpy, hefty, poorly wrapped present, obviously from her based on the look of utter delight on her face.

"It's from Kaylee," Olivia confirmed, smiling and tearing into the wrapping paper with gusto, revealing the two silver cubes we'd bought from Gordon as well as Kaylee's magic eight ball nestled between them.

Olivia stared down at the gifts in her lap. Then she looked up at Kaylee. "Where did you get these?" she asked, her voice gone cold and hard.

Kaylee took a step back, the smile fading from her face, her eyes latched onto the eight ball.

Shit. This wasn't good.

"Reiny and Lonan's uncle had the cubes," I jumped in, hoping to salvage the moment. "He found them in the desert. And the eight ball displaced with Kaylee and me. She didn't mean to upset you. She's never done a birthday before, so she gave you the things she values most."

"The eight ball displaced with you?" Olivia asked, sounding shocked. "That doesn't make any sense."

Suddenly, Kaylee reached out and touched Olivia's arm, mind-speaking to her.

The ball followed David, Kaylee said, *because you put his memories inside to keep them safe. And I brought you the cubes so you could restore them to him, but something is wrong. The ball has gone all blurry since I wrapped it, and I don't know why.*

"What?" Olivia and I both blurted at the same time.

"What's going on?" Olivia's mother asked in alarm. "What's she saying?"

"She said David's memories are inside the eight ball," Palmer explained. "But something's wrong with it now."

"I knew it!" Passion blurted, looking at Samantha. "I told you there was something weird about that eight ball."

"But I didn't put Marcus's memories in there," Olivia insisted. "I don't know what she's talking about. I pulled that ball from some CAMFer soldier at the Eidolon out of desperation. And when I saw it wasn't a weapon, I tossed it into the river. Oh, shit." Her eyes flashed to me. "You were in the river, and I grabbed for something to save you. To save us."

I found myself staring at the eight ball. Could it be true? Had Olivia somehow preserved my memories and Kaylee and I had been carrying them around with us all this time? If so, did I even want them back—these memories of horrible things? Did I want to remember being someone who'd led his sister and his friends to the slaughter at the hands of the CAMFers? Olivia was obviously a much better leader to them than I'd ever been. And then there was the whole issue of loving her. I had a horrible feeling in the pit of my stomach that maybe I'd been using her. What if that's what I remembered? What if that's the person I became again when those memories were restored?

"Kaylee, what do you mean they've gone blurry?" Palmer asked.

The ball doesn't look right, Kaylee said, taking it out of Olivia's hand and turning it this way and that. *Something is distorting its resonance. I can't even see if the memories are still there or not.*

"Samantha," Palmer said, turning to her. "What do you hear? Does the ball sound different than before?"

"I—I can't hear it," Samantha said, glancing from Passion to Olivia. "There's been some kind of interference blocking my ability since we came to Umatilla. But this morning when I woke up, the static in my ear had changed. It's louder now and more tonal—like a hum. I was going to tell you after the party," she said to Olivia.

"I've run some scans of the building and surrounding areas," Chase said, "but I haven't found the source of the interference."

"If they don't measure PSS resonance, you wouldn't," Palmer said. "But we might be able to modify something in the CAMFers' arsenal of tools that could trace it."

"I'm sure you could," Mrs. Black stepped up, putting her arm around Kaylee and glancing at Olivia. "But right now, why don't we let Olivia open her last present while I get the cake."

Palmer nodded and sat back down. Olivia set the cubes on the present table and Kaylee laid the eight ball next to them. Mrs. Black nodded, smiling at everyone, and left to retrieve the cake while Olivia picked up the large flat package wrapped in black plastic garbage bags. I guess we all just wanted to guard that one bastion of normalcy, to sit and enjoy a birthday party like normal everyday people.

"That's from Kaylee and me both," I said as Olivia began to unwrap the painting. "I found it in the desert, near the compound's old location. I guess it never displaced."

Olivia pulled away the last layer of garbage bag and stared at her father's portrait of Kaylee.

Then she looked up, pinning me with her eyes, some deep, indiscernible emotion swimming in them. "Thank you," she said, her voice breaking a little. "Thank you both." She smiled at Kaylee.

After that, it was one of those awkward moments at a party when the hostess has stepped out and nobody knows exactly what to do. T-dog and Chase tried to lighten the mood by recounting one of their humorous hacking adventures, but it quickly became clear the rest of us didn't have enough technical knowledge to understand most of it, let alone the punchline.

When ten minutes or so had passed, and Olivia's mom still hadn't returned with the cake, Passion and Samantha went off to see what was taking her so long.

The rest of us got up, stretched our legs, and made small talk.

I don't know if I heard the yelling and pounding of footsteps first, or if Palmer did, but I saw him reach for his gun as I turned toward the sound.

Passion and Samantha came charging through the door and it banged shut behind them.

"She's gone," Passion panted, looking terrified "Olivia's mom is gone."

"What do you mean she's gone?" Olivia asked, pale as a ghost.

"There are signs of a struggle in the kitchen," Samantha said. "The cake is smeared all over and there are boot prints in the icing."

"Was there any blood?" Palmer asked, putting his gun away, but I could still tell he was wired for combat.

"I don't think so," Passion shook her head. "We didn't see any."

"Good." Palmer turned to Chase. "Whoever took her, they're probably still on the Hold side. Get to the security room, check all the camera feeds, and try to get a visual. Marcus and Lonan, you're coming to the armory with me. Every one of you should have been armed a long time ago. Peter and Reiny, I want you in the infirmary working on some kind of sedative or lachrymatory agent we could use to gas a room. T-dog, as soon as we're gone, lock the dome down tight. The rest of you stay here and make yourselves useful. This dome is still the most secure location in the compound."

Mike, I can find her faster than the cameras, Kaylee mind-spoke. *You know I can.*

"No," Palmer snapped at her. "It's too dangerous."

But she was already moving, running toward the door of the dome leading to the Hold side.

It was closed, but she didn't bother opening it. She just faded to a pale blue outline and passed right through, disappearing from sight.

32

KAYLEE

I hadn't waited my whole life to be reunited with my mother, only to have someone snatch her away from me. This compound was my home. My realm. In the few weeks after I'd discovered my ability to phase through solid objects, I'd explored both sides thoroughly, and I'd done most of it at night while avoiding the camera feeds. Ultimately, though, I suppose, that's what had gotten me in trouble. At some point, the CAMFers must have caught me on camera and told Dr. Fineman. That is when I'd become too much of a liability for them to keep around.

Now, they'd taken my mother. At least, someone had, and my ability was our best chance for finding her as quickly as possible, no matter what Mike said.

So, I disobeyed him.

I ran for the dome door and phased through it.

First, I went to the kitchen, but I found nothing but smeared cake and a few boot prints, just as Passion and Samantha had described.

After that, it only took me about ten minutes to search the entire Hold side. I stuck my head in every room, every closet, every nook and cranny. It's amazing how fast you can move through a building when walls and doors and floors are no longer barriers.

But my mother and whoever had taken her were nowhere to be found.

I even stuck my head out one of the outer doors, but all of them were heavily alarmed and we'd heard nothing, no evidence that someone might have escaped through one. No, they had to be inside still, but where?

There was only one logical explanation—if they weren't on the Hold side, somehow they'd made it to the CAMFer side. Perhaps, when we'd all been paying attention to Olivia opening that last present, my mother's captor had dragged her through the dome without being seen.

I flew back toward the dome, phasing through everything in my path.

When I slipped through the door, I caught the quick look of surprise on my sister and her friends' faces as I whipped by, passing through to the CAMFer side. They would understand what that meant. They would have Chase look on this side now, and Mike, Lonan, and David wouldn't be far behind me.

I moved methodically and carefully, phasing from room to room and floor to floor. The CAMFers had more underground levels than The Hold. The building went darker and deeper, and there were more places to hide like the prison blocks and the morgue.

I'd been to the morgue before, once, when one of the CAMFers had told me my sister had killed someone. I'd phased there that night and found an old cut up man in a metal drawer. Of course, it was obvious to me right away that he hadn't been killed by Olivia's PSS. He'd been killed by his own. Then, much later in Gordon's house, I'd felt his resonance again, pulsing from a box in the den. When I'd snuck into that room and gripped that knife, I'd finally understood what had happened. Dr. Fineman had warped it's resonance so much, it had turned on its owner.

No, my sister wasn't a killer. Nor was I.

Even so, as I phased into the lowest level of the CAMFer compound, I took out that knife—the one Gordon had found in the desert—the dangerous, twisted thing from inside Major Tom—and I slipped it up my right sleeve, the handle firmly cupped in my palm the way Mike had taught me to hold a knife. As long as it had contact with me, it would phase with me, and back again.

I checked all the cells, quickly, efficiently. And then I heard muffled voices drifting from down the hall. A softer voice, pleading. A deeper voice, responding.

I raced down the corridor as fast as I could, and stood outside the morgue, pressing my ear against its door.

"If your minus bitch of a daughter doesn't stop whatever it is she's doing, I'm gonna kill you," the deep voice said. "Do you want to die, or are you gonna help me stop her?"

"I wouldn't help you, even if I could," my mother replied, her voice soft and strained, but strong. "I've never been able to make my daughter do anything, so good luck with that."

"You think this is a joke?" the deep voice asked, vicious and angry. "Let me prove to you how serious I am."

I heard a scuffle of movement and a whimper of pain.

I didn't think.

I felt no fear.

I phased through the door and flew at the back of the man looming over my mother, my knife raised.

I don't know how he knew I was coming, but he did. Just as I changed to solid form, he turned, putting up his right arm to block my blow, and I saw the knife in his left hand, sweeping up toward my belly.

"Kaylee!" my mother cried.

I reacted just in time. His arm and his knife went through me, his momentum carrying him staggering to my right and crashing into the metal morgue drawers built into the wall, something strapped to his back clanging against them.

I went solid and sank my knife into his side.

He cried out and swung toward me, but I was already gone, a mere wisp in the air, a ghost of a girl hanging between him and my mother.

I could see the absolute terror in his eyes as they took in my ethereal form. I had seen him before, of course, my sister's cruel guard, Anthony, though he'd lost a hand since then. He was afraid of me, and that was good. So afraid, in fact, that he stumbled back, clutching at the knife in his side and pressing himself against the crumbling cement wall, stumbling on a fallen stone rather than take his eyes from me.

I was completely unarmed. Still, he'd literally have to go through me to get to my mother now, and I doubted he was willing to do that.

Suddenly, Mike, Lonan, and David were at the door, rushing in and pointing guns at him. Behind them, in the hallway, I could see my sister, her frightened eyes taking it all in.

"Drop the weapon," Mike yelled. "Put your hands up."

Anthony slowly raised his arms and let his knife drop to the floor.

"Search him," Mike told Lonan. Then he turned to David and said, "Help Mrs. Black. Get her out of here."

He has a weapon on his back, I told Mike, returning to material form as David came and helped my mother up. She was bleeding from a shallow cut on her neck and another on her cheek, but other than that, she seemed uninjured. The two of them headed toward the door and slipped out into the hallway where my sister put her arm around our mother and led her away.

"Check his back," Mike relayed to Lonan. "Kaylee says he has a weapon there."

Lonan had already deposited several more knives on the floor, but when he grabbed Anthony to turn him around, Anthony didn't budge.

"Don't be a fool," Mike warned, moving closer, his gun raised, as Lonan tried to yank Anthony from the wall a second time to no avail.

"I'm—not—doing it," Anthony grimaced, clutching at the knife in his side which seemed to be sinking deeper and deeper. "Something—is—pulling me," he gasped, obviously straining to move away under his own power.

"He's telling the truth," Lonan confirmed, trying to slip his hand between Anthony and the wall. "It's this thing on his back. It's adhered to the stone or something."

"Please," Anthony panted. "Pull—the knife—out."

Lonan reached down and clutched the handle of the knife, his muscles straining.

Slowly and bloodily, inch by inch, the knife emerged from Anthony's wound, but as soon as Lonan had it free, it sprang from his hand, flying through the air and sticking point first into an eroding crack between two cement blocks just to the right of Anthony's head. And then it began to drill, carving its way into the wall, mortar dust crumbling as it went.

"What the fuck?" Mike stared at it. "Kaylee?" he turned to me, an eyebrow raised.

It's not me, I said. *I have no idea why it's doing that. But the knife's resonance is blurry, just like the eight ball's, except much worse.* I could see that even as it carved deeper and deeper, the blade spiraling into the hole it was making.

"Please," Anthony begged. "Get me off this wall."

"Plug his wound with this," Mike told Lonan, tossing him a handkerchief from his pocket. "Then cut that strap and let's get him out of here."

Lonan handed the handkerchief to Anthony to apply to his own wound. Then he picked up a knife from the floor and sliced carefully at the black plastic, freeing Anthony from the wall.

When they moved away, I gasped.

Embedded into the deteriorating cement was the PSS knife Dr. Fineman had created out of Passion's blades. I could see it was the knife even though its resonance was blurred and distorted. But that wasn't what surprised me the most. Leaking through the cracks and holes in the wall surrounding it, was a radiant blue glow, a spectrum of PSS resonance like I'd never seen before.

There's something on the other side, I told Mike, taking a step toward that light. *It's pulling the knives.* Was it my imagination or was it pulling me too? My body wanted to go there as if the space behind the wall was my new center of gravity.

"Stay back," Mike warned, grabbing my arm. "We need to get out of here."

Lonan shoved Anthony in front of him, out into the corridor, and Mike pulled me gently with him, closing the door behind us.

As soon as it was closed, I felt better. At least like I wasn't going to fling myself through that wall toward whatever was beyond it.

"Let's go," he said, pointing us down the hallway. "We'll deal with whatever the hell that was once we secure the prisoner."

33

OLIVIA

"**H**e's a young CAMFer guard named Anthony," Mike explained. He'd gathered us in the library for a debriefing, except for my mother and Reiny who were in the infirmary. Oh, and Pete and Lonan, who were tending to her kidnapper's wounds. "And as far as we can tell," Mike continued, "he was working alone."

"But how did he get in?" Passion asked anxiously.

"We think he was unconscious and was never displaced," Mike said. "Just like Pete."

"You mean he's been here the entire time we have?" Samantha asked, appalled.

"It appears so," T-dog said. "If he'd come in one of the doors, it would have set off an alarm. And being a guard, he knew how to avoid the cameras. That's why we never saw him on the CAMFer security feeds."

"Yes, but how did he get into the Hold side?" Grant asked. "You changed the code to the dome door and we've kept it locked."

Marcus and I exchanged a look, guilt flashing across his face.

"That would be my fault," he admitted. "I accidentally left it open for a short time last night."

"I'm as much to blame as he is," I jumped in. "I couldn't sleep, and I know it was stupid, but I went over there. He was just following me to make sure I was okay."

"Yeah, but I should have closed and locked the door," Marcus insisted.

I could feel the rest of them staring at us, hypothesizing about what Marcus and I had been doing over on the CAMFer side together in the middle of the night. But they couldn't be more wrong. That was the last place either of us would go for a private make-out session or romantic rendezvous. Still, my face began to flush, betraying my innocence, and Marcus was looking anywhere but at me.

"Who's at fault is immaterial," Mike said. "Drawing him out was the best thing that could have happened, given the circumstances. We'll put him in one of the CAMFer cells for now, and he'll have to be guarded. But we're going to have to decide what to do with him long term."

Did Mike mean kill him? Even after everything Anthony had done to me, I wasn't sure I could condone that.

"But the more pressing issue is what's happening down in the morgue," Mike said, just as a loud clunk emanated from the area of the present table, echoing through the dome. Everyone turned, startled. Mike reached for his gun, and Grant and Marcus bumped into each other trying to step in front of me and my sister.

I pushed between them and walked over to the table. The magic eight ball was on the floor. It had rolled off and landed on the tile below, its flattened answer window face down. Based on all the laws of gravity and physics I knew, it should have stayed right there. But it didn't. Instead, it moved, tipping up on its rounded surface and rolling away across the floor.

"What the fuck?" I heard Chase murmur behind me.

I followed the eight ball. So did everyone else.

When it got to the threshold of the dome door leading to the CAMFer side, it rolled up against it. Then wobbled back, rolling to tap against it again. And again. And again.

It was eerie, like something out of a horror movie, making the skin crawl at the back of my neck.

It's being pulled, like the knives were downstairs, Kaylee said.

"Olivia," Mike said, staring at me and I followed his gaze, looking down, to see the dog tags hovering in the air just below my chin.

It hadn't been the skin of my neck crawling. It had been the chain dragging against it as the tags lifted, straining toward the door.

I grasped them and stuffed them down inside my shirt. They stayed, but I could feel them trembling against my skin.

The tags are blurry too, Kaylee said.

"Do you have your father's stone?" Mike asked me.

"Yeah," I nodded, reaching into my pocket and pulling it out.

As soon as I did, it flew out of my hand and hit the door with a loud thunk, sticking mid-way up, as if magnetized.

"What the hell is going on?" Marcus asked.

I went up to the door and grabbed the rock, pulling it off, though it was like fighting a strong magnet. I held the rock out to Kaylee and she nodded. It was blurry too.

"Whatever it is," Mike said, "it's affecting all the artifacts. He turned to Kaylee. "The knife you had down in the morgue—where'd you get it?"

I stole it from Gordon, she said, giving me a worried look. *But it came from a man named Major Tom.*

Just hearing that name sent a shock wave through me.

"You stole it?" Marcus asked, surprised. "Why?"

It wasn't safe for Gordon, Kaylee said. *The artifacts— they only listen to Olivia and me.*

"Well," Mike said, "that explains why it stuck to the wall. Something is down there distorting and attracting the artifacts."

"Then we need to know what it is," I said, turning to Chase. "Can you pull up blueprint files for the dome and the compound? Maybe there's a hidden room or passage we weren't aware of."

"Or it could be something that was here at Umatilla," T-dog pointed out. "I can look up blueprints and layout images for the depot centering on this location."

"Excellent," Mike said. "And I think Kaylee and I should go back down and have a look."

I don't want to, Kaylee said, sounding terrified. *It was pulling me too. It still is. But it's not as strong up here as it was down there. It could be affecting our PSS.* She glanced at my ghost hand. *I think, maybe, Olivia's hand is beginning to blur.*

My hand looked fine to me but, obviously, Kaylee could see something I couldn't.

"What about the rest of us?" Mike asked her. "Kaylee can see everyone's PSS," he explained. "External and internal."

My sister's list of talents never ceased. Was there anything PSS related she couldn't do? I seriously doubted anyone in our group would bat an eye if Mike suddenly claimed Kaylee could spin PSS into gold and poop PSS rainbows. Fuck. Was I jealous of her? Maybe. My ghost hand had once been able to tell if someone had internal PSS. It used to want to reach into people and touch what was inside of them. But not anymore. Not after Anthony.

Everyone else looks normal, Kaylee said, after a quick inspection. *And it's too hard to see myself, but I feel it. It's pulling me. And it may be doing something to the rest of you I can't see.*

"When you were all down there saving Mrs. Black," Samantha said, "the sound in my ear changed again, almost like notes being added to an underlying chord. Maybe, if I got closer, I might be able to understand what I'm hearing."

"I could go with her," Grant said. "We know I don't have PSS, so I should be fine."

"Okay," Mike agreed. "Grant, Samantha, and I will go down to the morgue. Kaylee, you keep an eye on any changes to Olivia's PSS and the artifacts. And put them in a sealed container as far from the CAMFer side as possible. Maybe distance will reduce the impact."

"I have a small faraday cage in the van," Chase said. "I have no idea if it will block what's happening, but we can put them in that and Kaylee will still be able to see them. And the van is on the far side of The Hold compound, so we'll probably be safest over there anyway."

"Excellent." Mike stuck his hand in his pocket and pulled out his matchbook. "Put this in there too." He tossed it to Chase. "Let's go." He gestured for Grant and Samantha to follow him, then turned back to his brother and added, "And do that blueprint search like Olivia suggested."

It hadn't been a suggestion. It had been an order.

Of course, now that Mike was here, he'd naturally take charge again.

Still, I had a good plan and I truly believed it could work. I would not give it up.

We should put the cubes in the cage too, Kaylee said, running to the table to get them, and I didn't miss the worried look she cast at Marcus.

My sister had certainly dropped a bomb when she'd revealed that I'd somehow captured Marcus's memories in the eight ball and the cubes could be used to restore them. But not now, not with all this going on, and probably not afterwards either.

I hadn't missed the look on Marcus's face.

He didn't want his memories back.

34

MIKE PALMER

'd been in the dome one day and things had already gone to shit. Anthony kidnapping Mrs. Black had only been the beginning. I'd been an idiot not to arm everyone the minute I'd entered the compound. If anything happened to Chase, our parents would never forgive me. Well, that was already true, but they would hate me even more.

Thankfully, Anthony hadn't taken Chase. He'd taken Olivia's mother, probably because she'd been alone and injured, and he was a coward. That boy hadn't learned a thing since I'd goaded him into getting his hand cut off. Some people never learned.

And when Kaylee had rushed through the wall of the dome after him, unarmed, I'd feared the worst.

She didn't have the skills or guts to face an opponent like that. Or so I'd thought. Imagine my surprise when we'd arrived at the morgue door to find she'd pinned the bastard to the wall.

Unfortunately, it was no ordinary wall.

So, now, here we were. Grant and I had guns, but Samantha had refused to take one. I'd let that slide since she wasn't a great shot anyway. Besides, whatever was happening to the artifacts and Olivia's PSS, I doubted firepower was going to be the solution. Still, having a gun in my hand always made me feel better.

I opened the door and stepped into the morgue. Samantha and Grant followed me.

The wall was a crumbled mess, stones and mortar piled on the floor in front of a gaping hole about the size of a small window. It was at chest level, and there was no sign of Major Tom's knife or the Fineman's PSS-severing device, though a pulsing, blue glow was pouring through that hole.

Samantha stepped toward it and I held out my hand to stop her. "Listen first," I said. "What do you hear?"

She tilted her PSS ear toward the wall. "An underlying hum," she said. "That's the constant, almost like the bass. There's something faint and high-pitched on top of that. And then two more tones, more mid-range. By the acoustics, I'd say there's a room behind that wall, and something inside is the source of what I've been hearing."

"Grant, go take a look." I motioned the boy forward.

Grant crossed the room and stuck his head through the hole.

"It's hard to see," he said, leaning further in, his shoulders brushing the edges. "There are a bunch of pipes here, just inside, and some kind of big tank directly to the right. That's where the glow is coming from. The room is large and circular. I think we could squeeze through if we opened this wall up a bit more."

"Any sign of the artifacts?" I asked.

"Not that I can see," he said, pulling his head out.

"Okay." I slipped my gun into its holster and crossed to Grant. "Samantha, you watch the top of the wall near the ceiling. If you see any sagging, let us know. I don't think this is a supporting wall, but better safe than sorry." I grabbed a cement block and pulled, and Grant quickly joined me. In about ten minutes, we had the opening big enough for us to pass through one at a time.

"I'll go first," I told them. "Samantha, you come second. Grant will take up the rear."

I pulled out my weapon and climbed through the hole, immediately confronted by a series of large pipes. To my right was the curved wall of the tank glowing with PSS, and I had a sinking feeling in the pit of my stomach that my day had just gotten a whole lot shittier.

I climbed over and under pipes, and Samantha and Grant followed. Some of the gaps were a tight squeeze but eventually we were all through, standing in a large round room, empty except for the three dead bodies lying on the floor.

"Oh my God," Samantha whispered. "Are they dead?"

"Yes," I answered, scanning the room, assessing quickly that there was only one door. I crossed to it, and slowly pulled it open, looking down the long tunnel-like corridor it led to. I didn't hear or see evidence of hostiles, but the tunnel verified what I'd suspected as soon as we'd climbed through the wall. This wasn't a hidden room of the compound. The architecture was different and the tunnel too expansive. This was old Umatilla infrastructure and the compound had landed on top of it. I closed the door. Unfortunately, the locking mechanism was broken, but we should hear someone coming down that tunnel from a fair distance.

"Who are they?" Grant asked, he and Samantha keeping their distance.

"These two are military." I pointed at the bodies closest to us, stepping carefully over the nearest one, my boot squishing in what was undoubtedly brain matter. "They were each shot in the head from behind at close range." I was glad it was dark, so Grant and Samantha couldn't see the gory mess that had made. I walked over to the third body, a woman. She was lying face down in a pool of blood near some kind of machine built next to the tank. She'd been shot in the chest, instead of the head.

I rolled the stiffened body over and Muriel Peretti's pale dead eyes stared back at me.

I hadn't seen her for over thirty years, and her face was bloated and purple with lividity, but it was definitely her. Muriel had briefed me on Umatilla and what to expect right before I'd gone into the facility with Gordon's NAM group. She hadn't been FBI. She'd worked for the government as head of some department at the depot. I didn't remember much of what she'd told me, but I was sure she'd neglected to mention the possibility of temporal displaced to Norway and the global contamination of human DNA.

If Muriel had come here with military backing, that did not bode well for us. Then again, it hadn't boded well for her either. Whatever she'd been trying to do, someone hadn't liked it. At least now I knew the military had arrived, and it looked like they were trying to be covert, which could play to our advantage. If I had to guess, I'd say they'd come down here to get rid of this tank and cover their tracks.

"Do you know her?" Samantha asked. She'd walked over and was staring down at Muriel.

"No." I stood up, turning to the blinking machine next to the tank. "But whoever she was, I think she was working with this when she got shot."

"It looks like it's on," Grant said, joining us. "Maybe that's what started the change Sam heard last night."

"The timing for the bodies is about right," I said. "I'd say they've been dead about twelve hours."

"I don't see an off button," Sam said, stepping up to the machine. "Just a bunch of meters and sliders, almost like a soundboard."

"Is that what the hum is coming from?" I asked.

"No." She shook her head. "It's coming from the tank. The extra notes too. But this machine has something to do with it." She reached out a tentative hand for one of the sliders.

"Don't touch it yet," I said. "Let's have a closer look at the tank first."

"Yeah, okay." she nodded, putting her hand on the tank and walking along its smooth curve. "It's vibrating," she noted.

Although the tank appeared to be metal, the PSS glow from within somehow permeated it, giving the impression of a translucent tank full of swirling gasses. Whatever this tank had originally been made of, it had been changed by the contents inside of it. And I was pretty sure I knew what those contents were. The question was what was being done to them? And could we, or should we, stop it?

Yes, this was shaping up to be a shitty, shitty day.

"Hey, I found something," Samantha called from the other side of the tank, back near the pipes and the hole in the wall. "It looks like it has been damaged over here."

Grant and I both walked over.

"It's hard to see in the dark, but put your hand here and feel." She pointed to a lower portion of the tank hidden in shadow.

I reached for it first, my fingers easily finding the small divot in the tank.

"It feels like a bullet hole," I said, pulling my fingers away and letting Grant have a turn. But that didn't make sense. If a stray bullet had struck the tank when Muriel and her men had been killed, it would have ruptured the tank or ricocheted off, not left a perfect, bullet-shaped indentation.

"And it's not the only one," Samantha said, reaching higher up and to her left. "Feel here."

I reached up and felt a strange outline, long and thick on one end, with a ridge in the middle, then tapering to a fine point on the other end.

"It's shaped like a knife," Samantha said.

"Yes, it is." I pulled my hand away, moving to give Grant room.

"There's one more," she said, pointing further to my left. That indentation was bathed in enough light that I could clearly see the strange outline of the PSS-severing knife Fineman had created out of Passion's blades.

"Hey, guys," Grant said, staring at the portion of the tank in front of his face. "I think I just saw something floating around in there."

"Where?" I asked, and Samantha looked too, both of us scanning the swirling blue vapors.

And then I saw it. Major Tom's knife. It floated toward me, spinning end over end and then disappeared again, fading away as quickly as it had appeared.

"Did you see that?" Samantha asked. "How did it get in there?"

"It phased through the tank just like Kaylee phases through walls," I said. "I think both the knives did. Whatever's in there sucked them in."

And the bullet shape? It could have just been a manufacturing glitch in the forging of the tank, an anomaly having nothing to do with what was happening now, but I knew it wasn't.

This tank full of PSS gas was attracting artifacts, and a bullet-shaped artifact certainly existed. Jason's bullet. Which meant Jason had been down here or close enough that the pull of the tank had gotten the better of him.

I turned and looked at the three bodies.

No, the kid was a decent shot, but there was no way he could have pulled this off by himself.

"But how could it do that?" Samantha asked, backing away from the tank.

"I don't know," I said, because I didn't. We needed more information and I was hoping Chase and T-dog had found something. If not, bringing Kaylee down to look at the tank might be our best bet, even if it was affecting her. But first, there was a little matter of getting rid of the corpses.

"We need to clear this room," I said. "Samantha, I want you to go to the staff suites on the second floor and grab some sheets and towels. Get as many as you can so we can mop up this blood and wrap the bodies. Oh, and see if you can find some rubber gloves and bleach too."

"What are we going to do with the bodies?" she asked.

"Well, conveniently, the room next door is a morgue," I pointed out. "Once they're wrapped, Grant and I will carry them over and put them in the drawers." Hopefully, we could get the bodies through the pipes. We probably could. Besides, it wasn't like bending them a little was going to hurt anything.

35

OLIVIA

"I found it," T-dog said, turning his monitor toward the middle of the van where Kaylee, Marcus, Passion and I were squeezed in around him and Chase. There was a roughly-sketched blueprint on the screen, looking more like a labyrinth than any building plan I'd ever seen. "This circular room in the center is some kind of storage facility from the old Umatilla days, and there's a system of underground tunnels all around it, leading to many of the bunkers. None of this was on the original blueprint. It was added during the decommissioning. I really had to dig to find this image, and there are a shit-ton of encrypted files associated with it, but I have a program working on them already. Whatever the government was doing down there, they really didn't want anyone to find it."

"So, the compound landed practically on top of that room," Chase said. "Tee, pull up a blueprint of the compound's lowest level and superimpose it onto that one to give us a better visual."

"Got it," T-dog tapped his keyboard and the image on the monitor changed, showing the CAMFer compound's basement floor over the top of the labyrinth image. "That's the morgue," T-dog pointed to a small square room now butted right up against the curving wall of the circular one. "They definitely made contact. That's probably why the morgue wall crumbled."

No. Kaylee shook her head emphatically. *The artifacts pushed through the wall, or they were pulled. Something is down there acting on them.*

"Both could be true," Chase pointed out.

"Um, this is weird," T-dog said. "I was running a basic image scan of the blueprint of those tunnels and I got a hit on one of the external camera feeds."

"Are you sure?" Chase asked. "That doesn't make sense."

"I know," T-dog said. "Let me pull it up. It could be a glitch in my search program and maybe I can—" He stopped, staring at his screen. "What the fuck? Look at this. It's some couple holding up signs like those sappy videos on the internet."

It wasn't some couple. It was Jason Williams. And he was with a girl, an athletic-looking red-head wearing a black NASCAR outfit or something, and there was a small motorcycle in the background. T-dog had frozen the feed on a picture of Jason holding up a piece of cardboard with a crude drawing on it—a drawing of the blueprints of the Umatilla tunnel labyrinth and the round room T-dog had just shown us. In the corner of the picture, I could see more cardboard signs on the ground at Jason's feet, all with writing on them.

"Rewind it," I said, standing up and leaning over T-dog. "That's Jason Williams."

"That's Jason?" Chase peered at the screen. "Are you sure?"

"Yes, I'm sure. Find the beginning," I said, gripping T-dog's shoulder.

"She's right," Marcus said. "That's definitely him."

"Okay, okay, give me a second," T-dog said, clicking his mouse and scrolling the video back five minutes. "This is where it starts." He clicked play.

On the monitor, I could see the muddy camps in the near distance, looking beaten and bedraggled after last night's storm. The motorcycle appeared, weaving between two tents and heading straight for the camera. The red-haired girl was driving and Jason was riding behind her, one arm slung around her waist while the other clutched a stack of cardboard signs. They parked the bike, climbed off, and Jason handed the signs to the girl. Then he looked up at the camera, waving exaggeratingly, like a castaway on a deserted island flagging down a passing plane.

The girl handed him the first sign and he held it up. LAST NIGHT I SAW FINEMAN WITH SOLDIERS, it read in sloppy black-marker lettering.

"He's warning us," Marcus said from behind me.

IN A ROOM UNDER THE COMPOUND, the next sign read.

"Fuck!" I exhaled. Of course, this was Fineman's doing. I thought I'd gotten rid of the man, but no such luck.

HE TURNED ON A MACHINE NEXT TO A TANK, the third sign said.

AND THEN HE SHOT 3 OF THEM.

"Shot who?" Passion blurted, her voice full of panic. "Mike, Grant, and Samantha are down there right now."

"This is from hours ago and he said he saw it last night," T-dog reminded her. "I think he means Fineman shot three soldiers."

On the screen, the next sign came up. It was the hand-drawn map that had triggered T-dog's search, and smack in the middle was a round room with a large red X marking its position.

Then came the final sign. TELL MIKE YOU ARE IN DANGER. Jason held that sign up the longest, and we could see the girl talking. Then, they both picked up the tossed signs, got back on the bike, and rode away, disappearing from view between the tents.

"So, whatever is happening downstairs, Fineman caused it," I concluded.

"I think Mike and his group should have been back by now," Chase said, sounding worried.

"I'll go check on them," T-dog volunteered, getting out of his seat, and we all shuffled aside so he could get to the door.

"At least we know Jason is okay," Marcus said. "I felt a little shitty leaving him out there."

"He didn't look like he was doing too badly," I said, trying to stay calm. "That red-head is pretty cute."

"Hey, what are you all doing in here?" Pete asked, sticking his head in the partially-open sliding door. We'd closed it all the way at first, but it had gotten stuffy way too quickly in the crowded little van. "When I didn't find anyone in the dome, I got a little freaked out," he admitted. "Did I miss something?"

We caught him up to speed on our discovery about the morgue wall, the room behind it, Jason's message, and the changes happening to the artifacts and my PSS. "We've put the artifacts in that faraday cage." I pointed to the small screened box near my feet. "And this van is supposed to protect Kaylee and me. Maybe. We hope."

"If your PSS is being affected," Pete said, "Reiny and I should run some tests. All the PSS research equipment from our study is still here. A workup on everyone wouldn't take long. We might catch something Kaylee missed or can't see."

"That's a good idea," I said. "What about Anthony?"

"He's patched up," Pete said, "and I gave him some pain medicine that should sedate him for a while. Even so, I left Lonan outside the cell. Mike didn't want him left alone."

"I wasn't asking if I should send him a get-well card," I clarified. "I meant can you run the tests on him too? He was down there in the morgue longer than most of us." Wouldn't it be ironic if Anthony, who hated everything and everyone having to do with PSS, actually had it and we could prove it to him?

"That shouldn't be a problem," Pete said. "The equipment is fairly portable so we can take it down there. I'm curious to know myself, given that his step-brother manifests PSS outwardly, and there's almost always a genetic link, but the fact that—"

"Wait a minute," I said, grabbing Pete's arm. "What the hell are you talking about? What step-brother?"

"I thought you knew." Pete looked from me to the rest of the group and back again, his Adam's apple bobbing up and down. "Anthony and Jason share the same father. Mr. James has familial records on all of you. But we know the link for PSS came from Jason's mother, not his father, and since Anthony was staunchly on the CAMFer side, we never had the opportunity to test him or access his medical records."

"Anthony and Jason are brothers," I said, turning to Marcus. "Did you know this?"

"I don't think so." Marcus shrugged. "At least not that I remember."

Right. Marcus had no clue if he'd known or not. The old Marcus had kept many secrets from me, and this could have been one of them. But I guess it didn't really matter now.

"How long will the testing take for all of us?" I asked, turning back to Pete. "And how long for the results?"

"A few hours at the most" he said.

"Then do Anthony first, but don't tell him what it's for. Let's save the fact that he probably has PSS for later."

"You do realize he won't believe us, no matter what we show him?" Pete asked, his brow creasing. "Anthony would sooner cut off his other hand than believe he has

PSS. Some people can't change, or they won't, even given overwhelming evidence that they already have. Even when they see it with their own eyes."

"Maybe," I said. "Did you know Kaylee can see internal PSS?"

"No," Pete said, glancing at her. "I wasn't aware of that."

"Well, she can. And if we could give everyone Kaylee-vision, if they could see all the people with internal PSS—their mothers and fathers, their spouses and children, their siblings and best friends—not just those few of us with it on the outside, I think things would change."

"You might be right." Pete nodded. "But we can't make people see. We can only present them with the truth. How's your mom doing?"

"I don't know." I pulled the van door open wider. "I should go check on her."

"I can do that and come back and give you a full report," Pete offered.

"Mike wanted us to stay here," Passion reminded me.

"I'll be fine," I said, hopping out. "The infirmary isn't much closer to the morgue than the van is."

"I'll come with you," Pete said, "and grab Reiny so we can set up those tests."

"Do you mind if I come?" Marcus asked, looking to me for permission. "I'm a little claustrophobic."

"Sure," I said. I hadn't known that about him. He'd never told me. I looked at Kaylee, thinking she might want to come too, but she appeared deep in thought with a strange expression on her face.

"I'll stay with her," Passion said. "We can keep an eye on the artifacts."

"Thanks," I told Passion. "Let's go," I said to Pete and Marcus, leading the way.

36

DAVID MARCUS

Olivia's mom was going to be okay. Reiny had stitched her cuts and also discovered that her leg wound had opened back up. So, it had required new bandages, some pain killer, and apparently a sedative, because Mrs. Black was out like a light, stretched out on one of the gurneys snoring lightly.

"She's fine, but she needed some rest," Reiny explained to Olivia as soon as we walked into the infirmary. "All this has been hard on her."

"I know," Olivia sighed, slumping into a chair, her expression awash with guilt. "She never should have come with me. She would have been safe back in Portland."

"No mother is safe when her children are in danger," Reiny said. "She's as much a part of this as you and Kaylee are." She turned to Pete and asked, "How's our other patient?"

"He'll live," Pete said. "Lonan is guarding him. And Mike, Grant, and Samantha went to check the morgue. Apparently, there's evidence that something down there is affecting the artifacts, and Olivia's PSS and Fineman is somehow involved. So, I'd like to run some tests on everyone and see what we can find out. I'd really appreciate your help."

"Of course," Reiny said. "You two okay to stay here for a bit?" She asked me and Olivia.

We both nodded and the two of them left, hand-in-hand, Pete beginning to fill Reiny in on all she'd missed.

I turned to see Olivia watching them go, a half-wistful, half-envious look on her face. Then she noticed me watching her, and she frowned. "Did you know they were in love?" she asked, "back on the farm when they revived you?"

"I had no idea," I said, "but honestly, I was a little self-absorbed."

Suddenly, her face broke into a smile, transforming her. And then she was laughing, not a dainty fake giggle, or with her hand shyly over her mouth like some girls, but a gut-busting, head-thrown-back, complete-body guffaw.

I couldn't resist. Before I knew it, I was laughing too, both of us eyeing her mother, wondering how our uproarious laughter wasn't waking her, and that made us laugh even more as we tried, unsuccessfully, to suppress it.

Finally, I was able to stop and catch my breath long enough to pant out, "What's—so—funny?"

To which she laughed even harder, but finally choked out. "You—said—*was*."

It took me a moment to get what she was referring to. I'd said, "I was a little self-absorbed," in the past tense, and that's what we'd been laughing at for ten minutes. Because she thought I was self-absorbed still. Or always.

I stopped laughing and stared at her.

She stopped and stared right back.

"Listen," I said, sitting down across from her and trying hard not to sound defensive. "I'm sorry I'm not the guy you remember from before. I lost my memory, and it sucks, but there's not really anything I can do about it."

"Maybe not," she said, unable to mask the disappointment in her voice. "Even if your memories are in the eight ball, they may be messed up now. Believe me, I understand there's no going back to the way things were. For either of us."

I looked down at my hands, clenched in my lap. I really didn't want to have this conversation. How could I tell a girl I barely knew that I was terrified of finding out I hadn't loved her? And I was terrified of finding out I had. I couldn't. So, I decided to change the subject.

"I'm curious," I said. "What comes after you show that movie? I may not remember you, but I can tell there's way more going on up in that head of yours than you're letting anyone in on."

She frowned at me again. "That's an interesting accusation, especially when everything I know about scheming, I learned from you."

"I guess I was a good teacher then," I said.

"That remains to be seen." She looked at her mom, her expression an unreadable mask. She reached out and took her mother's hand in hers, stroking it gently. "My mother used to be terrified of my ghost hand," she said, but I wasn't sure she was talking to me. It was almost as if she were telling a story to the unconscious woman, or herself. I was merely an afterthought. "I didn't understand back then why she hated me so much, or what I had done to deserve that fear and loathing, so I just threw it right back at her. I made a barrier with it to protect myself, and we both lived inside that barrier together, hurling each other against it in our efforts to escape."

"She obviously adores you now," I said, pulled into her tale. "How could that just change overnight?"

Olivia smiled, a soft, gentle curve of her lips. "It didn't just change overnight," she said. "Our lives had to be utterly destroyed. Everything we thought we knew about ourselves and the people we'd loved and the world we'd lived in and who we really were had to be completely unraveled. It's still unraveling now, and I don't know if it will ever stop. But that process—that horrible, unpredictable, devastating process—changed us. It finally got us working together to break down the fear, rather than trying to break down each other." Olivia looked up now, her eyes capturing mine. "So, my plan is to pull as many people as I can into that unraveling—you, Anthony,

Pete, Reiny, Lonan, Grant, Samantha, Passion, Chase, T-dog, Mike, Kaylee, and all the people camping outside this dome. All the people with PSS all over the world, internal and external, and all the people without it. All the people scrolling the internet, or sitting at home watching television, or lying in the hospital. And all the Holders and CAMFers too. I'm going to confront them with the very things my mother and I have been confronted with, and then I'm going to sit back and see what happens."

"And you don't think that's a little too ambitious?" I asked. "You're talking about changing the world."

"No," she said, staring me down. "The world changes. That is an unavoidable fact. I don't have any illusions about being The Chosen One, I assure you. But maybe, as a group, we can influence the direction of that change. Or maybe we can't. There's really only one way to find out. And since you started me on this great unraveling in the first place, I expect you to help me."

I was surprised at her brashness, and somewhat turned on by it.

"Well, I'm here," I said, smiling. "And I don't really have anything better to do."

"Good." She bestowed another amazing smile on me.

That was the moment I knew I was in trouble. Whatever I'd felt for Olivia Anne Black before, I was definitely intrigued by her now.

37

OLIVIA

"**S**o, Fineman was involved and somehow Jason saw him down there," Mike summarized.

We were back in The Hold's computer lab, against the far wall beyond the van. At least some of us were. Grant had taken a shift guarding Anthony, my mom was still conked out in the infirmary, Chase and T-dog were in the van hacking, and Pete and Reiny were looking over the PSS tests they'd run on everyone an hour ago. But Kaylee, Marcus, Mike, Lonan, Passion, Samantha and I had met for another pow-wow.

"I'm just guessing," Mike went on. "But I think that tank contains a sample of the original PSS gas released during the Umatilla accident thirty-three years ago. The military brought in Fineman and their own scientist to get rid of it—to cover their asses now that so much public attention is centered on the depot. But obviously, there was a disagreement and Fineman won. Which means whatever that machine is doing, it isn't good. I hate to say it, but we need to get Kaylee down there to take a look. She's our best chance at stopping whatever it is doing."

"The machine connected to the tank looks similar to a soundboard," Samantha said. "And I could hear the resonance of the tank and notes that I think might have been the artifacts inside of it. With my ability to hear PSS and Kaylee's ability to see it, we could experiment with the settings of the machine. We might be able to figure out how to shut it off, or at least how to counteract the effects it's having."

"No," Marcus said. "We need to keep Kaylee and Olivia as far away from that thing as possible. Why risk either of them if we don't have to?"

"Because I think we may have to," Pete said, walking up with Reiny, a stack of papers in his hand. "These are the results from the tests we just ran." He looked at Kaylee, then back at me. "Everyone's PSS was normal, internal or external, except for Olivia's, Kaylee's, and Anthony's."

"What's it doing to them?" Mike asked. "Can you tell?"

"We think so," Pete said, putting his nurse face on. "It appears that their PSS is being extracted, much like what a minus meter would do, but more slowly. Our theory is that the machine and tank down there are siphoning the PSS straight out of their bodies.

We can't be sure how long that process will take, but we believe within the next twenty-four hours, the three of them may not be functional anymore."

I didn't know what to say. Despite my noble speech to Marcus earlier about not being The Chosen One and understanding that the world was always changing, I had not seen this turn of events coming. I wasn't even feeling sick. Maybe a little tired and run down, but certainly not like I'd be bedridden in a day or so.

"What do you mean, 'not functional anymore'?" Marcus demanded. "They'll get sick?"

"Yes," Pete nodded. "And if the process isn't stopped and reversed relatively soon," he paused, struggling to voice what I feared was coming, "they'll die."

"Then we need to get them out of here," Marcus said, looking around at the group, his eyes gone wild. "We can sneak them out tonight and take them as far away from this compound and that tank as possible."

"We don't think that would help," Pete said. "And by the time we were far away enough to know for sure, it could be too late. Think of it as someone losing blood from an internal injury. It isn't enough to remove the person from harm and patch them up. You have to figure out the source of the bleeding and stop it, or they can't heal."

"What about my blood?" Passion blurted. "Couldn't we give Kaylee and Olivia a transfusion or something?"

"Possibly," Reiny said, sharing a dire look with Pete. "In fact, we believe the reason the tank isn't affecting the rest of us is because we've had the vaccine made from Passion's blood, and obviously

Grant and T-dog aren't affected because neither of them have PSS."

So, T-dog was one of the rare people without PSS.

"But I never got that vaccine," Marcus said to Reiny. "You said I didn't need it."

"Because you had a full transfusion of Passion's blood in the ambulance after we found you," Reiny explained. "That's how we discovered the protective properties of Passion's plasma in the first place. After we gave it to you, your chest could not be disrupted. I discovered that purely by accident when I dropped my stethoscope into your chest while you were unconscious, and you didn't reboot. Your PSS remained stable. So, we ran some test and confirmed what we'd discovered. As soon as we were sure, your uncle insisted everyone at the farmhouse be given that vaccine, including Olivia's mother when she arrived. I'm pretty sure everyone who worked for him got a dose, and I acquired one for Lonan, just as a precaution, which I gave him later back at the reservation."

Marcus couldn't reboot anymore? He looked as shocked as I was to find that out. His ability had been such a defining aspect of who he was: the boy who died repeatedly but always came back to life. Still, I was happy for him. Now he'd be even harder to kill than he'd been before, without all the inconvenient ten-minute death-naps.

"But that's good, right?" Samantha piped up. "We can give Olivia and Kaylee the vaccine and it will protect them."

"We're afraid that won't work," Pete said. "The vaccine takes twelve to fifteen hours to become effective, and it would be similar to giving someone a vaccine after they'd already contracted the disease. Passion's plasma protects against PSS extraction, it doesn't prevent it once it's already started. And again, there's the urgency issue. The time it would take to see if the vaccine would work may exceed the time we have left."

"You mean the time *we* have left," I said, finally finding my voice. Shit. I was dying. Kaylee and I were dying. Well, and Anthony too, but I didn't give a shit about him.

I looked over at Mike who had been way too quiet for way too long. His face was pale and he looked stunned.

"You're sure you didn't see the effect in Chase?" Mike asked in a hushed voice. "He hasn't had the vaccine."

"He hasn't?" Pete said, shocked. He began shuffling through the paperwork in his hands, finally pulling one sheet out. He scanned it, then handed it to Reiny and she scanned it too.

"We'll have to test him again," Reiny said. "If he's being affected, it hasn't reached a level we can detect yet. We just assumed you'd given him the vaccine."

"No," Mike shook his head. "I didn't have contact with him between the Eidolon and the displacement. And the extra vaccines I had on me in the compound didn't displace with me."

"Wait," I stared at him. "You had this vaccine when Kaylee and I were captives here, and you didn't give it to us?"

"I couldn't," he said, his eyes guilt-ridden despite his protest. "Alex believed the vaccine might disable Kaylee's ability to pass through material objects.

And I couldn't give it to you, or Anthony wouldn't have been able to sever your hand, which was the key to getting you and her out of the CAMFers' grasp."

"Well, that rescue may have been completely pointless if we're going to die in the next twenty-four hours," I said.

"You're not going to die," Marcus insisted, his jaw clenched. "We're going to go down there and turn off that tank."

"It might be the best course of action if it can be done quickly," Pete said. "Anthony shows the most damage, we assume because he was near the tank the longest. Kaylee's is not quite as severe because she was the second most exposed. And Olivia has slightly less damage than Kaylee because she was only downstairs briefly. That could explain why Chase is showing no signs. He's been upstairs, mostly in the van, far from the tank. Based on that, we can assume proximity and duration of exposure play a significate role. Sending Kaylee and Olivia down there would result in more damage to their PSS. But if the end result was figuring out how to stop the process, I believe Passion's blood could counteract it."

"So, it's an all or nothing game," I said. "I suddenly feel very motivated to go down there and turn off that machine."

"Don't be ridiculous," Marcus snapped. "You and Kaylee should stay up here where it's safe. The rest of us can figure out what's going on downstairs."

No, Kaylee said. *Mike and Pete are right. Olivia and I aren't safe, even if we stay upstairs. I will go down and* look at this thing. *I was afraid before, and I'm still afraid, but if it could save us, I must do it.*

"And I'm sure as hell not letting her do it without me," I said, giving Marcus a look.

"Then you'll need to do it soon," Pete said. "And I'd like to take some of Passion's blood so we'll have it ready, as well as give Chase a dose, just in case he hasn't been affected yet. I could even give it to you and Kaylee in hopes that—"

No, Kaylee interrupted. *Not until I've seen the tank. Olivia and I may need our powers. We can't do anything that might impede us.*

I thought for sure Mike would take over then, but he didn't. He still appeared stunned. And the rest of them were looking at me.

"Okay," I said. "Mike, Kaylee, Samantha, Marcus and I will go down to the tank. But I need to arrange a couple of things before we do."

"And we should all eat something first," Passion said. "It's almost dinner time and I don't think any of us have eaten since before the party. Sam and I will go throw some sandwiches together."

The party. Had that really been this morning? It felt like days ago. This couldn't still be my eighteenth birthday—the day I was born and the day I was given a death sentence. I needed to talk to Chase. If I was going to die, we had to release the movie tonight, and I had to sit down with him and Marcus and T-dog and outline the rest of my plan for them step-by-step. Fineman couldn't win. I wouldn't let him.

"Everyone meet in the kitchen in half an hour," I said. "We'll leave from there after we've eaten."

I turned toward the van and suddenly Mike was beside me.

"I can't tell Chase," he said. "He trusted me and this is my fault and I can't tell him he might be dying because of me." I had never seen Mike like this, and it scared me.

"We don't know he's dying," Marcus said gently, coming up and gripping Mike's shoulder. "And you freaking him out about it isn't going to help. Pete will explain it to him when they give him the vaccine. Now, go pull yourself together because we need your head clear and in the game when we go down there."

"Yeah, okay," Mike nodded, focusing on me with clearer eyes. "I'll do everything in my power to keep the three of you safe."

"I know you will," I said, hugging him impulsively. He stiffened at first, but he settled into it, patting me on the back like he was burping a baby. Then he pulled away, rubbing his hand across his face.

"I'm going to give Anthony a quick visit," he said, returning to the hardened Mike I'd always counted on. "He *deserves* to know what that thing down there is doing to him."

"Knock yourself out," I said. "But he won't believe you."

"I can be very convincing," Mike said, turning and walking back toward the dome.

38

JASON

"Jason, wake up," someone said, shaking my shoulder. "The dome is doing something, and I think it might be a response to our message."

I sat up in the camper bed and found Allie standing over me. She looked neat and well-rested. She'd obviously been up for a while and probably out telling everyone she was the newest secret agent of the PSS rebellion. I just hoped her story drew the heat to her and away from me.

"What time is it?" I asked.

"It's around six. Get dressed and come outside." She tossed a shirt at me. "Hurry up." As she opened the camper door, and I got a glimpse of people standing silently looking in the direction of the dome, light flashing across their watching faces before it closed behind her.

I pulled on my shirt, then threw on my boots.

By the time I got outsides and looked toward the dome, it was playing some kind of movie.

"It was running the sky stuff at first, but this is new," she explained.

Once, when I was little and my old man and my ma were actually getting along, we went to an old drive-in, one of the last ones in Texas, before they'd closed it down. Tony and I had sleeping bags in the back of the truck, and my mom had filled a gallon bucket with popcorn and drenched it in butter. We each had our own two-liter of Coke too, and my parents drank beer after beer. I don't remember what the movie was. It wasn't the movie that was important. It was the excitement in the air, and us leaning over the top of the cab, shoulder to shoulder. It was my parents not fighting, and the sea of families just like us parked in their cars, enjoying that one night together.

That was the feeling in the air while the movie on the dome played.

Mostly, I couldn't believe what I was seeing, even though I knew it was true. The captivity of Kaylee. The torture of Marcus. The death of Danielle and everything Olivia had been through. It was almost too much to take in. But I had to hand it to whoever had created it. It was a kick-ass piece of propaganda.

Allie kept glancing at me through the whole thing, her eyes huge and full of understanding.

This was the exact fucking story I'd told her.

When the black screen appeared at the end, the crowd

around us began to murmur and chatter, but then the final frame flashed up and their cheers erupted like thunder, rippling across the mob, as they took up the chant, "Come Home to the Dome. Come Home to the Dome."

Allie joined in next to me, shaking her fist in the air as she chanted.

And I joined too, raising my own, a smile breaking across my face.

This was going to piss off my old man like nothing ever had.

After the euphoria of the movie settled down a little, Allie convinced me to meet with Matty and the rest of the bikers at the bunker to tell them I was part of the dome resistance. She was sure they'd want to help. She said many of them had PSS, small marks like hers, and all I had to do was show them my leg and they'd follow me.

I wasn't thrilled with that last part, but I knew Palmer would want me to risk it. The CAMFers and The Hold might have gotten into Umatilla while I'd slept the day away, and I'd need all the protection I could get. Talking to Matty confirmed the worst. The locals had been monitoring the fences, and a group matching the description of my old man's crew had breached the eastern fence around noon. Shortly after that, a group of black SUVs had been let through at one of the official road blocks. Mr. James must have pulled some strings, now that he was back on top of The Hold.

"Yeah, that's not good," I told Allie's people. "Those are the two factions that once had control of the dome. They did all that bad shit you saw in the movie. Things are going to get violent fast, if we can't squelch them."

Even as I said it, we heard gunfire in the distance. They all turned and looked at me, expectantly. And I hadn't even shown them my leg yet. "Do you know where they parked their vehicles and set up operations?" I asked.

"We can find out," Allie said, signaling a couple of guys who quickly took off on dirt bikes. "What's your plan?" She turned back to me.

"Well, they've come very late to the party," I said. "And there are a lot of people between them and the compound. I say we set up various perimeter lines all the way around, and we don't let them through, no matter what." Of course, that would protect me too. The more people I could put between my old man and me, the better.

"We should tell my grandpa," Allie said. "He served in the army and he has a big group with him. They're pretty well armed and disciplined. He'd know how to set everything up and organize people."

I was tempted to pinch myself. Maybe I was still back in the camper asleep and this was all a dream. People didn't invite me to lead them and suddenly start taking orders from me. That was not my life.

"We can use the bikers to spread the word," Allie continued. "They can go from camp to camp and recruit, and we can tell people to sign up at my grandpa's tent. He'll love to have more people to order around."

"That sounds good," I said.

And that was the beginning of my very short career as a rebel leader.

39

KAYLEE

The morgue had changed significantly since my knife-fight with Anthony. The hole in the wall was larger, the PSS glow emanating from it pulsing and more intense than before. There was a pile of stone and rubble pushed off to one side, and blood on the floor, wiped here and splashed there, various red footprints trodden through it. One of the morgue drawers was partially open, the corner of a crimson-stained sheet trailing from it, and I couldn't help thinking that Major Tom finally had company.

Mike went through the wall first, stepping into the light, his gun out in front of him. My sister went next with me following in her shadow. She stopped at the first pipe, instinctively putting out her ghost hand to brace herself against the tank as she stepped over it.

Olivia, don't—I cried out, too late.

Her hand went straight through, followed by her arm up to the shoulder and she pitched sideways, falling into the tank.

I lunged forward, wrapping my arms around her waist and pulling her back. We both fell against the pipes, panting and terrified, just as the tank pulsed back into material existence.

Don't touch it, I warned, making sure we were both steady on our feet before I let her go. *It's phasing in and out, and I'm not sure what would happen if it went solid with part of you in there.*

"Okay," she nodded, looking shaken and eyeing the tank with renewed caution. "If it's phasing, wouldn't the gas just empty into this room? How's anything even still in there?"

I don't know, I said. *I need to get a better look at it.*

"Well, thanks for saving my ass," she said, turning and maneuvering through the rest of the pipes ahead of us.

I followed, carefully, and Samantha and David came after me.

Once I stepped fully into the room, without the shadow of the pipes masking it, the pulse of the tank was almost blinding.

"That's new," Mike said, nodding at it grimly. "It wasn't doing that earlier."

I could barely look directly at it the way the rest of them were. It was like staring at the sun. And yet I tried, tried to see and understand what was before me. The tank was no longer a tank. That much was clear.

What had once been a metallic man-made thing was now PSS itself, one minute material, the next ethereal, pulsing in and out of existence. And yet somehow it still contained the PSS gas inside of it. Not only that, just as Pete had said, I could see it pulling PSS into itself, like a black hole sucks in matter.

The brightness was too much. Spots flashed on my retinas, so I glanced down and away, my eyes landing on Olivia's ghost hand.

She followed my gaze and lifted her hand, flexing and turning it different directions in relationship to the tank. But she couldn't see what I saw. She couldn't see how bad the blur had gotten since she'd inadvertently dipped that hand into the tank. Her PSS was stretching away from her in misty wisps, slipping through the air toward it and disappearing into its overwhelming glare.

For a moment, I felt suddenly dizzy and clammy, like I might throw up.

Olivia couldn't see what was happening to her, but she must have read my expression because she caught my eyes and shook her head ever so slightly. We'd both known the risks of coming down to the tank, and she didn't want me to alarm the others when there was still a chance we could stop it.

We need to hurry, I said, looking at Mike. The PSS glowing from the muscles across his shoulders was strong and steady, completely unaffected by the pull of the tank. *Where is the machine?*

"This way," he said, leading us around to the other side of the room.

I bent over the blinking device, carefully inspecting each dial, meter, and slider, but they meant nothing to me, and I felt a panic rising in my chest. Mike expected me to know what to do. They were all sure I could save them. If I were the heroine of a book, I would know exactly what to do, but I wasn't, and I didn't.

I don't know how this works, I confessed to Mike. *We'll have to experiment.*

"I trust your instincts," he said.

What were my instincts? I wasn't a creature of machines, I knew that much. But Samantha had said she might be able to use it, to tune it like one of the many instruments she played.

Samantha should adjust the dials, I told them. *If they control the resonance of the PSS, she will be able to hear it, and I will be able to see it. Perhaps we'll discern a pattern we can work with.* I was making it up, just guessing like any of them could have. But I had to believe in our ability to solve this. There was no other option.

"Okay," Samantha said, stepping up to the machine, laying her hand gently on the first slider, and tilting her PSS ear toward the tank. "Let's see what this one does."

Wait. I turned to David and Olivia. *Go stand over there. It will be safer.*

It was a lie, and probably my best so far. I already knew in my gut there was no safe distance for me or Olivia. Still, I'd directed them to a slightly darker part of the room where I would be able to see more clearly the rate at which my sister's PSS fled her body. That was the only real way I could think of to gauge the effectiveness of what we were about to do. I couldn't look at the tank too long or discern anything about its resonance, not the way it was pulsing. And for some reason, I couldn't see my own PSS streaming away from me, though I knew it must be. But I could watch the effect on Olivia get better, or worse, and adjust accordingly.

She and David moved away, into the darker shadows near a hatch-like door, his chest glowing through his shirt like a beacon. They were standing side by side, awkwardly, their shoulders touching a little. I could tell David was warming up to my sister again, his heart already remembering what his head could not. Even if the tank had wiped his memories from the eight ball, the two of them would be okay. I wanted them to have another chance together.

I turned back to Samantha and said, *Okay. Now.*

As she moved the first slider up, slowly, carefully, the speed and brightness of tank's pulsing increased. Within seconds the flashing was so fast and intense, it was as if the world was cut into black and white shards of moment.

There was Sam, her face pinched.

Black.

There was Mike, frowning at me.

Black.

There were David and Olivia, her ghost hand's PSS streaming away from her toward the tank like a shooting star.

NO! Turn it down! I yelled at Samantha, and the flashing stopped, the pulsing returning to its original pace and intensity. *That's not the one,* I reiterated, my stomach churning with anxiety. *It's not working. It's too dangerous.*

"Kaylee, it's okay," Mike said, putting his arm around my shoulder. "You can do this. Maybe we got the worst one out of the way."

"That sounded very soprano to me," Sam said. "Almost like the whistle of a firework, so if high is bad, maybe low is good. Let's try this one."

I braced myself, terrified, but this time the pulsing slowed and deepened. It had a heavy thrum to it, a vibration I could feel coming up through the floor into my bones. And the tank looked all wobbly like I was seeing it through the waves of heat that often rose off the desert outside the dome.

I turned and looked at Olivia, hope against hope, but what I saw was even worse than before. Her PSS was looping away from her in great fat ribbons of energy flowing from her fingers. Even as I watched and yelled at Samantha to stop, my sister slumped against David, her face pale and drawn.

"This isn't working," David said angrily, as the pulsing went back to normal. "Olivia almost fainted on that one." He was holding her up, his arm around her waist.

"It was just a moment of light-headedness," she insisted, propping herself against him. "I'm fine. We can try again."

This isn't working, I said, mind-speaking only to Mike. *That was worse than the first one.* I was beginning to feel sick as well. I wasn't sure if things looked blurry because of the tank or because I was growing faint. *Mike, please, we need to go back upstairs.*

"It's up to you," he said, looking down at me, earnest and trusting. "I think we should try one more, but it's up to you."

I knew he was right. If we gave up now, I'd just made Olivia and myself much worse for nothing. We would still die. We would just die faster. And Mike couldn't lose Chase. I understand what his brother meant to him. We had to try again. No, we had to keep going until we found the answer. Or until we couldn't keep going anymore.

I turned to David and Olivia. *Get ready*, I said.

I looked at Samantha and said, *Go ahead*.

This time, the room felt bigger around me, the air heavier and thicker, and everyone's movements seemed to slow down like time was spiraling away from us.

Out of the corner of my eye, I noticed Mike slowly raising his arm to point at the tank, his mouth open with strange, garbled sounds coming from it. In the background, Samantha was just standing at the machine, her hand frozen on the slider.

When I tried to turn my head to look at Olivia, it seemed to take forever. Halfway there, my eyes traveled across the tank and I saw what Mike had been pointing at. The artifacts had come swimming out of the swirling blue, pressing themselves up against the inside wall, their outlines and details as clear as if they were right in front of me. There was Major Tom's knife, which I'd stabbed into Anthony, and next to it the PSS-severing device Dr. Fineman had created, and finally, the small metal bullet I had seen shining from Jason's pocket the moment I'd met him.

I stared at them, transfixed, completely forgetting for a moment that I needed to check what was happening to Olivia.

And then everything sped up.

Not to normal speed.

No, this was much faster.

The artifacts flew backwards and the wind rushed toward me, the room sliding back, my feet slipping.

People were yelling, but it was chipmunky and just as garbled as before.

I slammed into the tank before I understood it had pulled me to itself, my face pressed against its cool, pulsing surface. My head started to phase through, and I tried to jerk my neck back, but the pull was too strong. Suddenly, my right eye went all blurry, like I was seeing underwater, and I realized half my face had phased into the tank. I started to panic, to try and scramble away, but then a strange calm came over me and I looked up toward the light, the beautiful streaming light.

The top of the tank was a desert sky full of stars. Millions and millions of stars flashed toward it in amazingly fast sparks of PSS energy. I could see up and up, past the contents of the tank, through the ceiling of the round room and all the floors of the compound above, and out into the wide world where all those sparks were coming from because they were coming from everywhere. A spark from every person camped outside the dome in the desert, except the rare few who didn't have PSS. A spark from every pronghorn and burrowing owl and red ant. From every resident of Hermiston and the other nearby townships. Every living creature on the planet that possessed a hint of PSS was slowly losing it to the pull of the tank. The closer to Umatilla they were, the faster the sparks flew, coming from every direction, as far as I could see and beyond the horizon.

Then the artifacts floated into view, the two knives and the bullet pulsing with my sister's PSS resonance, and I could see the tiniest strands of energy flowing away, up and out of the tank, back into the world.

At the same time, while I was seeing all that with the eye that was in the tank, out of the corner of my other eye, I could see David and Olivia. He was holding onto the hatch-like door of the room with one bulging arm, his other wrapped around Olivia's waist. And she was bent in half over it like a rag doll, her arms flailing out like banners in the wind, her legs being pulled under it, the expression on her face one of determined agony. The blur from her PSS was like a solid column of light beaming straight into the tank.

Then I blinked, and the pull stopped, and I was hurled to the ground at the base of the tank, my head slamming against the floor, my ears ringing.

"Kaylee, are you all right?" Mike knelt down next to me, his face a shattered mask of concern. "I'm so sorry. I should have listened to you. We never should have tried another one." He pulled me against his chest, cradling me like a baby. "I'm so sorry, little one. I'm so sorry." I felt something wet drop on my face and I looked up, bewildered, to see that he was crying.

Then the darkness took me, and Mike slowly faded from view.

40

DAVID MARCUS

"**O**livia is asking for you," Pete said, looking down at me. Mrs. Black stood behind him, her eyes desperate and devastated, a woman facing the imminent loss of both her daughters, and I wondered if she'd survive that.

I wondered if I would.

I stood up and followed Pete, leaving the library where we'd gathered for our vigil after we'd rushed Olivia and Kaylee back up to the infirmary and handed them over to Pete and Reiny's care. That had been hours ago and Olivia had finally regained consciousness, which Pete said was a good sign, but I wasn't sure I believed it. I'd seen Olivia transform from a vibrant, healthy girl to a walking corpse after only twenty minutes of messing with that fucking tank. When I'd visited Kaylee's bedside in the infirmary earlier, she'd looked just as bad, and she still hadn't regained consciousness. And it was my fault. I'd brought Kaylee here when I could have kept her at the reservation, safe and sound. It was just like Danielle. Perhaps I was destined to relive this one deadly mistake over and over, whether I remembered it or not.

I knew I was in shock. Probably, we all were. My body moved, following Pete through the dimly-lit dome to the far side where we'd moved Olivia's bed so she could rest undisturbed. I stepped between two privacy screens and my eyes saw her and my brain said, *There she is, barely alive, looking at me with those gorgeous, haunting eyes, and I will never forgive myself for this.* But I didn't feel any of it. I was just there, watching it happen.

"I'm going to check on Kaylee," Pete said, disappearing behind the screens and leaving me there to fend for myself. To face Olivia alone.

She was hooked up to an IV just like Kaylee was. It was administering fluids, plus a dose of Passion's plasma, though we all knew that was a long shot. Pete and Reiny had told us they had no idea how to stop the tank's effects. All they could do was make Olivia and Kaylee comfortable. There wasn't anything any of us could do.

And it was even worse than that.

On the way back up from the morgue, Olivia limp in my arms and Kaylee limp in Palmer's, Kaylee had regained consciousness briefly and begun to speak in a horrified whisper straight into our minds.

It's taking the whole world, she'd said. *All the PSS, like stars, rushing toward it, and when it can't hold anymore, it will destroy us all.*

Palmer had stopped, leaning against the nearest wall, but she was already unconscious again.

He'd looked at me and Samantha and said, "She hit her head when she fell. She doesn't know what she's saying."

Both of us had just nodded.

And none of us had said anything to the others about Kaylee's rant.

Why would we? Even if it was true, what could we possibly do about it?

"Don't look so depressed," Olivia said, her weak voice still strong enough to draw me back to reality. "I'm not dead yet, you know?"

"You're not going to die," I told her, wanting to believe it. I sat down in the chair next to the bed and took her ghost hand in mine, stroking my fingers across the soft flesh of her inner wrist. Her PSS was faded, her hand so thin I could barely see it.

She closed her eyes and a slow smile crept across her bluish lips. "Some part of you remembers how much I like that," she sighed.

didn't remember, but it didn't matter. I wanted to make her feel better. I couldn't lose Kaylee or Olivia. I couldn't be responsible for another death. It would break me.

"Marcus," she said, squeezing my hand, and I looked up to see her eyes drilling into mine. "Don't you dare give up on me. I lost you to the bottom of a river, and I didn't give up. I lost you to lies and torture by the

CAMFers and I didn't give up. I lost you to your own recovery, and I didn't give up. You don't get to give up. Not ever. Even if I die, you go on with this and execute the plan I laid out for you and Chase before we went down to the tank. Do you understand?"

"Yes." I held her gaze and nodded. "I understand."

"How are Kaylee and Chase?" she asked. "Pete and my mom wouldn't tell me. They just kept saying they didn't want me to worry. Of course, that just made me assume the worst."

I was tempted to evade or lie to her. In fact, that's what I'd been instructed to do. And I was good at lying. It was pretty much my default mode of communication. But after the leadership and determination Olivia had demonstrated over the last forty-eight hours, she deserved to know the truth.

"Kaylee is still unconscious," I said. "Pete thinks she might have a head injury. And Chase's PSS is showing signs of the effects now."

"How is Mike taking that?"

"Not great," I said, keeping it simple. There was a difference between straight-out lying to her, and leaving out the details of what a frantic mess Palmer was. He blamed himself for the disaster in the tank room—for using his influence over Kaylee to nearly destroy her. Whatever we'd done down there had actually increased the rate of the effect on Kaylee, Olivia, and Chase. So, that was on him too, and the man was desperate. He'd had T-dog and Chase at their computers all night, searching the Umatilla database for anything on the tank that might help us stop it. And he hadn't left his brother's side, other than to check in on how the girls were doing.

"My mom told me you showed the movie," Olivia said, smiling. "She said people cheered so loud you could hear it in the dome."

"It's gone viral on the internet too. It has half a million hits and counting."

"That's good." Her fingers twined with mine as she lay her head back on her pillow. "I'm so cold," she said, trembling, "And you are always so warm." She pulled her hand from mine and patted the edge of the bed. "Come here."

As soon as I understood what she meant, I glanced around self-consciously. What would Pete think if he came back and found me in bed with his patient? What would Olivia's mother think if she caught us like that?

"You're going to deny a girl her dying wish?" she teased, but there was an edge of desperation to it I couldn't ignore.

So, I got up, pulled the blankets back, and slid into the bed next to her.

She smiled the hugest, most radiant smile I had ever see, and rolled straight into my arms, nestling her head under my chin against my chest.

"Thank you," she sighed, clinging to me. "It makes me feel better, you know, because I could never die, here, in your arms. Not with you to hold onto."

I think she fell asleep, even as she said it. I felt her relax against me, and her breathing slowed, the palm of her ghost hand pale against my chest, and I tried to imagine that I could feel my strength, vitality, and energy flowing into her.

I must have been pretty tired myself, because a minute later, I was asleep too.

Later, much later, a strange rattling woke me, and I opened blurry eyes to see Kaylee and Samantha standing at the side of the bed.

"What are you doing?" I demanded, guilt washing over me. I should have been at Kaylee's bedside, not sleeping with Olivia. "Kaylee, you should be in bed."

"I told her the same thing," Sam said, "but she wouldn't listen."

I know what to do, Kaylee said. *I know how to stop it and save Olivia and Chase and everyone.*

Olivia stirred in my arms and opened her eyes. She turned her head and saw the girls too. "What's wrong?" she asked groggily.

I know how to stop the tank, Kaylee said again. *But I need the three of you to come with me, and we'll have to use the artifacts and the cubes.* She reached down to the floor, hefting up the faraday cage and setting it on the edge of the bed. That had been the rattle I'd heard earlier.

I wasn't sure which surprised me more, that Kaylee had gotten out of bed, undone her IV without alerting Pete and Reiny, commandeered Samantha, walked to the van, and brought back the heavy faraday cage, or that she was insisting we all go back to the tank.

"We can't go down there," I told her, sitting up. "You and Olivia barely survived last time."

We have to, she insisted. *And we don't have much time. If we don't do this, everyone with PSS dies.*

"Everyone? What do you mean 'everyone'?" Olivia asked, sitting up next to me.

I saw what it was doing when my face went inside, Kaylee

explained, her voice desperate. *It's pulling PSS from everyone, not just from us and Chase, but everyone in the world. And when it reaches its fullness, it will displace to—somewhere else—somewhere different than our plane of existence—it's hard to explain—but it will take all the PSS with it.*

"And when the PSS goes, anyone who had it dies?" Samantha asked.

Yes, Kaylee whispered. *Unless they had Passion's vaccine before the process started. Her plasma blocks the connection.*

"How can you know that for sure?" I asked.

I saw it, she said, jutting her chin out at me. *I saw it all in my head while I was asleep, but it wasn't a dream. And I saw how to stop it too. The machine is changing the resonance of the PSS in the tank—reverting it back to its original state before it became PSS. As a result, PSS everywhere is being called to it and changed back as well. I don't know how to stop the machine. But the artifacts have an effect on the PSS in the tank as well. One or two aren't strong enough to reverse the pull. But all of them combined with the cubes might be, especially if we can tune the machine to just the right resonance. But I can't do it alone. I need your help.*

"I think it's our only option," Samantha said.

"Okay," Olivia said, reaching down and carefully detaching her IV. "We'll help you."

"No." I grabbed Olivia's arm, determined to stop her. "This is crazy. It's going to kill you both, and I can't be responsible for that."

Olivia turned and stared at me. "Before you got here Chase found some of Fineman's experiments and files," she said. "They indicated that he was working on a method for reverse-engineering PSS, a way of eliminating it from human DNA altogether. He was just missing one key ingredient—a sample of the original PSS gas from the Umatilla accident. That sample is downstairs in the tank, and we know Fineman had access to it. So, it doesn't take a leap of logic to assume that machine is doing exactly what my sister says it's doing. Fineman and the CAMFers would like nothing better than to rid the entire world of PSS, but we're not going to let that happen if Kaylee thinks we can stop it. Now, you can either help us or get out of the way. That's your choice, but what we do IS NOT and never has been your responsibility. If I die going down there, make no mistake, it was my choice, not yours."

We need you, Kaylee said to me, pleading. *I have a plan, but it will not succeed without you.*

"Fine. I'll help." I let go of Olivia's arm. "But we should at least tell the others what we're doing."

There's no time, Kaylee said, handing me the faraday cage. *And they'd only try to talk us out of it.*

"She's right," Olivia said, getting up to slip on her shoes and pull on her sweatshirt.

"Okay," I stood up, hefting the faraday cage onto my shoulder.

The entire way through the CAMFer compound and down into the morgue, I marveled at the bravery of my cousin and the two Black sisters. Olivia had been so physically weak she could barely stand, but adrenaline must have kicked in because she was walking on her own, clamoring between the pipes into the tank room, following Kaylee.

Once inside, the artifacts in the cage bounced

around, shifting toward the tank, and I almost dropped them. I held on, though, stumbling up next to Samantha and Olivia.

I can't see, Kaylee said, raising a hand to shield her eyes. *It's so bright. We have to hurry.*

To me, the room and the pulsing looked the same as before, but it was obvious Kaylee was being blinded by it. She wasn't even facing the right direction as she took a tentative step, leading us toward where she thought the tank was.

"It's this way," Olivia said, taking her sister's hand. "Tell us what to do."

Samantha must go to the controls of the machine, Kaylee said. *I've already told her what to do and what to listen for. And you must guide me over to the tank. The three of us need to be next to it.*

Samantha gave us a nod and crossed to the machine.

Then Olivia took Kaylee by the arm and guided her as I followed with the cage. When we got to the tank, Kaylee reached out to touch it and her hand immediately phased through.

Good, she said. *We're not too late. Now,* she turned, looking slightly to the left of Olivia and me as she addressed us. *I must phase all the way into the tank, and Olivia must hand me the artifacts as I call for them, exactly in the order that I call for them, while Samantha moves the sliders on the machine. But Olivia can't pass the artifacts to me without protection for her ghost hand. Direct contact with the gasses in the tank would suck her PSS dry before we could finish. That is why, David, you must stand next to the tank, but not touching it, and, Olivia must hand the artifacts to me through your chest.*

"Through my chest?" I asked, hoping I'd misheard. While it was true that kind of maneuver wouldn't disrupt my PSS anymore and turn me into a flopping corpse, I still wasn't thrilled with the prospect.

Your PSS contains elements of Danielle's healing and Passion's vaccine, Kaylee explained. *It is the best protection we have.*

"Why risk Olivia when I've had the vaccine?" I asked. "Why can't I hand you the artifacts?"

You wouldn't be able to control them, she said. *And if the tank materialized while you were handing something to me, you'd lose your hand. Now, please, stand against the tank.*

"Wait," Olivia said to her sister. "If reaching into the tank would hurt me, won't phasing into it hurt you?"

A little, Kaylee said, *but my phasing ability will protect me.*

"Okay," Olivia said, positioning Kaylee facing the tank.

I set the faraday cage at Olivia's feet, stepped up to the tank next to Kaylee, with my back a couple of inches from it, and then realized I was going to have to take off my shirt. I stepped away, pulling my t-shirt over my head and tossing it on the floor.

"It would be better if you faced the tank," Olivia pointed out. "That way you won't accidentally touch it or something."

She was right. It made sense. But then I wasn't going to see when she reached through me. I'd have no warning.

"I promise, I'll be gentle with you," she said,

teasing me, attempting to keep the mood light despite the dire circumstances.

"You'd better be." I turned and faced the tank's swirling blueness, positioning myself as close to it as I safely could without touching it.

I heard Olivia fiddling with the faraday cage's latch, readying it to open quickly. Then I felt her step up behind me, her left hand settling on the bare skin of my lower back for balance, sending a shiver up my spine. Her face was near my right shoulder, looking over it so she could see into the tank.

"We're ready when you are," she said to Kaylee, and I felt her warm breath against my neck.

Kaylee hesitated just a moment, and then she stepped past me, phasing into the tank.

41

OLIVIA

I had no idea if Kaylee's plan would work, but I'd thrown together a few creative solutions of my own in the past, and they hadn't been complete disasters. Besides, it was either this or die a slow, agonizing death in bed like my dad. I preferred death-by-doing-something-crazy than death-by-doing-nothing-at-all, thank you very much. And the vaccine would protect Marcus. Reiny and Pete had said so, and Kaylee had confirmed it. Marcus and my mom would survive, as well as many of my friends. These were the facts I tried to focus on as my sister stepped into a throbbing tank of PSS gas.

As soon as Kaylee phased through, she floated up a little, hovering slightly above and to the right of where Marcus and I stood, which was good because I could see her clearly, and she seemed to be able to see again as well, her eyes scanning the interior. As I watched, she turned away, raising her left hand, and something came whooshing out of the fog toward her. It was the PSS-severing knife Fineman had made out of Passion's blades, and Kaylee caught it, gripping the handle firmly.

Olivia, the dog tags, she commanded, holding her right hand out to me.

I reached down, flipped open the faraday's lid, and grabbed the tags, the other artifacts batting at me but staying inside the cage.

I stood up, facing Marcus's bare back. "Here we go," I said, warning him as I pressed my ghost hand into his PSS.

Once, in a steamy bathroom back in Indy, I'd touched Marcus's PSS chest with my PSS fingers. That had been intimate and sensual. This was something completely different. I don't know if it was because of the effects of Passion's vaccine, or his own resistance and fear, or just because I was doing a hell of a lot more than touching him, but his PSS resisted. A lot.

I had to push hard, ignoring the weird sensation of my hand passing through his ribs and organs. Not only that, but I also had to resist the subtle, intoxicating pull of some artifact buried deep inside him, making my hand want to drop the tags and search for it. Whatever it was, its resonance was strong. It took every ounce of willpower I had to press on, pushing my hand through the front of him, and I could feel his PSS coming with it, surrounding my hand like a glove as it phased through the wall of the tank and I handed the tags to Kaylee.

Samantha, move the first slider, she called, snatching the tags from me.

Over Marcus's shoulder, the tank's pulsing effect sped up, just like it had last time, strobing my sister in black and white relief, and fear clenched my gut. We couldn't take that kind of abuse again. We wouldn't survive it.

But then Kaylee raised the artifacts in her hands, swirling them in the gas above her, until the strobing slowed, then stopped. As it did, a whirling funnel of air appeared over her head, and she gently released the knife and the tags into it where they continued to spin, caught up in its vortex.

I slipped my hand from Marcus, and he staggered back against me before quickly righting himself. "I'm sorry," he gasped. "I wasn't—I didn't realize it would feel like that."

I glanced at Kaylee, but she had turned from us again, and this time something small and metallic was flying to her hand inside the tank. She caught it, pinching it between her thumb and forefinger, and I realized it was Jason's bullet. As soon as she had it, she called out, *Samantha, the second slider*. Then she raised the bullet upward, just like before, and it joined the knife and the blades in a spinning dance over her head.

Now Major Tom's knife, she said, and I thought she was talking to me but that knife wasn't in the cage. I looked up, confused, to see Major Tom's knife hurtling toward her inside the tank. She'd been commanding it, not me.

She caught it just before it struck her, holding it at bay, her hands bleeding a billow of PSS around her as the blade drilled toward her.

"Kaylee!" Marcus called in alarm, and I grabbed his shoulders, holding him back.

Samantha, the third slider, Kaylee said, her voice strained as she wrestled the knife into submission, straining to lift it over her head. And she did, freeing it into the swirl with the other artifacts, where it spun as obediently as the rest. But they began moving faster, whipping round and round.

Olivia, the eight ball. Now! Kaylee demanded, holding her hand out to me.

I grabbed it from the faraday cage and lifted it to Marcus's back. Shit. What about his memories? Would they be lost forever?

"Olivia, do it," Marcus said, sensing my hesitation, and I did, slipping the eight ball through him. Again, his PSS cushioned my hand, surrounding it as it went into the tank.

Kaylee called to Samantha for the fourth slider and raised the eight ball over her head into the swirl.

Our father's rock, Kaylee said, her eyes drilling into mine, and I handed it to her through Marcus, ignoring the nostalgia that washed over me as she placed it with the other artifacts swimming above her. With that addition, the PSS in the tank grew brighter, making it hard to see Kaylee and filling the room with a blue-white glare.

Now both the cubes, Kaylee said, her voice panicked, *and Mike's matchbook. Do them all at once. We don't have much time.*

I couldn't really see the faraday cage anymore, but I reached for it, feeling inside, grabbing both the cubes awkwardly in my hand and then finding the matchbook with my fingers, elongating them a little to latch onto it.

I turned toward Marcus and felt for his back.

My hand went in, pressing, pushing, too full, but his PSS accommodated it, and then I felt Kaylee's hand take the artifacts from me.

I looked over Marcus's shoulder, straining to see her.

I'm sorry. Her voice was a weak whisper in my mind. *I love you both, and Mother, and Mike. That's how I know you will understand.*

I was still processing those words, trying to make sense of them, when I heard a familiar sharp snap, the sound of a match being lit, and darkness flared out of the middle of the tank, eclipsing the glare of light around it.

Kaylee was floating there, the artifacts spinning above her, her hair caught up in the motion and hovering around her head like she was a mermaid or an angel. In her left hand, she was holding the two cubes, stacked one on top of the other. In her right, she held Mike's matchbook, the entire thing going up in flames, engulfing her hand like a torch.

Don't be angry with me, she said, smiling lovingly at Marcus and me as she brought those two hands together in front of her, baptizing the cubes in fire. *This was the only way.*

"Kaylee, No!" Marcus yelled, but it was too late.

She raised the burning cubes over her head, touching the swirling mass of artifacts, and the world went supernova.

There was a high-pitched whine in my ears as I flew backwards. I landed hard on the floor and Marcus fell on top of me, his body heavy and limp over mine.

Then, everything went dark.

I had a vision while I was unconscious. Not a dream, or a nightmare, but something I knew was true.

In it, Kaylee floated above me as I lay on the tank room floor, Marcus slumped across me, and PSS was all around us, and in us, and connecting us. I could feel Samantha in the round room with us, and my mother and friends sleeping upstairs in the dome. I could feel Anthony in his cell, and all the people in the crowd outside the compound. I could feel the pronghorns, and the people in Hermiston, the people in Portland, and further, and further, all over the world, as if my senses and nerve endings had been stretched to encompass the entire planet. It was the most amazing thing I had ever felt.

What are you doing? I asked Kaylee, speaking into her mind.

I'm giving everyone a gift, she said, smiling, *so they can see what I see. I know you and mother will be sad that we couldn't be together as a family. I'm sad about that too. But this is the best ending I could possibly imagine for my story, and the best beginning for yours.*

And then she was gone.

42

JASON

Some people remember where they were when we landed on the moon, or when the President got shot, or when the planes struck the two towers in New York City, but everyone remembers where they were when The Change happened. It doesn't matter if they were there, knocked on their asses into the desert sand next to the dome itself, or they were sitting in their living room at home. It doesn't matter if they were in the US, or South America, Europe, or Asia. What happened, happened to all of us, all of humankind, all at once, a global phenomenon. That's what they called it.

All I knew is one minute I was in an underground bunker, planning how to use Allie's resources to keep my old man off my back, and the next minute we were hit by a blast of light and energy. It threw me to the ground, washing over me and through me, and then the world went black.

That's how most people describe The Change, no matter where they were when it happened.

What they won't describe is the vision they had while they were unconscious, at least not in any detail. Oh, they'll tell you they had one, because everyone did. But visions from The Change are considered a very personal matter. I've never told anyone mine, and I don't plan to. I do believe that without the visions, the world after The Change would have descended into utter chaos. As it was, things still got a bit crazy after the blast—after Allie and I woke up side-by-side on the ground of the bunker.

"What the hell was that?" Allie mumbled, sitting up.

I fumbled to get up as well, dizzy and disoriented. When I finally managed to stand, I turned toward Allie and I could see the glow of her PSS birthmark, the one on the back of her neck, even though she was facing me. I could see it right through her—like she was transparent, except she wasn't—but I could see her PSS glowing at me as plain as day.

She was looking at me too, staring at my leg.

"I can see your PSS through your pants," she said.

I turned, scanning her crew, all the locals who'd gathered to help us protect the dome from the CAMFers and The Hold, and it was like looking at a sky full of stars. Everyone sparkled and glowed, some part of their body radiating PSS. Some had it on their skin, others had it deeper inside. And there were a few who had it like a pinprick of light in one or two of their cells.

I turned back to Allie. "Um, can you see that?"

"Yeah," she nodded, her eyes panning the room.

Some of the others were beginning to get up and it was obvious they could see it too. Everyone was glancing around and beginning to question each other, just like Allie and I had.

Suddenly, the bunker door flew open and Matty charged in, his left pec shining with PSS like a fucking headlight. "Something happened at the dome," he said, panting. "There was an—explosion or something—and now—come and see."

Allie and I ran to the door. Others followed, pushing and shoving to get out. We had to run around the hummock of the bunker to see the dome and there it was, glowing like the moon, a stream of iridescent particles flowing out the top of it and up into the night sky. Was it radiation? Had Fineman set off a fucking bomb? Is that what he'd been rigging down in that tank room? Fuck.

"Look." Allie pointed, but not at the dome. At the people.

Everyone had come out of their tents and vehicles, thousands and thousands of people, spread across the desert floor and glowing like lightning bugs, because almost every one of them had PSS.

A murmur rose from the crowd as they looked around at their neighbors. It grew louder when they realized they'd been changed as well. I saw people reaching out, trying to touch the PSS of a family member or friend, but there were cries of fear and alarm too. The sound of the response grew like a rumble of thunder. Some people panicked, shoving their stuff into cars and campers, desperate to escape, but there was no quick way out of Umatilla. Other people began to celebrate, great cheers and chants sounding from various areas around the dome.

"Your friends in there did this," Allie said. "Didn't they?"

"I don't know," I said, but she was probably right. This had Olivia and Kaylee's signature written all over it. At any rate, I was sure now it hadn't been Fineman. The last thing he'd want to do was give all these people PSS.

Over the noise of the crowd, I heard the rattle of gunfire off to the west.

Allie and I turned in that direction, but I couldn't see anything through the swirling, glowing horde.

Matty's phone rang and he answered it. "Okay. I understand. We'll be ready," he said, before hanging up. "The CAMFers are making a run for it," he told Allie and me. "They're plowing through the crowd and running people and camps over if they have to. And they're headed this way. Jay doesn't think we're their target. He thinks they're just taking the path of least resistance to the closest exit."

I almost laughed. My old man was having the worst night of his life. And I was glad he was coming my way. Maybe I'd get to see his PSS.

"Should we try and stop them?" Allie asked.

"No," I said. "They're running scared, and we want them gone, so let's do our best to clear the way. But get everyone armed and ready, just in case."

"Got it," Allie and Matty said, heading off to organize our people.

Fifteen minutes later, a caravan of armed, glowing CAMFers blew past our bunker, my old man's truck in the lead.

As he drove by, I know he saw me standing there surrounded by my army of locals.

And I saw the glow of PSS shining from his left arm as he gripped the steering wheel.

It was impossible to miss.

43

DAVID MARCUS

"Well, this confirms it," Reiny said, running a hand-held imager over Olivia's ghost hand one last time. "Your PSS is completely back to normal."

Sam, Olivia, and I had woken up in the infirmary a few hours ago, and Reiny had been running tests on us ever since. And not just on us, but on everyone in the dome. As she finished up Olivia, Chase came in for his final check, and Reiny turned her scanner on him. "Yours is back to normal too," she told him, smiling. "And Pete, Lonan, and Mike are downstairs checking Anthony, but we expect the results to be the same. Whatever Kaylee did last night, it saved the three of you."

"And it killed her," I said, slumped in a nearby chair. I had fucking failed again. I had promised Kaylee I'd keep her safe and now she was dead.

"It was her choice," Olivia said, her voice full of emotion. "She knew what she was doing. You heard her say it was the only way."

"And you believe that?" I asked, standing up. "There had to be something else we could have done. I could have gone in her place."

"That wouldn't have worked and you know it," Olivia insisted. "I have to believe Kaylee weighed all the options, and did what had to be done. Besides, it was her gift of seeing PSS that everyone needed. You couldn't have given that."

"And you really think that's going to change anything?" I scoffed. "It doesn't matter what people see, they'll always think they're better than someone else. Maybe their PSS is brighter, or it's near their head instead of their ass. It's human nature to compare ourselves to others and fight about it. Nothing is going to—"

"Shut up!" Olivia snapped, jumping off the gurney and getting right in my face. "You think you feel her loss more than I do? Or my mother does? You knew Kaylee for what? Two weeks? And that's about twelve more days than we had with her, but you're not going to see us bitch about it. You're not going to hear us complain about how she didn't let us rescue her so our poor, bruised egos would feel better. I lost my dad to cancer, and it was pointless. You lost Danielle and it nearly destroyed you. I get it. Death fucking sucks. That's exactly why we have to make Kaylee's count for something. I know what she told me at the end. I believe in what she did. And now we're going to go on with the plan, just like she would have wanted us to. So you can either shut up and help, or get out of my way," she finished, storming past me and out the infirmary door.

There was a long, uncomfortable silence after she left.

Part of me knew what she'd said was true, but some other part just couldn't let go of the loss. It was stuck inside of me, something I couldn't dislodge any more than I could remove my own heart. But I could bury it and face the task at hand. I'd done that all my life. And so that's what I did.

The next time I saw Olivia, she was typing away on Chase's laptop up in the dome library. I came around a partition, surprised to find her alone. If she noticed my entrance, she chose to ignore it. I sat down at the table across from her and cleared my throat.

She kept typing.

"What are you working on?" I asked.

"A speech." She looked over the top of the screen at me. "The people out there deserve an explanation for what has happened to them, and the internet is exploding with questions and theories. Chase and Tee have confirmed that the effect is global and comprehensive. Everyone in the world can see PSS, and they want me to be the first to make an official statement about it. I'm on in less than an hour."

"What are you going to say?"

"Oh, you know, that my sister sacrificed herself in vain and everything is hopeless. That sort of thing."

"All right. You made your point. I know what I said was out of line but—"

"Really?" she interrupted, returning to her typing. "I guess I'll say something else then."

"Olivia," Palmer called, coming around the partition. "Chase said you wanted to see me."

"Yeah." She looked up. "I want you and Marcus to go down and get Anthony. Then I want you to take him to the nearest exit and put him out of the dome."

"You want us to just throw him out?" Palmer asked.

"Yes." She nodded. "I'm tired of wasting time and people guarding him. There's too much to do, and Pete's says he's healed up enough to get to the nearest hospital himself. He's no longer our problem or our responsibility."

"Okay," Palmer said, glancing at me. "Let's go get rid of Anthony."

I followed him out. What else was I going to do? Olivia had obviously dismissed me.

Palmer and I went over to the CAMFer side and made our way down to Anthony's cell. Grant was standing outside the door, guarding it, and we told him what Olivia wanted us to do.

When we opened the cell, Anthony cowered in the corner, the PSS in his left knee joint now clearly visible. I could tell he thought we'd come to kill him.

Palmer went over and grabbed him, pulling him to his feet. Then Palmer and I each took one of his arms and led him out, heading toward the main level with Grant following behind us.

"Where are you taking me?" Anthony asked.

"We're letting you go," Palmer told him, as we approached the same side-entrance Chase had used to let us in.

"What?" Anthony dug his heels in, struggling against our hold. "No. Please. You can't put me out there. Not after what you've done to me."

"Your stump is almost healed," Palmer said. "And we've pumped you full of enough antibiotics and pain-killers to last until you can get to town. You'll be fine."

"No!" Anthony cried. "You don't understand. It's not this I'm worried about." He shook his handless wrist at Palmer. "It's this." He gestured at his glowing knee. "I can't go out there a freak. I'll have no place with the CAMFers. My old man will kill me. You have to ask her to take it back. I know she did this to me. I can't live like this. I'd rather die." He collapsed on the floor, clinging to Palmer's leg.

Palmer yanked away, crossing to the door's security keypad and punching in the code while Grant and I grabbed Anthony by the arms and pulled him to his feet.

"Please," Anthony begged. "Just take it away first. I'll do anything."

Grant and I shoved him forward, pitching a weeping Anthony out into the desert sand, and Palmer slammed the door behind him.

"Well, that felt good," Palmer said, turning to head upstairs.

And he was damn right.

44

OLIVIA

I had never been great at speeches. I'd gotten a C minus in my junior year communications class, but that seemed like a very long time ago. I doubted what I'd learned was going to come in handy for a speech to the entire world about why they could now see PSS they'd never known they had. But I had my mom read over my notes and she thought they were good. She was sitting nearby, putting on a brave face for the daughter she still had left. She was grieving Kaylee. We both were. But we'd learned a long time ago that you just had to keep going after you lost someone.

As I sat down in front of the microphone, Chase pointed his hand-held camera at me, smiling. Overhead, the dome's sky projector program ran its final skyscape, alerting the crowd outside to pay attention. "We go live in two minutes," Chase said. "I'll give you a count down at three seconds, so you know when to start."

I had assumed we'd record my speech before we showed it on the dome or posted it to the internet, but Chase thought it would be more impactful live. He said it would give an immediacy and personal touch that would increase our reach. He was the internet and computer expert, so I went along with it, but now I was regretting that. What if I froze or completely messed up? I looked down at the papers in my hands, already crumpled and sweaty.

I heard one of the dome doors open and looked up to see Grant, Marcus, and Mike returning from releasing Anthony. Marcus caught my eye and nodded. They'd done it.

"And three, two, one," Chase said.

I glanced back at the camera, caught off guard, staring into its lens and forgetting everything I'd prepared.

Shit.

Chase was still smiling at me encouragingly, so I opened my mouth to begin. But then I made the mistake of looking up, and there I was, my head bigger than a house, projected onto the surface of the dome, my mouth hanging open like a giant idiot.

"Olivia, you'll do great," my mother whispered from behind me.

So, I looked away from the dome straight into the camera and went for it.

"Hello and good morning," I said, my voice a little wobbly. "My name is Olivia Black and I'm speaking to you from inside the dome at Umatilla Chemical Depot in Northern Oregon."

I didn't expect the cheer that suddenly roared outside the dome, as if we were at a sporting event and everyone's favorite team had just scored. I paused for a minute, waiting for it to subside. "Late last night," I continued, "there was an event here—a surge of PSS energy emanating from the compound which we understand has had a global impact, and we know you have questions."

I tried not to smile—I wanted people to take me seriously—but that last part was probably the understatement of the century.

"First, let me say, you are not in any danger," I went on, which was followed by another cheer. "All of us inside the dome, who were exposed the most, have been tested and have been given a clean bill of health. Well, except for my sister, Kaylee. She was— lost," my voice broke on that sentence, and I gulped back the tears rising in my throat. This was for her. I couldn't get emotional and mess it up. Not after all she'd done to make this possible.

"The truth is," I said, my voice gaining strength, "she sacrificed her life to keep us safe. And in the process she gave us a gift—the ability to see the PSS inside of others." The crowd went utterly silent then. "Now, I know rumors are already circulating that what happened was some sort of disaster, or that what you're seeing as a result is an optical illusion that will soon wear off. However, we have reason to believe it is a permanent alteration of human perception. As soon as this video is done, we'll be releasing documented scientific research that proves ninety-eight percent of the world's population had PSS before this event ever occurred. We just couldn't see it until now.

And we know there will be people who will not believe the evidence, but that's their problem, not mine." That got a rumble of laughter from the crowd.

I looked down at my notes, shuffling to the last page.

"For those of us inside the dome one thing is clear," I said, letting the conviction ring in my voice. "Something has happened today that cannot be ignored or suppressed. You deserve to know the true origin and nature of PSS." A cheer rose up. "The world deserves to know the truth." Another cheer, louder this time. "So, we in the dome are dedicating ourselves to researching and uncovering that truth. We will be releasing videos and documents that have long been hidden."

"If you're already here with us at the dome," I continued, "thank you for all you've endured, but our fight is not over. We need your continued presence and support, so our message cannot be stifled." That got a roaring cheer. "And if you are watching this on the internet, or the news, or on your phone, we invite you to join us." That's when they started chanting, "Come home to the dome. Come home to the dome," and they didn't stop so I had to speak over it. "We're not going to hide here forever, or continue to keep you out. Our goal is for this dome and our cause to belong to every one of you." That got the biggest cheer of all, a roar that went on and on.

"Thank you," I concluded, and then T-dog shut off the feed and the dome over my head went opaque.

"Great job," Chase said, lowering the camera. "The crowd loved you, and you hit every bullet point we talked about."

45

DAVID MARCUS

When my jet landed on the dirt tarmac just outside of Umatilla, I recognized Gordon's old truck parked there waiting for me—the same one Lonan and Reiny had driven onto the depot eighteen months ago, before The Change. It was nice to see that truck. Nice to know there were still things in the world that hadn't changed since I'd left the dome over a year ago. Because most things had.

As I descended the stairs of the plane, Lonan jumped out of the truck and strode toward me, the glow of his PSS temple visible, even in the bright afternoon sun. We met at the bottom of the steps and he grabbed me by the shoulders, pulling me into a hug.

"David," he said, stepping back and grinning at me. "It's good to see you. It's been too long."

It had only been three months since we'd seen each other at Gordon's funeral, but Lonan had been understandably distracted then. Prior to that, it must have been Reiny and Pete's wedding on the rez. At least Gordon had gotten to walk his niece down the aisle before his heart had finally given out. And I had gotten to dance with Olivia. More than once.

"It's good to see you too," I told Lonan. "How's Reiny?"

"Busy. And stressed. She would have been here to greet you, but she's in the thick of this FDA approval process and they needed her at the lab. We'll see her later though. And Pete."

"So, the FDA is still dragging their feet on Passion's vaccine?" I asked. "How can they possibly justify that?"

"They can't," Lonan said. "Not after what happened at the high school in Oklahoma and the theater in Idaho. Those people would still be alive if they'd had Pass-1. The CAMFer attacks have strengthened our case to push through approval for global distribution as soon as possible. The momentum is on our side now. Reiny says it's only a matter of time."

"And my uncle's been cooperative?"

"He didn't have much choice," Lonan said. "Thanks to you, we had the money for a good lawyer and his case completely fell apart once it came out he'd used Passion's samples without her knowledge or permission. They seized his stock of the vaccine and his research. Of course, none of the Holders who got the vaccine are complaining. In fact, we've been able to use their data as proof of a successful human trial, which has sped up the FDA process somewhat. But enough about all that. You must be eager to get to the dome and see all the changes."

Eager is not the word I would have used. I wasn't eager to revisit the place Danielle and Kaylee had died—the place I had failed them—which is exactly why I'd gotten out of there as fast as I could after The Change. I had run away, but I hadn't bailed on Olivia completely. I'd flown back to Indy, gathered my financial resources, and hired the best lawyers I could find. They immediately set up a foundation for The Center for PSS Research and Acclamation and negotiated legal possession of the dome. But I hadn't stayed like everyone else, living and working by Olivia's side, and I knew that had disappointed her.

Instead, ironically, I'd gone recruiting, traveling the world convincing young, impressionable college students and professionals to donate their time and knowledge at the very facility I had fled. Maybe I was trying to make up for not being there. I don't know. I did know I was good at my job. Over the last year, I'd sent three hundred and thirty-two volunteers back to the dome. And occasionally, I'd returned to Oregon for a wedding, or a funeral, and a few times I'd met Olivia in a coffee shop in Portland and we'd caught a movie and dinner together.

So, no, I wasn't eager to get to the dome. Terrified would be a more appropriate word, and I was nervous to see Olivia again. Away from the dome, we'd become good friends. Okay, probably more than friends. But I wasn't exactly sure because we'd never really talked about it. And to complicate matters, she was maybe my girlfriend, but she was definitely my boss.

Which is why I was there, finally, climbing into the truck with Lonan. Olivia and I had to talk. I had to tell her face-to-face.

On the way to the depot entrance, I didn't miss the shiny new fence towering along the property line or the signs designating it as *Private Property of The Unified Umatilla Association*. Lonan had done that. He'd gotten all the special interest groups to enter into one lawsuit against the government for joint possession of the land. And they'd won. Of course, that hadn't been too surprising given the Umatilla documents Chase and T-dog had released exposing the original PSS event and the subsequent cover-up. The government and military had been so busy facing fall-out from that, they would have done anything they could to make themselves look better. As a result, the Umatilla property was now a community trust managed by a board of directors and presided over by Lonan himself. From what I'd heard, it was a thankless, difficult job trying to get such a diverse group to work together, but if anyone could do it, Lonan could. He was one of most level-headed human beings I'd ever met.

We pulled up to the new main gate of the UUA. It had a manned booth now and the attendant stuck his head out and greeted us with a glowing smile, literally. He had PSS of the mouth. "Good afternoon, sir," he said to Lonan in a lilting accent. Then he saw me and his face broke into a huge grin. "Mr. Jordan, we heard you were arriving today. I don't know if you remember, but you recruited me six months ago in Belfast."

"Of course I remember you, Sean," I said. "But you seem to have forgotten I go by David, not Mr. Jordan. And if you've been here that long, you must be a full-time staffer now. How do you like working at the dome?"

"It's a privilege," he said. "I can't thank you enough. Really."

"I'm glad to hear it," I said. "Now, how about letting us in?" I gestured at the gate.

"Yes, sir." He punched a button in the booth and waved us through.

"You have quite a fan club here," Lonan said, smirking. "I hear the female recruits hang posters of you over their beds."

"What?" I blurted, mortified. "Where the hell are they getting posters of me?"

"Someone on the internet is mass-producing and selling prints of Gordon's Ghost Heart mural," he said. "There are several different versions. I'm surprised you haven't seen them."

"Can't you sue them or something? Don't you own the rights to Gordon's work?"

"I do, and I could," he said. "But I'm not going to. It's free PR. You'll just have to get used to being a sexual icon."

"No, I won't." I crossed my arms over my chest and stared out the window. Lonan thought it was funny, but it wasn't. The more I'd traveled, the more I'd noticed people treating me differently. They knew who I was before I arrived. They respected me without question.

They acted like I was better than they were, that I somehow deserved more. And it wasn't my money. Most people didn't know I had any. Other than the jet, I traveled simply and humbly, sleeping in hostels and cheap motels. No, it was because of my PSS chest and the rumors about what it could do. Rumors that weren't even true. I couldn't die and reboot anymore, and I made that clear any chance I got. But people treated me like some kind of Messiah anyway, and it was really starting to get to me.

That was just another reason I couldn't recruit anymore. It didn't feel right. That's what I'd come to tell Olivia. I had come to quit.

Off in the distance, the dome appeared on the horizon, shining like a pearl in the sand.

Just a few more miles and we'd be there.

46

OLIVIA

My morning had been full of meetings, as usual. First, I'd gone over the weekly security report with Mike Palmer and Jason Williams. Mostly, it was about vetting and background checks for the newest batch of recruits coming in. Three of them had been flagged for further investigation, and I'd signed off on that. We had always been careful about who we let into the dome, but with the recent CAMFer attacks, we'd stepped it up a notch. That last thing we needed was a CAMFer mole in our midst.

Then, I'd met with T-dog and Chase for an IT update. Our website and social media hits were spiking. The call center had been busy as well. People were scared. They were demanding the vaccine.

Which was one more thing we could use to push the FDA along.

My third meeting was just a brief stop-over in our training center to check in with Passion, Samantha, and Grant. They were revamping our two-week orientation track and they wanted me to look over the changes, but I had every confidence in the three of them. They were excellent teachers and the volunteers adored them. In fact, one of the recruits, Claire, adored Grant so much she'd become a full-time staffer and they were dating now. They weren't the only ones. Jason and Allie had been an item for over a year, and the rumor going around was he'd been shopping for a ring. Love was in the air, and that's exactly why I kept myself too busy to breathe.

Anyway, after I left the training center, I'd gone over to see the progress on the renovation of the CAMFer side of the compound. Of course, both Mia and my mother had been there, overseeing every tiny detail. The Black-Lightfoot Memorial PSS Arts and Community Center was their shared vision and they wanted it to be perfect. The art gallery portion would feature the complete works of Gordon and my father, and they were working on collecting other PSS-inspired art as well. They were even going to have a listening studio for music, including some of Samantha's original compositions. I hadn't been over to the CAMFer side in a while and it was barely recognizable. My mother and Mia, with the help of some recruits and several contractors, were transforming the place of my nightmares into a beautiful, serene, space that would honor Psyche Sans Soma and everyone who visited it.

I was so glad Mia and my mom were sharing this project. They'd become good friends in the process.

After oohing and aahing over their progress, I headed to the new staff food court in the dome, grabbed myself some fries and a sandwich, and sat down next to the Kaylee fountain. I loved sitting by the fountain. In fact, there was a table reserved for me that no one else used, so close I could feel the spray of the water on my skin. As I stuffed a fry in my mouth, I looked up at the life-sized sculpture of my sister, beautifully rendered in melted metal and blue anhydrite by Mia. My sister's hands were spread out, her pale eyes looking down at me, the clear water pouring over her like a blessing, the desert sky hanging above her.

She had saved the world from itself. She'd given us all eyes to see what we were really made of, the part of us that was magic and stardust, energy and light, the eternal portion we'd always possessed, revealed by the consequences of a freak accident, yes, but still as real and significant as the flesh and bone we'd focused on for so long. I understood now what Kaylee had been trying to tell us. PSS had always existed. It wasn't the composition of humanity that changed after the first accident at Umatilla, or the second. It was our ability to see and understand who we were that had been transformed.

Even as I sat eating, people bustled back and forth, their PSS shining from within them. We'd gotten so used to it now, it was hard to remember when we couldn't see it. It was like noticing what someone was wearing or the color of their eyes. The only big mystery left was why a few rare people didn't have it at all, like Grant and T-dog, but Pete and Reiny were working on that and they had several interesting theories.

"A French fry for your thoughts," said my best friend, Emma, snatching one of my fries and plopping down across from me as she stuffed it in her mouth.

"You're supposed to pay for thoughts, not steal for them," I pointed out.

"Yeah well. We both know you're going to tell me anyway, but at least this way I get some food out of it. Let me guess," she said, stealing another fry. "Were you thinking about your boyfriend?"

"As a matter of fact, I wasn't," I said. "Because I don't have a boyfriend."

"Right." Emma rolled her eyes. "When's your not-boyfriend supposed to get here?"

"I don't know," I said. "He was vague." Which is exactly why I'd been keeping myself so busy all morning. I loved Emma, and I'd been thrilled when she'd come to work at the dome after she'd graduated from Greenfield High. She fit right in. Anyone who'd known Emma before The Change hadn't been surprised to see PSS shining out of her belly button like a laser pointer afterward. That was Emma. Straight and to the point. But that also meant I couldn't hide my feelings from her. She knew I was a nervous wreck about Marcus's arrival.

"He's been vague for a year and a half," she said. "That's the problem. So, are you finally giving him an ultimatum? I've seen the way Chase looks at you, Liv. You can't wait around for Marcus forever. There are other fish in the sea."

"Em, it isn't that simple. And in case you haven't noticed"—I gestured at the dome, the people and everything I'd worked so hard to build—"I haven't just been waiting around. There are more important things than—"

"Olivia," I heard Lonan call from across the dome.

Emma and I both turned, and there they were, Lonan and Marcus, walking right up to us.

We all exchanged the typical greetings. "Good to see you. How are you? It's been so long."

Then, Emma excused herself because her phone center shift was starting, and Lonan said, "I'm going to check in with Reiny and let her know we've arrived. I'm sure you two have some catching up to do. Olivia, can you bring David by Reiny and Pete's quarters for dinner? You're invited too, of course."

"Sure. Okay," I said, as Lonan walked away.

Marcus glanced around the dome, taking in the food court, the people, the Kaylee fountain. "I like what you've done with the place," he said, his eyes lingering on the sculpture as he sat down. "It feels right."

"Thanks." I sat down across from him and pushed my food aside. "We've done our best to honor her."

"Olivia, I don't want to drag this out." He reached across the table and took my hands in his. "I think I've already done that enough."

My heart was in my throat, pounding like a drum.

"I came here to tell you I can't recruit anymore. I'm tired of life on the road, and I don't like the way people have started to idolize me. It feels too much like The Hold, and the last thing I want is to become my Uncle Alex."

I looked down at our hands. Was he quitting or breaking up with me? Because if it was the latter that seemed grossly unfair given I'd had no idea we'd been together.

"So," he continued, "I talked with Sam and we came up with a plan. She thought we could create a new track for the staff and volunteers who want to become recruiters themselves, and I can train them. I'm not sure if I'll be a good teacher or not, but with her team helping me, I think I could learn."

"And you would do that here, at The Center?" I asked, daring to hope.

"Yeah," he said, twining his fingers through mine "But only if you're okay with it. Either way, I'm not traveling anymore, but I was hoping we could—I mean, I know it's been a long time, and we'd have to start from the beginning, but I think I finally know who I am, and what I want—so, I thought maybe, if you're still interested—"

"Yes, David Marcus Jordan," I said, beaming at him. "I'm still interested."

Then we both stood up, stepping around the table, and he took me in his arms, kissing me beneath the fountain of Kaylee.

THE END.

If you enjoyed this book, please support the author by leaving a review right now on the venue you purchased it from.

ACKNOWLEDGEMENTS

I would like to thank my imagination, which has kept me company all these years and been a great source of comfort and entertainment.

I would like to thank my penchant for worry. Without it, I couldn't possibly have conceptualized this story into being with all its complex twists and wonderful surprises. Spending a lifetime envisioning every possible bad scenario really can come in handy.

I would like to thank the terrors and horrors of my mind, the things that scare me most, because they drove me to write my fears away (or at least onto the page where others can read them).

Finally, I would like to thank myself for being strong and giving me permission to do this thing I always wanted to do.

If I never write another thing, I'm proud of this series.

P.S. I'm totally going to write another thing.

ABOUT THE AUTHOR

Ripley Patton is an award-winning author who lives in Portland, Oregon with one cat, two teenagers, and a man who wants to live on a boat. She has also lived in Illinois, Colorado, Georgia, Indiana, and New Zealand.

Ripley doesn't smoke, or drink, or cuss as much as her characters. Her only real vices are eating M&Ms, writing, and watching reality television.

To learn more about Ripley and what she's going to write next, be sure to check out her website at www.ripleypatton.com. You can also sign up for her monthly e-newsletter there to keep up-to-date and win cool prizes.

www.ingramcontent.com/pod-product-compliance
Lightning Source LLC
Chambersburg PA
CBHW021424240626
47153CB00001B/17